NEW YORK REVIEW BOOKS
CLASSICS

LAST TIMES

VICTOR SERGE (1890–1947) was born Victor Lvovich Kibalchich to Russian anti-czarist exiles, impoverished intellectuals living "by chance" in Brussels. A precocious anarchist firebrand, young Victor was sentenced to five years in a French penitentiary in 1912. Expelled to Spain in 1917, he participated in an anarcho-syndicalist uprising before leaving to join the Revolution in Russia. Detained for more than a year in a French concentration camp, Serge arrived in St. Petersburg early in 1919 and joined the Bolsheviks, serving in the press services of the Communist International. An outspoken critic of Stalin, Serge was expelled from the Party and briefly arrested in 1928. Henceforth an "unperson," he completed three novels (*Men in Prison*, *Birth of Our Power*, and *Conquered City*) and a history (*Year One of the Russian Revolution*), all published in Paris. Arrested again in Russia and deported to Central Asia in 1933, he was allowed to leave the USSR in 1936 after international protests by militants and prominent writers like André Gide and Romain Rolland. Using his insider's knowledge, Serge published a stream of impassioned, documented exposés of Stalin's Moscow show trials and machinations in Spain, which went largely unheeded. Stateless, penniless, hounded by Stalinist agents, Serge lived in precarious exile in Brussels, Paris, Vichy France, and Mexico City, where he died in 1947. His books *Memoirs of a Revolutionary*, *Notebooks*, and *Midnight in the Century*, as well as his great last novels, *Unforgiving Years* and *The Case of Comrade*

Tulayev (all available as NYRB Classics), were written "for the desk drawer" and published posthumously.

RALPH MANHEIM (1907–1992) translated more than one hundred books, primarily from German and French. His first major commission was *Mein Kampf,* which was published in the United States in 1943. Among his prizewinning translations are *The Tin Drum* by Günter Grass, *Castle to Castle* by Louis-Ferdinand Céline, and *A Sorrow Beyond Dreams* by Peter Handke. After Manheim's death, the PEN Medal for Translation, which he won in 1988, was renamed in his memory.

RICHARD GREEMAN has translated and written the introductions for five of Victor Serge's novels (including *Unforgiving Years* and *Conquered City,* both available as NYRB Classics). A veteran socialist and co-founder of the Praxis Center and Victor Serge Library in Moscow, he splits his time between Montpellier, France, and New York City.

LAST TIMES

VICTOR SERGE

Translated from the French by
RALPH MANHEIM
with revisions by
RICHARD GREEMAN

NEW YORK REVIEW BOOKS

New York

THIS IS A NEW YORK REVIEW BOOK
PUBLISHED BY THE NEW YORK REVIEW OF BOOKS
435 Hudson Street, New York, NY 10014
www.nyrb.com

Originally published by the Dial Press in 1946 under the title *The Long Dusk*.
First published as a New York Review Books Classic in 2022.

Library of Congress Cataloging-in-Publication Data
Names: Serge, Victor, 1890–1947, author. | Manheim, Ralph, 1907–1992,
    translator. | Greeman, Richard, contributor.
Title: Last times: a novel / Victor Serge; translation by Ralph Manheim; revised
    with a foreword by Richard Greeman.
Other titles: Dernier temps. English
Description: New York: New York Review Books, [2021] | Series: New York
    Review Books classics | Identifiers: LCCN 2020016147 | ISBN 9781681375144
    (paperback) | ISBN 9781681375151 (ebook)
Classification: LCC PQ2637.E49 D4713 2021 | DDC 843/.912—dc23
LC record available at https://lccn.loc.gov/2020016147

ISBN 978-1-68137-514-4
Available as an electronic book; ISBN 978-1-68137-515-1

Printed in the United States of America on acid-free paper.
10 9 8 7 6 5 4 3 2 1

INTRODUCTION

THE PANZERS of the Wehrmacht were already in the northern suburbs of Paris when Victor Serge left the city. He was without papers and, as usual, nearly broke.

Serge was accompanied by his young companion Laurette Séjourné, his teenage son Vlady, and a Spanish friend, Narciso Molins y Fàbregas. On the outskirts of Paris, they joined the huge southward exodus of refugees toward the unoccupied zone, a "flight," he would write in *Memoirs of a Revolutionary*, "accompanied by a sense of release bordering at times on gaiety."

The gaiety waned as they made their way through Vichy France. From the Dordogne, Serge wrote Nancy Macdonald, the wife of Dwight Macdonald, his editor at *Partisan Review*:

> We have been traveling in freight trains, spending nights in the fields. In a little village in the Loire country we were so tired that we lay down behind some stones and slept through an entire bombardment. Nowhere, in this completely chaotic world, were we able to find any asylum . . .
>
> Of all I once owned—clothes, books, writings—I was able to save only what my friends and I could carry away on our backs in knapsacks. It is very little, but fortunately includes the manuscripts which I have already begun. This letter is a sort of S.O.S. which I hope that you will also communicate to my known and unknown friends in America. I have no money for stamps; I will be able to send off perhaps one or two letters, but that is all. I must ask you to immediately undertake some action

of material aid for me. I have scarcely a hundred francs left; we are eating only one meal a day and it is a very poor one at that. I don't at all know how we are going to hold out.

The Macdonalds responded to Serge's call for help by setting up the Fund for European Writers and Artists. As to Serge himself, however, his past membership in the Communist Party made it impossible to bring him to the United States.

After weeks of wandering, Serge finally arrived in Marseille. The harbor of Marseille had been officially closed, but the city was crowded with refugees of every political stripe competing for the last visa and the last berth on the last (hoped-for) boat to the New World (whose doors remained largely closed). There, in October 1941, Serge heard from Daniel Bénédite, who, from the Paris police prefecture, had helped him with French residence permits. Bénédite, a literature graduate and a left-wing socialist, was now working in Marseille with Varian Fry at the American Emergency Rescue Committee, or Centre Américain de Secours (CAS), as it was known in French. This improvised organization snatched hundreds of political refugees—artists, intellectuals, left-wing militants—from the clutches of the Gestapo in the months following the fall of France.

Bénédite had found an eighteen-room Second Empire house, the Villa Air-Bel, on thirty hectares and with a magnificent view just outside Marseille, which he hoped to turn into a phalanstery of radical thinkers and artists. Serge was the first person he invited to come live there, and Serge in turn pressed him to take in André Breton and his wife and daughter. Fry also moved into the dilapidated villa that Serge humorously renamed Château Espère-Visa (Castle Hope-for-Visa). Thus began the adventure of the "surrealist château" of Air-Bel, with its famous Sunday-afternoon fêtes to which Breton's friends—among them Wifredo Lam, André Masson, Jean Arp, Marcel Duchamp, René Char, Max Ernst, and Benjamin Péret—came by tram from Marseille to play surrealist games.

The safe haven of Air-Bel was too good to last, however. To protect the operations of CAS, Fry left, and Serge and his family, hounded by the police *and* the Communist Party, soon followed. They ended up living in a downtown hotel "on the advice of the Sûreté police because it was inhabited by a half-dozen German agents. For this reason it is heated in winter," as he wrote the Macdonalds. The winter of 1940 was especially severe in Marseille, and it came just as the results of Nazi requisitions were felt most deeply. In another letter, Serge describes whole crowds gathering "in front of the window of a rotisserie just to watch a single chicken turning on a spit."

The Macdonalds in New York and Julián Gorkin in Mexico finally succeeded in arranging a passage to Mexico for Serge. On March 25, 1941, Serge and Vlady along with André, Jacqueline, and Aube Breton, and other refugees whom Fry's CAS had helped to save, set sail from Marseille to Martinique on the SS *Capitaine Paul Lemerle*, a ship that Serge humorously described as "a sardine can with a cigarette-butt stuck on top."

These experiences were to be the inspiration for *Last Times*, the novel that Serge began in Mexico early in 1943. Arriving in the New World, he had at first turned to finishing *The Case of Comrade Tulayev*, his novel about the Stalinist terror of the thirties that he had begun in France. He had also written *Memoirs of a Revolutionary*. Macdonald and George Orwell did their best to help Serge find publishers for these two great books, but their efforts were in vain. The Soviet Union was a wartime ally, and literature critical of the Soviet regime was unwelcome.

Serge was by this time in desperate financial straits. With *Last Times* he bet his survival as a writer on the construction of an American-style novel of topical interest that, he hoped, would win a wide, popular readership. The book's politics are accordingly uncontroversial, focused on the struggle against fascism, with discussions turning around broad themes of optimism versus pessimism, historical destiny, and the catastrophe of Western civilization; and though there is one Communist villain, when it comes to the villainy of Stalinism—silence. Formally, too, the novel presents few challenges.

It is a straightforward story told by an omniscient narrator, with none of the stretches of stream of consciousness found in Serge's earlier novels. Following the lead of Balzac and Zola, Serge aimed to present a panorama of Europe descending into war, while he looked to the movies for scenes of rousing drama. From Eisenstein, Serge took his epic description of the head-on collision of two monstrous locomotives, and I am nearly certain that Serge saw *Casablanca* in Mexico City and that the famous singing duel at Rick's is the model for a similar contest that Serge stages in a French prison camp.

Last Times begins on the eve of the fall of France, with a detailed description of a cheap Paris hotel in the Marais, not unlike Balzac's immortal description of the Pension Vauquer at the start of *Le Père Goriot*. Serge uses this classic device to bring together the disparate characters whose intertwined destinies will work themselves out in the novel. From there he opens up on a description of Paris in her last days, from the sinister wall of the Santé Prison to the splendid silence of the empty Place de l'Opéra. This includes marvelous vignettes of a couple of philosophical winos under a bridge on the Seine and a tragic view of the old Jewish quarter on the eve of an inevitable pogrom.

After the arrival of the Germans, Serge follows his characters to the South of France, where they fight for survival, escape, perish, or join the Resistance. His protagonists are to an extent types: the Jew, the Spanish refugee, the woodsman, his daughter the ingenue, the good bad guy, the rich eccentric poet, the tough young woman from the German underground, the bitter demoralized soldier. Together they form a kind of fictional family (similar to the multiethnic platoon in so many US war movies of the period) with which the reader can readily identify, though by today's standards, Serge's treatment of female characters seems unfortunately clichéd. There is a madonna (Angel) and a plethora of whores and abortionists. Hilda, the German revolutionary, does have an inner life and interesting backstory, but Serge fails to develop her.

There is plenty of action in the novel, however: several sordid murders, a suicide, a torture scene, an aerial bombardment, a number of close escapes, skirmishes in the maquis, and those colliding locomotives. And there is a happy ending, sort of, since Serge provides alternative endings, one tailored to his own vision of the historical situation, the other meant to cheer his wartime audience. The dark and the light. On the dark side we have the fate of the two young good guys: Maurice Silber, the Jew, beaten to death, though defiant to the end, while the Spaniard Ortiga lives on, but only barely, in a Saharan work camp, dreaming of escape. Meanwhile the character who could be said to represent Serge himself, old Ardatov, miraculously saved from occupied Europe, is murdered on the ship to the New World by the Stalinist Willi Bart, a killing that symbolizes what Serge saw as the inexorable extermination of his whole generation of revolutionary militants and intellectuals, crushed between Nazism and Stalinism. It also draws on his continuing and entirely realistic worries for his own safety in Mexico, where Trotsky had not long before met his end at the hand of a Soviet agent.

Such is the end of the tragic symphony. But then comes a coda: "Dawns Break Everywhere." We are in the world of the Resistance, and the book ends with an optimistic flourish: "... but nothing has ended."

A conventional novel, in many ways, though one to which Serge brought all his skills as a novelist. He sketched maps of his Marseille locales the better to imagine them; he blocked out his plot and characters scene by scene on a long roll of paper as in a screenplay. He did a professional job and took pride in doing it, coming to accept the compromise he had made in taking it on. "I prefer practical compromise with social censorship to a deliberate dive into despair," he writes in his *Notebooks*, where he also records moments of creative exhilaration:

> Occupied these past days with Félicien Mûrier, I suddenly felt the need to return to Karel Cherniak. I knew, without being sure, that his fate was leading him to suicide. For several days I was tormented by the presence within me of Karel Cherniak, especially while falling asleep, and probably as I slept. He prevented me from seeing the other characters. I finally found a key phrase, insignificant and empty in appearance, "Cherniak

opened the window," and I knew that the solution was ready within me, that all that was left was to write, but I didn't know what this solution was. It would have been impossible for me to recount it in advance.

And yet he continued to have mixed feelings. Serge the writer held himself up to very high standards. His ideal was "literary creation that is free and disinterested," and he dismissed writers who were "merely suppliers to the book trade." He was ambitious, too, to break the mold of the "impoverished and outmoded" bourgeois novel, centered "upon a few beings artificially detached from the world." And yet beset as he was by poverty, persecution, isolation, and ill health, he could hardly bring himself to, as he said to his friend Herbert Lenhof, "let myself go all the way, shake off the weight of external and internal censorship" needed to truly make a novel live, and then there was yet another obstacle that made it "psychologically impossible" to transform his recent experiences—his "last times"—into a work of fiction. In December 1944, he writes:

> I am at the end of *Last Times* and experiencing extraordinary difficulty finishing this book...It is more that a novel—for me—ought to have an internal justification, internal to its characters and to its atmosphere, and that in reality all the men that I have tried to bring alive here strike me as condemned men walking through fog. They need a solution, I need a solution for them—and there is none. History can impose its solutions only by passing over their corpses.

And yet *Last Times*, once finished, was the success Serge had hoped for. He had mastered the genre of the popular novel and won his bet. It was published in French as *Les derniers temps* by Les Éditions de l'Arbre in Montreal at the end of 1946 (it would not appear in France until 1952), and in *Le Canada* it received a rave review: "The Great Novel of 1946." Other Canadian reviews unanimously praised Serge's mastery of French style, and even the Catholic *Revue Dominicaine*, though deploring the book's depiction of "the vices of the flesh displayed in all their impudicity," concluded that it was a "masterpiece" of realism. Ralph Manheim's English translation, entitled *The Long Dusk*, came out that same year from Dial Press in New York, and was extensively and more or less positively reviewed in *The New York Times*, *The New Yorker*, and *The Saturday Review*, as well as in daily papers across the country. Irving Howe in *Partisan Review* patronized Serge's writing as "journalistic" but placed it well above Arthur Koestler. After the novel's publication, on receiving a fan letter from an "indulgent" and "qualified" reader of *Last Times*, even Serge warmed to his book. He replied:

> You have felt the sincerity of my characters, and that's the most important thing. Maybe I conceived my people a little bit stronger, more courageous, more complete, than they are in everyday life. It seems to me that the novelist has the right, if not the duty, to purify reality a bit, to look for the best and the purist in man—and that he thus serves the truth.

Read today, this novel of the mid-forties about refugees in a time of civilizational collapse remains vivid, exciting, and strikingly contemporary. Today, an estimated sixty-five million refugees across the planet are fleeing tyrannies (many supported by the West), civil wars (often big-power proxy wars), starvation (in countries which, like France under German occupation, are exporting agricultural products), and ecological catastrophes (mostly caused by carbon-based capitalism). The novel's apocalyptic title is if anything more to the point now as the planet totters on the brink of extinction—whether through a nuclear winter following an atomic war or through the destabilized climate reaching a catastrophic tipping point. In January 2022 the *Bulletin of the Atomic Scientists* has just moved its Doomsday Clock forward to two and a half minutes before midnight.

—RICHARD GREEMAN
January 2022

A NOTE ON THE TRANSLATION

THERE is a story behind Ralph Manheim's translation of Serge's novel and my decision to revise it which also bears telling. Manheim translated from both French and German and became known as one of the most distinguished translators of his day. When Dial Press employed him to translate the novel, he was already familiar with Serge's work—he had translated his pamphlet "From Lenin to Stalin" for the Trotskyist Pioneer Publishers in 1937—though there is no mention of this in the ensuing correspondence between author and translator. "Cher Monsieur Ralph Manheim" and "Dear Mr. Victor Serge," they address each other respectfully, and Manheim makes it clear how much he appreciates Serge's writing, especially about the Marseille underworld, and, hoping he is not offending, asking him to "write some short stories dealing with this or a similar milieu? I believe stories of this type could be sold to the magazines for a ridiculous amount of money." Far from being offended, Serge found Manheim's offer "very seductive...These are worlds I know well and can imagine even better. Such stories could be really interesting to write." Manheim also encouraged Serge to submit *The Case of Comrade Tulayev* to Dial Press, since, with the war now over, the book's prospects should be improved. He advises him to wait to see how the new novel fares, however, offering to take the manuscript elsewhere if it is rejected.

When work on the translation began in February 1946, Manheim, extremely scrupulous, submitted to Serge a list of queries about unusual words and expressions, which Serge went to great lengths to answer. One query concerns the locus of a passage from Psalms quoted by the pious Protestant mayor of La Saulte. "Nobody around me has a Bible," Serge replied from Mexico. "I just went to the largest public library downtown; they don't have a Bible." He shared the amusing anecdote of being directed to the Library of Parliament because it is suspected there are "some Jews there." Serge, who had obviously quoted the passage from memory, finally identified it as "a French Protestant Canticle translated from Luther's adaptation of Psalm 46" and provided Manheim with the corresponding English passage.

In other words, all seemed to be going well, and on February 22, Manheim wrote: "I have incorporated all your comments in the MS as well as the changes you had sent to Sidney Phillips"—the head of Dial Press. Unfortunately, this involvement of the editor/publisher between the author and the translator was soon to lead to confusion and serious problems. Indeed, some of Serge's "comments" never made it into print (until this edition).

These problems surfaced when the galley sheets appeared from the printer in August 1946. On August 8, Manheim wrote: "Now we come to trouble. I am not at all pleased with the galleys. Dial has done a good bit of editing . . . There are stylistic 'improvements' which are very much for the worse." These "improvements" were apparently made by Phillips without recourse to the original French, and Manheim reported that unfortunately the boss was "very pleased with his editing job" and would probably be unwilling to accept the many corrections Manheim had sent him, pinned to the galleys. Numerous other changes may have been made by an anonymous editor whom Manheim humorously suspected was being "paid by the number of corrections."

Manheim urged Serge to write the publisher and protest various changes. He added: "I assume you approved the cuts in Chapter V [Serge hadn't] but I am sorry they left out the incident of the bomb-throwing." Sadly, Manheim concluded, "this is the first time in my career as a translator I have encountered such editing and I am very sorry it has to be in connection with your book."

However, two weeks later a euphoric Manheim wrote:

To my great surprise, Sidney Phillips is accepting all my re-corrections. Apparently my alarm was groundless. But believe me, I have translated books for ten different publishing houses and I never saw such an editing job before. I felt sure that having made their mistakes, they would try to defend them. Nothing of the sort. The war is won without a battle. Now at least you can blame me for any Americanization of the book ...

He added: "Except for the matter of cuts. They should have consulted you and they said they were going to consult you."

Alas, Manheim's alarm was not groundless. On September 3, 1946, he was forced to write: "I'm afraid it is too late to do anything about the text but protest. It has already gone back to the printer." He tells Serge: "You would be completely within your rights" to demand to see proofs and to "refuse authorization if the text is not to your liking," but he advises against it. He himself has obviously gone to the wall for Serge's text and found it pointless. "In my battle for the text, I created so much bad blood that Phillips, after correcting my corrections of his corrections, wrote me a letter telling me that it was all my fault. This is what is known as having the last word." Manheim concludes: "These people, on the grounds that they publish radical literature, think they can treat everybody like coolies."

This troubled history accounts for the unreliability of the translation as finally published, which omits sentences and paragraphs and whole pages and contains obvious mistranslations, some rather comical. Two Parisian winos (*clochards*) sleeping under the bridge in chapter seven get up at dawn in search of *jus* (juice)—wine—not "coffee" as the Dial translation would have us believe. Women's nipples and pudenda get pudically excised, as do other explicitly sexual references like *entremetteuse* ("go-between"). A "mole hole" metamorphoses into a "squirrel hole."

Thus in reviewing Manheim's work with an eye to revising it in the way that even the most expert translations may call for, I soon found myself involved in something more like a restoration of Serge's novel, and as I restored substantial passages to the text it became necessary to revise the translation as a whole to bring it closer to modern standards of translation. Seventy years ago publishers were, as we have seen, accustomed to taking big liberties, and translations were more like paraphrases or imitations of the original, "explaining the idea" rather than closely rendering the author's choice of words and stylistic devices. With Serge, the result is that his rapid, allusive, paradoxical style, noticeable even in this most popular of his novels, became watered down. I hope that in this restored and revised translation I have been true to and have helped to bring out the life of a book of which Manheim was so respectful and worked, for all the obstructions he encountered, hard to carry over. I hope, too, that this new edition of Serge's novel, out of print in English for decades, will find the new readers that in our own last times it deserves.

—R. G.

LAST TIMES

For Laurette, Vlady, and our friend Narciso—
companions in escape

1. MENACE

EVERYTHING doesn't all collapse at once. Within the overturned anthill a few corners remain almost peaceful; and there the ants may imagine their universe going on as usual. Probably this Parisian street, which we will call the Rue du Roi-de-Naples, in a section of the old city over which the centuries seem to have passed with royal indifference, has not changed and will scarcely change for some time to come. Most of its houses date from the end of the seventeenth century or the beginning of the eighteenth. They witnessed carriages passing through this street on their way to the Louvre in the time of noble town houses and exalted personages in powdered wigs. Later, the tall, gloomy dwellings of the bourgeoisie heard much talk of the profits promised by the East India Company and many prophecies regarding the schemes of Monsieur John Law. Its paving stones often resounded with the tread of the insurgent people on their way to attack or defend the Hôtel de Ville. Was it, in those days, the thoroughfare of a prosperous neighborhood inhabited by moderate revolutionaries (moderate beneath their bloodthirsty aspect); or the gathering place for the rabble, roused by the words of Jean-Paul Marat? The Faubourg Saint-Antoine is close by, but the quiet Rue des Francs-Bourgeois and the aristocratic Place des Vosges, formerly Place Royale, are also not far off.

The struggles celebrated in history books have attached memories to these stones, but no such souvenirs are revived in the minds of the present inhabitants, exclusively preoccupied with the miserly present. "What skin is it off my ass whether duchesses and sans-culottes danced around bonfires here or somewhere else?"—Monsieur Anselme would say—"I just tend to my own business." Even the light shines stingily on these houses and these lives; gray days are desperately sad; days of white sky are dim and dingy; while sunny days are cut in two by a dividing line. This broken line starts at the level of the fifth floor and traces a jagged diagonal across the cracked wall of a building owned by the Metropole Insurance Company—behind whose faded curtains vegetate the scheming spawn of fifteen families—then drops abruptly, in a cascade of impalpable gold, pale but singularly gay, down to a fruit stand on the sidewalk. There a little joy rains down, though what with their worries, people pay little attention to it. Still, it makes them feel better. "It's a fine day, Madame." "Yes, isn't it, Monsieur? You won't believe me, but my sciatica has calmed down." Here the sun is not the same as in the rich neighborhoods near the Bois de Boulogne. Maybe there is a secret affinity between the sun and wealth; maybe it is no accident that gold is the metal that most closely resembles the sun.

All things considered, there is more gold than sunshine in the Rue du Roi-de-Naples and its adjacent streets. Small fortunes, middling fortunes, prudent, unsatiated, still-hungry fortunes, amassed in silent, devious ways, some of them risen from the sewers and smelling slightly of drainage. On its way, the gold has been transformed into symbolic papers bereft of light, some of them filthy, others deceptively gilt-edged. But produce, humbler, cleaner, less insidious but more perishable, still continues to dominate these streets. Rue Rambuteau, Rue de Rivoli, Rue Turbigo carry nightly floods of organic matter in a mild state of decomposition down toward the central food market. Factories and home industries feed more stores between Boulevard Sebastopol and Place de la Bastille than there are stars on a clear night. There is a monotonous kind of variety about these stores, more variety than in the faces of the people—which reveal merely the souls of shopkeepers and merchants.

There are shops like traps, as alluring as magic grottoes, proposing 100,000 SHIRTS to the embittered passerby who owns only the shirt on his back; jewelry shops into whose windows teenage girls peer, longing for the necklace of a Hollywood Scheherazade, as does the anonymous personage who carefully calculates the risks and profits of a well-planned burglary. Secondhand-clothing stores exhibit, for the benefit of phantom customers, trench coats that might come in handy as camouflage. In their doorways Jews from Lithuania were awaiting—unawares—their atrocious final hours. Mme Sage's herbalist shop and M. Louis Lempereur's tripe-butcher shop stood next door to each other. All shades of decomposed blood and edible viscera in vague tints, ranging from grayish-pink to yellowish-violet, filled M. Lempereur's cavern, frequented by impoverished housewives and mysterious forlorn old women who in all likelihood had never been young... Mme Sage's sanctum, greenish, dark, and smelling of suspicious herbs, was visited mostly by worried ladies of a dangerous age and by teenage girls in love and in need of help: "An herb to pass it off, Madame Sage, there must be one?" Alas, there is no herb that can destroy the seed of human life in the womb of the innocent; but, charitable and eager for gain, Mme Sage did know a thing or two; she knew of probes, potions, pills, injections—you can tell them, my dear, that you took a nasty fall down the stairs. For psychological cures, however, Mme Sage referred patients to Nelly Thorah, the clairvoyant, a little farther down the street, at Number 16, next door to the Hôtel Marquise.

The glaring marquee of a movie theater sent a feeble red glow over the roofs bristling with old-fashioned chimney pots like pointed hats. "Just the right lighting for a guillotine," said Charlie l'Astuce. The silhouette of his soft felt hat could be seen as he glided through the violet shadows on his rubber-soled shoes.

The Hôtel Marquise exercised a vague attraction on people within a range of a hundred yards or so; beyond this radius, other hotels and other bars neutralized its malignant power. It was five stories high with three windows to a floor. Its front had been repainted a watery green around 1925. Though stained by rain and soot, its façade looked suspiciously clean amid its grimy plaster neighbors. The hotel's corridor, up three steps, was decorated in green porcelain. The glass-paned mahogany door swung open discreetly when anyone came in, but it set a little bell on the other side to tinkling hysterically behind the bar presided over by M. and Mme Anselme Flotte. The adjacent doorway leading into the bar was narrow but hospitable. The zinc-covered bar, with a vase of flowers by the cash register, disclosed three bluish siphons. The mirror behind it, polished every day by M. Anselme's own hand, displayed the prices of the day's specials, TRIPES À LA MODE DE CAEN or BŒUF BOURGUIGNON, in great round letters. BIÈRE LA MEUSE, BYRRH, DUBEAU-DUBON-DUBONNET, A PERNOD FOR ARTHUR! These signs inspired agreeable obsessions in the customers. Signs of the present times were posted to the left of the entrance: a helmeted soldier, looking like a blue penguin, and a civilian in an overcoat, resembling a plucked crow, exchanged confidences, doubtless concerning the secret plans of the General Staff, while failing to discern on the wall behind them the giant shadow of an enemy ear. Another poster transformed, by naive magic, old iron junk into tanks and gleaming bayonets beneath a victorious tricolored sky...

Here M. Anselme Flotte reigned over eighteen rooms, two of them rented by the hour; forty-seven bottles within arm's reach; a score of faithful clients, made even more faithful by their little debts; four to seven ladies of the evening; his capital, his parcel of real estate, his cellar, his stocks, his clientele. He only added up the serenely increasing total of his domain in moments of warmest intimacy with Mme Alexandrine Flotte.

"Flotte,"* as he would often say, "is obviously not a name for a wine seller; but I started out in the navy, Monsieur."

This old joke would relax the features of his pasty, rather expressionless face. What was left of his colorless hair was plastered down neatly on a flat, fleshy scalp. The lower part of his face, heavy and soft, contrasted with the alert shrewdness of his small red eyes, shifting back and forth behind their thin slits.

"My husband sees straight into the heart of things," Mme Alexandrine Flotte liked to say. "He gives a quick look, so quick you wouldn't notice, then he sits there rinsing his glasses, with his eyes half-closed like a big good-natured tomcat. You'd say he was falling

*In French, *flotte* means both "water" (slang) and a "fleet" (of ships).

asleep, but he's thinking all the while, don't doubt it for a moment, and that's when he sees what's going on inside people. At night he says to me: 'Sandrine, I can see right through so-and-so like he was an empty bottle,' and I know he's telling the truth. You can't pull the wool over his eyes. He can floor a man with one little innocent question, like when he said to Monsieur Bœuf the other day: 'You've come for Émilie again, eh?'—or Monsieur Tartre, the old skinflint who doesn't order anything but brandy and coffee every three days: here's what my Anselme says to him: 'They're not exactly safe deals, are they?' he says, 'but they'll bring in at least 40 percent.' You should have seen old Tartre jump, as though he had caught himself thinking out loud, and you can be sure that doesn't happen often. He was so flabbergasted it made him stutter: 'W-what's that you s-say, Monsieur Anselme? W-where d-did you hear that?' 'Don't worry,' my Anselme says, smiling up his sleeve because he was only kidding, 'I'm a little in the same line—' Tartre took to his heels all upset, he must think there's something fishy going on, but maybe that will make him order a little more, and after all, he knows we wouldn't make trouble for anybody."

M. Anselme Flotte would take it all in as he sliced a *zeste* of lemon peel between his thick red fingers, and in his rather piglike eyes you could see a gleam of contentment. And to please his audience, he would suddenly begin to sing:

> "Everybody's got to make a living.
> Everybody's got to work!"

"We're good folk," Mme Alexandrine Flotte would say. "You can count on that." The tone implied that there were other kinds of people, and not too far off either. But these simple expressions of the truth about humanity could scarcely be a guide in the choice of a clientele. After all, scoundrels pay the same price for an aperitif as the apostles themselves would, in case they should decide to take a place at the bar. And besides, you could count on the apostles to kick up a fuss in the neighborhood.

The hotel had originally been called Hôtel des Îles Marquises, in memory of Marine Corporal Anselme Flotte's station at Hiva Oa—where the sea is a giant platter reflecting the sky; and the sky is infinitely, ineffably radiant, as though the whole world were sheer transparence, warmth, and light—it's unbelievable. Playful waves, singing, foaming, roll endlessly over coral reefs covered with moss, velvet seaweed, and marine flora. Some of the isles are especially blessed, crowned with palms and trees riotous with red foliage; the women, brown and smooth, their flesh fresh, put flowers in their hair; their mouths are too large, they have gold teeth, and they all have the clap. Damned islands! Corporal Flotte had nearly got himself tied to a stupid bathing girl with exotic flowers in her black tresses. He took hold of himself in time, thanks to Pernod. It's not a world, the Pacific. It's the aphrodisiacal plague. At the time when Anselme Flotte moved into the Rue du Roi-de-Naples, investing the funds realized from the sale of his father's property in the Nièvre, he was seized with an absurd nostalgia and said to his Alexandrine—still slender, with a vigorous bosom, and a provocative bun over her forehead, "Sandrine, I think I'll call the place Les Îles Marquises! That's where the two of us should have lived. You just can't imagine!"

Fifteen years of smoke, noise, night lights, rain, cold, business deals, and local news items passed by; and when he came to have the lower floors renovated, Anselme Flotte simplified his sign by omitting mention of the islands, and added in italics, today nearly effaced: "*She is doing quite well.*" For according to the chorus of the latest hit, Madame la Marquise was doing quite well, though her stable, her château, and even her husband had just gone merrily up in flames.

The building next door, Number 16, property of the Widow Prugnier, GROCERIES, FOODSTUFFS, WINE, lived a life of stagnant finality. The hotel represented the stability of adventure, the adventure of life in the heart of Paris, that giant cesspool; the respectable house next door embodied average life, without adventure. It was not often that anyone even died there: a little blond girl whose very presence in the gloomy pit of the courtyard had seemed incongruous had been carried away, swathed in white muslin inside a little coffin decorated with paper lace. An ailing old man had departed, driven away on the trot in a ramshackle third-class hearse, and the old women had said, "It's none too soon, why, he had cemetery written all over him. What good is it to live so long? At least he was alone, he didn't bother anybody —He stank though —Do you think, Madame Sage, that there's a place in heaven or hell for trash like him?" Mme Sage didn't think so. She believed that heaven and hell were inventions of the priests; as for hell, we were more or less living in it down here, alas! But the *Psychic Review* shed a different light on the life beyond the grave, a life in which, to be sure, an old fellow like that could scarcely take part in. Even in his lifetime you could see that he had lost his soul— and what was left of his body, well, that wasn't worth talking about.

The Widow Prugnier tended her shop with the help of a short Breton girl, broad of hip and shoulder. Both of them dressed in black, had the same protuberant chins, the same shallow eyes quick at small calculations, the same gimlet-like glances, lighting up now and then with a sparkle of malice—as though they would like to poison somebody but could never get up the courage, said Dr. Ardatov, one of their customers. CREDIT WILL BE GIVEN TOMORROW, promised a sign perched on the blue tapioca sacks, but another sign, newer and more conspicuous atop the sardines, announced that CREDIT IS DEAD AND BURIED, and don't you forget it.

Mme Prugnier dispensed with a concierge, and looked after the house herself. When she went to collect the rent, she climbed the six flights of stairs, resting on each landing so as not to be out of breath in case of arguments. Since her good-for-nothing son had left for the Maginot Line, she would lose her breath anyway, and alone in the dark stairway she sometimes took her head between her hands and groaned "Holy Mary!" But there was no help for it. Life was like that. Her only bad tenants lived in the attic rooms on the sixth floor, and yet they could hardly have found cheaper lodgings. So much relentless severity, so much regret sublimated into reproach was stamped on her sharp features when she knocked on these three doors that a sort of panic, like the panic that seizes men in the dusty corridors of police headquarters, threw the indigent foreigners into humiliating confusion. Dr. Simon Ardatov, who had stood under the gallows without trembling, opened the door a few inches and, suddenly overcome with nausea, promised to pay "by the first without fail, Madame, you can count on it." Yes, yes, count on it and drink ammonia. He calls himself a doctor and he doesn't have the right to practice. The Widow muttered something about the bailiff, in the unhappy knowledge that she could never cover a bailiff's charges by selling these people's bric-a-brac; and turning her back, she knocked on a low door marked by a visiting card fastened with thumb tacks: MAURICE SILBER, BROKER. Broker of what, ye gods! What gall!

Moritz Silber(stein) opened with alacrity. "Come in, come in, Madame Prugnier! You are well, as usual?" Lively and voluble, in a jacket somewhat too tight for him, Silber smiled with his lashes, his eyelids, his nose, his thick lips; his affability was intolerable; he was a redheaded Polack, under sentence of deportation but enjoying a temporary reprieve. He took his rent payments lightly, made up all kinds of stories, suggested deals. He would pay at once in merchandise, on favorable terms. "Just haven't had time to raise any cash. You can't imagine, Madame, how irregular some people are with their payments. Take that leather-goods man in the Faubourg du Temple, a reputable firm. They owe me three thousand six hundred francs. Would you believe it?" Mme Prugnier didn't believe a word of it. Samples of gloves, leather, and zippers were strewn about the table, intermingled with newspapers in Yiddish, Arabic, or Russian characters. Moritz Silber danced around the landlady with amiable little gestures, and she felt uneasy as though he were having a huge joke at her expense, as though, with the dexterity of a magician, he were going to spirit away her antique brooch with its three little diamonds; or suddenly ask her for a loan—and spellbound she would grant it in spite of herself, just to escape from the room without him touching her—or even without him giving her a friendly slap on the behind, and she wouldn't dare to cry out or complain to a soul! Madame Prugnier fled, taking her rent receipt with her. Under the attic window that opened out onto the roof tiles, she paused and tried to regain her self-possession.

"Let's see now, what did he promise me, that beast?"

Then she knocked furiously at Pepe Ortiga's door.

Pepe was not home. Or he was pretending not to be home. But in that case how would he manage to slip out without her seeing him? He usually came home at one in the morning, climbing the stairs four at a time, like a nocturnal ape. She would have to chase him for ten days at a time, then in the end she would catch him on the run and thrust her rent bill under his nose.

"Do you know what this is, Monsieur Or-ti-ga? Eh? Why, no, I'm sure you have no idea."

The handsome, curly-headed, curiously elegant lad would cast a negligent glance at the paper and reply in his deep, moving, singer's voice, "Don't worry, Madame, and don't inconvenience yourself. I'll catch up with you one of these days. But you're going to make me miss my Métro. Excuse me, please."

He would fly off. Some Saturdays, payday, he would come home in the evening accompanied by a girl of his type: round, pale face, smoldering black eyes that looked at the world with sultry insolence, as if you were seeing her naked through her pupils, her nipples hard. They would come into the grocery together and pick out expensive canned goods, lobster, Portuguese sardines, artichokes, and a bottle of good wine; they would whisper to each other with amorous indecency, as though they were kissing, and when it came to paying, Pepe Ortiga would throw forty francs extra on the counter, as part payment on his rent—don't bother giving me a receipt, Madame, I trust you! His trust was both infuriating and touching. He checked neither the prices nor her addition. Where had he learned to trust people?

"He's the sort of guy," said the Breton servant, "who used to burn convents and rape nuns."

Madame Prugnier objected: "Don't be silly, girl." And she added with a sharp little laugh, "It's not as easy as you think to rape somebody."

Below the sixth floor lived people who paid regularly: all of them highly respectable. On the fifth, the Sigues; they worked at home, making paper flowers and hats; the Dupins, M. Dupin worked for the PLM (Paris-Lyon-Mediterranean Railroad). On the fourth floor a strange doormat of gray horsehair, with a heavy black triangle in the middle, marked the door of Nelly Thorah, the clairvoyant, whose real name was Mme Jacques Lamblin; she was a woman of experience who had been to Port Said and Monaco. She had her picture in the advertising pages of the newspapers—and never caused any trouble. Then there was M. Kaspar, bookbinder, a Russian who had been very rich in his own country before the revolution; and M. Tartre, JOBBER, TRANSPORT, occupied the entire third floor.

M. Tartre lived alone with his maid, Mlle Marcelle (forty-five years old, the soul of discretion and thrift, a woman who never said a word too many). M. Tartre was a fat, bald little man who wore tortoiseshell glasses and suits of British homespun and smoked cigars. He wasn't a man to let money slip through his fingers, you could tell that just by looking at him. From time to time police inspectors came to inquire about his habits, but when Mme Prugnier mentioned this to him, M. Tartre disclosed his gold teeth and his own yellow teeth in a broad episcopal smile: "I am under protection, Madame, since an attempt at blackmail."

On the second floor, the Boitelles, who worked in a printshop and had a son in the Army; and M. Klaus, a salesman of pharmaceuticals, an Alsatian who spent a fortune on taxi fares. On the first floor, Mme Florence, a dresser in a vaudeville house, who probably did a little hooking in high-class bars, a nice girl in any case, with big green eyes and long lashes, and a radiant freshness in spite of her night work; a good, reasonable girl, she never brought a man home with her, used a good deal of water in washing herself, spoke little but with "exquisite" manners, and reminded you of a movie star. Next door to her, the Lancier sisters, two pious little old ladies with white hair under bonnets trimmed with black lace. They had two little Pekingese dogs with wet eyes, so old they had forgotten how to yap; they lived on an income provided by the textile mills of Lancier Successors at Valenciennes.

There were no children in the house, for children make noise. The only child who had ever been admitted by Mme Prugnier was now resting in the cemetery, as if these lives and stones had sent him on there. And Mme Prugnier would say, "Children, ah, it's too sad. They make noise and then they die."

"And what about us, Madame, what do you think the rest of us do?" replied Augustin Charras.

And he would add into his mustache, "The only difference is that we make hypocritical noise, unpleasant noise. As for me, I'd rather be playing marbles."

A foot of masonry separated Widow Prugnier's grocery from the shop of AUGUSTIN CHARRAS, COAL AND WOOD, a little black cave, black with anthracite, with solitude, with hardened sadness. The sacks of coal were piled up to the ceiling; paper bags, briquettes, coal, and wood obstructed the entrance, pieces of kindling took up an entire corner, and more of it was strewn over the flagstones. At the age of sixty, Augustin Charras, a war veteran, Croix de Guerre with palms, had lost his taste for work. He spent the day on a chair in the midst of his coal, chewing on a dead pipe. His mustache was yellow with tobacco smoke, the wrinkles in his face were full of black dust, his shoulders were stooped, and the veins on his big hands were swollen; he read humorous papers, *Le Canard Enchaîné* and *Le Merle Blanc*—the latter whiter than ever because of the censorship. A shady character, all in all. He was believed to have "ideas," the kind of ideas that do no one any good. The day war was declared, he was heard to sneer, "Oh men can be such asses! Do you remember the war to end wars? And now they want us to die for Danzig, as they say. And twenty years from now for Shanghai. Or maybe for the moon." And he spat great slimy gobs of spit on his sidewalk.

Mme Prugnier could not restrain herself from saying "Don't go on like that, Monsieur Augustin, or people will be taking you for a Communist."

"And suppose they do? Maybe they're not as lousy as we think."

But after that he scarcely spoke, except on the day when his customers found him almost in a stupor, a newspaper dropped onto his knees, understanding nothing that was said to him and repeating, "Rotterdam! Rotterdam! What wretches! No, they are no longer human. What has become of us, I ask you! Oh God, oh God, oh God!"

Angèle Charras, a seventeen-year-old student at the Pigier School, was "as innocent as a plaster saint," "a model of virtue"; yet she somewhat scandalized the neighborhood by replying with a nod of her head or a bright smile to the "good evening, M'selle" of the streetwalkers whom dusk brought into the neighborhood as regularly as if they were reporting to a steady job. Angèle would cook an *omelette au lard* in the kitchen behind the shop, lay the white tablecloth for M. Augustin, light the old-fashioned hanging oil lamp. A little later, as the girls were taking up their posts at the approaches to the Hôtel Marquise, Angèle would sit down to her piano. She played strangely, and well. "It makes you want to laugh or cry for no reason," said Raymonde, who at times would ignore a passerby for the sake of the enchanting music.

Looking in from the darkened street at a certain angle, you could see Angèle's pure profile and her hands running over the keyboard. And you could see the ponderous shape of Augustin Charras, slumped in his chair amid the coal and wood, his hands flat on his knees, his head bowed.

When she had finished playing, Charras would close the shop and go out to Anselme's for a glass of wine.

"What's the good word, Monsieur Augustin?" was the proprietor's ritual question.

"Me? Nothing."

Charras always seemed to be returning from far off when anyone spoke to him. (What a waste of money, putting a piano in that ramshackle old shop of his and having his young miss learn Chopin, as if that would be of any use to her! A little crazy, no doubt. A proud one.) Once, when some of the regulars were talking about the war, the Siegfried Line "that we'll have to smash through one day," the "Maginot Line of the air" demanded by one newspaper, the English who weren't doing a damn thing, the Russians and Americans, so egotistical it made you puke, the Italians who were no doubt cooking up some macaronic betrayal—Augustin Charras, not looking at the proprietor, said to him in a low voice, "Take it from me: we're screwed."

He thrust his hands into his pockets and went out alone, beneath the night sky, black with a vague purple glow, toward the Bastille or the Seine. He thought of nothing but only murmured, "It's not worth hollering, it's no use crying. There's nothing to do."

Don't deny these houses have a soul, a soul compounded of habits, nameless diseases, frustrated hopes, petty crimes, and the vain but unending search for an impossible escape. Stand in one of these courtyards shaped like an enormous chimney, and raise your head. In some window at the edge of the sky you will see flowerpots, a pink brassiere hanging on a wire, a birdcage, and you will seem to see the very breath of that soul—the soul of poverty itself—which doctors once thought to be cancerous. For years, anguish had been eating its way into these lives, as drops of water falling continuously on the same spot ultimately pierce a rock.

The five-cent franc was no longer dependable, the future war cast a nightmare shadow over the world. It was still possible not to believe in the calamity to come, to believe in the continuity of things present. Yet the anguish persisted, in the stones and in the people. M. Anselme joked ponderously, "There won't be war tomorrow, that's for sure." "Well, we have at least one optimist," said M. Bœuf, inspector of the vice squad. "Not for three days," continued the optimist sarcastically.

The three days passed inexorably. At M. Tartre's, at the Sigues', at the Boitelles', at the Dupins', at Nelly Thorah's, at Augustin Charras's, at the Marquise bar, everywhere people sat by the radio listening with anxious hearts to a raucous German voice bellowing invective, imprecations, and vague threats. Untiringly it clamored for war, war, war, war, war! Grief, grief, grief to you, grief to us, grief to the world, grief, grief, grief!

"That Adolf is quite a guy, you can't deny it," said Anselme Flotte. "He knows how to make his poor bastards march four abreast—he keeps them on their toes! Not like Daladier or Blum or the lousy Popular Front!"

"Twelve bullets in his hide would be too good for him," commented Charras.

"Quite a guy, I'm telling you," confirmed a drunk.

On the day war was declared, Anselme Flotte flew into a great rage that made the sweat stand out on his forehead. "The dirty bastards!" The men leaning against the bar were silent under the weight of their emotion. Anselme Flotte, the owner, the richest, the strongest, felt that he must speak.

"This time, I'm telling you, we mustn't stop halfway. We were too soft in '18, Clemenceau was right. We can't keep starting in all over again every twenty years, hell no! We've got to put an end to it, and there's only one way. No more Germany. We've got to wipe them out from first to last, from the old men to the snotnose brats, they're a murdering breed, the whole lot of them!"

This utterance fell upon cowardly silence. Near-empty siphons hiccuped. Augustin Charras snickered as he examined the amber transparency of his Martini as though doubting its quality—and doubting something else too. But M. Anselme heard him perfectly when he quietly growled "Then you go fight, you faker, you're over-age!"

The grown sons went, the young husbands went, the reservist fathers of families went, silently, silently. No one got drunk, no one burst out into the "Marseillaise" at the East Station: young Gaston Prugnier, shy and friendly; young Boitelle, said to be as clever as a Polytechnic student; young Dupin. The pimps went, Charlie l'Astuce first. He was blond Émilie's man, blond Émilie with her misty blue eyes, her vaguely bluish teeth between parted lips. Charlie stood drinks all around, even for M. Bœuf of the vice squad. Charlie said out of the corner of his mouth, "I know I won't come back. What do I care? As long as it helps other people, France, and the kids on the block! I wish I could be sure of that!"

"Don't talk nonsense, my boy," said M. Bœuf amiably. "You'll be back in six months and we'll have plenty of little scuffles in dark corners. You're tough."

"That's just why I won't come back," Charlie insisted.

There was something like friendship in the look they exchanged. And Charlie was killed at Lauterbourg or somewhere else at the end of the third week. His last letter, addressed to his "beloved little wife," was passed from hand to hand. "We're leading a cozy little life," he wrote, "only the airplanes are a pain in the ass. I miss only one thing in the world, our Saturday nights at the dance hall in the Rue de Lappe and our boating trips at Suresnes, and how sweet you looked in a bathing suit, and my peaceful little corner at Anselme's. You can tell Anselme that I wish him well, he was never a mean son-of-a-bitch. Say hello to Fernande for me. I still advise her to stop being such a sucker. I kiss you in all the little nooks and corners..." A letter that made you proud of your man.

Émilie didn't go with anyone else for four whole weeks, and then it was only on the insistence of her girlfriends and because after all she was a little afraid of M. Bœuf. "Your man was a hero," said M. Bœuf, as he possessed her, and told her of his own experiences at the battle of the Somme in 1917. She had the letter framed and hung it over her bed with a photo.

The milliner at the end of the street displayed in her two shop-windows mourning styles for women of all ages, for all the faces of the grief to come. Some of them were very becoming. She was never at a loss for a business angle, not her; you felt like throwing a brick at her windows with their smiling wooden heads, blonds, brunettes, and redheads—some even with white hair—done up in black turbans, with veils drooping gracefully over their ears. "There are going to be plenty of widows, plenty of widows," the display seemed to gloat. On a wall nearby bills were posted. A ladies' committee continued to publish its illustrated protests against vivisection. Pity the poor guinea pigs sacrificed to an inhuman science! Augustin Charras solemnly urged his customers to read these posters, which he found particularly moving.

The war, muzzled by the Maginot Line, absolutely impregnable, was mild. A seven-minute walk away, the Jewish quarter of the Rue des Rosiers, where for centuries no rosebush had ever bloomed, existed in a state of heavy, continuous lamentation—the Jews have been sort of in the habit since the fall of their famous Wall in Jerusalem—because their Warsaw was succumbing under shellfire. Of course, no one could do anything about it. Warsaw was on the borders of Russia, at the edge of the snow and of Bolshevism, not much closer than Ethiopia... When the war was finished over there, perhaps there would be peace.

"If you ask me, I don't believe it," said Augustin Charras. "Once the dance has begun, I have a feeling that it will circle the globe. It will take more than the Maginot Line to stop it."

M. Anselme Flotte gave him a dark look. "You wouldn't be a defeatist by any chance?"

"Me. Not at all. I wish every general on the planet the most thundering victories. We deserve them, don't we?"

M. Bœuf gave him a sidelong glance and adopted his good-natured tone. "Don't get your dander up. Everything will come out all right. As long as business is good, everything's good."

Business was good. The rooms in the Hôtel Marquise were taken every night. From five in the afternoon to two in the morning there were always three girls gossiping in the entrance. Five others prowled the sidewalk, each enjoying the right of a whole housefront, in accordance with a tradition perhaps dating back to Louis XIV.

An old-fashioned streetlamp, smeared with blue blackout paint, threw a stingy, malevolent light over this nocturnal world. "It's funny," said Annie l'Étoile (so called because of the pink, star-shaped scar on her neck), "like they've invented a light that gives darkness; you'd think you were in the morgue." But it wasn't the morgue, it was a place of business. Not every spot on the sidewalk was equal; the best of them provided enough dingy light to bring out a silhouette, to give a certain venomous charm to a harshly made-up face, to lend a black mouth the seduction of a wound or of a gaping vulva. The zone of almost complete night should have been set aside for the homely women—but try to make them listen to reason before they've been on the job for twenty years. If M. Bœuf had not watched over his wayward flock like a good shepherd, they would have torn each other's hair out fighting over the spots close to the lamp, the convenience of a dark doorway surmounted by a faun's head. But M. Bœuf was there, and his favorite was the girl from Nantes, Émilie, with blond curls pressed to her forehead and eyes like two little drops of blue water. He was sociable to the point of occasionally sitting down at a table with the pimps and discussing business with them directly. "You see, Messieurs, what I say is that everyone has got to live. Each in his own way. We can't all work for the government, can we? That would be too much of a good thing. But duty is duty, until they pension me off. The least I can do is pull in a couple of them once or twice a week. They can get off with two or three days if they don't raise a stink. After all, I can't have people taking me for a grafter or saying I've got my eyes in my back pants pocket. And besides, I have three other streets under me, that gives them plenty of leeway—" They understood each another. While he took his favorite upstairs to the room with the mirrors, an olive-skinned man in a suit with small checks kept nervously ordering drinks (which M. Anselme, charitable soul, did not refuse him after hours) and looking at the clock more often than there was any need to.

The bar was flourishing too. During the hours when it was legal to serve drinks, soldiers on furlough filled it with their dilapidated uniforms, khaki or horizon blue, and their discordant voices. "At the front," they said, "we twiddle our thumbs. Take our sector, the Meuse—" In short, there was nothing happening—except for one event of minor importance. A soldier on a bicycle brought a letter for the Boitelles. Mme Boitelle came home from work at five o'clock, and shortly after descended the stairs emitting sobs that were more like loud hiccups. She issued from the hallway of Number 16, holding a handkerchief in front of her mouth as though she had a toothache. Angèle Charras was practicing the piano. Slow chords drifted over the graying sidewalk like phosphorescent disks over colorless water. Stunned, Mme Boitelle stopped under the WOOD AND COAL sign and whirled about strangely. She was a large woman with a mannish look, an upright head, and a fine head of hair. She burst out, "Make her stop, Monsieur Augustin! Make her stop. It's so awful."

They saw her sobbing into her handkerchief like a child, like a madwoman, and she was holding, clenched on the top of her dress, a large envelope from the Ministry of National Defense. When ministries write to taxpayers, it is not to inform them that they have won the lottery. It transpired that young Gustave Boitelle, the merry plump lad with a weakness for loud neckties, would never return, never again be seen here or anywhere else, having fallen "on the field of honor," in a forest in the Saar—he who hated trees. Mme Sage, the herbalist, consoled Mme Boitelle at great length and even brought into her bedroom a little tract with a blue cover, published by the Psychic Society and entitled *Communications with the Beyond*. "It is scientific, my poor Madame. Turning tables, you know. It wouldn't surprise me if he spoke to you someday." Mme Boitelle only sobbed all the more desperately. Then she bought herself a black crepe hat, rather pretty, at a neighborly discount. Time passed.

One May evening M. Bœuf came striding in, abandoning his usual sagacious amble. He seemed in such a bad temper that Marthe, Monique, and even Émilie took refuge in the hallway; but he passed without paying them any attention, burst into the bar, letting his manicured hands fall on the counter, and stared stupidly at himself in the mirror.

"A strong Pernod?" suggested M. Anselme, who never let anything surprise him.

"They're at Sedan, can you believe it," gasped M. Bœuf, who seemed prostrate. "Good God! Now all we need is a Bazaine!"*

Sedan! The two belote players seated in the corner by the door heard the whispered word and their cards dropped from their hands. Through the mind of M. Anselme, who was scarcely aware of it, ran a memory of the Marquesas Islands in the midst of an incredibly azure sea—and a childhood Épinal print: the Emperor, bareheaded, on horseback, surrendering his sword to the King of Prussia. Round cannonballs sprayed flames of red ink about them as they burst. A camp follower gave a drink to a wounded man. The King of Prussia was a noble, fatherly old fellow in side-whiskers. "That's too much!"

"We're done for," said M. Bœuf tranquilly. "Trapped like rats, you can take my word for it."

Obeying a presentiment, Mme Alexandrine came in. Her face,

---

*In 1870, during the Franco-Prussian War, the French were disastrously defeated at Sedan after Marshal Bazaine allowed his army to be encircled in Metz.

still betraying a certain grace despite the increased heaviness of her features, seemed to rest on the bouquet next to the cash register.

"What's wrong, Anselme?"

Mechanically wiping a glass, the boss muttered, "Sedan."

Mme Alexandrine preserved her outward calm, but her stomach writhed within her, as on the day when Clémentine, the chambermaid, came and whispered in her ear, "Madame, there's blood under the door of Room 11."

"Oh well," she said, "Sedan isn't Pantin. They're not at the gates of Paris, after all."

"It may be pretty much the same thing," said M. Bœuf darkly.

The air was charged with so much emotion that two of the girls outside pressed their faces to the glass panes of the door. M. Bœuf turned toward these feminine masks blurred with anxiety. He opened the door.

"Émilie," he said gently. "Come in and have a grenadine."

And in a tender stupor he contemplated the blond girl's profile. "There we go," he thought, "France is done for." And he could think of nothing else.

An avalanche of catastrophes followed. It became known that M. Hyppolite Lunaire (the house across the street: WHOLESALE LACE), who bought in Antwerp, Brussels, Malines, had dismissed seven out of fifteen of his female workers "until the end of the war." That the Lancier ladies had fallen abruptly into destitution since the textile mill of Lancier Successors in Valenciennes, founded in 1881, had been occupied by the Germans; rumor had it that the mill had been destroyed. That the generals or tank drivers had been guilty of treason on the Meuse, giving up the bridges, etc. That the line of the Somme was pierced. That our aviation did not exist; that the Belgians, that the English . . . That the government was going to defend Paris to the last ditch, that there would be another Battle of the Marne, that the taxis would be mobilized. That Paris would be declared an open city and that the real battle of France would be fought on the Loire with every chance of success against a tired enemy. That Georges Mandel was going to arrest Georges Bonnet and that Georges Bonnet was going to arrest Paul Faure.

Suspicious foreigners were rounded up at the Bastille, in the Hôtel de Ville quarter, at the Châtelet, in the Faubourg du Temple, at Saint-Paul; and these measures inspired both panic and comfort. It was plain that parachutists dropped in the Bois de Vincennes would not get far. Thank God for that! (Unless by chance they had French identification papers in good order.) At Neuilly a parachutist was arrested disguised as a priest and armed with a submachine gun. Trucks carried away to an unknown destination groups of Jews and well-dressed foreigners guarded by taciturn Mobile Guards in black helmets. Wholesalers raised wine prices. In the midst of this confusion Mussolini declared war on France. Tears of rage glistened in the eyes of men in the Métro. "We must be done for if that coward is joining the fray!" *L'Action Française* uttered a pained comment upon the unexpected attitude of the "dictator of Latin civilization." *L'Humanité*, in a letter-sized mimeographed version distributed at night by devoted comrades, continued to denounce the "Franco-Anglo-Saxon imperialist plutocracies" and to hold up the peace policy of the Soviet Union as an example to the toiling masses, small businessmen, and sincere Catholics. "For a strong, free, and prosperous France!" It was said that now America would— The ministries evacuated their archives, Rouen was in flames, Amiens in ruins.

One morning a beer truck from Lille strayed into the Rue du Roi-de-Naples. At the still-uncertain hour when the first stores were opening, this enormous phantom, dusty and unbelievably battered, lumbered along beneath its burden of furniture, mattresses, roped-down bundles, and children sleeping in the poses of angels or tired animals. There were weary housewives, a freckled madonna nursing her newborn, soldiers wearing the insignia of mixed-up regiments, the 32nd, the 321st, the 126th . . . The confusion was complete.

"Where are you from?" someone asked the madonna, and she answered, "From the mines of Fismes. My husband has disappeared."

She smiled politely, revealing bad teeth.

"Is there much damage in your section?"

"No, not at the mines . . . In other places I don't know." She apologized: "I slept the whole way."

The phantom truck departed slowly through an oblique solitude. Angèle Charras came out of the black coal shop and ran after the truck with a little package which she put into the grimy hand of a little boy. On her way back she seemed to emerge from the dreary blue morning. The truck turned the corner and only a few remembered the picture that it made, like something out of a shipwreck.

Several stores closed. Cars overloaded with people and baggage passed through the neighborhood, mattresses on the roofs, trunks, bicycles, baby carriages piled high on the luggage-carriers—one even carried a white refrigerator all splattered with dry mud. "Well, it's the great escape," mused Mme Alexandrine. "The rich ones are heading south. We'd do the same in their place."

But it wasn't only the rich. The strangest spectacle was the parade of jalopies from shortly after the first war, recovered from auto graveyards and rebuilt from pieces and parts, squeaking and panting, bearing license plates from Meurthe-et-Moselle, Artois, Côtes du Nord, Ardennes. The refugees riding in them had left nothing behind, were carrying away old saucepans, cats in baskets, dogs, and unwashed children. "I don't get it," said Mme Alexandrine. "What are they running away from? What have they to lose? I suppose Hitler wants their old clinkers." These must be people with neither property nor patriotism, nondescript rabble tied up with the Spanish Reds, running away from the prospect of punishment which—well, it might be excessive.

The tone of conversation in the bar became profoundly bitter. Was Anselme Flotte losing his grip? Or rather, in view of the days to come, was he not showing courageous foresight? The things he said nowadays would have been impossible for him a month earlier. "It serves us right," he said, "we were taking it too easy, the forty-hour week, paid vacations, the Ministry of Leisure Time—why not a ministry of pleasure, if you please, and free whorehouses for the working class? That might be an idea to take up in the Chamber. Some of the workers at Renault's were making their two hundred francs a day, and maybe you can tell me what they were doing that was so special. And all this time Léon Blum was having his château refurnished. More Spanish than French, I'm telling you. And now we have to foot the bill for the Reds."

M. Louis Lempereur, the tripe butcher, was getting green around the gills, torn between the desire to flee and the fear of flight. He exaggerated the same opinions with particular awkwardness, mingling invective against foreigners, strikers, Communists, and pacifists with imprecations against the Boches and the fascists. "They've been vandals and brigands ever since they came out of the forests of Prussia. When will the world be rid of this vermin?" He suggested the formation of a national guard. M. Bœuf, though he himself saw things none too clearly, reacted against all this incoherence.

"The Boches are the Boches, there's no doubt about it." A sigh. "But they, M. Lempereur, know what they want. And they work. No forty hours for them, you can bank on that, but fifty or sixty. And in Germany they send demagogues to Dachau. They have put their house in order. They're too strong for us, that's all."

With an air of infinite boredom, Augustin Charras spat heavily on the floor. Anselme Flotte watched him with a kind of hatred.

"Take me, for instance. I'm on my feet from five in the morning till after eleven at night and I'm lucky if I get in a little nap in the afternoon. Nobody thinks of a paid vacation for me. I go to the central market before dawn, I carry the whole hotel on my shoulders. And even if I'm not satisfied I can't go on strike. Taxes rain in on me, and the rates go up and up. The franc is falling on its ass, and the tourist trade is dying out, and as for the Hotel Owners Association, the government treats it like the fifth wheel on a cart! Look out for yourself, Anselme; no one else will."

Two sewer cleaners in rubber boots were drinking white wine at the bar. "Not much, this white stuff," one of them muttered quite audibly.

Anselme Flotte, accepting the challenge, turned toward him,

furious beneath his feigned good temper. "Shall I tell you M'sieu, what this white wine wholesales for? Would you like to see my bills? Or maybe you'd like me to tell you what goes on at the wine market?"

"Oh, I wouldn't want to put you to that much trouble, boss," said the sewer cleaner.

The threat of a storm hung over the glasses. The second sewer cleaner wiped his thick mustache with the back of his dirty hand, gazed into the void around him, and muttered, "Balls!" And suddenly he addressed M. Anselme Flotte in the most familiar terms:

"You're scared shitless, boss. If you could carry your whorehouse on your back like a snail—and mighty poor eating that would be!—you'd light out of here in high. You probably wouldn't stop running until you got to Lake Chad. But you can't do it. You're afraid a Boche shell might wreck your beds and set fire to the bedbug and syphilis nests that that bring in all your dough. You're scared to blow because it's your pile, your property, but you're just as scared to stay in your rathole. You'd really like to be on the right side of the fence—but there's your trouble: you don't know which *is* the right side."

The movement of his hand, blackened by subterranean filth, had in it a somber threat: "You might as well get set to shit green, boss. This is only the beginning—"

Anselme Flotte kept his dignity: "That will be one franc sixty, Messieurs, and I hope never to see you again in my establishment."

"You won't have to lose sleep about that, boss. You're more likely to see the Boches. They'll probably come and smash your bottles and kick your ass."

The glass doors rattled sharply. A tall, swarthy soldier, his helmet dangling from his shoulder, his garrison cap askew over his sunken cheeks, threw his backpack—so heavy it seemed to be full of scrap iron—on a chair, ordered a pint of red wine, and sponged his forehead with a filthy rag that he used as a handkerchief. No one spoke to him. He drank and smiled, showing the teeth of a carnivore. Happy, he talked to himself: "Nothing's changed here in old Paname. Except for the rats that are clearing out. That's what rats are for. It's a grand old town, Paname. At Saint-Claudien, everything is in flames . . ."

"Saint-Claudien?" asked a voice hovering feebly in the void. "What do you mean—everything?"

"Maybe I meant Saint-Germain. The whole place is on fire, you should hear it crackle, oh là là! The whorehouses and the gin mills," said the soldier with a broad grin. "Just listen to it!"

He threw the door open. At the edge of the sidewalk, at the edge of the void, beneath the slated twilight, alone in the anxious air, the slender outline of a streetwalker stood tense. She was listening— In rhythmic bursts, from the distance, from beyond the suburbs, came the deep, gasping breath of artillery...

"Good evening, everybody!" said the soldier politely.

A blue curtain had already been lowered over the window of Widow Prugnier's grocery store. Night fell like gray panic. The soldier, readjusting the straps of his backpack, entered the hallway of Number 16 and silently climbed the stairs.

2. LIQUIDATIONS

ON THE fourth floor the soldier stopped in front of a dark door, struck a flame from his cigarette lighter, and read on a copper plate: ACHILLE TARTRE, JOB LOTS, TRANSPORT. The bell in the apartment emitted a low, insistent buzz. The floor in the hallway squeaked beneath quick slippered steps. M. Tartre opened the door in person, as far as the safety chain would permit, and pointed a flashlight through the crack.

"Ah, it's you," he said in a hesitant voice.

"Yes, it's me," said the soldier. "I hope your maid won't mind making me a little black coffee."

"No, of course not. Come in."

No sooner had he opened the door than M. Tartre confusedly regretted having done so. In his military uniform the visitor was too unlike himself—that is unlike the tall young man generally attired in a well-tailored suit. The soldier stooped to pass through the doorway; in the narrow hallway, between the cupboard with the mirror door and the green hangings covering a filing case, he awkwardly drew up to his full height, like a wild beast stretching in a narrow cage.

"Nothing has changed here either, Monsieur Tartre. That's funny. You can't imagine what a funny impression that makes."

M. Tartre blinked. At home he wore no spectacles, as his eyesight was excellent. Short but powerfully built, with a bit of a paunch, he wore a warm house jacket of beige wool with blue facings. A skullcap covered his bald head. A Moorish lantern of wrought iron and colored glass dimly lighted the corridor. M. Tartre passed around his visitor, permitting him to enter first: *politesse oblige*. "Turn to your left and go into the dining room."

The visitor, not hearing perhaps, for M. Tartre spoke in a low voice, took the door to the right and entered the office. A metal lamp concentrated an intense light on the desk.

"It's not very gay in your place," said the soldier in a tone that seemed to M. Tartre full of hidden meaning.

"I enjoy myself away from home," said the little man, forcing an easy manner. "You know, Paris hasn't run short of pleasures. Upon my soul, it would take the end of the world for that to happen."

In the haven of his office M. Tartre felt better. The desk put a certain distance between himself and his visitor. There was a telephone on the desk. On a board beneath the right-hand drawer was a good automatic. A small safe stood beside the swivel chair. Next to it stood the liquor cabinet, which contained a blackjack and another revolver.

"Armagnac?" suggested M. Tartre, still blinking.

"Armagnac!" The soldier accepted joyfully.

The soldier listened enraptured to the silence in the apartment. A silence without the ticking of a clock, without the nibbling of mice, without the snorting of horses, without the roar of distant motors— insidious as buzzing mosquitoes—a silence without the least reminder of time and of danger, a magic silence. This man could still hear within him the crashing of planets being pounded by maddened artillery, the roar of bombers, enormous explosions, metal screeching, and the ripping apart of tanks, earth, tires, stones, and men's chests. "Good God," he said to himself as in a dream, "what wouldn't we have given, on the Somme or on the Marne, for a moment of this silence!" More audibly he murmured, "There's nothing left but stinking ruins."

"Where?" M. Tartre asked.

"In lots of places."

"War," M. Tartre sighed.

Above the triangular beam of the lampshade, the soothing half-light disclosed shelves full of samples, glass closets containing bottles of perfume, musical instruments, surgical tools, silverware, a microscope, traveling kit. Stuffed birds were perched near the ceiling. The soldier dropped his heavy backpack on the carpet, bent himself double, and sank into a leather easy chair. His head, a little higher than the surface of the desk, was just at the dividing line between light and shade, and he leaned sideways so as to remain in the shade. On the desk there was only an old solid silver inkstand, an account book—opened—a folded copy of *Paris-soir*, a detective story with a colored cover showing a curtain being raised by the spread finger of a hand in a yellow glove. Below the curtain a star-shaped spot of blood. The book was called *The Mystery of the Eleventh Hour.*

"That mystery must be stupid," said the soldier softly. "Stupid like *Pourrissoir.*"*

M. Tartre raised his head, which he had lowered to fill two little glasses with alcohol. His face was wide and blotchy with broken veins, his mouth round like a mollusk. From between his yellow eyelids, dark agitated pupils cast glances like quick bites.

"What mystery?" asked M. Tartre.

"The crime in the book. Since I have seen crime on the scale of the Pyramids, I know that there's nothing simpler. There's no mystery about it. Especially at the eleventh hour."

M. Tartre's hand extended his glass. "Your health!" "And here's to yours!" They clinked glasses.

"Got to read something before bedtime," M. Tartre explained. "These stories are sometimes entertaining."

"I don't find anything entertaining about crime," said the soldier. "I'd rather read stories about little blue flowers."

His vigorous animal features lit up. His hollow cheeks and tanned skin gave him an air of savagery and physical decisiveness. A sense of violent fatigue emanated from him.

"You've come from the front?"

"More or less. From a blazing furnace, rather. There are lots of them—"

"On leave?"

* Popular term for the newspaper *Paris-soir.* A *pourrissoir* is a vat in which rags are left to rot in a paper factory.

"That's the word for it. The longest leave in the world, Monsieur Achille."

Several times within the last few minutes M. Tartre had regretted opening the door. Now the turn of the conversation and the weariness of his caller half reassured him. He was determined to retain his advantage.

"If you'll wait a few minutes, my maid will be back. She'll make you a good cup of black coffee, there's nothing like it."

"I should be surprised to see Mlle Marcelle back for some days," the soldier answered dreamily. "I saw her taking the express at Austerlitz Station."

M. Tartre's breath came heavy at this news. The solitude and the silence seemed to crush him. Pretending to scratch his leg, he pulled out the board with the Browning on it. The next exchange was meaningless:

"You must have been mistaken."

"It's possible."

The soldier stretched his legs out on the carpet. He watched the shadows at his feet. He listened to the seashell vibration of nothingness. He thought of nothing. That was good.

M. Tartre placed his left hand on the lighted edge of the table, where it lay like a strange shellfish. His right hand hung beside the automatic. He did not like making loans that would never be repaid—or vague offers. He waited.

"I've brought a deal," said the soldier finally, as though the object of his visit had returned suddenly to his memory.

"Go on."

The soldier bent over, picked up his heavy backpack, tossed it on the table, and with a flick of his thumb slid the zipper. M. Tartre stood up, breathless. His little round belly protruded and the fleshy wrinkles in his face were gathered in an expression of extreme attention. Beneath the lamplight the backpack took on the shape of a voluminous tropical fish whose wide open belly revealed a treasure. Everything sparkled: heaps of wristwatches, brooches, pendants, necklaces. The diamonds stood out against the black silk bands of the ladies' watches. The tiny white or gilded dials shone like stars amid this plunder of the thousand-and-first night.

"All the watches run," said the soldier with childlike gravity. "They all give the correct time. I wound them while I was tearing the tags off. Look."

His eyes gleamed as, leaning over the treasure, he pressed a little square watch set with fine diamonds to M. Tartre's ear.

"A golden deal," murmured M. Tartre.

"There's a little platinum too."

The soldier plunged his hand into the gleaming pile and finally drew out a bracelet of a metal duller than silver.

"And not a drop of blood," he said with pride. "I didn't take the soiled pieces."

M. Tartre, embarrassed, said nothing.

"There must be a hundred thousand francs' worth."

It was clear that a hundred thousand francs seemed a fabulous sum to this young man.

"Well," said M. Tartre, highly pleased. "I'll give you twenty-five thousand in cash . . . No, look here, for you I'll make it an even thirty thousand."

The soldier passed his hand over his forehead. He was pale now, he seemed faint. M. Tartre hastened to pour him a glass of Armagnac.

"If you knew," said the soldier, "in what a corner of hell I took all this—to prevent the Boches from taking it. If anyone on earth could even imagine—"

M. Tartre tapped him gaily on the shoulder. "It's all over for you, my boy. Thirty thousand right now. And if it brings in any more—you know the difficulties in this kind of business—you can count on me for a bonus. You won't find a fairer man than me to do business with."

The soldier fell back heavily in the leather chair. The greyhound was exhausted. M. Tartre felt that he was master of the situation. Most likely this pillager of ruins didn't have a franc to his name, and every step he took in the streets was at the risk of the firing squad. He had no money for a hotel room, not even for a forty-franc whore! M. Tartre decided that his offer of thirty thousand had been unreasonable.

Twenty thousand would have been plenty. You look all shot, my boy, you're in no state to debate the friendly price that I'm willing to give you. The soldier's eyes elsewhere, far away. Amid a flood of unrelated visions—the defense of a little hog-backed bridge beneath fine old oak trees, the bursting of a comrade's skull, burning buildings—one image forced itself on his memory. In the smoke-saturated air, amid the wreckage and the hysterical crackling of flames, the jewelry store had remained strangely intact. The shop was open to the sky; nothing but the little hand of a child, fingers soiled, neatly cut off at the wrist, fallen from heaven onto a velvet-lined tray displaying timepieces guaranteed for five years; droplets of blood, black pearls, were spread over the velvet and the watches.

"I would wash my eyes out with vitriol," said the soldier, "if it could make me forget that. Holy God!"

"Twenty-five thousand, will that be all right?" M. Tartre repeated.

The soldier returned to the present moment and shrugged. "Didn't you say thirty?"

"Twenty-five, my friend. It will be thirty or more when the account is liquidated. Nowadays, you know—"

An unspeakably luminous smile came into the soldier's eyes. A singing voice within him repeated, "I'll give five thousand never to see that hand again. I'll give ten thousand! Done!"

"Out with the bills, Monsieur Achille," he said joyfully.

M. Tartre turned around, opened the safe. The vertical slit in the safe was like the opening in a monstrous piggy bank kept by the children of giants, nasty giants. M. Tartre's repulsive, pink hand was thrust into it. Perhaps the steel edging of the safe would cut it off clean, and the abominable hand would fall into the treasure. Above all, thought the soldier, I must not go mad. He forced himself to concentrate his attention on the old solid silver inkstand. He took out the two ink bottles, first the black ink, then the red ink—hideous red ink.

In a rage the soldier lifted the inkstand and weighed it in his hand. M. Tartre, seen from behind, was pudgy, his neck padded with lard, his scalp a yellowish pink, and he noisily licked his fingers as he counted the bills. The massive inkstand descended on his skull with the deadly force of a bomb exploding. M. Tartre collapsed slowly, giving a prolonged sigh. He slid slowly from the swivel chair and vanished into the shadow of the table.

"It's funny," said the soldier. "Beats the shit out of me."

His hands trembled and he watched them tremble. He listened to the buzzing of the void.

"Well that's that," he said, and now he was calm.

His hands no longer trembled. He closed his backpack and threw it over his shoulder. On his way out of the room he bent down over the desk, thrust his fingertips into the black maw of the safe, seized a packet of bills which he stuffed into his trousers pockets. It never occurred to him to take the second packet that lay beneath the first. His jaws were clamped tight, and between them he mumbled stupidly, "Thirty minus five is twenty-five, minus five, I'll give ten thousand not to see it again, I'll give ten, I'll give the whole thing."

The cannon were silent, not a motor in the sky. You could fill your lungs with this silence. The soldier closed the apartment door after him slowly. The balustrade was cool to his touch. Before going down, he listened again to the incredible silence. A sound of voices reached him from the upper floors. The talk was about flight—what else could it be about?—about a car, about money, or rather, no money.

"I tell you, Maurice, we have to leave tomorrow, and better in the morning than the afternoon." (This voice had a Spanish accent.) "You can't count on the last train. Either it leaves before you get to the station or it never leaves. If we can't do better, we leave on foot . . . as long as we leave."

"Twelve hundred in all, twelve hundred for the two of us, we won't get far, José." (The other voice was low, sibilant, and lisping.) "Do you know what the fare is to Lyon?"

The voices died down and then rebounded. "We can't leave him in the lurch, he's been fighting for forty years, an eternity—"

"That gives us twelve hundred for the three of us!" said the lisping voice desolately. "We won't get farther than the Loire. Balls! Come with me to the Rue des Écouffes, I still have a chance—"

The speakers descended the stairs. The soldier preceded them without the least sound. Pressed against a door in the darkness, he saw two young men pass him, one of them bareheaded, the other wearing a felt hat.

"It would be enough," said one, "if we bought tickets to Tours."

The soldier followed them. A smile of savage satisfaction lighted up his face. He was no longer alone. He followed the strangers. He felt strong. And relieved. The bag of treasure weighed heavy on his hip. The night air cleansed his soul.

"You are saved, my boys," he thought. "And you don't know it. Isn't that a good one?" He laughed softly to himself, overcome with joy. An elasticity as of resurrection returned to his limbs. High heels tapped on the sidewalk behind him. A streetwalker came running up to him and took his arm. The oval of her face was deathly pale, her mouth a black wound.

"Beat it," said the soldier pleasantly and hastened his step. "It's not the right time—"

As she removed her arm, he remembered the banknotes in his pocket with his snot-rag and his pipe.

"Hey, don't run away so fast, little night flower." He put a crumpled bill into her hand and she ran to unfold it under the dismal blue light of the streetlamp.

3. ENCOUNTERS

RUE DES Écouffes and Rue des Rosiers, narrow and plunged into anxious darkness, were full of silent animation. The sheer cliffs of their wretched housefronts rose from sidewalks lined with garbage. Laborious yet stagnant poverty lurked beneath the old masonry—as on similar streets in Vilna, Cracow, Odessa, Saloniki. In this asylum for the wretched of all nations a dozen languages were spoken, not to mention dialects. Cap makers from Lodz, moneylenders from Bessarabia, shoemakers from Berdichev, diamond merchants from Amsterdam, artisans from Sub-Carpathian Ruthenia, ex-shipowners from Athens, ex-merchants from Smyrna, ex-barkeeps from Chicago, furriers from everywhere, fugitives of every trade that throve between the pearl-gray shores of the Baltic and the blue coasts of the Aegean, between the Danube and the Dnieper, between the pawnshops of the Old World and the great banks of America, fugitives from all the Gehennas of toil, money, persecution, and faith, lived here together and read newspapers printed in graceful characters devised on the banks of the Euphrates or the Jordan some three thousand years before the age of linotype. Here beat the tenacious heart of a landless nation, dispersed throughout Paris as throughout the continents of the world. Invisible spokes converged on these streets from the heights of Belleville—whence suddenly you glimpsed, on the horizon, the Eiffel Tower set nobly between gray sky and gray city—from the broad boulevards near the Place de la République, where repose seems to flee at your approach; from the Faubourg du Temple and the Bastille, where industries and dramas have so little space to feed on; and even from the Champs-Élysées where, thanks to the earthly radiation of wealth, the Paris sky takes on a perfect softness.

This quarter was home to incredible exports unknown to serious economists. You could sell anything and buy anything here: a Hebrew, Yiddish, Mohammedan, or Christian name; a cleanly laundered passport issued by one of the fifteen sovereign states of Central Europe, the Balkans, the Baltic; an authentic and pure fiancée, who was submissive to the ancient Law and would in truth become an irreproachable wife; girls with big dark eyes and redheads with pale pink lips for the brothels of Valparaíso, Montevideo, Shanghai, or the fabulous City of the Moon which drunken sailors claim exists; banknotes, genuine or forged, devaluated or magic, originating in Paraguay or Manchukuo; visas for Siam, Honduras, and other promised lands known only to stamp collectors; odd volumes of Maimonides, the mysterious writings of the Kabbalah, the psychoanalytical novels of Sholem Asch, the Life of Theodore Herzl, the preachings of Ahad Ha'am—found a homeland where the Temple was built!—of Lenin, Tolstoy, Gorky, and of Stalin, Father of Peoples...

Here you could buy or sell a little more than all the merchandise of the universe, with the exception, to be sure, of consciences and beliefs—for trafficking in these is more common among the Gentiles. The old Law and young ideas retain here a vigor bordering on a materiality of the spirit. Men who think they no longer believe still believe in themselves. Here, when men go bad, they know it. Even traitors sometimes look into an interior mirror and say to themselves, "I am rich, I eat well, I wear silk shirts, I shall build a villa with a swimming pool, I shall buy up the business of that incurable imbecile who has never betrayed anyone, I am happy"—but how sad it is, stern God! to be such a rotten bastard under it all. "May my children, may my children's children never know what I was, what I am, beneath my well-tailored clothes!" (And they send big contributions to relief committees.)

Here menders of eyeglasses, tinkerers of watches that will never again show a right time for luck or sunlight, patchers of suits worn down by lives of heartbreak, men resembling Rembrandt's models worked under a skylight and dreamed that on one day of the week the Creator Himself assumes human form and goes walking with His beloved beneath orange trees in bloom.

No one in these streets was unaware that a misfortune was approaching for which there was yet no name—no one uttered a sigh. These people remembered having survived several pogroms—thanks to one blue-eyed cutthroat who chased a terrified family down into a cellar, shut the door, and turned around, crying that Glory be to God there are no more vermin left in this place so let's go. "If the Eternal wants us to perish, what do our wishes matter?" said the old men familiar with the revered texts. "If the Eternal wants His people to be saved, who can destroy us?" they added. And they advised the young people to procure false papers.

The engineer Chaim, owner of the Tel Aviv restaurant, declared: "If they come, well, the soldiers will sell what they have looted on the way, and there are plenty of them who like Ukrainian borscht, chopped herring, stuffed carp! It won't be so bad, take it from me, until there is nothing left to eat."

When that time came there would be some way to escape—through the lines, the last frontiers, cemeteries, no doubt, God be praised. The weakest, considering themselves the purest, fortified themselves by fasting; the rich had already departed.

At this time of night the shops were neither open nor closed. Most of them had their shutters down and their doors ajar. The streetlamps, globes painted blue, bathed the crumbling plaster of the housefronts in a desolate undersea glow. A beam of oddly luxurious light filtered through cracks in the blackout blinds of certain upper-story windows that by day sported pink or cream-colored curtains. Here were mirrored parlors, garishly lighted. Over grocery stores and leather workshops, over the apartment of a highly respectable family in a courtyard edged with flowers, the establishments of "Judith" and "Rachel" were carrying on business as usual. They were perched at the top of narrow stairways, freshly repainted like those of good prisons, under too-bright lighting; the caller was admitted through an iron door after an assistant madam, with a triangular face incredibly ravaged by thirty years of baseness, had looked him over. Safe little dives for respectable businessmen, legal hangouts for well-dressed hoodlums. The piously bearded man would be ushered behind a bead curtain into a little room where he could sit without being seen and select a brightly adorned body for himself. Exhausted, shipwrecked swimmers, struggling and gasping for air like shining fish leaping and asphyxiating in nets, were ringing the bells of these establishments. Days of great events are days of good receipts.

On the edge of the sidewalk an obese mother and her overgrown little girls were murmuring tender goodbyes to a young cyclist who was setting out for the South and safety, taking with him his threatened adolescence and the wealth of a family: a few diamonds sewn into the buttons of his jacket. "Don't undress when you go to bed, my darling child—"

A dry cleaner's delivery van lumbered down the street like an awkward, square beast; the open rear doors revealed a whole tribe crowded upon trunks and comforters. On the roof a man was perched on top of a pile of bedclothes, asleep. He had a thin beard, his mouth was closed and his neck extended, proffered to the sacrificial knife of an invisible high priest.

Maurice Silber and José Ortiga dodged the truck, slipped on some vegetable peels, and stopped outside a door emitting a feeble ray of light. The shop had been built in other days, beneath a carriage entrance. It was long and narrow under a high oval ceiling. A flowered screen at the rear separated the store from the living quarters. The grain chests were empty, the boxes of noodles, beans, lentils, sugar, rice— all empty; the shelves of canned goods had nothing on them but a few disdained samples. The sacks had collapsed into useless rags. There remained on the counter a few fresh onions and some kosher sausage, some Yiddish newspapers, sewing thread, children's penholders, small bottles of ink, mint pastilles, licorice, candles. Seated behind the counter, an old man was reading a New York magazine beneath a waxed-paper lampshade. Foreigners when they saw him recognized at once the vaulted forehead, the leonine white beard, the sensitive nose, the spectacles of a Karl Marx; Frenchmen were reminded of Victor Hugo or Rodin. But it was only Moïse Mendel the grocer, Zionist and Socialist, with brown eyes illuminated by a wise benevolence. People consulted him about a book to read, a disturbing dream, a small investment, a question of conscience, the political situation, ideas.

"Monsieur Moïse," said Silber, ill-concealing his agitation, "you're the only one who can help me. I must get out of here, tomorrow."

"Yes," said M. Moïse, "you must."

"And I'm broke. I haven't been able to sell my samples, thirty pairs of ladies' gloves—of good quality I assure you, one of doeskin and one of pigskin with a slight defect; I still don't know how I'm going to manage to leave, there's no way I can take all that with me."

Old Moïse lowered his head to get a better look at the young man over his glasses. "Such is the egotism of youth; it never entered his head to ask what old Moïse was going to do. Sorry, sacred egotism. And he is right. Old Moïse doesn't matter to anyone anymore. Alone on earth, alone with his stars and his memories—and the memories are fading."

Moïse reflected. Then: "Go down to the Faubourg du Temple and see Aron-Durand, tell him I sent you. He is a man with a bad conscience and he wants to get rich quick. He is piling up stocks of everything now. He'll give you a third of what the stuff is worth, resign yourself. Wait, take these fifty francs too. Old Moïse has already given away half his cashbox. I'll give you an address in Marseille."

At this point the two young men suddenly realized that the old man actually existed. "And you," they exclaimed, "what will become of you, Monsieur Moïse?"

M. Moïse had sallow lips, his skin was the color of old linen. With mischievous calm, he said, "My father, a pious man, had his beard cut off by the Cossacks during the Kishinev pogrom in 1905; he was too pious, and this indignity hurt him as much as the death of a little eight-month-old girl, my daughter, my Deborah, trampled to death by men who did not know what they were doing. My oldest son was killed in 1919 in the pogrom at Proskurov; he was a brave boy, a militant of the Bund, and we were in disagreement. He defended the synagogue with an automatic. Our blood will not die out, for I have a daughter who is a dentist in Detroit and a son who is a precision mechanic in Chicago. I have seen many things come to an end in my life, and I know that our people survives every massacre and that a new greatness is in store for it. If they cut my beard, it will grow again. If they cut my throat, I know that pain is brief, that death is as eternal as life, I know that the life of the earth and of men continues, and that the oppressed consciousness awakens."

He perceived that he was speaking too solemnly, changed his tone, resumed his air of a fatherly shopkeeper who can only be swindled if he wants to be.

"People don't move out at my age, *Kinder*! I'm shrewder than Rothschild himself. With an operating capital that has never exceeded a thousand francs, I have drawn enough to live on—thanks to a steady turnover, of course. Liquidation today would be bad business. I have refused the dirty money of the rich men who betray our people. A man's days are numbered when his beard is as white as mine. And besides, perhaps they won't get here. As long as a misfortune has not come to pass, who knows if it will come to pass?"

"They will be here in forty-eight hours, Messieurs."

A tall, thin soldier with hollow cheeks spoke these words as he entered. There was a somber, joyous vibration in his eyes. He was not a Jew.

"Have you any shoelaces?" he asked. "And a pencil, and a little cake of soap?" He would have purchased indiscriminately a Chinese vase, a picture postcard of Marlene Dietrich, neckties, anything at all! Moïse wrapped his purchases in a Yiddish paper.

"Is that Arabic, Monsieur?" the soldier asked with a broad, enraptured smile.

"No, those are Hebrew characters. That will be three francs twenty-five, soldier."

The soldier drew from his trousers pocket a banknote which he looked at strangely: *One thousand francs.* Christ Almighty! That's a good one. For *one thousand francs* you could buy this whole shop with its eternal misery, and this old saint as well—of the race of Judas—and his whole clientele, probably. The soldier burst out laughing. No one had laughed so loudly in this place for a long time. Moïse thought the young man must be drunk, looked at the bill, set his glasses straight to read its absurd value, shook his head, also laughing, but discreetly.

"I have no change, Monsieur."

"So what?" answered the soldier irritably. "What do I care if you have no change?"

He put his purchases into his pocket, tossed the banknote, crumpled into a ball, among the little fresh onions, and turned toward Moritz Silber and José Ortiga. "Will you two have a drink on me?"

Moïse smoothed out the big bill with his ivory fingers. "Very well," he said, "I'll try to change it. One moment, if you please." The three men made way for him.

"Let's get out of here quick." A hysterical laugh twisted his mouth. "I'll buy a round of drinks."

"Why not?" said Silber absently.

The street was dark. A little girl, running in the darkness, stumbled and dropped the loaf of bread she was carrying. The soldier picked her up.

"Don't run away, little snotnose. Look, here's a beautiful picture for you." He placed a crumpled bill in her hand. "Don't be scared, pretty babe, I'm telling you it's really a beautiful picture." The child ran away. They were approaching the Tel Aviv restaurant.

"Just a word before we go in, comrade," said Ortiga. "Are you sure you haven't had a bottle too many?"

"I'm no comrade," said the soldier. "I don't like phrases from meetings. Everyone for himself in this son-of-a-bitching life. In the second place, my stomach is more than empty, not a bite to eat or drink since noon. In the third place, I'm in a royal good humor. In the fourth place: all three of you in that old Saint Judas's joint looked like you were in trouble up to your neck. I know what that is. And you don't look like murderers, that's sure. I know what they look like too. So you've nothing to fear from me."

"I am a comrade," said Ortiga gently. "Perhaps not for you, of course. I am a soldier in an entirely different war, and I don't give a fuck for phrases and meetings. But let's go drink something if it gives you pleasure. We still have time."

The last diners in the Tel Aviv restaurant were talking quietly under the foggy lighting. A waitress with a delicate profile, but unfortunately cross-eyed when you looked at her full face, raced about the room like an excited ant. Her black hair was done up in an enormous knot, her apron stained. Silber, Ortiga, and the soldier sat down at a table covered with pink oilcloth decorated with little yellow flowers that seemed to fade into the fog.

"Give us anything," ordered the soldier, "something good and tasty and the best bottle you've got in the house."

He accepted the cigarette proffered by Silber, took it between his lips, struck his lighter, gave his chance companions a friendly look, blew out the little flame, and chewed on his unlit cigarette.

"It's a funny thing, Messieurs, how much you look like . . . It's really phenomenal."

He studied the mobile face of Silber with its lined forehead, heavy eyelids, long slender nose; a convulsive and aggressive firmness marked these unbeautiful features. He shifted his glance to Ortiga, the harmonious face of a young Mediterranean fisherman, with a low, smooth brow and deep-set brown eyes, calm and full of reflected light like the eyes of an animal at rest. One crafty, the other strong.

". . . how much you look like a lot of dead men I've seen. There must be only a few hundred models for human heads. When you've seen a few thousand dead men, almost dead men, and maybe dead men, and some who are neither dead nor alive, you've seen every possible face, including their expressions before and after bombardments. The whole time, in the train, in the Métro, it seemed to me that I recognized some of those stiffs. There's nothing pleasant about it, I assure you. Is it an obsession—or do you think it's simply the truth?"

The waitress brought chopped liver, stuffed peppers, bread, and wine. They emptied the first bottle right away.

"I fought in Spain," said Ortiga. "Teruel was a gigantic, senseless massacre. I saw more dead men in a week than a man should see in a whole lifetime. I looked at them without seeing them. I saw them without thinking about them. I missed my old lively friends. There is nothing in common between men and corpses."

"I've seen one dead person," said Silber. "That was when I was a child. My grandmother. She didn't look like herself anymore, she was petrified. She frightened me. You are mistaken, Monsieur. We living creatures are profoundly different."

"Perhaps not," said the soldier dreamily. "After all, where is the difference?"

He opened his eyes wide and leaned in toward his two companions confidentially.

"Take a good look at the waitress, for instance. See how she distorts her mouth as if she were screaming. But she isn't screaming. I could swear that I've seen that mouth, that bun crushed against a rock, and those squinting eyes, lying beside a road between Épernay and I don't remember what other godforsaken hole. Is it true or not, what do you think?"

"It's possible," replied Silber, who was beginning to feel rather uncomfortable.

"You agree that it's possible? I've wondered several times in the last few days if I wasn't going mad, or if other people weren't all mad—after all, what is the difference between mad people and people that aren't mad?"

"That's enough of you bringing us down and spreading the blues!" cried Ortiga. "Suppose you drown your own in wine. Have a drink!"

Ortiga filled the soldier's glass. "Drink it down!" He went on, "I've heard enough of your dead men and your madmen. We have other things to do tonight. We're in a hurry."

"You're right," said the soldier, suddenly calm.

He gulped down his wine, licked his lips, and introduced himself: "Laurent Justinien, sales broker in civilian life . . . Let's talk about business. I've never seen myself like this before, it's stupefying. It's as though I had never understood anything up until now, do you understand?"

"Enough of that," said Ortiga. "Check, please."

"No, I'm not done. You don't understand anything. You're getting out, eh? You have reasons for running away from the Boches, eh? You're broke, eh? Haven't you read the ad in the papers: 'Gentleman offers free of charge . . .'?"

"He's a phony," said Silber.

"Possibly. Maybe it's me. I've become as serious as the dead. Every word I say is as solid as a stone. Maybe I'm done with being a swine. Look at your faces in the mirror back there: you are drowned men, ready for the morgue. —I'm throwing you a line, that's all."

The two young men judged him by his hard features, by the direct unwavering look in his pupils, dilated by a sort of hysteria, by his deep, measured, self-assured speech. There was both frenzy and decision about him. A little off the beam. And irritating. Like a man who has just committed a crime without giving it a thought. He seemed to have suffered a concussion. They were impressed by the thousand-franc note and the way he picked up the change without looking at it, leaving a twenty-franc tip for the waitress.

One of them said, "Your half-drowned men have a tough hold on life. Don't worry about us, we've seen worse. But what's this line you're throwing us?"

"Come along."

They took a few steps together in the trembling blue shadows, beneath the abandoned cliff dwellings.

"Here," said the soldier without stopping. From his trousers pocket he took a fistful of banknotes. "Take this with you. It's not worth much, but it can come in handy."

Silber took the notes, recognized them by touch, but showed no surprise. "How clearly you can hear the cannon. Thank you."

"No call for thanks," said the soldier, and they detected a dull anger in his tone. "Goodbye and good luck."

He outlined a military salute, turned on his heel and strode off in the opposite direction. A heavy backpack weighed on his right shoulder.

"I think we're rich," murmured Moritz Silber. "Let's go home now. We're getting out of here at daybreak."

Ortiga's eyes followed the soldier's tall silhouette receding toward the end of the street, the end of the world. "Poor bastard," he said. "How well I understand him! Wait just a minute!"

Ortiga ran after him, elbows against his sides, a bounce in his step.

"Hey you, Laurent!" The soldier turned around all at once, moved by a kind of muscular suspicion. An evil little glint appeared in his eyes.

"What more do you want?"

"Nothing," said José Ortiga calmly. "Absolutely nothing. We expect to cross the Loire day after tomorrow at Nevers. There is a bar as you approach the main bridge. If you feel like meeting us there—"

"I don't feel like meeting anybody," said the soldier joyfully. "Nobody. But it's nice of you just the same. So long."

The night was the color of ashes, enormously refreshing. Even its noises did not disturb the appeasing silence. The soldier moved through the night with lips pressed tight and head high. Freshness, silence, sounds pressed in on him. The city was enchanted, asleep in the midst of a dream, a nightmare. The soldier laughed. "Life is big, how big it can be!" He wanted a woman.

4. SIMON ARDATOV

DOCTOR Ardatov often worked past midnight at S.I. (Scientific Information), an encyclopedic agency that assisted its clients in the preparation of "theses, documentary and statistical studies..." What the agency actually did was to slice up several hundred specialized periodicals in more than a dozen languages, providing its subscribers with clippings from the *Neurological Review*, the *Review of Ethical Sciences*, the *International Philatelist*, the *Review of Metaphysics*, *Blue Humor*, the *Annals of Seismology*, and even such recondite publications as the *Bulletins of the National Association of Sorcerers* and of the *Society for the Study of Ritual Cannibalism*.

It was necessary to clip these papers in such a way as to utilize as far as possible both sides of the page, which was an arduous task. Somehow or other this enterprise managed to provide a living for some half dozen political refugees who had fled Prague at the last minute and by luck escaped the Polizeipräsidium in Berlin; survivors of the Karl-Marx-Haus in Vienna, of the battles and prisons of the International Brigades of Spain; men released from the Lipari Islands—arrested the following week by the French police and set free with temporarily suspended deportation orders. The S.I., conceived by a Viennese sexologist and directed by the Italian jurist, was always on its last legs; but by skipping a month's rent, by allowing a great historian who had immigrated to the United States to make up the deficit from time to time, it furnished learned expatriates with "a job."

Dr. Simon Ardatov made twenty-five francs in an evening, considerably less than if he had been a porter; yet the carrying of heavy loads requires muscles a man does not have at the age of sixty-three; and Simon Ardatov knew from experience that half a century of study does not equip a man for washing cars or peddling patent medicines. The sad thing about surviving several historical catastrophes is that you grow old like everybody else, and after spending your strength resisting fascism you still need one or two meals a day.

The S.I. had its office in the Rue Jean-Jacques Rousseau, under the eaves of a building that the Solitary Walker, dogged by poverty, would have recognized at first glance—he who, while writing *Émile*, was dropping off his newborns at the foundling hospital. The stairway with its nobly forged bannisters led to spacious landings with parquet floors that for generations had seen neither light nor elegant dress. Mimeographing machines in disuse, bundles of books remaindered for all eternity (*Applied Chiromancy* and *The Art of Pleasing at All Ages*), miscellaneous objects such as an antique loom and a lantern-slide projector constructed under the Second Empire by students of Nadar, encumbered the landings, which had double doors that had once been white with gold tracery. The building shook to the obstinate vibration of machines. The S.I. occupied a single room. It was singularly peaceful, being situated on the upper floor, where the grumblings and rumblings rising from the lower stories were distilled as wisdom is distilled from tumult. The adjacent rooms contained only stocks of merchandise disdained by burglars; the two attic rooms on the side street housed the Selecta Publicity Agency, known for the little ads it still published: GOOD WRITERS WANTED... Ardatov had gone there one morning to offer his services, scrupulously wondering whether his pan-European French justified his pretention to literary ability. He had found twenty convicts whose rags, ravaged faces, curved backbones, and stench of municipal flophouses attested to their decline. All twenty, bent over mangy address books worn at the edges by crowds of dirty hands, were addressing labels with maniacal haste—for they were paid by the thousand. Half a dozen of them, profiting from modern technology, had the benefit of typewriters dating from before the First World War. A sort of ex-noncom with a cop's mustache and a celluloid collar, apparently afflicted with incurable jaundice, watched over this staff of derelicts to see that they did not steal labels and two-penny penholders. He was not unaware of the silent rage provoked by certain long addresses with "triple-hinges and furbelows" like "M. Bonaventure Duchemin-Larévérence; pharmacist, first class; at Rives-des-Lavendières near Sainte-Nicolle-lez-Boibénit"—plus the département. The staff was capable of improvising the most unexpected abbreviations and pornographic deformations. Dr. Ardatov, informed of the piecework wages, had withdrawn . . . Later, sitting at his desk at S.I., he could hear the comings and goings of Selecta employees, and on the stairs the mustachioed jailer would greet him with two fingers raised to the brim of his derby.

Ardatov clipped foreign pamphlets, pasted them on sheets, or made little packages of the clippings and filed them in envelopes. The work was giving out, and so much the better. Of the four members of the staff, he alone had come this evening, to receive a hundred or so francs for an incomplete week. Tullio, the director, was typing and stamping the envelopes himself. The two men were working face to face, under a single light bulb, magnificent metallic moonlight shining through the window frame. The sound of quiet steps and talking in the corridor made them prick up their ears.

"I'll wager," said Tullio, "that Selecta is firing its gang of bums. Simon, I think the best thing to do with our envelopes tonight is to throw them in the wastebasket . . ."

The sound of talking and scuffling steps increased. Someone was feeling his way along the wall, tapping on the floor with a cane. The voice of the mustachioed jailer became distinct: "Let's go, gentlemen. On the double. If the firm is closing, it means that the firm is closing. It will open after the war or at Bordeaux. Now that you have been told, messieurs, on the double, I tell you!" Probably he was herding his miserable troop of pen pushers toward the stairway. Tullio smiled. His wrinkled face seemed to be modeled in warm earth; the four horizontal seams in his forehead, his dilated nostrils, his goatee sprinkled with white hairs gave him the look of a faun—but of an academic faun too well accustomed to riding second class in the

Métro. Former member of the bar in an Italian city, former Venerable of a Masonic Lodge, former coin collector ("the most incredible thing," he said), he now belonged only to Giustizia e Libertà (Justice and Freedom). "Wisely, we demand two absolutes," he said in speaking of this organization. "These metaphysical ingredients will help us perhaps to prepare a soup that will not be altogether inedible."

"Simon! We're shutting down. We shall reopen at San Francisco or at Buenos Aires. The outcome of the battle of Europe has for the moment deprived the S.I. of its raison d'être. Let's throw the paste pot out of the window."

He drew Ardatov toward the moonlight. The roofs and fantastic chimneys of Paris were dripping with light. High in the heavens, the moon revealed its pale continents. The sky covered the city with a bluish vault. In the distance, the continuous sighing of the cannon was like cosmic breathing. Tullio threw out the paste pot and it bounced on a black roof ten yards away.

"The clippings too!"

Torn into pieces, the press clippings awaited by several academic and literary egos scattered in the night like swarms of great white butterflies. They had never been so beautiful.

Tullio held out his fine apelike hands and said in a fury, "At long last! Good Lord! Millions of imbeciles imagined that bombs were for Barcelona or Helsinki, that tanks rolling in the streets were for Vienna, Prague, Amsterdam, Brussels—and that their sleepy little existences would go on until the end of time: bridge, belote, Saint-Émilion, the gazettes, stocks on margin, and steak not too well done!"

Simon Ardatov said, with bowed head, "Tullio, it will be an unimaginable catastrophe. Paris, Paris!"

His voice stuck in his throat.

"Because we lack imagination, Simon. We have been collecting catastrophes for twenty years now; we have been warning and prophesying, and writing articles of an irreproachable dialectic in our little papers that nobody reads. The only exit leads to the abyss, and that's the whole story. There's nothing to do but jump. That's the one thing we did not fully understand, for lack of imagination. What's more natural than an old world crumbling? People had forgotten that it's just as natural for the human animal to wait for the massacre, flee along the roads, hide in forests as to be born, grow, struggle, and die of old age..."

The agency's funds, kept in a cigar box, amounted to 180 francs, which the director and the scientific collaborator divided.

"Let's get out of here."

Tullio tossed the office key into the garbage can on the street.

"The garbage man will pick it up. He'll understand a good many things."

"Listen, Simon. Once in Florence, after my house was sacked, a garbage man brought me back the *Sonnets* of Petrarch, marked with my ex libris. 'I think, Signore,' he said, 'that this souvenir will be dear to your heart. They are beautiful sonnets.'"

They passed through streets cut into broad zones of soft darkness and vast light. The last streetwalkers, slipping along on their high heels, stepped aside as they passed. Some of the women stood leaning against the iron shutters of the shops, and the tiny glow of their cigarettes made circles around their shadowy lips. Policemen on bicycles, continuing their rounds in search of probable crimes, passed quickly, carried off by the soft sound of tires.

"In a few days Paris may be no more than a heap of corpses," said Simon Ardatov, "but those black crows will keep riding around the ruins."

"I expect so," said Tullio.

The great food market of Les Halles was beginning its nocturnal life. Trucks discharged their cargoes of vegetables on the sidewalks. The two men were walking through the damp leaves; there was a strong smell of rotting vegetables. The church of Saint-Eustache formed a little island of somber stones dedicated to silence. The friends talked, wondering what miracle might save this city. They allowed for the miracles of endurance, of chance meetings, of patience, of intelligence. Reality to them sometimes seemed woven of miracles and of accidents, at the core of which energy, aided by chance, struggled victoriously to save what must be saved. This time the miracle of the armies seemed impossible to them.

"I'll jump on my bike," said Tullio, "and head down toward Toulouse. With an excellent voting card issued by the City Hall of Suresnes to one Jean-Marie Têtu (Stubborn)—I made up the name myself—and with no baggage. I sold my treatises on international law this morning on the quays at a fair price. I had fun dedicating them to Benedetto Croce; that brought me ten francs, two packs of Gitanes."

He smiled gaily.

"Simon, I wouldn't advise you to wait more than twenty-four hours. The panzers might get here this very night. There's no resistance except in the newspapers."

"No bike. No more leg muscles. No dough. I hope to pick up a thousand or two tomorrow. If I don't manage to get the next to last train, I'll start out on foot. In '21 I crossed the Polish border that way, in '37 the Pyrenees. If I still had a life ahead of me, I wouldn't despair at the thought of retreating across the Himalayas or the mountains of Colorado. The historic cycle is growing shorter . . . I've got a travel permit: the rats in the préfecture took me for a White Russian."

"Where are you going?"

"As far away as possible. Common sense tells me to get close to the ports and the frontiers; but Spain is a trap and the ports will be occupied. Maybe there won't be anything else for us to do but hide in the caves of the Massif Central. In that as in other things we would be pioneers: the return to the caves."

Hands in pockets, they lingered under the dark mass of Saint-Eustache. The immense radiance of the sky was growing pale over the food markets. Tullio declaimed, "Christ on the cross glittered like lightning."

"Who wrote that, Simon?"

"Dante."

They felt themselves overflowing with a joy that had no need of words.

Ardatov said, "Do you remember what the good soldier Schweik said to his buddy: 'Meet you after the war, at the little corner café, about five o'clock—' Goodbye, Tullio."

They shook hands like young men.

The following day Dr. Ardatov combed the city for money. In the Avenue Henri-Martin the houses and gardens slumbered. The gentle sun, the clean asphalt, the absence of traffic, the expressionless faces of the few people in the streets created a sense of stupor.

Dr. Bedoît was packing his bags. He was well disposed toward his fellow men, with a good humor that came from the correct balance of his internal secretions. He was a gourmet, absorbed by affairs of the heart, and a highly successful practitioner. When the maid brought him Dr. Ardatov's shabby visiting card, he made a gesture of annoyance. This old colleague, with his antediluvian diploma from Moscow, a survivor of prisons, hangings, uprisings, emigrations, and flight, interested him as a man of another species, not exactly superior—for the suspicion that anyone aside from universally accepted geniuses like Montaigne, Descartes, Shakespeare, Goethe, and Pierre Curie might be superior to him never clouded Dr. Bedoît's mind—but completely and disturbingly strange. The downside was that these excellent, perhaps heroic, refugees were so badly dressed. Dr. Bedoît humorously recommended the foundation of an organization named GSIAR, "Good Suits for Intellectual Antifascist Refugees."

"I'm not at home," he said to the maid, but then he remembered that he owed Dr. Ardatov seven hundred francs for some anatomical sketches. "Hey, Marinette, I'm in, I'm in! —For you I am always in, my dear Ardatov—"

Ardatov entered. His square head was a little too heavy for his weakening frame, tufts of white hair stood out on his temples, he had shaggy eyebrows and a sad hard-blue gaze in the depths of his gray eyes. His shoulders were beginning to droop. His brown herringbone suit was no longer presentable except in the inelegant neighborhoods between the Place de la République, the Belleville Métro station, and the Seine.

"Sit down, Ardatov—sit here..." Bedoît threw a pile of clothes on the carpet.

"Look, my friend, France is paying for her errors, for her easy life—I agree, I who love an easy life—for the total noodlism (the word comes from noodle, my friend) of the Popular Front and of the reactionaries who let themselves be intimidated by policemen. (And yet what is civilization if not an easy life and the repudiation of violence?) I am leaving all this, the fruit of twenty years of work. My wife is already in the South. I am abandoning my practice. It is true that my most adorable patients were the first to make tracks. Soon I shall be on the road without knowing what's in store for me, what's in store for us all—"

"But he isn't going to offer me a seat in his car," thought Ardatov.

"I owe you seven hundred francs, my friend—here. Forget the change. Consider it an advance on future work, I beg of you. Work that we shall do after the liberation of our territory." (His voice broke.)

Ardatov rested in the deep white easy chair. The atmosphere of intelligence created by the books in this quiet room was agreeable to him. A man must lose all fighting spirit living in a roomy candy box like this. The curtains sifted the light as in a painting. A canvas by Domergue showed a nude adolescent girl with lips like two joined cherries against a background of cobalt blue. Dr. Bedoît's discomfiture rather amused Ardatov. The whirlwind would carry this amiable bourgeois the devil knew where, but his spirit would never rise from the ground. He was like the dead leaves stirred by autumn gales, that never rise more than a foot or two from their resting places.

"But why are you leaving?" Ardatov asked at length. "What have you to fear? I don't think Paris will be defended."

And his faint smile deepened, for he thought of himself. Had he been ten years younger, he would have stayed behind; with a bitter joy he would have overcome the physical fear, he would have said to himself, "The hurricanes are coming. It is the moment to take root.

It is impossible for France to die. Form secret organizations, prepare ourselves for the events to come." Now his irony was only for himself: "Absurd how out-of-date I have become."

"Stay here? How can you think of that, my friend? See Paris crumble hopelessly under the bombs? Stay with the Nazis? With the Gestapo? See their uniforms on the boulevards? Good God! To see them arm in arm with our little ladies? Anything rather than that!"

When a man lacks the spirit of a fighter, the spirit of a fugitive is the next best thing. There is courage and revolt in flight.

There was a score of years' difference between their ages, but there was still a strong similarity between them. The Frenchman was putting on a little weight, the shoulders of the Russian showed signs of fatigue; they had the same prominent heads, the same broad faces, one well rested and grown somewhat heavy at the chin, the other worn and seamed with dry wrinkles. Both were interested in the statistics of cancer and of mental illness.

Dr. Bedoît exclaimed, "You, with your past, must understand me!"

"If I looked at you from the perspective of the past," thought Ardatov, "I would refuse to understand you. What have you done to deserve a different future? To deserve a victory that wouldn't have been vile and conservative? What cause have you served?" But he immediately rejected this thought. Fish, after all, can live only in their native waters, they are what the water, the temperature, the degree of salinity, the quality of the bottom, the currents make them—

"You're right, Bedoît. I understand you. Well, good luck!"

Rising, Ardatov sensed around them the immense overturned city suddenly beginning to seek its soul in the abyss beneath the lightning flashes, while in the North, in the East, a little beyond the suburbs, artillery, aircraft, motorized columns were massing in accordance with an inexorable plan to torture it, destroy it, degrade it . . . There was really nothing to say.

"Forgive me, Ardatov, you know I'm your friend. Who knows if we'll ever meet again. My wife is already in the South. What was I saying? Oh yes. You won't be offended if I ask you to take one of these suits here? We're about the same build, you'll have it altered a little by a good tailor, won't you? Damn those bunglers who ruin good material. Take it, I beg you."

Dr. Bedoît picked his best suit up from the carpet and threw it affectionately over his visitor's shoulder. "Take it, please," and with his fists clenched on his hips, he moaned like a wounded animal.

"Ah, damn it all, I could lie down and cry. I don't know what I'm doing anymore. Forgive me, Ardatov—Marinette, Marinette, quick, wrap this up, Monsieur will take it with him. A neat package, eh? And serve us something quickly, a martini, Ardatov, you've a political mind, what's happening to us?"

"The same thing that has happened elsewhere. Just the sequel."

"Our poor old Europe's teeth are chattering with a fever of 106. Is it dying?"

"Irrevocably."

Accustomed to diagnosis, the two physicians were calm.

"The important thing is that the totalitarians will be carried away in their turn. We are at the edge of the pit, but the pit has been dug for them too. They're taking Paris, one day Berlin will be taken or destroyed, you don't need astrology to know that. And neither France nor Europe can die without being reborn. Something new must be done, and they're doing it, but with the oldest implements in the world: madness, war, chains, the inquisition."

"It does me good to listen to you, Ardatov. But it's hard just the same."

"It is hard to die, but natural. If we knew how painful it is to be born . . ."

"Yes, yes, Ardatov, the trauma of birth."

In the vestibule they shook hands effusively. Marinette, correctly disdainful, handed the visitor a well-made package. It displeased her that her master, one of the most respected doctors in Paris, should lose his head to the point of giving one of his best suits to a foreigner smelling of hunger and boiled cabbage, and who gave himself condescending airs in the bargain. (Let's hope that the Boches will rid Paris of this breed!)

"Where are you going, my friend?"

"To the Basses-Alpes," Dr. Ardatov, who had no idea, replied ironically.

In Rue Bonaparte, under a pretty pastel representing Marie-Antoinette in the Trianon days, Dr. Morlin-Lesobre, director of a medical publication, paid Dr. Ardatov four hundred francs out of eight hundred owed him for translations. "The rest next Friday," said Dr. Morlin-Lesobre. "That's our day."

Ardatov didn't budge from his chair.

"But you see, I am leaving."

Dr. Morlin-Lesobre raised his little round head with the sparse hair plastered on its scalp. He crossed his arms on the beveled glass of his desk.

"I can't help that, Monsieur. The review is continuing. Our preoccupations cannot be subordinated to reverses that can hardly be more than temporary."

Ardatov looked at him with pleasure. "At last I am seeing one of them close up, one who is not an idiot, not a complete idiot, at least. One who is waiting for them. You'll be served, Monsieur, they'll own your very soul." As amiably as possible, but in spite of himself showing his old teeth stained yellow by tobacco—like a grotesque bulldog that grins before biting:

"I really admire, Monsieur, your calmness in moments such as these. I shall doubtless spend no more than a couple of weeks at the Riviera. If I am away any longer, I should like you to contribute the remaining four hundred francs to your personal charities."

"You may count on me, Monsieur, to give them to the Red Cross," replied Dr. Morlin-Lesobre coldly.

A clown's smile flattened itself over Dr. Ardatov's face as, with a nod of goodbye, he picked up the package he had left on the typewriter cover. Dr. Morlin-Lesobre was able to hear the brief dialogue that passed between his secretary and the translator in the waiting room.

"Will you take the last two numbers of the review, Monsieur?"

"No," replied Dr. Ardatov dreamily, "you may deposit them for me. Don't fail to do so," he reflected a moment, "in the garbage, if you please."

The shopwindows of the St. Sulpice quarter still peacefully exhibited their church statuary and antiques. The modernized profiles of the Virgin seemed suitable for boudoirs with indirect lighting. Bronze Christs echoed Rodin's manner: they expressed just enough carnal suffering to make the purchaser think himself in possession of a work of art. Ardatov was amused by the medals designed to protect the soldier's heart both by supernatural power and by the doubtful resistance of thin metal . . . "What remains of faith in these trinkets? They answer to a meager yearning for timidly conventional consolations. Spiritually, they're the equivalent of the china hutch in the parlor. A real cry of faith would immediately show them up as the futile trinkets for futile souls that they are. But these days that kind of outcry is not to be heard, though there will be cries enough to come."

Several times a day Ardatov suffered sudden attacks of fatigue. If the wounded of victorious armies recovered more rapidly than those of defeated armies—as at least one physician claimed—then the old age of victorious men must be healthier and stronger than that of the last surviving warriors of defeated parties. A good deal of physical weakness can be overcome by clear thinking, by the will to hold firm, by the sense of history that will bring us revenge, by stubbornness in clinging to one's opinions—yet there are some weaknesses that cannot be overcome. Perhaps the hardest struggle is that between the mind and the (undernourished) flesh which nourishes the mind, exalts it above the flesh, and sometimes suddenly debases it.

Ardatov found a bench in the Place St. Sulpice and sat down. The newsstand displayed *Marie Claire*'s insipid charms, *Ric et Rac*—in which laughter, that expression of human plenitude, had degenerated into idiocy—and treasonous *Gringoire*. The morning editions were filled with lies inspired by anguish, with phrases about American sympathies, Weygand's military genius, last-ditch resistance, the memory of Jeanne d'Arc, the memory of the Marne, the enemy's fatigue. Not a living word, not an authentic cry of courage amid the disaster—that was plain for all to see. These were the depths to which the printed word, sold and domesticated, had fallen.

The Q bus stopped between the newspaper kiosk and the Bric-a-Bracum antique shop. The posters of the Bonaparte Cinema displayed the faces of women who do not exist in life, poised for kisses bereft of proud simplicity—kisses that do not exist in life either. The square itself remained real: the two flat unequal towers of the church, of a color between ocher and gray, the somber trees, the children busy with their games, the pious and almost clean beggar, who might have had an account in the savings bank, the ladies in black moving along the façade of an ecclesiastical building. There was next to nothing here of the exalted, drunken, ludicrous, childlike, and desperate ideas that burned with a low flame in the cafés of Montparnasse—or of the rationalized delirium of the naked women in the nightclubs...

If the bombs did not disperse them in a cyclone of smoke and shattered stones, the docile troop in the Sphinx would not stir from between its mirrors. Fifty naked women would await the coming of the victorious soldiers who survived the tank battles—as though they represented nothing more than good business and hard work. All hungry males are equally avid, equally brutal and tender, equally empty afterward. Their infinitesimal and infinite diversity never breaks the common circle in which they all move, anonymous, without individual face or voice. None emerges from the crowd for more than an instant, though each feels himself charged with a vital force belonging to himself alone. For all males living under threat of death, to lie on an unknown woman, to forget oneself in her, and to rise with moist forehead and a drunken, half-mad grin is proof of and recompense for a survival snatched from proximate nothingness.

The prostitute knows this: she distinguishes between races and gestures only in the space of a brief present. Belgians, Spaniards, Poles, Englishmen, Frenchmen from Meuse, from Franche-Comté, Bretons, southerners, and, if they come in tomorrow, boys from Prussia, Brandenburg, Posen, the Rhine, the Tyrol—all the same: there are dirty ones and clean ones, some are ugly brutes and some are nice fellows, some are vicious and some are bashful, some are cheap, some pretend not to care about money, and some really don't give a damn—and these last are the best of all. This is how the women would talk. War, peace, dictatorships, for them nothing changes... And while his wandering thoughts carried a hint of vaster truths, Ardatov himself saw nothing more there than a libidinal urge.

He felt better. The sun of this eleventh day of June shone through the branches and warmed him. He remembered an evacuation of Kiev in the year '18; it was hard to tell who was doing the shooting and who was being shot at the outlying crossroads. Every night the city was plunged into panic. Wild shooting went on everywhere, without design or plan. Terrified sentries shot into the darkness to give themselves courage; roving figures fired into dark windows; bands of assassins fired point-blank as they advanced down the streets; little boys shot at cats meowling in heat. The Jewish quarters, hearing all this fusillade, foresaw the throat-cutting to come. A venerable old man with a yellowish beard suddenly fell into a trance. The children lamented at his feet while he intoned a strident plaint, beating on a kettle with a spoon. Around him arose sighs, sobs, prayers, incantations, delirious cries. The delirium spread from narrow street to narrow street like a wave; the entire city howled continuously, like an animal being slaughtered. It had seemed to Ardatov, standing sentry at the door of an obstinate staff headquarters, that this clamor arose from the depths of forgotten ages; that the cities sacked in the dark days of the Middle Ages might have howled in the same way; and he had thought of besieged tribesmen, thousands of years before that, beating the tom-tom in a cave with red animals painted on its walls... Now Paris, in the expectation of night bombings, gave off the same howl through its powerful standardized sirens operated by electricity, at the signal of officers who were mathematicians. Thus there was continuity in all things.

... In 1920 the Reds had taken a city in Ukraine. At the entrance to the freight station some anarchists had just engineered a collision between two squat locomotives manufactured at Seraing... Blocking railroad tracks is often a useful tactical operation; moreover, there was the pleasure of waving to your comrade leaning out the door of the other engine, then releasing the steam and jumping off at the risk of your neck; the pleasure of turning around in a daze to contemplate the terrific shock of two black comets skimming the ground, the pleasure of breathing in the explosion ... Sometimes men get drunk on the joy of destruction, and it is natural that they are tempted to avenge themselves on machines. The two vehement metallic carcasses were smoldering. One bent over the other and seemed to be biting it with its monstrous wheeled teeth ... A few hundred yards away the Reds (they were half-drunk, cadaverous, filthy, enraged, laughing; among them there were as many saints as deranged bandits) came upon the last car of the last White evacuation train. As the men in black leather tunics approached this abandoned railway carriage, they heard a whining lamentation. The faces of terrified women—grotesque in their hats and makeup, forcing smiles through their tears—were pressed against the windowpanes. Their images blurred as they drew back in a wave. These women were perfumed, perspiring, wearing revealing gowns cut from draperies: probably the whole seraglio of the Parisiana Summer Garden, abandoned at the last minute by nationalist officers who called themselves "The White Eagles." ... The comrades discussed what was to be done with this troupe of females captured from the world bourgeoisie; the history of revolutions from Spartacus on offered no solution to this problem. Robespierre was pure, but Théroigne de Méricourt was not. What would Engels or Bebel have done? Some of the workers suggested shooting the whole lot of putrid, diseased sluts who had slept with all the executioners of the people. "What social usefulness can they have under a regime of free labor?" asked a young student furiously. Nonetheless, the silent bearded men gathered around the captives' carriage seemed to have trouble breathing, mouths half-open with bubbles of saliva between their lips. Behind the carriage windows, the smiles remained fixed on them, on life. "Enough talk!" someone finally cried—"The men are hungry. Give them the women. Let them make love with the triumphant proletariat!" Someone else pointed out that the prostitutes too were children of the working class, exploited from time immemorial—and that there was no human being alive without consciousness, and who knew if some among them might become conscious along with us? This opinion, supported by Commissar Ardatov, was officially accepted, while the silent bearded men were rushing the car, carrying its sentries with them. At the entrance stood a little Mongolian who kept repeating in a breathless voice, "Discipline, discipline, comrades!" He was brushed aside and probably followed the others in their indiscipline. "There are no problems of this kind to discuss in Western capitals," thought old Ardatov.

5. THE SILENCE OF PARIS

MÉTRO stations would suddenly fill up with crowds and then just as suddenly seem abandoned to Sunday torpor. The Saint-Placide station was animated only by the idiocy of the posters: VISIT PRAGUE, GREAT VACATIONS IN THE RHINELAND, THE CHARM OF TOURAINE, TOURS AT REDUCED FARES. On a day like today there should have been inflammatory posters crying: DESCENT TO HELL AT EXORBITANT PRICES! FORCED DEPARTURE WITHOUT RETURN! VISIT THE RUINS AND THE CEMETERIES! RESURRECTION IS PROMISED!

The most ironic of these colored compositions showed a map of the world in red, white and black. The Allied empires were spread over the two hemispheres, from Labrador to the Cape of Good Hope, from New Zealand to Senegal, surrounding the enemy empire that seemed like a crushed spider in the center of little Europe. WE SHALL WIN BECAUSE WE ARE STRONGER, said the inspired caption. A little old gentleman with a head like a stuffed owl, either obsessed, mad, or drunk, was standing in front of the map of Paris and adjusting his bow tie as though the map were a mirror.

The people in the Métro were different from their usual selves. The men were no longer occupied with crossword puzzles or the attractive passenger across the aisle. The office girls were no longer reading love stories. The men's eyes were set in a desolate obsession, as though their minds were saying over and over, "What's to become of us? Holy God, this can't be, it just can't be happening!" Money, work, pleasure, illness, intrigues, the ordinary little dreams were forgotten beneath the huge leaden cloud of humiliation and danger. Clothes had lost their banal correctness, they seemed to have been designed by trembling hands, cut of cloth without body, pulled out of shape by the weight of suitcases. In the station stops the pushing and rush was brutal with clenched mouths, muttered oaths, silent, aimless rage or fevers without heat or vision. Three ladies were talking within Ardatov's hearing. The first, age forty-five, imitated the mannerisms of a young flirt in the movies, and her mouth was painted a deep red—her mean, sensual mouth with its artificial contours traced with appalling self-love.

"What a calamity," this lady was saying, "my husband has taken the car full of our furniture—old furniture, you understand, is money—and I can't forgive myself, no I will never forgive myself for leaving fifteen kilos of lump sugar behind. And I wonder if we'll make the express, it seems there's been rioting at the stations, if I don't have a nervous breakdown with all this, my God! and my son-in-law hasn't written in two weeks, he was in the fort at Thionville. This sugar, you know"—her lisping voice mounted an octave for the benefit of the public—"we saved it up out of our rations, yes indeed, out of our rations, but even so, Monique and I just couldn't carry it by ourselves, and there are no porters anywhere. Everything is so disorganized, you can't get a taxi, and nobody will give you a hand. A fine government we had. We've fallen very low, Madame Amédée."

"Yes, we've fallen very low," Madame Amédée replied. The lines of her flabby cheeks were gathered around a hard, pink, fleshy mouth. "In our apartment house, for instance—" and there followed whispered remarks about the Jews and the foreigners.

The third lady was a young woman wearing a large graceful hat hiding half her forehead. Raising her lowered eyes, she looked at Ardatov, and it seemed to him that in an interior voice, so low she herself was hardly aware of it, she was saying, "Forgive them, Monsieur, that is how they are, they can't help it; forgive me for not being like them and for being shamefully glad I'm not; forgive me for suffering from what they are, and yet being unable to detach myself from them." Ardatov averted his eyes.

Madame Amédée said, "I only hope to God that our punishment purifies us!" She looked at everybody with aggressive dignity.

"Speaking of punishment," drawled a man's voice, "it'll be more than a little pinch in the ass. Isn't that your opinion, Monsieur?" The man had a drooping mustache and ravaged cheeks beneath an old felt hat. He turned to Ardatov, who replied cordially, "And how!"

The other winked. Big dark pupils against yellowed whites streaked with tiny broken veins.

"Where do you think the little billions for national defense have been disappearing for the last twenty years? Not into sugar cubes that melt in your tea, eh? And those fine young men, the cream of our Military Academy with their plumed helmets, have turned out to be real geniuses, haven't they? Of course these are things charming ladies who stuff their tummies with pastries, pinky in the air, don't care to think about."

A crowd of uniforms came rushing into the car. And although the soldiers remained silent, something incredible was observed. Under posters stating that it was forbidden to smoke "even a Gitane," they were puffing calmly away at their pipes of black Algerian tobacco, and this gesture expressed the power of indiscipline and of violence they carried inside them. A civil servant, recognizable by the forlorn shadow of green lampshades visible on his receding chin, pointed a rigid finger at the sign.

"Not to worry, old man," said a helmeted young thug amiably, his Adam's apple bobbing with each word, "there's no more government. The government's taken a powder. Got that, citizen?"

A kind of comic horror floated above this group of tanned faces bristling with three-day beards and sculpted by hard fatigue. Was nothing left of state regulations, of injunctions not to smoke or urinate against respectable walls; was nothing left of the security these prohibitions implied?

Two human masses, too tightly packed, it seemed, either to move or to be absorbed, stood stagnant on the platforms of the Denfert-Rochereau station; they were pieces of electrified crowds whose silence, bathed in low murmurs, whose watchful eyes, stretched necks, shoulders stooped under the weight of their burdens, whose very immobility expressed mad haste. The surge of this crowd shook the already overcrowded car. Repulsed by the new wave, carried along by a brusque contrary current, Ardatov found himself almost running—his neat package torn open and transformed into a shapeless bundle—in a passageway where two files of human ants were rushing blindly in opposite directions.

"These are the final hours," he thought. "There will be neither battle nor bombardment, there will be nothing, nothing but the end…"

Place Denfert-Rochereau hovered in a pale light of tranquil devastation. Like certain paintings by de Chirico. Lofty arcades bare in the sunlight dominated an arid perspective, a geometrical crossroads somewhere in the capital of solitude. A dark human silhouette is lost there, its movement sucked up by the immobility of the stones and of the air like translucent crystal, permanently hardened over the strange images it encloses. The insignificant presence of a human silhouette presages a nameless, bottomless tragedy, whose dim presence tarnishes the bright colors. That woman with Egyptian haunches is only the fossil of an unknowable but simple suffering. Here on the square the enormous bronze lion was somber and the soft blue sky seemed misty white. The solemnity of the monument recalled a catafalque. The converging avenues and boulevards, empty of traffic, whose rare pedestrians resembled dark beads rolling between the closed shutters of shops and cafés, were mere geometric figures. The buildings were fixed vertically on the unwrinkled asphalt. Paris had lost her soul and her sounds. There was no one at the entrance to the catacombs, no one! At the corner of the Avenue d'Orléans, a waiter, in black and white with his napkin over his arm, stood like a specter in the doorway of a restaurant. With crossed arms, he stood facing the pale desert and waited with empty eyes. His eyes were without pupils, like the eyes of certain statues.

Ardatov crossed the square toward the peaceful and sinister Boulevard Arago. Under the chestnut trees a black man dressed in light gray came toward him with a dancer's step. He was young and sumptuously black, and he was chewing on the stem of a red carnation. Under his arm he carried a large portfolio. It took this Negro, coming from the wall of the guillotined,* at the edge of the bright void of Paris, to complete the symbolism of the moment. As they were about to pass each other the Negro greeted Ardatov with a broad smile, without removing the red carnation from between his teeth. If he had said, "Monsieur, you will go no further, it's all over"—Ardatov would have felt no surprise. But the Negro said, "Bootiful pictures to sell, Mossieu, very bootiful modern pictures."

Opening his portfolio, he showed Ardatov great fantastic butterflies painted on gray paper, with the eyes of panthers—or were they women—on their wings. Fat mollusks, emerging from absolutely white shells, were devouring the bodies of the butterflies.

"I leaving," said the black man nonchalantly. "Me artist. Got to leave for West Indies. No money. You buy."

His eyes were cheerful. Ardatov gave him a hundred francs, explaining that he understood nothing about the new schools of art.

"Really?" said the artist. "It's too bad. I would like to explain to you—" They exchanged smiles. "*Bon voyage!*"

Along the prison wall the trees formed a lane as in an enchanted park, leading nowhere. The chestnut trees lived in the shadow of the wall; the shadow of their foliage relieved the flat surface of the wall that stood like a massive guillotine blade between the earth and the sky.

The streets around La Santé are full of little cafés where the prison guards eat. These men were diminished by long years of confinement, shuffling through the dingy light of the corridors, handling big shiny keys, vaguely discerning through the traitorous peepholes in the doors the prisoners moving at the bottom of a well of indifference. The comings and goings of the warders distinguished this street even on summer Sundays when clouds like celestial toys chased each other through the perfect blue of a First Communion sky. The cafés were somnolent and greasy.

"The prison in Liège is at the end of the Rue d'Amercoeur, at the end of the Rue d'Amercoeur—" Ardatov climbed the red wooden

---

*Wall outside La Santé prison, at the foot of which the guillotine used to be set up.

steps of one of those houses that are called "bourgeois" by a sort of irony. "How can they live in this annex to the prison?" he wondered. "After all, they are alive." Yet so many living or nearly living beings grow accustomed to a captive destiny.

These living beings, the Thivriers, both schoolteachers, received Ardatov in a dining room stupidly furnished on the installment plan. Torn newspapers and pieces of string were scattered over the linoleum near the empty bookshelves.

"Excuse us," said Florine, "we've spent the day emptying our bookshelves. We've already buried three cases of them out at Plessis-Robinson. Now we are perfectly prepared for house searches." Their tranquil courage was mingled with a subconscious fear of adventure, a need for domestic stability, the habits of discipline of conscientious civil servants still a little afraid, in spite of everything, of the school inspector.

"You're staying?"

Lucien Thivrier answered, "The school is staying. Eighty percent of the children are staying. Neither the Ministry nor the Teachers Federation has recommended evacuation. But even if that weren't so, I think we would stay."

"We would stay," said Florine. "Coffee?"

She laid her bare arms on the table. They seemed the arms of a washerwoman steeped in cold water.

"We feel a kind of relief. We were in a suffocating impasse. Danger was approaching, we felt we were lost—there was nothing to defend and no way of defending ourselves, everybody realized that more or less vaguely. Republic, Parliament, universal suffrage, Popular Front, one farce after another, no way left to believe in anything... Socialist Party, Communist Party, General Federation of Labor, all flat on the ground because nothing was standing up...Whatever remained of democracy, what with the directors of the Bank of France, the Chamber of Commerce and Industry, the Sarraut decrees, and concentration camps for Spanish republicans, whatever was left underneath this decomposition was indefensible and unable to resist anything... A war to maintain that? Enough to die laughing or tear out your hair…We did both. We'll see what happens now. What we need is a different France in a new Europe. Or else there will just be death."

"I see a dialectic of large numbers, of economic necessities, in intertwined events," said Ardatov. "No one in the world understood, I mean had a clear conception of a situation that had come about by itself; no social force existed capable of intervening strongly enough or consciously enough. Big numbers, necessities, events advanced on their own, blindly…The Nazis are the monstrous offspring of old, conservative Europe. Paid to defend it, they're betraying it, dividing it against itself and digging its grave. They are intelligent enough, but they are wedged in. They have put the blinders of anti-socialism, irrationality, inhumanity, anti-Semitism over their own eyes—too many blinders for good technicians and good organizers. They embody, perhaps, the ruthless, and therefore stupid, despair of a people whose revolution was drowned in blood and intrigue. In three, five, or ten years they will be carried away by the tempest they themselves have unleashed. Now it's too late for them to stop."

"And our hour will come?"

"Most probably. But it's quite possible that none of us will be here. But even so, it will be our hour, the hour of all of us. Possibly its reality will be different from what we imagine, possibly we would be incapable of recognizing it."

Ardatov usually talked this way. He spoke with assurance, slowing his speech to find the right expression, questioning himself, but concluding with certitude. He was confident, he called himself an optimist, but his optimism, his confidence were colored by an almost cruel impassiveness and, in immediate matters, by a sadness that came close to despair. "You and I," he might say, "have no real importance. We are grains of sand in the dune. Sometimes we have a glimmer of consciousness, which is essential but which may well be inefficacious. The dune has curves in its surface, caused by the wind. The consciousness of the thinking grains of sand can do nothing to change them… We exaggerate our own importance to the point of ridicule; we would be much more human turning away from ourselves the better to perceive the vastness of life and the truth of which we are only the tiniest fragments...This could become discouraging, for we might discover that at a certain moment in history, there is no more place for us and that the best we have might no longer be useful...

"Now, if you ask me how the world is doing, I believe that it is following the course it must follow and that we must foresee; that it is moving toward the object of our hopes, rolling over our bodies and our skulls on the way. Neither revolutionary rhetoric nor the spirit of sacrifice can compensate for our impotence. The Spanish Revolution was lost in advance, the strikes of May '36 were lost in advance despite the apparent victory, the Popular Front betrayed itself in advance, the European democracies, tender mothers of fascism, were defeated in advance by the totalitarian machines; and these last are equally defeated, defeated by the defeated and by the industrial machines of America and Russia, which in spite of themselves will take over the acquisitions of the Nazis, adapting them to the mentality of Anglo-Saxon democracy and to the spirit, as yet unforeseeable, of an immense revolution seething with contradictions.

"In all this, the conscious grains are precious; let us not underestimate ourselves! It is a matter of the rise or fall of man. This may be pride, but it sustains us, provided, of course, that it be a pride without self-complacency and without concern for appearances. A number of precious grains will be crushed or inexplicably buried. However, a century will not pass before Europe, Euramerica, Eurasia see the birth of a rational, balanced, intelligent organization capable of re-conceiving history and guiding it, and at last attacking seriously the problems of the structure of matter-energy and its galaxies. Human destiny will brighten..."

Florine served the coffee. It was not a moment for philosophizing. They spoke little. Ardatov had come to ask the Thivriers to hide a few books and papers that he would leave behind, and they promised to do so.

"We shall bury them with our own. The soil of France," Lucien Thivrier jested, "will be filled with spiritual treasures for the first time. It would be impossible to calculate how many people are burying or walling up books, manuscripts, documents, portraits. These and not gold or jewels are our wealth. Isn't that a sign of the times?"

The Thivriers resembled each other, as is often the case with couples brought together by a profound choice and molded by common habits. Both faces were frank, honest, average, and hard to remember. They both wore glasses, they had the same accentuated features, the same half-playful, half-serious expression; they got along well sexually no doubt, as well as otherwise. They differed only over points of doctrine, which they discussed to the point of nervous irritation, until the only thing to do was to kiss and head for the bedroom.

"We will try to live under the iron heel," said Lucien. "By resisting the iron heel." Florine added.

Seen for the last time, objects take on unprecedented relief. The Wallace Fountains with their hosts of sparrows had acquired a special grace. The empty chairs along the balustrades in the Tuileries cast shadows like surrealist tracery on the gravel paths. Not a single child was sailing a boat in the large basin. Nearby a sign said: SHELTER, 80 PERSONS. There some little boys were building earthworks, with a tunnel through which a tiny yellow train was going to pass. Ardatov was curious to know what their mother was reading. It was a novel about an orphan adopted by a countess and courted by a viscount. The lady posed the book on her knees, looked sadly at the trees still bathed in sunlight, turned toward this old poorly dressed gentleman who seemed decent enough.

"Aren't all these events terrible, Monsieur! I spend the day here with the children in order to be first inside the shelter in case of bombing. We sleep with our clothes on. What will become of us small businesspeople if the Boches come?"

The old gentleman, who perhaps had his own reasons for being upset, only sighed politely, but he raised his hat as he left.

Ardatov stopped by the Seine to take a last look at the fishermen who were still dangling their lines between the flat, colorless stones and the dreary water. They did not suspect that a large part of Europe was about to collapse over their heads. As usual, the gudgeon mocked them. They did not know that at this moment the Seine strangely resembled a broad distant river, the Neva, which had flowed through other dangers on certain days heavy with history. Its greenish waters, like those of the Seine today, had taken on a somber tone, reflected a pale light, a vast expectancy. A great unmoving panic had hung over the quays, the equestrian statues, and the shuttered windows.

Since his youth Ardatov had forced himself not to think of himself any more than was necessary. If he liked remembering, it was because his memories did not belong to himself alone; his memories allowed men, cities, vanished ideas, fragments of a world in movement survive within him. We learn with time that the present has less reality than the timeless and that what we believe is the past survives and persists in a thousand stubborn ways. The future grips our shoulders with its inexorable or beneficial hands and is already pulling us forward when the present moment seems so simple and stable to us. Why do men need a finished world, like a solid home whose stones would never change? They would be startled to learn that beneath their cities underground waters and, perhaps, invisible movements of sand or lava are at work well below those waters; that in their familiar skies storms are building up as consequence of atmospheric depressions in equatorial regions; that an infinitesimal slippage in the earth's crust could suddenly displace the oceans; that centuries-old walls crumble one day all on their own; that steel beams wear out, and that the essential thing—to be different from woodlice—is to grasp this obscure dynamism, to second the work of the underground streams, of the storms in the sky, of the fatigue of the beams. For the old human dwellings are stifling and soporific; they must, they must collapse to make room for the houses of the future which human intelligence itself will construct! "They have forgotten the meaning of natural catastrophes and of escape..."

Riches and collections inhabit both banks of the Seine. The royal façade of the Louvre, the crouching Scribe, the perfect Victory of Samothrace, decapitated, arms broken, wings mutilated, her élan thrusting forward the most meaningful of victories! These collections, open to all, confront the passerby with mummified faces of dead civilizations which still retained a marvelously inspired expression.

Other collections, like heaps of commodities, call forth more bitter reflections. The man who cannot, who will not, fully live a dangerous and unstable life, relying on the mixture of truth and error that we barely glimpse, collects butterflies, Chinese prints, bound editions on fine paper, autographs, postage stamps, and what else? He constructs for himself a narrow world of cabinets and display cases, of knowledge limited to philatelic history, and thus he has filled the void of his soul; through covetousness and avarice he has built a shelter in which he can ignore earthquakes, strikes, murders, wars, revolutions, counterrevolutions until the time the conflagration comes. This man has even found a kind of nobility in his love of things whose symbolic language he discerns with solitary disinterestedness.

The other Louvre, the Louvre department store, a mammoth collection of merchandise, receives more visitors by far. If fire doesn't devour it, they'll change the price tags. Calculate the consequences of the defeat of France on the price of walnut bedroom sets, imitation Smyrna carpets, fountain pens, vases, G-strings! The conquerors—down from their bombing planes, out of their tanks, escaped for a few days from hellfire at the edge of nothingness; eighteen-year-old parachute troops, calm technicians from Headquarters, soldiers in uniform with puffed-out chests sporting decorations—they will all be good customers. And they, too, are collectors, perhaps the most forgivable of collectors. The bookseller and the antiques dealer on the quay will also do good business.

Flowing from one river to another river, this memory emerged. On the quay of St. Petersburg, on one of those limpid mornings that extend the white nights of spring into broad daylight, two young men sitting on a bench of the Summer Garden were exchanging inconsequential remarks and profound looks. The Neva flowed a hundred yards off. Children of the rich were playing, accompanied by French governesses, in front of Peter the Great's Dutch house. Each of the two young men in student uniform was carrying, delicately wrapped like a purchase from a confectionary shop, his little infernal machine.

The envoy from the Combat Organization who approached them at the entrance of the park, had given them their final instructions in a lighthearted tone of voice, for they had to keep smiling as they talked. Kolia would throw the first bomb: Simon Ardatov, posted fifty paces farther on, would throw the second if necessary... On the other side of the river, within the low prison-fortress whose bunkers stretched out above powerful tides, whose golden spires penetrated the sky, nooses were made ready for them (the very idea of them makes you involuntarily reach for your throat). Is being hanged really that painful? They felt themselves to be (conscious) instruments of history and in this way stronger than the fortress with its nooses, than the brief pain of the cervical vertebrae snapping, than the more intolerable pain of expecting it. Kolia poked Simon with his elbow and suddenly burst out laughing.

"Think of it, brother, his collections!"

"Right, his collections!" repeated Simon, amused.

The sky was filtering through the sea-green foliage; for them, the moment was tinged with pitiful irony. The great imperial dignitary for whose end they had armed themselves, the unscrupulous policeman, the man of torture chambers, of perfidious secret services, this man was known to have but one passion: Chinese art—pottery, masks, fans, screens, jade seals, carved crystal... He had whole display cases full of them, the envy of the British Museum! The man-machine in his brocaded court dress functioned to repress; the faithful-man with the bent backbone lived for sacred precepts as devoid of humanity as the rich brocade on his uniform; the man himself, forgetful of the interests of the Empire, of the court and its factions, of interrogations and prisons, would awaken to another reality in front of a crystal vase dating from the Song dynasty.

"He may never have really thought about what he is," said Kolia as much in contempt as in dismay.

"What do you want from them?" answered Simon, who was a little pedantic. "They live under the sign of unconsciousness in a sort of traditional animality. So they need collections to comprehend something beyond it."

The hour rang out. The two young men clasped hands while looking deeply into each other's eyes; Kolia went off without a word, to meet a young student, a pretty young student whom he would never kiss, toward the Trinity Bridge, toward the deed, toward the hospital, toward the gallows... Simon took another path toward the same probabilities.

"Early on, we had the sense of history," concluded the old Ardatov. "And that abstract divinity has treated us harshly..."

At the top of the Champs-Élysées, the Arc de Triomphe resembled a monument in a cemetery. There were no idlers in the arcades of the Rue de Castiglione. Except for one, the stores all had their iron shutters down. Two showcases offered luxurious toilettes in the Parisian taste to rich Americans, silk scarves in French colors, handkerchiefs with tender designs, little bottles, powder boxes. Such showcases would doubtless appear in museums toward the year 2500, when the present wars would be studied as curious cyclical crises bringing the sick collectivities of the capitalist era toward their ends or unforeseen rebirths. And they will say "the Second European War, the Third World War," in exactly the same tone that teachers use nowadays when they say "the Third Peloponnesian War..." The Place Vendôme and the Avenue de l'Opéra were almost deserted. A dull light hovered over the asphalt. No lovers waiting outside the opera, no newspaper hawkers, no distracted gentlemen absorbed in slyly watching the passing girls; no businessmen, with potbellies and the stooped shoulders of domesticated apes, commenting on the stock quotations. Nothing. This desert preserved a cold elegance of geometry, the nobility of a Paris stripped of its agitated daily life, a Paris as sovereign as an exalted idea. There remained only the vertical planes of the housefronts, the horizontal planes of the street, distributed light and shadow, and the transparence of evening falling upon these lines and spaces. Ardatov still recognized a city of Europe, a city of the world reduced to an algebraic common denominator.

"I have seen beneath this decanted light, equally naked, the Winter Palace Square in Petrograd in 1919, the Plaza de Cataluña in Barcelona in 1939. And other men will see the Schlossplatz in Berlin, the Red Square in Moscow, the Graben in Vienna, equally naked." This he could not doubt.

The black capes of policemen appeared at the opposite corner, in front of the Café de la Paix. At the corner of Boulevard des Italiens and Rue du Quatre-Septembre, Ardatov made out three forms—two men and a woman, They had stopped, undecided, outside the Café du Brésil, which was closed. An auto passed before the opaque façade of the opera, leaving behind it a wake of unreality. Sandbags formed an absurd ant heap covering Carpeaux's statue *Dance*. The policemen dozed standing up, dark and gloomy as beetles. What use was it to go on checking the papers of foreigners? Who knew if tomorrow the Fifth Column might not be in power. And besides, what do we know, where is the Fifth Column? Might it not, by chance, be us? The slowed-down breathing of cannon in the distance foretold clearly enough the approach of the four columns of the Apocalypse.

"Well, my boy, I guess we're cooked," said the elder of the two policemen, who had been through the other war, the Chemin des Dames, Tonkin, Morocco, night duty on the Place d'Italie, and the February 6 charges on the Place de la Concorde—the whole shake. And now it has come to this, shit, shit, shit! and not to know whose fault it was. Stavisky or the Cagoulards, Chamberlain or the Communists, the Two Hundred Families or Léon Blum?

The younger of the two policemen was worried, for he had received his appointment through pull under a Socialist ministry. "I guess they'll fire me."

He smiled at the distant image of a hooker leaving the Neapolitan Café—which remained stoically opened but empty and, with its café terrace removed from the sidewalk, disfigured like a toothless face. The girl, a walking statuette, bore her round breasts before her toward the emptiness of the boulevards, sure, despite everything, of meeting the last male and taking away his last one-hundred-franc note with her caresses ... And then the others would come, wouldn't they? A beggar on crutches emerged from the Boulevard des Capucines, magnificently alone. He seemed to be reading an old recruiting poster of the Garibaldi Legion. Then he contemplated the bare avenues beneath the jumble of buildings. "Ah, Paname, aren't you beautiful, without your mob of tamed baboons!"

For a moment these solitary beings gave the Place de l'Opéra a human soul.

Ardatov and the three figures coming from the Rue du Quatre-Septembre recognized each other without surprise—for no surprise was possible on these inclined planes of emptiness. Together they repaired to the wicker chairs and tables of a forgotten little café on Rue Auber across from the Opéra, and sat down, pursued by the empty gaze of the policemen. A bald waiter, belonging to the old days, came to take their order.

"There's nothing but beer, you know."

It was nearly night but the sky was filled with a white fog. The dead lamps of the side entrances to the Opéra vaguely recalled the festivities of the Second Empire, as obelisks and sphinxes recall the Egyptian Middle Empire or Sixth Civilization, the civilization of the Twentieth Dynasty, Thutmose the First, Seti the First. Dead learning. Was the Duc de Morny any less dead than Thutmose? The Second French Empire was terminated by the second invasion . . .

"It reminds you of ships," said Jacob Kaaden with a gesture of his hand.

And in reality the grand prows of the angular façades were like the prows of phantom ships upon water long frozen. "It's an enchantment," murmured Hilda, her frail frame huddled in a trench coat, her hands in her pockets, her face that of an anemic Minerva at a distance from everything.

"Hilda," said the poet Cherniak, "you're not even conscious. It's not enchantment, it's asphyxiation."

After a few years of exile the poet Cherniak had worn himself down to the web of his being, preserving only a poor childish egoism and a sort of limping eloquence: "I am an echo of myself / with stalactites of foolishness / I have lost even my suspenders / In a low-priced River Jordan." He wrote these rhymes in Czech on paper napkins picked up in little restaurants: "My ideal for an omelet / And your eyes of blue, my beloved / For an Identity Card." He had also written for twenty francs a tale called "The Hanging of Adolf Hitler." He read it to some friends and said with tears in his eyes, "Not bad, eh?" Then added, "The only trouble is that it is he who will hang us."

Cherniak was only about thirty-five years old, but his face was all flabby wrinkles, his mouth twitched as though he were chewing air, his gaze was muddy and spent. He drank and probably took drugs. He had suffered for sacrificed Vienna, for Prague, for burning Warsaw, for the ghettos, for the destroyed libraries, and now he suffered only for himself, though the sum of his personal hardships had been a few weeks in prison. "The profoundest tragedy of Comrade Prometheus," he said, "is not being hanged in a cellar by Nazi beasts, but not being able to pay Mlle Muserelle for his week's board." He wore a tourist's suit with a tie the color of dead leaves. He detested Ardatov, that desiccated doctrinaire who could perhaps cure a toothache by a Marxist formula.

"Here we are at the end of the line," he said. "I don't know, Ardatov, if your transcendental optimism will sustain you for long inside this rattrap. They'll invade England in two months—and we'll never get our American visas. Can you recommend a little intravenous injection absolutely reliable and more or less painless?"

"There are such injections," said Ardatov, "and I'll note them for you." He took out a mechanical pencil and a slip of paper and began to write in the darkness.

"You're nothing but a wreck, Cherniak," said Jacob Kaaden who had the hard face of a miner beneath his felt hat. "Give him a good prescription, Ardatov, and I'll see that he gets the stuff."

"And you, Jacob, you think you're a strong man, don't you? And you admire yourself a little, in the manner of Nietzsche and Trotsky? You all have good recipes, big ones."

Jacob Kaaden shrugged his shoulders.

"Yes, we do have some of those, it's true. I don't feel any stronger than anyone else, unless that someone else is a bohemian incapable of going down into a mine or putting in his eight hours at Renault's.

I've seen a good many fellows, better than you or me, die even before the real battles had begun. Now they've begun. Nothing can prevent them from reaching their logical conclusion. I'm satisfied. Go on and drink your beer, and don't get peevish."

"I like you well enough, Cherniak," said Hilda. "But you can be mighty annoying."

Hilda, at twenty-five, was familiar with the dungeons of *Polizeipräsidiums*, *Maisons d'arrêt*, and model prisons (as they say in Spain); she knew the concentration camps of Austria, Germany, Valencia, Catalonia. Her first lover, Wolf, theoretician of the *Neues Denken* Leninist group, had died in Oranienburg camp; a small urn of ashes, standard issue, had reached her in a calm provincial prison haunted by whistling blackbirds. Kurt, her second, had been killed at University City in Madrid by the Moors—or the Communists—and legends of blood and treachery had come to her in the women's prison in Barcelona—where, among comrades, she might have felt quite at ease despite the bedbugs, if not for her hunger and indignation. Her third lover, Sasha, a dissident Marxist, had been interned in the French camp at Gurs and had strayed into revisionism. She detached herself from him as he detached himself from her—"because in our epoch the couple is only an accident or a relic." To make a living, she designed jewelry or worked in a munitions plant—which had just closed—at Suresnes. "It doesn't trouble my conscience," she said, "to check the quality of grenades. All roads pass through war today. And besides, it's impossible to tell which might be the good grenades."

"Here it is, my dear poet," said Ardatov. "I have indicated the permissible doses. All you have to do is multiply them by five."

Cherniak took the prescription and examined it with an incongruous smile. Would it be so easy? So simple? The temptation bordered on fear. Does this old man, this old doctrinaire, believe there is no better solution for me? What insult can I throw at him that would cut through his armor of impersonal reason and hurt him? Should I tear this paper to shreds and scatter them on the sidewalk? —Ah, you people, you have no pity. You have no understanding for the loneliness, the anguish struggling deep inside a soul! But he could not tear up the little slip of paper—and besides, it would be a poor gesture.

Cherniak put it in his memorandum book. "For me or someone else, who knows?" These prescriptions did provide a sense of security after all. Would he never find security except on the frontiers of despair? Cherniak declaimed as he improvised:

> "The good doctor said: 'Monsieur,
> A swift descent to Hell
> Will cure your hemorrhoids.'"

"You are the good doctor, Ardatov. I thank you. A humorist has called pessimism the hemorrhoids of the soul."

"If the soul exists," said Jacob Kaaden rudely, "it has no asshole."

"I am of the contrary opinion," said Cherniak.

As often happened, he felt a desire to cry. He was pursued by human baseness. Only the day before yesterday his temporary residence permit had been renewed for a month, and now Paris was going to fall, undefended. In every glance he encountered offense, lack of appreciation. He was better than all these healthy brutes and not a single one of them realized it. Every morning he was destroyed by the effort of awaking in a hotel room on Rue de Vaugirard. Once again to shave, to dress, to wonder if his soiled shirt could be worn one day more. The sense of suffocation he got from this room with the dirty yellow flowers on its wallpaper sent him running out to little bars near the broad, airy squares, where he was seduced by the shapes of women in the distance. Close up, women are stupid; not one is able to understand three lines of Baudelaire, they are greedy, you only have to know how to read the lines of their mouth, the shape of their chin, to know what kind of deplorable clay they are modeled from . . . He wanted women, but when he dared speak to them it was only to utter subtle sexual innuendos, for which he had a childish facility. When they finally caught on they would say, "Why, you're nothing but a little creep." And then he was pleased at having hurt their feelings and enjoyably sad at the hurt they had inflicted on him.

At this moment no one was taking the least interest in him, he thought, not even Hilda, who was watching wide-eyed as the darkness deepened over the deserted Paris night. Ardatov and Kaaden were talking about papers, buses, trains, hiding places, addresses in Toulouse, Brooklyn, Buenos Aires. Detestable creatures. Full of themselves, they could spend their whole lives revolving in the same circle of ideological formulae that nobody was interested in anymore. They were not defeated, they were dead, wrapped in bandages printed with a thousand phrases from Karl Marx. The thoughtful voice of Ardatov came to him from the depths of a vast darkness.

"You seem very aggressive, Cherniak. What's on your mind?"

"Oh, no, I am benevolence itself. I was thinking that we are the last of the last."

They could no longer see one another. The waiter, his white shirt-front moving through the void, came to tell them that the café was closing. "No one else is coming in tonight, that's for sure ..."

They counted out the change under a flashlight. A necropolis silence descended over the Opéra. Kaaden spoke with irritation. His silhouette seemed desiccated, his voice harsh.

"The last, you say? Don't you understand that if Paris dies, if Europe is dead, the world is going to explode? We are the first to realize it. And I didn't promise you a place in my car just to hear you whine. I warn you that if this goes on, I'll throw you out in the middle of the countryside, no matter where. We'll hold firm as long as necessary. The "last of the last" at the end of this story, who'll be kicked to death one day by his own bodyguards, is named Hitler. The three-quarters-dead intellectuals won't live to see that day, they'll be buried by that time ..."

Once again Cherniak took safety in humiliation. He whistled derisively, but very softly, between his teeth.

"And you, Hilda, what's to become of you?"

Hilda stood on the edge of the sidewalk, tightening the belt of her trench coat, as though about to vanish into the incorporeal darkness. She was moving away from them, ready to depart into that total night, alone, bound for no foreseeable destiny.

"I don't know." (She was speaking in a hushed voice, but distinctly, full of a feeling of peace which made her whole being smile.) "I feel like staying. I never liked Paris before; now I feel enchanted here . . . Breathe in: it's marvelous . . . I would like to stay. I won't be running much risk with my Swedish papers . . . Farewell, farewell, farewell. I feel as if I'd been drinking champagne. I can't understand why I feel so happy. I haven't forgotten anything."

Her hands were cold. They parted. Big trucks with blue headlights rumbled down the street. The black helmets of the Mobile Guards gave off a dull reflection. Ardatov went down the steps to the Métro. The city was without light, except in these underground crossroads.

6. DIALOGUES

THE ANXIETY hanging in the opaque gray of the night sky had taken on a sulfurous quality. The pathetic blue light of the streetlamps was stifled under layers of black. Signs in absurd hieroglyphics clung to housefronts that seemed to have lost all light forever. Night against night. A cat jumped out of a garbage can at the sound of human steps and turned around, bristling; its green eyes glared and then it was gone, absorbed by the stones and the void. The door of the Marquise bar was ajar, and through the crack a feeble red glow oozed out over the sidewalk. A few steps away a prostitute was negotiating with a stout man whose shape emerged, as in an aquarium, like the huge head of a dark fish emerging from a mysterious grotto. The woman laughed, and her laughter was cut off by the empty blackness. A dog barked plaintively on an upper floor. Somewhere the siren of an ambulance rose and fell and died away. Ardatov nearly bumped into two human forms clinging to the wall between Number 16 and the hotel.

"G'evening, doctor," the woman's greeting sounded like a sigh. Anselme and Alexandrine Flotte were waiting—what could they be waiting for? They stood pressed together close to the wall, their faces the color of ashes.

Numb with fear, Anselme Flotte whispered, "Doctor, someone has been killed at Number 16. It's horrible. Sandrine is beside herself."

"Who was it?"

"M. Tartre."

"Ah!" Ardatov sighed politely. What should he say? It was so simple to be killed in this world—to kill is far more complicated— admirable people were killed every hour.

"It's a pity," he said stupidly and made a move to pass them.

"Do you hear?" said Alexandrine Flotte.

Snatches of explosions on another planet combined with an electric silence. The bell inside the hotel jangled as a couple passed through.

"You go in, Anselme, the doctor will keep me company for a moment, won't you Doctor?"

"With pleasure, Madame."

"There's something funny about the air, haven't you noticed? It seems like smoke . . . Say, could it be gas?"

"I don't think so." He sniffed the air. It had a faint unfamiliar smell. "It's probably the smoke screens they spread as they advance. Or gasoline dumps burning."

Sandrine Flotte gasped in her handkerchief. "I'm no coward," she said. "But it's too much for me." The doctor felt her wrist, it was plump and warm.

"I don't think anything so terrible will happen to an open city, Madame. Take a sedative and go to bed. Would you like me to bring you some Luminol?"

The woman replied convulsively, "Oh, yes, doctor, a pill that will make me sleep." The word Luminol appealed to her like magic.

Anselme returned and forced himself to say things reassuring in their very everydayness. "Imagine, Sandrine, it was Fernande again. She sure doesn't lose any time. Makes no difference to her if the Boches are coming, she attends to her business. Oh those whores, doctor, all they think of is money—what filth!"

Ardatov, whose face they could not see, smiled wryly. "A bad lot," he said. With a heavy step he climbed the stairs where the corpse's stench was discernible. In his room he found a tube of pills, which he carried down to the little café.

"Give this to Madame, and let her sleep tomorrow as long as she likes." Anselme thanked him and offered him a little something. His face was flushed, his thick hands fumbled, but his shrewd eyes retained their self-possession. He drank with Ardatov—just a little glass of white wine, a little refreshment after so sad a day. They clinked glasses.

"Are you leaving, doctor? Something tells me."

"Yes, at daybreak."

"Oh là là, all the decent people are leaving. What's to become of us?"

He held out both hands over the bar. "Good luck, eh? I hope we'll be seeing you back soon, when Paris is recaptured. But when will that be? We're up to our necks in trouble." His fleshy lower lip trembled. "Take this old brandy with you, Doctor, for the trip."

"I never drink hard liquor," said Ardatov, suddenly aggressive.

"I didn't know," Anselme Flotte apologized. "It was meant well."

"I know that, Monsieur Flotte."

Ardatov left a great emptiness behind him. Flotte mechanically wiped off his clean bar, his hand reaching for the rag of its own accord. The little café was afloat in disintegrating reality. Gendarme pushed open the kitchen door and sauntered in. The old gray tomcat resembled the proprietor like an inferior brother, noble in his own way and distant. His animal instincts were long since sated, he was stuffed with leftover stew, and he had a good warm place to sleep under the stove. He purred rarely, digested his food in tranquility, took an interest only in himself, and that in moderation. But his colorless eyes, with their vertical line of yellow, observed everything that went on under the tables; he knew by profound intuition where it was best to look for rabbit bones. He had a white spot just under the chin, closely resembling the napkin Anselme tied on himself before sitting down to table. Gendarme sensed his master's solitude. In two leaps he was on the bar, stretching and arching his back, as though to say: I am here, Anselme. You're not all alone. M. Flotte stroked his back and was comforted.

"You're lucky, Gendarme. You can't understand..."

Ardatov returned to his room, carrying his day's fatigue like the burden of still being alive. The sixth-floor landing was lighted. Moritz Silber, tense and beaming, welcomed the old man.

"Come in, Doctor. We are waiting for you." A candle filled the attic room with shadows. Ortiga was tying bundles. His eyes glittered beneath his low forehead. Silber explained, "We've got to clear out,

Doctor. We're taking you with us. We have money. The big shot in the Faubourg du Temple is lending me his truck on condition that we take a load of merchandise."

"If there's not enough room, we'll chuck his merchandise out," said Ortiga joyfully.

"Then I'm in luck. Let me get my breath."

That's how salvation comes when it comes—simply. A great wisdom commands us to trust in chance, but with a rational, tenacious will. Ardatov lay on the battered couch and thought aloud, "The worst enemy of luck is fatigue." Ortiga turned toward him his energetic young fisherman's face, cut in two parts, one black and one golden, by the feeble light.

"You're not tired of living, though?"

"Let me think a moment, José, though I have already thought about it more than I should."

Ardatov half-closed his eyes, crossed his hands over his heart and abandoned himself to the unexpected relief of not being alone, of knowing that tomorrow's tasks were simplified, of observing the movements of two young men for whom long and unknown roads led to landscapes, faces, events almost without end. At twenty-five a man does not imagine that life has an end. He has the confidence of muscles and brains well irrigated with fresh blood; a confidence based on truth, for life has no end.

"We had a fantastic piece of luck," said Silber.

A splendid silence spread over them while the two young men cut some resistant substance with scissors, tore some cloth with a sound like a lashing sail, cooked some bouillon cubes over the gas. Ardatov spoke without opening his eyes.

"I shall never be tired of living. This planet is a marvelous place, no doubt about that. And history is made in spite of us, through us, with us, even if it crushes us. It goes where it has to go."

Ortiga handed the doctor a cup of bouillon. "Watch out, the cup is chipped. Isn't there a bit of fatalism in what you just said?"

"No, not at all. There is no fatality in the growth of children. There is no fatality in the growth of societies. And if my old muscles begin to weaken, that has nothing to do with discouragement. We need several lives and we have only one—and we have them all."

"That's a bit obscure."

"Obscure like everything that's true. Formulas can be transparent, but reality is not. And reality will continue when we are no longer here." Ardatov raised himself slowly. "Well, my suitcase is ready, and it's not heavy. Wake me about five o'clock. By the way, do you have safe-conducts?"

"I made them myself," Moritz Silber said proudly.

"*Entonces, buenas noches.*"

As Ardatov went down the corridor, he reflected that he did not say it all to these young men, because they could not understand it all... An essential part of human experience remains incommunicable. How could they understand that a crowd of dead men walked with him at every moment and pulled him gently toward them? We have thought all that you have thought, wished for all that you have wished for, loved all that you have loved, we have been so much like you that it would be hard to make out where you differ from us, some of us better than you, some stronger, we are gone, but soon you will be gone too, and others will remain... These absent men erased a boundary whose edge we move along, finding it natural, prodigious, a boundary which perhaps doesn't exist... Some good psychologists believe they have discovered a death instinct in us; but this doesn't have to do with fatigue, wouldn't it be something more like our sense of accomplishment and continuity? It would take a lifetime of study to elucidate it, I can only intuit.

He pushed open the door of his room and saw Hilda sitting there with legs crossed, reading. The light bulb, shaded by a stamped envelope, cast an aura around her smooth blond hair.

"What are you reading, Hilda?"

"Freud's *Interpretation of Dreams*. Are we as sexual as all that? Do you think so?"

"I think that old Sigmund has sometimes gone to the bottom of things. But soundings in such a deep ocean—"

He took a few steps around the room, without reason, because he always felt the need to move. A black curtain covered the window; on the white walls the dampness had made great stains with vague shapes like clouds. Hilda detected the contours of an enormous rose, a sailboat riding on a wave, a forehead surrounded by hair—and this hair was also the wave.

"I'm dreaming wide awake."

Ardatov's opaque form moved slowly through the room. There were gray pockets under his eyes, and only his firm hands reflected the light.

"I have come—"

Occupied by his thoughts and his physical weariness, Ardatov had almost forgotten her. He raised bright eyes to the young woman.

"Welcome. I can guess. You walked an hour in the darkness of Paris, through lethargic streets that have lost their names and lead nowhere but which are beautiful as never before. At first you felt exalted, proud in your solitude, you admired this enchanted labyrinth, you were exalted by acceptance of everything that is to come—and then suddenly you discovered that it was a blind alley, a useless risk, and you came."

"I thought you might leave on foot. There are no more trains or, if there are, you can't get to them. The stations are hell, I've seen them. I want to go away with you. You aren't petty. You have confidence. The others are so worn out."

"Not Kaaden."

"No, not he, or a few others. But they're so narrow. Strong and limited by their very strength."

He had not really seen her before this moment: her vigorous ash-blond hair, her obstinate little forehead, the childlike freshness, naive hardness, the hidden charm of this unaffected face. Her eyebrows were only a faint line. Her blue eyes, slightly slanted, were calm and veiled. She leaned on the table with both hands, her bust forward; she was slight but strongly built, gifted with the tenacious, unviolent strength of plants. Her knapsack, with her mess-gear on top of it, lay at her feet, calling out for a trip to the mountains.

"What peaks shall we climb, Hilda?" asked the old man heavily, but with a kind of joy.

"The most difficult," she said, laughing, and her whole face lit up.

"We must get a few hours' sleep," said Ardatov. "We shall be leaving under good conditions. Let's let the night in, all right?"

He turned out the light and drew aside the curtain. A dull glow reached them from the misty sky. Only the seven stars of the Great Bear were distinctly visible. The roofs formed angular masses. "I'll sleep on the spring and you, Hilda, can have the mattress, it isn't bad."

"It's all the same to me."

They undressed in the half-light, indifferent to each other's presence, but anxious not to cause each other embarrassment. Ardatov stretched out on the iron bed and watched the young woman in her nightgown lie down on the mattress he had put on the floor for her. After long days, a current of dense fatigue rose from his legs to his brain, dulling his sensibility, confusing his thoughts. "Perhaps this is the instinct for the last sleep..." This time he was falling asleep in contentment.

"Are you already in bed, Hilda?"

After a moment's wait, she replied softly, "Yes."

He was already asleep, his breathing regular and strangely strong. Hilda, lying hardly above the floor, saw the faintly blue square of the sky. It had few stars yet was infinite, embraced the whole universe, covered the whole of France. Tranquil landscapes lay forgotten below, insensitive to the mists, the human noises of the night, the suffering of the wounded, the annihilation of the dead. The humidity invigorated the sap. Each blade of grass was a living thing, each stream followed its path toward daylight. Somewhere, some villages had just finished burning, they were no more than flaming dots scattered on a darkened map. People watched as their earthly abodes were eaten by the flames... Along the rails and the roads, the columns of tanks, the supply columns, the medical columns, burdened with fevers and agonies, covered the earth with advancing motors, animals, killing machines, men dominated by machines, forward march, forward march: silence, no smoking, it's at night that armies bound most confidently toward hellish days... All these movements were made in obedience to telephonic orders. Fear, momentum, and instinct magnetized them. Under this unimaginable pressure, another army collapsed and Paris slept like a sick man, confined to a bed defined by the contours of the Seine, at the bottom of a moving abyss. Carried away by visions, Hilda descended toward the mystery of sleep: Four soldiers were drinking red wine in a spectral house. Suddenly they stood up. They were four brothers, exactly alike. They had a single face, repeated four times, and a single soul. These four proud men, united like the four luminous branches of a somber cross, decided at dawn to defend a little hog-backed bridge surrounded by juniper bushes in blossom and by wisps of fog. In the middle of the gray roadway an emerald-green tree frog opened human eyes. Hilda felt the anguish of a long fall; she was falling naked like a meteor through a cold fire, toward this little bridge. "They are going to be killed, all four of them! What shall I do?" She made an exhausting effort to wake up and warn them, "Don't go, don't go." But the cold fire devoured her words, she lost sight of the four soldiers, and then under a little hog-backed country bridge four naked bodies, incredibly white, came floating by, carried by the gentle current, and on the four foreheads, all so alike, were four black stars. Where was the tree frog? Moaning, Hilda broke the painful spell of sleep. The sky above Paris was beginning to brighten. The rectangle of the Great Bear glittered feebly.

7. FÉLICIEN MÛRIER

A SUFFOCATING dawn was rising. From the heights of Montmartre and Belleville, you could see slate-colored fog crawling across the suburbs, and drowning their distant reaches. Dense at ground-level, the fog invaded the sky, becoming thinner only at the zenith. The Eiffel Tower stood out like filigree in the distance. The Seine, gently rolling, flowed between its stone ramparts, its overhanging trees, its motionless barges, the somber arches of its bridges a shelter for gaping anxiety. The two sleepers who awoke under the Pont de Sully saw the outline of Notre Dame blurred by the unaccustomed fog.

"Do you remember the Thames in the fall?" said one. The other, who knew his classics, replied grandiloquently, "Even if the justly angered gods are preparing for us this noon an end worthy of rodents, even if they mean to send asphyxiating clouds down upon us, is that a reason not to go and get some of the grape at Antoine's? Coming, Bonapartist?"

Well read, both of them. The shorter of the two limped and sported a goatee; the brotherhood of ill luck called him "Bonapartist" because he carried about with him a single book, *The Memorial of St. Helena*, and no French genius was greater in his eyes than the Emperor—revolutionary, conservative, builder, legislator, lunatic, "amazing strategist, my boy," whose very defeats were attempts at victory over the impossible, brilliantly conceived. "Just take a look at the campaign of France in 1814. —And what a contempt for the ideologues! Almost as great as my own!"

The other, the friend of the classics, signed the invitations to business meetings, which he occasionally scrawled at the bottom of certain theatrical posters, with the name of Croche. His close friends called him sometimes Phynance and sometimes Sourcerer, for having, thirty years earlier, managed a mortgage bank that had unfortunately gone under. Then, ten years later, after a few years in confinement, he had devised an ingenious system of international accounts for Europe. Croche, sickened by the symmetrical cretinism of financiers and the customers of savings banks, now believed only in divining rods that point the way to subterranean water and hidden treasure. A member of the National Association of Diviners, once each year he transformed himself into a more or less respectable but by no means commonplace gentleman, donning a suit of half mourning rented from an old-clothes dealer in the Rue André-de-Sarte, and went to attend the conferences of the Association, even when they were held in the most boring and provincial places in the depths of Brittany or Roussillon. In the 1934 competition, equipped with a hazel rod, he had vied with his fellow members of the association in hunting for a golden ingot buried in the presence of a notary beneath a yard of humus in a park one kilometer square. He had finished a respectable seventeenth, a little less than three yards away from the treasure. "If I hadn't drunk so many aperitifs that morning, I would have found the treasure, it was in the palm of my hand, I would have won the prize, old man. But I don't mind, I strictly deserved my bad luck, because in my heart I didn't give a good goddamn about their ingot and their prize. The whole thing was absurd. But what breaks my heart is to have known for the last ten years that there is a treasure on the Île Saint-Louis—I can even tell you where: between the Rue Bretonvilliers and the Quai d'Anjou, you'll pardon me for not being more exact. And it's one hell of a treasure. The only trouble is, you'd have to tear down a bunch of buildings to get at it. Again I find myself in conflict with the real-estate interests . . . But it does my heart good just the same to know that it's there and that no one will get it. Now do you understand why I prefer to lodge beneath the Pont de Sully?"

More silent than in better days, Croche and Bonapartist put away their bedding—cushions stuffed with old newspapers to keep out the cold—in a tool box belonging to the Department of Waterways; for a moment they contemplated the Île Saint-Louis, their treasure island, noble and forlorn with its steep embankments, its severe old houses, its slender trees: it seemed to be drifting away into the fog. Shall we ever again see the soft pearl-gray mornings of the Seine? What if this lousy war even changes the climate! Bonapartist became angry, and foraging in the fleece of his chest, said, "All this, old man, is the fault of the circumcised, it can't be denied."

Both of them were bearded and ravaged, as disparate as old rags, as alike as brothers. They could be readily distinguished only by their gait, the one limping, the other proceeding by easy jerks. Their rags had the same sordid color—piss-and-flea color, they called it.

"Enough of your absurdities," Croche replied. "Why did the Roman Empire fall, why did the empire of the Pharaohs fall? Because the earth turns. There's a guy who predicted all this, Oscar Spengler, a Boche scholar. I've read him, it's all worked out. But let us proceed:

"Aurora, cloven-footed,
To the grape doth invite."

They were alone on the embankment. Every morning at this time, the little tugboat *Odalisque*, spouting soot, would steam up the Seine toward Berry. This morning there was no *Odalisque*. The *Odalisque* was on strike. No cyclists riding to work, toolboxes strapped to their saddles. Croche contemplated the desert. "Pure Sahara. Say, maybe the Claridge is empty. We could move into the first floor. I don't like the upper stories."

"No soap. It'll be full of Boche generals by tonight. The patriotic staff is getting the champagne ready for them, I'll bet you three sous. What we could do, we could go tell the Quakers that we're Belgian refugees. You have lost your villa at Ostend and I've lost my library in Louvain."

"They won't believe us," said Croche sadly. "We're professional refugees from the ruins of civilization, but we've been at it too long.

Philanthropists have a remarkable nose for permanent misery, and there's nothing that makes them sicker."

Bonapartist picked up a box of matches, a useful article. Having unbent himself—"Oh, my back"—he returned to larger problems.

"I've been wondering if Adolf doesn't sort of take after Napoleon. The Emperor's masterpiece was his defeat. We won't really know about Hitler until he falls. There are ways and ways of doing these things."

"We'll see. You don't imagine someone could take Paris and not come a cropper? It's as if I had found the treasure on the Île: there would be only one thing left for me to do: to die without heirs."

They advanced at a limping pace toward Le Joyeux Matin, a bar that opened at daybreak for a clientele of boatmen, street sweepers, workers at the food market, early-rising bums. It nestled in the ground floor of a little tumbledown house on the quay, incongruous among a row of more recent buildings—though they too were old and decayed. It was a pleasantly somber place, furnished with square tables and straw-bottomed chairs. None of the usual customers had yet appeared on this strange morning. Not even those night workers, initiates in the mysteries of the sewage system, who emerge from the tunnels of the Métro by little secret doors or rise from manholes, carrying with them the smell of subterranean putrefaction; not even those strange young men with feeble chins and bright, furtive eyes, who, it could be guessed, had just hidden away under the beds of their hotel rooms packages worth a one-way ticket to Saint-Laurent-du-Maroni, a place specializing in hard labor and banana trees, Negresses and pink flamingos, jungles and death.

A stout gentleman in an overcoat, wearing the red button of the Legion of Honor in his lapel, eventually came in and ordered: "Black coffee with old brandy." His hat was tilted back, revealing the face of a silent and heavy eater; as a young man, he might have resembled a rat, now he looked like a pale-faced wild boar. His chins were getting bluish; the fatigue of a sleepless night weighed on his lower lids. He sat down heavily, put his elbows on the table, and placed his thick hands in front of him; they were well manicured but dirty. He dropped his head and his presence was so oppressive that Antoine the proprietor looked for something to say.

"I open at the legal hour, Monsieur. I mean the hour of Monsieur de Paris—the first morning hour, the freshest, the bluest. And this is the last morning."

The gentleman said "hmm" like a lazy hound who was being disturbed. Antoine continued more or less to himself: "This is the hour when on certain days his worship, the chief executioner, officiates—just at the moment when I pull up my shutters, when I put my coffeepot on the gas. And then I say to myself: he's a man like you or me pushing the button—and the head of a man like you or me too that's dropping into the basket of sawdust, and the fellow has just about a quarter of a second to take in the idea that he's had it."

The gentleman removed his hat, perhaps in honor of the fallen heads. Sparse pomaded hair divided by a white line more or less covered his powerful skull. He seemed to be coming out of a stupor. His manner of speech was polite, his voice hoarse but pleasant.

"Extremely interesting what you say there, *patron*."

Antoine, vaguely irritated, thrust his thin jaw forward. "It's not interesting at all. In fact, it's idiotic. I don't even know why I said it. People talk without thinking, they'd do better to hold their tongues."

The decorated gentleman (the phiz of an actor at the *Comédie Française* or of a respectable pederast) considered Antoine with cordiality.

"I am entirely of your opinion. But sometimes the great art is to speak without knowledge."

With the movement of a man chasing flies, he chased ideas from his face.

"... Apropos of the guillotine, Monsieur, I will tell you something that is not very well known. Our good Dr. Guillotin invented nothing at all. Contrary to what is taught in the schools, his philanthropic machine was not a French invention but a Scotch one. James Douglas, the fourth Count Morton, an adversary of the tender Mary Stuart (between ourselves a worthless slut), invented the decapitator about 1560—I have not been able to establish the precise date. History is the science of uncertainties. He was of course an assassin, this Count Morton, and he died by his own invention, as was fitting. The Scots called their machine 'The Maiden'—perhaps because even when you sleep with Lady Death, she keeps her maidenhead. But I don't believe they thought about it, they spoke without knowledge like the great poets and like you, Monsieur. The French, more subtle, called it 'the Widow.' Virgin and widow at once, what could be truer?"

"No use trying to understand," said Antoine somberly. He disliked this well-dressed lecturer.

The reassuring shapes of the two winos staggered up to the door. The gentleman ordered cold ham, mustard, and white wine. He was one of the foremost men of letters of the time in Paris, and thus in the world. "It bores me," he said sometimes. "What bilge literature is. I recognize only poetry, impure poetry." He amused himself by inventing names for vague beings, intermediate between plants, animals, phantasms, and the word; these colored specters peopled his work, like bacteria in puddles of rainwater. He detested the poses he himself assumed in salons and cafés. "There's no help for it. When you're with two or three persons who admire you a little, or pretend to, you turn into an old whore. If you blow your nose or move a little finger, it's as if you were saying: Yes, I am the great man. Pah!" From time to time he roamed the city all night, until his back ached and his legs grew cramped in the exaltation of dawn. He was led by an almost intolerable pain—the anguish that makes a man want to be the invisible witness of a crime or of a fantastic, depraved embrace. Torpid, full of self-contempt, he wandered along the Seine haunted by the phantoms of the drowned, and suddenly he felt intelligent, because well-balanced phrases on the crisis in Europe, that luxurious drunken boat, on the pataphysics of the newspapers, etc., spontaneously took shape in his mind, like a song. And just as fireworks burst forth like geysers, in a sky empty with boredom, beautiful verses without beginning or sequence traced dazzling parabolas through his mind. He was too lazy to stop and note down these inspirations, and so most of them were lost. At the Café de Flore he could recollect only snatches that needed filling out, erasures, devices, and research in the *Petit Larousse Illustré*. "What stillborn poems ferment in garbage pails: There are imbeciles who say that I have genius. It is the nights of Paris that have genius. The whole mystery of the creation and the disintegration of humanity chants its lament in the shadow of a public urinal on the Quai Montebello at three o'clock in the morning. The night owl who thrills at this apparition is at least a distant relative of Shakespeare. If I have talent, it is because I love good French according to Littré, according to the night workers at the central market of Les Halles, and because I am afraid, afraid. —Do you follow me?"

Since he made these remarks to the first journalist to appear while devouring his sausage-and-bean hotpot on the marble table of a cheap restaurant, young critics thought him a supreme actor. Overeating increased his enchanted malaise.

He had just been walking through the darkest hours, stopping in unsavory crannies to distribute his cigarettes to the most wretched of prostitutes, to bargain with sinister young men and then to disappoint them, to watch the couples at the approaches to the hotels, to watch a pack of dogs chasing a bitch in heat—this last in the Rue Mazarin beneath the black cupola of the French Academy. "Fame, that fascinating bitch ... no good, no good ..." His obsession was that France was crumbling, that Paris, literature, elegance of wit, all were crumbling beneath a base defeat that was well deserved—or utterly undeserved. We were governed by morons. Yes. And the others? The conquerors? Are sadists and murderers any less morons? We lived for absurd values, the only true values. Valéry, Claudel, Fargue, Gide, Nathan, myself, are absurd. What we needed was corporals, corporals in leather tunics, shut up in steel boxes rolling on caterpillar treads. —Lord!

He devoured the ham with mustard, the white wine, and more black coffee. He noticed the two personages from the Pont de Sully, to whom the proprietor was serving some leftover cold cuts.

"If the gentlemen will give me the pleasure of ... They are my guests, *patron*."

Bonapartist and Croche had taken the man's measure. Better than anyone else here below, they vaguely understood him. And nothing surprised them. If a ravishing American woman, alighting from the most sumptuous Chrysler, had invited all three of them up to her hotel, they would simply have said, "Yes, ma'am, but we've lost the habit of sheets, princess, and even of the sweet little trifle—but we can always try." They amused themselves by telling stories of this kind.

"We appreciate good company, amiable Amphitryon," they replied, and bringing their plate of leavings they sat down with the man of letters, who greeted them with a lunatic smile. "What do you think of the guillotine, gentlemen?"

"I don't wonder you bring it up this morning. Did you see the sky, like a backdrop for a descending blade?"

"By God!"

A delivery truck stopped on the brightening quay, and people poured out of it. A blond young woman entered first, then another with dark eyes, followed by an impassive, rather elegant old man, and then a few more people, filling the little room with a tumult that was almost gay. Young voices asked all together if there was any coffee.

"Lucky bastards, going on a little tour to the Pyrenees, I take it," murmured Bonapartist.

"Or perhaps to the pampas of the Argentine. Are we beating a retreat, ladies and gentlemen, like the General Staff?"

Augustin Charras set his two fists on the edge of the table.

"Not I. I'll stay here and croak with Paris, if Paris croaks, and that won't happen so quick. The others have their reasons; they are stronger than me. Those who are getting out today are the ones that will return to settle past-due accounts." He turned a quarrelsome look on the gentleman with the Legion of Honor. "Isn't that your opinion, Monsieur?"

"My rule is never to judge, Monsieur. But to have the prettiest girls leave is an affliction for those of us who stay. The three of us are staying, just like you, Monsieur, to croak if..."

Augustin Charras's ill temper melted into sudden sympathy. He sat down at the table with an air of familiarity.

"Agreed. And all of us won't croak. We'll hold out. We're tough customers, we are."

"Yes, tough..."

Augustin Charras insisted. "They'll break their teeth on Paris. They won't be dealing with ministries and army staffs anymore, but with us."

"With us," the poet repeated in a muted voice. That was hard to say, and hard to think. What are we? Have we not become accustomed, living in the ease of egotism—an intelligent, benevolent egotism—to being no force at all? A hard secret voice added, "And those who have no force are nothing in a time of force. I am *nothing*." Did not the two winos chewing so repulsively with their cadaverous jaws belong to the same nothingness? They had fallen beyond all possibility of redemption—but what an infinite capacity for resistance they had, to subsist like the grass trodden underfoot, burned and befouled, but growing back again, unceasingly, patiently. Each of them with his quarter of a century of degradation behind him... and yet they existed! That was impressive.

Charras stared down at the wooden table and frowned. Perhaps it was the first time in his life that he felt strong and sure of his strength without knowing what to do with it. He took little notice of his chance companions at this table, the two poor devils from under the bridges, the sad, fat, gloomy bourgeois blown into this place by the aimless breezes of dawn—but nothing separated him from them. A man is what he can do, this is the moment to be real men, my poor friends, we had stopped thinking about that. For some of us it is too late, no doubt. Lord, have pity! No one in the world can know, it is true, when it is too late and for whom. Dogs that have been run over have been known to show their teeth and bite. Augustin Charras showed his teeth joyfully and turned to the gentleman with the decoration: "Are you are not of my opinion, citizen?"

"Yes," said the poet, who did not know whether he was agreeing for the sake of politeness or because he was beginning to discern a truth. "Besides, all is not lost, my friend. We will defend the line of the Loire."

"Did you read that in the *Canard Enchaîné*? They have crossed the Albert Canal, the Meuse, the Sambre, the Somme, the Marne, the Seine, and you, you imagine we'll stop them on the Loire? If General Weygand says that, he doesn't believe a word of it, any more than I do. They will stop where they want to, or when they're out of breath. This war, I tell you, isn't the business of the military anymore, it's our business, do you understand? The business of civilians, of poor civilian suckers, you'll see."

What is the relationship between thought and the passage of time? Sometimes you think more and better in a fraction of a second than after endless self-questioning. A star shines where there was nothing before. Does it appear in time? In the space-time continuum? Is it intemporal? The poet was questioning himself this way because a wave of ideas were suddenly passing through him. Zigzag flashes, drunken magnetic fields?

"Obviously you are right, Monsieur, now our turn has come."

For fear of being ridiculous, he did not utter the rest of the discourse his mind had framed: "I let myself be carried along by the current of appetites, chance meetings, success, loves, ideas that at bottom were only the ghosts of ideas. I looked at the universe as an amateur, I juggled words charged with unknown radiations as an equilibrist plays with the magnetic balls that pass through his dancing body like magic. And I am not among the worst. Here we are, all of us: on the mat, floored by a good uppercut to the jaw, awakened from ourselves— a whole nation and what a nation! Decadent, do you think? That's the name barbaric vigor gives to truly civilized people. Our culture and our great well-being had disarmed us, we had forgotten the ferocious natural laws, had put to sleep some instincts that are still indispensable, the instinct for mass murder for example. A few little crimes were enough to maintain a hint of sadism in us. We preferred Eros, the Muses, Apollo, Dionysus to warlike Mars, dripping with fresh blood. Were we wrong? That will be seen much later. We have been beaten to the ground. It is from today on that we shall see whether we are capable of living." (I'll write a magnificent article—that no one would be able to publish anywhere anymore—ah, I don't give a damn about good articles, in the NRF or any of those places! It's like Rimbaud said in "Vertigo": "Empires, Parliaments, Republics all perish... I am here, I am still here!" Now that's good.)

Augustin Charras leaned confidentially toward the man of letters. "That girl with the dark hair there in the corner, beside her blond girlfriend, that's Angèle, my only daughter. I'm sending her away with those refugees, a good crew, a couple of Spaniards, an old Russian, politicals. They were the first to pass through the fire and dirt, the barbed wire and all the rest, while we were still sleeping. I don't want Nazi brutes looking lustfully at my kid. I don't want her to see what's waiting for us. I'm staying here alone like an old tree, let the wood-choppers come—"

The calm violence inside him was not far from a sort of invigorating despair. He sniggered quietly. Returning to his abandoned shop frightened him a little after all. Having been a lumberjack in the Vosges, he knew it did not do much good for an old tree to stand still and resist the ax, but he also thought of his own hatchet, that fitted so snugly in his hand. It was the only bright object in his coal shop.

"Why," he asked abruptly, "why didn't the government quietly distribute arms to the people of Paris before clearing out? This isn't a war like other wars."

Bonapartist shrugged his shoulders with sage contempt: "Don't go talking ideology, Mossieu! All wars are the same, one government's as bad as another, they all get their turn to take the jackpot, and the higher the conqueror climbs, the further down he tumbles... All you need is the patience to wait, it'll happen all by itself."

"We need a social war," said Charras, pursuing his own thoughts.

The man of letters understood nothing about doctrines. He called Marx "the great unreadable Magus." Am I a bourgeois because I have a little bank account, fifty Japanese prints that no longer interest me, as much disgust for bourgeois stupidity as Flaubert, disgust for the vulgarity of the workers, and this sentiment of a world on the road to ruin, and this love of poor, lowly human—the most human—things? Filled with doubt, he replied, "I see bastards and decent people, all mixed together, often in the same people. But do classes exist?"

Bonapartist, stuffed full of ham and café au lait, felt himself almost in form. He replied in the affirmative, "They exist, amiable Amphitryon. Just look at the two of us. We are at the bottom of the heap. All the classes crush us without seeming to, each in its own way. We say shit to all of them, not very loud though, because we don't want any trouble with the stock exchange or the CGT."

Croche found that this strange day was beginning well. It is in those times when the planet begins to turn a little crooked that luck comes in reach of your down-and-outer. If by chance the Stukas bombarded the Île Saint Louis, perhaps the treasure there might even become accessible.

"As long as they don't blow up the bridges, fellows like us haven't much to lose. We are nonbelligerents par excellence. But remember, gentlemen, that we have never consorted with the enemy."

The people at the back table were rising. In the confusion of departure, the man of letters found himself next to Hilda. He liked her hard, fine features and her gray eyes.

"You are charming, Mademoiselle," he said to her. "I wish you the realization of your hopes. You are foreign?"

She replied affably, for now there could be no danger. "No, not foreign to these events. I'm a German refugee."

"Well, take my best wishes with you."

On the sidewalk the immense white morning surrounded them all with a surprising radiance. The winos went off first: "Our occupations call us, gentlemen." Like fat, crippled insects, they crept along the quay toward Notre Dame. Charras and the man of letters, an intimacy grown up between them, lit cigarettes. With the corner of his eye, Charras pointed to the departing foreigners.

"They're marked out for the concentration camps. They have guts. I've finally come to see that they're right. We should have started to fight a long time ago."

"Of course," said the man of letters. "And besides, my friend, we are marked out for the concentration camp ourselves. And we *are* right."

It was now the height of the morning. The two men were in good spirits. The man of letters introduced himself, feeling as he always did an irritating pride (for pride sustains a man, but confines him within vanity, and vanity is as slippery as spittle).

"I am Félicien Mûrier."

"Augustin Charras, at your service. Coal and wood, Sixteen Rue du Roi-de-Naples, a shop without pretensions. You're a doctor?"

"No—a writer."

"What do you write?"

"Mostly poems."

"In the manner of Victor Hugo? Say, won't there be *Chastisements* to write?"

It was good to feel himself unknown—the unknown poet. Strange never to have considered the poetry of revenge. Yet, if the mission of poetry is to create anxiety, doesn't it punish the torpor of the mind?

"They will be written, Monsieur Charras, don't doubt it."

Charras jumped into the truck. Hilda, Angèle, and Ardatov were already installed amid wooden boxes and traveling bags.

"I recognized the man you were talking with," said Ardatov. "He's a great man in his way."

Charras's eyes followed the poet, who was departing along the quay with a weary step, his shoulders stooped under his heavy overcoat.

"He seems like a good fellow," commented Charras, "but what's great about him? I don't get it. Maybe it's we who are great."

The truck, with Moritz Silber and José Ortiga in the front seat, drove off toward the Jardin des Plantes.

8. THE INDIFFERENT

"WHEN the shit gets as far as the police stations," said M. Carpe, "it means that..."

He finished his sentence with a gesture of despair. The ship was sinking. During the night of June 10 a great cold fear had invaded these rooms, where accumulated layers of dust gave routine a feeling of permanence. Even the dust seemed to pale when the radio announcer, first in a matter-of-fact voice, then tense and almost stammering, read the decision of General Hering, commandant of Paris, to defend Paris block by block. "In other words, slaughter and destruction everywhere! Like at Madrid when the anarchists were in the saddle." The walls of the police station had not been painted in more than ten years, light as wretched as the end of the world fell on the sheaves of records, and from the little courtyard came a stink of sewage that no amount of carbolic acid could drown out. From time immemorial an atmosphere of suicidal discouragement had pervaded this office.

"The last repairs were made when Tardieu was minister," said M. Carpe with indignation and sadness, for these were the things that a regime could be judged by. What if the fortifications had been maintained the same way?

"We're cooked geese," said Patrolman Blin, a stout good-natured fellow with a nose deformed by purple protuberances.

The others were so overcome they said nothing; merely tightened their belts and unhooked the collars of their tunics.

The préfecture sent down orders by the dozen, it would have taken twenty men to carry them out; then it gave no sign of life for hours at a time, and as there was too much to do, only routine duties were performed. A lieutenant of engineers on leave came in and shut himself up with the deputy precinct-captain for a whole hour. They studied the map of the quarter; sappers were expected. M. Carpe reckoned that four thousand sandbags should be urgently demanded from army headquarters. Officer Landois, said by malicious tongues to be the son of a Communard, sketched projected barricades on the map. "With fifty machine guns, I'll undertake to hold out for twenty-four hours."

"Fool, what do you expect to do with the Stukas?"

"And what about the RAF and our own air force?"

"Nobody's seen them except in the papers, which are no longer even good enough to wipe your ass..."

Officer Landois took his cap off to scratch his head. "Ah, damn, damn." His disappointment provoked a great burst of laughter.

The military authorities had secretly arranged to place a shortwave radio providing information to the enemy in a two block area—in other words, a thousand square yards worth of six-story buildings. A patrolman and a plainclothesman—M. Bœuf, who had volunteered—contemplated a block of old houses. The cigar store and bar of old lady Mahieu, widow of the First World War, occupied the corner next to the wash trough. A red horse's head, resembling a seahorse, could be seen against the white sky. No mysterious vibration betrayed the short waves.

"Ah, if we found those scoundrels, what a pleasure it would be to twist their balls," M. Bœuf dreamed. "But we might as well look for a needle in a hay barn."

Fardier suggested looking in on a few foreigners. At the top of a stairway filled with the stench of toilets, the detectives found a suspect denounced by the concierge on the ground that he seldom went out. But he had no radio. On the other hand, his residence permit had expired. This little redhaired Pole, probably a Jew, repaired old clothes—of course without a work permit.

"Better come down to headquarters with us. You're guilty of a double violation." He followed them without objecting, but his reddish eyes were like those of a sick rabbit. In the street, the two detectives exchanged a look.

"All right, go home. You'll be called. Don't you understand? We're telling you to beat it."

"Lord," said M. Bœuf in disgust. "Such characters aren't human. You talk about your Fifth Column. We round them up by the busload, a whole stadiumful of them, and what good does it do?"

The redhead ran off and they looked after him with amusement until he disappeared down a smelly corridor. Patrolman Fardier sighed and kept muttering, "What a pretty sight we make."

In the only presentable house within the "designated perimeter," they rang the doorbell of an apartment occupied by a South American. The maid, wearing a white apron, led them into a cream-colored vestibule. Through a half-open door, they saw the portrait of a general and a glass case full of decorations. "Monsieur is at Biarritz. Monsieur will not be back before the first part of July."

"Well, it's sure we won't find anything. Let's have a drink."

... M. Carpe, the deputy precinct captain, and Officer Landois took care of routine affairs by themselves. The precinct captain had been called to the préfecture and would return God knows when. The bicycle squad was out on jobs in the suburbs. (Fardier, having drunk two quarts of red wine to keep up his courage, was at home sleeping; M. Bœuf was wandering from bar to bar.)

The police station was squeezed into the ground floor of a tall building with a crumbling façade. Its green woodwork and murky windowpanes protected by gratings made it look like an old post office. The red lantern, surmounted by a flagpole for the Fourteenth of July, and the semicircular inscription, LIBERTY, EQUALITY, FRATERNITY, were marks of a humble personality. Within, a nondescript public, resembling objects in a lost-and-found office, was milling around behind the railing that divided the front room into two zones, the zone of the street and the zone of authority.

M. Carpe was attending to the public. In the captain's office, Officer Landois, his forehead moist with sweat, was answering the telephone and taking notes in his large, schoolboy script. The complexity of tasks necessitated this division of labor contrary to hierarchical order. Something incredible happened to Officer Landois. He shrugged his shoulders as he read an anonymous denunciation of "M. Léonce Durin, self-styled wine salesman, the lover of one Mélanie Truche, nicknamed Monique Trèfle. He has been seen making signals from his bedroom window on the fifth floor of the house at . . ." and so on. Every day letters of this kind were received. If you bothered to investigate, you would find nothing but jealousy and neighborhood squabbles behind them. Another letter, more serious because it was signed "Anselme Flotte, former Marine Corporal, veteran," pointed out to the captain that "the aforesaid Augustin Charras . . . utters Communist and defeatist remarks and, in view of the grave crisis facing our country, might become a suspicious and dangerous element . . . concerning whom it is the duty of good citizens to inform the vigilance of the competent authorities . . ." "All right, Flotte, we know you—we know you can't stand his guts, and if he gets on your case, maybe he's not so far wrong."

The telephone rang imperiously.

"Hello, police headquarters, Rue— Who? What? This is Landois, *L* as in Louis, *A* as in Arthur."

Without listening further, a low distinguished voice at the other end of the line said, "I recognize your voice, Captain Langlois. This is Colonel Broudouroudourou. Will you please inform your superiors: the bridge at Creil is still holding, but resistance is breaking down on the Oise. It's very serious. Goodbye, Captain."

Officer Landois made a grimace. The Oise, good God! Sunday-morning landscapes passed before his eyes bathed in the glare of doom. He leaned over and whispered to M. Carpe, "A colonel just telephoned, name sounds like brou-brou-brou, I couldn't get it. He says the Fritzes are about to cross the Oise at Creil."

"I was expecting it," said M. Carpe, stunned.

"And Blin telephoned, he wants to know if we should take action against pushcart women operating in prohibited locations."

"Yes, take action by all means. The regulations have not been suspended to my knowledge."

With his silver-rimmed spectacles and his black tie fastened by a horseshoe pin, M. Carpe had an especially arid look at this moment. He turned angrily to the public.

"Landois, you take care of these long faces. I just can't make out what they want. It gives you cramps just to look at them. Next. You, Monsieur."

A sawed-off little man with a triple chin leaned painfully across the bar and spoke in an undertone. His pudgy hands were at work crumpling the brim of his felt hat.

"It's to verify an adultery, officer. You've got to come right away, I beg of you."

M. Carpe reared up like a serpent, his eyeglasses sent forth swift lightnings. The gentleman could see nothing but his gnashing teeth.

"Next you'll be asking me if I'm a cuckold too. It's not the day for verifications. Read the papers, Monsieur. That's all. Next."

The gentleman felt the floor shifting under his feet. Were they already talking about him in the papers? Were there special days for verifications?

A lady with a pince-nez extended some papers and said, "Permit for a telegram, *please*. British nationality."

"You can't send wires to London anymore, Madame."

"Yes, Monsieur, I have inquired at the central office. And it's not for London, it's for Hatford, my castle at Hatford, Sussex."

The telegram said: KITTY GIVEN BIRTH TWO MALES ONE FEMALE ALL WELL STOP LOVE.

"Who's Kitty?"

"My little Pomeranian dog."

M. Carpe signed and stamped the blank, cursing under his breath. "Sussex, Sussex. I hope your mutt croaks. That's all. This world is full of nuts. Next, Madame."

The opulent bust of another lady whispered, "I am Madame Nelly Thorah of the occult sciences, that is, I am Madame Jacques Lambin, widow, née Thérèse Herminie Descourvieux. I have come to inform you that there has been a dreadful crime in our house. Monsieur Tartre has been murdered."

"The fence?"

"Oh no, Monsieur, Monsieur Achille Tartre."

M. Carpe stood up, lifted by impotent fury.

"And what do you want me to do about it? Call the public prosecutor, the judiciary police, the Pope ... Go on."

"And you?"

A personage with the face of a jockey boiled in vinegar announced gravely, "I wish to make a complaint. My bicycle has been stolen."

"In writing. You can bring me your complaint out of turn. If you know the name and address of the thief, the exact spelling. Who's left?"

M. Carpe was sick to his stomach and had a bitter taste in his mouth. Behind his eyeglasses full of chaotic reflections he was in fact in tears. An idea, one single idea, beat in his brain like the clapper of a broken bell: "We're done for, done for, poor Paris, poor Paris."

The victim of adultery stood in the half light and stared at the filthy stone floor; his hands moved slowly around the brim of his hat. Mme Nelly Thorah turned around, took a step toward the door, then two steps back, removed a bottle of salts from her handbag and took a long whiff. "It's unbelievable."

Officer Landois's neck had turned purple. He was listening to two timid old people neatly dressed in black, sexagenarian orphans. The woman repeated the story after her husband and Landois tried to understand, but the landscapes of the Oise were in his mind and all three of them seemed like suppliants with invisible ropes around their necks.

"We are from Rouen, officer, we had a hardware store for thirty years in the Rue des Bonnetiers. They came in along Rue Grand-Pont and the river. Our house was destroyed, even the cellar. We have nothing left. We are on our way to Niort, where our son-in-law's house is, he's in the Army. We lost our younger daughter at Argenteuil, there were explosions, a panic. We thought we'd find her at Montparnasse station, but she wasn't there, the train was three hours late, you can imagine. She's a good girl, but she's backward, she doesn't always understand what you tell her, you have to repeat it softly."

They opened a locket containing the picture of a young girl.

"Give me her description. I will communicate with the missing persons bureau. Leave the picture. We will find her."

"Do you need the picture? We have no other—and what if you don't find her?"

"No, I don't need it. We will find her."

It seemed to him that the whole police station and the millennial foundations of Paris were beginning to sway gently with a mad motion which made his heart beat fast and filled his very limbs with a sensation of savage energy. He looked down on the old man and the old woman in black.

"Blond, seventeen, beige topcoat, operation scar on her neck, must be spoken to softly—I can see her. We'll find her, I guarantee it."

The two old orphans went out, jostling one another as though they were going to fall together. The woman murmured, "Did you hear that, Guillaume? He said, 'I guarantee we'll find her.'"

Officer Landois walked like a sailor on a pitching vessel. M. Carpe took his arm. "It seems M. Tartre has been murdered, next door to the Hôtel Marquise. Go have a look. But you know it doesn't matter anymore."

"First I want to call the missing persons bureau. I tell you we'll find that girl. People have to speak softly to her."

"Yes, softly," echoed M. Carpe.

Landois spent forty minutes on the phone. Twice he shouted the description of a blond, stammering young girl in a beige topcoat, scar under her chin, lost in the tumult of the defeat between Argenteuil and Montparnasse. The ground of the city continued to sway distinctly, but somewhere amid the shifting crowds there was this child, intact and calm, who couldn't understand the world in which people spoke too loudly—and to say what? He had no doubt that he would save her. In the end a furious voice answered him. "Will you stop pestering us? This is the second time you've given us that description. Get it into your head that it's the three-thousandth and then some in two days. We're snowed under."

The ground stopped swaying. M. Carpe came in.

"Landois, it seems we're about to capitulate. The Boches may be here in a few hours. Some idiot just said on the radio that Paris is not France. I say there is no more France."

"You're wrong, Monsieur Carpe."

"Yes, I'm wrong—"

That aged him, made him seem thinner, took away his deputy-captain's dignity. He looked like the wino with glasses who had been locked up a few days before for pessimistic remarks.

"Do you remember that tramp, Monsieur Carpe? He said that Europe was doomed, that we'd all end up by being shot, and that there'd be a great plague."

"Maybe he was right."

They were immersed, as they spoke, in a strangely banal fear. By chance Patrolman Blin entered the public waiting room, followed by several screaming pushcart women. Carpe automatically recovered his old self. "Silence! I told you, Blin, not to bring action against them, it's not the moment for it." Then more softly, "My poor Blin, we are about to capitulate. You can set up your carts wherever you like, ladies. Tomorrow we shall see. —Ah, what shall we see tomorrow?"

And the swaying of the earth began again. Landois, to escape it, went out into the stupefying street radiant with sunlight and headed for 16 Rue du Roi-de-Naples. He stopped at the Marquise and asked Anselme Flotte to accompany him to the site of the crime. Mme Prugnier remained on the landing, her arms crossed beneath her black shawl.

"I think I saw a tall soldier pass last night, I heard him climbing up there like a cat. It gave me gooseflesh. But you'd better look in on the foreigners on the sixth floor, officer."

The door was unlocked, Landois and Flotte needed only to give it a shove. The stench of the corpse caught in their throats and made them cough. They turned on the desk lamp. M. Tartre had crumpled in his swivel chair and the safe stood open behind him. The murdered man's large face was turning green, his open eyes were also turning green. In his left hand he held the metal inkstand, in his right hand a rag. Both hands had fallen on the desk. Flotte and Landois tiptoed round the desk, examined the dark head wound and the blackened blood on the carpet.

"I can guess how it was," said Flotte. "He fell there, see, then he got up again and sat down—" And Landois concluded, "He didn't know what he was doing anymore. He began to wipe the fingerprints off the inkwell . . . He must have been mighty scared of fingerprints— In view of his own deals."

Landois burst out laughing so loudly that M. Anselme Flotte took fright and Mme Jérôme Prugnier crossed herself on the landing. Flotte pointed a finger at the safe: "That's a lot of dough in there!"

"You see where it gets you to have too much dough," said Landois joyfully. "Well, now we are informed, M. Flotte. I am not one of those who believe in the resurrection. Will you treat me to an aperitif? Don't touch anything before the coroner arrives, if the coroner hasn't taken the express for Bordeaux."

The building was swaying on its foundation. "To hell with the foreigners on the sixth floor," thought Landois. "I'll say that their papers are in order and that I've seen nothing suspicious."

Passing in front of Mme Prugnier, he said very gravely, "Everything is in order, Madame. Be careful to lock the door."

Mme Prugnier followed him to the bar where he drank three little glassfuls, one after another. Mme Prugnier asked, "Aren't you afraid there will be looting?"

Landois meditated a moment, but that was to permit the tonic warmth of the alcohol to expand in his brain. "Looting, Madame? It's quite possible, quite possible. But there's nothing much we can do about it with our reduced personnel." His slightly mad eyes gleamed with malice as he thought, "A little looting will shake up your fleas."

9. THE EXODUS

LEAVING Paris by the Porte d'Italie, desolate as the gateway to a dead capital overgrown with weeds, the little yellow truck traveled over roads almost devoid of traffic. The main wave of fugitives had already passed. The suburbs were lethargic. Mobile Guards, few and far between, were interested only in hearing the latest bad news. Near the last houses of Villejuif a Mobile Guard stopped the car. Silber and Ardatov leaned out.

"What's the problem?"

"Is it true that the Boches have entered by the Porte de la Chapelle and the East Station is burning?"

"Probably not true."

The soldier in his black helmet chewed on his cigarette. "All you hear now is rumors. You have room. I wonder if I shouldn't get the hell out of here with you?"

"And your mission?" Ardatov asked him softly. "Our mission was to defend the country I think," replied the man in the helmet. "Very well. You may pass."

"It's the deluge if they're not checking papers anymore," Silber observed.

Ardatov remembered the debacle of a White army fleeing toward Novorossiysk and the Black Sea in 1920, with a whole population of ex-bourgeoisie mixed in among its wagons, its cars, its lice-ridden ambulances; he thought of the people of Viipuri just last winter fleeing like this under the gray snow toward the lakes and forests of Finland. Ortiga remembered the golden roads of Catalonia only last year, covered with routed armies moving toward the Pyrenees, prosperous France, the hope of living after all.

Experts in defeat, Ortiga and Ardatov judged it best to avoid the main roads, crowded, perhaps clogged and perhaps bombed, in any case drained of gasoline. They headed for Limours, then through plains and thickets for Dourdan and Étampes. Unaware of the disaster, the villages seemed unchanged: scattered among the green fields, sparse woods and orchards, drowsing around their belfries. A dreary, parsimonious aspect: shutters closed on streets where no one passed, solidly closed portals, jagged zigzagging walls topped with broken glass, cafés half-open, but so drowsy that the only tremor of life was the buzzing of flies. Ancient old women by the roadside showed signs of surprise at the sight of a commercial vehicle from Paris—if anything in the world could surprise them after seventy years of petty toil, of God-willed sorrows, of penny-pinching, of distrust and perseverance. In a sunlit courtyard some men were shoveling manure with pitchforks.

Silber questioned them as to the shortest road to...Then: "Are you aware of what is happening?" The peasant spat into the palm of his hand the better to take hold of his pitchfork.

"What else could you expect? The way things are now, the sooner it's over the better."

Silber reflected that you couldn't carry your fields with you as a peddler carries his stock. The people of the earth thought they owned the land—in reality they belonged to it. As Silber took the wheel he realized that the massive, meditative presence of Ardatov beside him modified the course of his own thoughts.

"Is there such a thing as mental communication, doctor?"

"Often," said Ardatov. "We say only a part, the least important part, no doubt, of what we want to communicate. Anyone who hears only the words without forming a further contact with the man is performing only a superficial and useless function."

Hilda and Angèle, inside the truck, were watching the oncoming landscape over the shoulders of the two men in front and at the same time listening to their conversation.

"Then you think our conversations consist of two parts," said Silber. "One spoken and one understood."

"The essential part is not spoken but understood."

"Otherwise there would be no love," said Angèle, and if her cheeks were red it was from windburn and not from blushing at her boldness.

Among these strangers, so different from the men and women she had known up to now, she felt simpler, prepared for a kind of battle that she could not yet define.

"All falsehood," said Hilda resolutely, "resides in words. I hate words."

Ortiga, leaning on the tailgate, saw all in one piece the flowers, thickets, wheat fields racing by, and outlined on the glass partition, the profiles and windblown hair of the two young women. His contentment expressed itself in a mocking, almost cruel look and by the absence of any precise feeling; he felt like a body of water warmed by the sun, stirred by long waves, traversed by slow-moving fishes. The fishes were thoughts. This tranquility and this lovely land. But he was not duped. He was lying in the sierra, listening to the buzzing of insects, seeing only a sumptuous landscape in miniature, plants which seen from so close up looked like a tropical jungle and within it a beetle with wings of dull gold; and he desired nothing so much as to have lying beside him a girl whose eyes had the metallic sheen of those wings; his manhood rose within him ... But just raise your head two inches, at the risk of having your forehead plugged by a Moorish sharpshooter, and you will perceive the carcass of a friend, the bones of his hand—the flesh eaten away by ants—still holding a thermos full of fresh wine. The wine attracted him. It was near Huesca.

"Where are we, Doctor?"

"We're heading for the Loire. We're going to get on the highway, José."

The highway: the immense, mad, calm disorder of a sudden, hurried migration. Sometimes the dull roar of cannon fire seemed to draw nearer, and then again died away. Beneath tall comforting poplars the mass extended, molten humanity imprisoned between ditches and embankments, peril and safety. The stream was halted because of a bottleneck somewhere miles ahead. Silber hesitated to join the blocked traffic, but some army trucks coming on behind him on the narrow side road cut off his retreat.

The little truck advanced slowly, laboriously, through a crowd of people covered with white dust, each bent beneath his wretched burden. These were fugitives from a village on the Somme where the houses, the vegetable gardens, the farmyards, the post office, the cemetery had vanished from the face of the earth in fantastic eruptions of earth and fire. Evacuated in quartermaster trucks, they had been piled into luxurious first-class railway coaches in a last train that a stoical or stupid station master had dispatched on schedule, though the heavens at the end of the line were incandescent metal—and now they were again heading for some station in hope that another train would pass. Pathetic and commonplace. Some carried children in their arms, while others followed them. Fearful of being separated, they refused seats on the buses. Silber found a gap in the line behind a brewery truck from the North, drawn by two statuesque Flemish horses, their flanks caving in with weariness. A red froth caused by thirst had formed around the nostrils of the beasts. Their master, a teamster from Armentières, cursed highways without water, though he knew that he himself was to blame because he was afraid of separating himself from the current, in the midst of which his panic dissolved. Some soldiers suggested unharnessing his horses and leading them across the fields to "that farm you see over there." The man from Armentières repelled their suggestion with alarm. What if the stream began to move again, what if he should fall behind? Above all, he feared that he would not find his wife and daughter who had gone ahead in the Ford with all their family possessions, and were supposed to wait for him at the crossroads under the belfry surrounded by red tiles and roofs of violet slate rising over the gently sloping fields. He climbed breathlessly up the embankment from which he could see his destination. "That's where they are, Caroline and Marinette, they still have some cold chicken and a case of good old bottles, we haven't lost everything."

The plain rose like a woman's belly; to the right, between two clumps of round trees, tanks could be seen crawling along the other road toward the crossroads.

"Couldn't they fight?"

"They're going to bring the bombs down on us."

The eyes of the horses were vitreous globes, reflecting nothing.

At the top of the embankment the magazine-cover silhouettes of two graceful Parisian girls could be seen against the sky. They were smoking nonchalantly; bright silk scarves hung over their shoulders. A young soldier was joking with them. "You don't believe in love at first sight? Well, missies, you're a little behind the times." His words were cut off by the breeze. Two old people were pushing an antique baby carriage in which an aged woman lay on her back with her mouth open, apparently sleeping and not at all disturbed by the flies crawling over her ashen lips. Her feet in coarse black socks hung grotesquely on either side of the carriage. With her mummified hands she held a hen and a rooster in the hollow between her legs and her belly. The birds were tied together, their little eyes had circles of coral. "We're from the Eure," the people said. "This is our grandmother."

"What filial love," Hilda muttered.

Ortiga nodded his head. "Unless there's a question of inheritance."

"In either case," Ardatov interrupted, "we're taking them aboard."

He addressed the head of the family, an old man with a handlebar mustache: "How many of you are there? We'll give you a lift. Climb in."

An energetic woman of about fifty and a tall flat-chested girl with a chin like a horse disengaged themselves from the crowd.

"We thank you," said the man. "I'll pay you for your gas."

Some Moroccans helped them to hoist up the baby carriage, the infirm old woman, the poultry, the bundles.

"We do a small business in the markets of Normandy," explained the man with the mustache. "We are taking our stock with us, what would become of us if we didn't?"

Marketers' carts, drawn by horses of that discouraged breed seen at run-down country fairs, bore the most unlikely assortment of people and objects. Cyclists pushed along their bikes step by step. Autos caparisoned with bedding, deformed by heaps of trunks, scarred by collisions, remained enviable and strong, superior machines, the possession of which ennobles and saves. The men at their wheels had an expression of irritated energy, as though the pedestrians, the cycles, the carts, the trucks that had gone into the ditch had no right to the same road, the same flight. Ordinarily the possession of an obedient, efficient motor of a good make enhanced their dignity, but now that this privilege no longer had the power to abstract them from the common misfortune, it became a mockery. One car had been stopped by engine trouble. A peasant, leading the horses of his cart by the halter, was proposing the most fantastic arrangement to an impressive, decorated gentleman with watery eyes and an apoplectic expression.

"I'll tow your buggy with my two nags, you take my wife and two children aboard, and when your motor is repaired, you drop them across the Loire at Châtillon."

"But I'm not going to Châtillon."

The dignitary was torn between his fear of remaining by the roadside, where he would be swallowed up by the panzers, and the absurdity of the solution offered. He scratched his thigh furiously. Some of these refugees must be full of fleas.

"It might do to reduce the weight of your car by throwing some of those trunks overboard," Ortiga suggested amiably.

"It's easy to see they're not yours."

"Mine have been at the bottom of the ocean for some time. All right, don't get excited. The panzers are two hours away. If they pick you up with your trunks, that'll be your business."

Ortiga walked away, swinging his shoulders. A peppery-tempered old lady opened the door of the Buick.

"Bertrand, all you have to do is identify yourself to some high officer."

"Dreaming again, Mathilde."

She could never understand that all the high officers were at Bordeaux, Tours, Clermont-Ferrand, Quimper-Corentin! And if he were to say to the lowliest corporal, "I am a member of the Senate

Military Commission," the corporal might well be tempted to beat his face in!

Yellow and green, the 8 bus (Montrouge-East Station) stood by the roadside as naturally as if it were on Boulevard de Sébastopol, full of passengers eating lunch. Its platform was encumbered with rabbit cages. A gasoline truck belonging to the Compagnie du Nord was halted not far from the sick Buick. Its hood was raised disclosing the viscera of its engine, and men in blue were trying to fix it. Under this mass of fuel enclosed in steel that had suddenly become fragile, a mother and her children were taking the shade. The mother was spooning out condensed milk to the little ones. That family was traveling on the gasoline truck. Moroccan riflemen were prowling about in search of a providential truck, a basket of provisions that could be stolen, or some little job to do in exchange for a bottle of wine.

"Make way, make way for a wounded man!"

An old intellectual and a young medical officer, supporting a tall young man in a hospital dressing gown, cleared a path for themselves. The wounded man raised his pale face and turned a veiled look upon the world. He was immersed in other visions—to each man his own universe, and the universe of pain and death is exceedingly absorbing, believe me, and richer in images than liquor or opium.

"Papa," he asked. "Are we at Honfleur? I hear the sea."

And indeed the road sounded by turns like the sea rolling over pebbles and like the hollow sound of the ocean in a shell. High in the sky an airplane flashed in the sunlight, buzzing obstinately.

Ardatov led Hilda and Angèle to the edge of the field.

"And I wanted so much to see the country," said Angèle sadly.

"The earth is always an admirable thing," said Ardatov. "If the plane starts to dive, lie down in the ditch."

An old officer, his forehead bandaged beneath his cap, one arm in a sling, was standing near them. The plane worried him. "It is interested in those columns of tanks. Look."

The mechanical bird of diamond-studded steel, describing a great circle through space, became gray then black as it descended toward the other road. It was met by a few faint rifle shots, the rat-tat-tat of a machine gun. Several big explosions followed, the earth shook, and black geysers rose up in the fields and fanned out, white clouds forming at their edges. The officer adjusted his field glasses with trembling hands. He contained his oppressive anger.

"And not a single pursuit plane! It's been like this since Flanders. In the Ardennes, Monsieur, we were thrown against an army that was armored, motorized, etc. And what were we? The most gallant cavalry in the world."

The plane slowly regained altitude, flying in a spiral. The roar of the road was for a moment mixed with oaths, cries, the whinnying of horses. But there was a movement of joy when it became clear that the column of tanks that had been blocking the crossroads had passed, though probably its middle section had been destroyed. The people slid down from the embankment.

And the entire road moved, starting off like a single being. The bicycles, the handcart, the old wagon hitched to a chestnut mare were the first to pass between the under-repair gasoline truck and the stalled Buick. The Montrouge-East Station bus stood still and grumbled at the head of the narrow passageway beyond which an empty space beckoned like a mirage of escape. Shouts issued from the bus. Each second seemed weighted with unknown perils. From the inside of the Buick, still reassuring like the corner of a drawing room, two ladies in black hats and a boy holding in his arms a red terrier with little bells on its collar saw riotous faces gathering round them.

"There's just one thing to do, chuck them in the ditch. Come on."

The hysterical ladies, the boy with his terrier, the stout, red-faced dignitary desperate under the pressure of the crowd jumped into the ditch and started to climb the embankment, which was steep at this point. They climbed on hands and knees, tearing their hands on the brush. The elemental fury of the crowd, conspiring with the treachery of things, completed their annihilation. Sweet Jesus. Why dost thou permit so much iniquity?

"Bertrand, my friend, you aren't going to let those savages go on?" begged the lady whose bust was fuller than her hips.

Bertrand, the man of politics feared by Leftist ministries, sat with

arms folded in greater disarray than a child who has been unjustly
punished and looked on as the trunks were cut from their moorings,
as the trunks fell into the ditch, as Sidis, infantrymen, sweaty women,
a miserable intellectual with a pince-nez, thugs from the slums like
you see on the benches in Police Court, pushed against the car with
all their weight, pushed and lifted—a little more! Government, highway police, Senate, even wealth was going up in smoke, in broad
daylight beneath the calm poplars. "What rabble!" The 8 bus, like a
battering ram, gave the Buick a sidewise shove. The beautiful car
tipped over with a sigh, its wheels oscillated for a second, and then
the body hurtled down upon the trunks in the ditch. A sigh of deliverance rose from the crowd. A young priest with a square jaw,
speaking through his nose, tried to comfort the ladies.

"You will surely find seats in the artillery vehicles."

The ladies' bosoms heaved with exasperation. Ah, save your breath,
what use is your advice? The jewels, the bonds, the silverware that are
in the big trunk under the ruined car, I suppose the artillery will save
them. The artillery has something better to do.

For some minutes the wave rushed along on a road strangely dis-
encumbered. There was a long fire engine painted a flamboyant red,
topped with copper helmets, aviators' caps, heads of women and
children; a personnel carrier of the Moroccan Division, sending forth
a plaintive song beneath the trees; the camouflage nets of an airfield.
The red crosses of a medical detachment mingled with a squadron of
dragoons moving in single file to let the automobiles pass. Great oxen
drew a covered wagon reminiscent of the American prairies. A noncom,
riding alone at the edge of the squadron, inquired endlessly about his
regiment, which had become inexplicably lost somewhere in the region.

At the crossroads the flood spread out over the church square of
a large village celebrated for its good restaurants, in which at this very
hour prosperous families, apart from the tumult, were seated, their
elbows on white tablecloths, discussing the last menus of an era. The
square and the streets leading up and down the hills, with their pale-
colored houses and angular roofs were invaded by the commotion of
an insane fair. In answer to an age-old instinct, the majestic horses

of the teamster from Amentières trotted straight for the fountain in the marketplace. Their master stood up, no longer guiding them, and looked for his wife's Ford amid the chaos.

He was in greater physical distress than his beasts. The worst of misfortunes, the misfortune of being lost, could be read in his bloodless face. Behind the church passed the endless file of an army in retreat, ambulances, tanks, supply vehicles. The horses plunged their steaming nostrils into the water. Their master made inquiries and learned that a colonel had ordered the cars parked in front of the church to drive back toward La Roquette by the only road that was open. If it had left in that direction, the Ford could not avoid moving toward the enemy, unless it followed the low road through Les Saintes and rejoined the departmental road at the farm of Le Châtre—do you follow me? Only, a bomb crater made this departmental road impassable at a point five miles from the farm. The bomb fell yesterday at four o'clock, right next to a flour truck that was evacuating a summer camp. What a massacre, Monsieur, all those little children.

An angry gendarme appeared between the satiated horses and their panicked and desolate master. "I repeat that there is a watering trough at the end of the marketplace. Are you deaf? Do you want me to give you a summons?"

This thundering threat aroused joyous remarks among the soldiers. "Good old copper! You won't forget to give the Boches summonses, will you? They walk on the flower beds, you know."

A bareheaded officer grabbed the gendarme by the shoulder. "Go and bring me the mayor. Have the square cleared for the people who were wounded in the air raid."

This was quite out of the question, enormous moving vans had just blocked the only exit to the departmental road, hemming in the tanks between the Café du Départ and Lemaire's Bakery (where there was no more bread). A group of Belgian cyclists in bright shirts, raising their bicycles on their hind wheels like hippogryphs, and isolated horsemen of the Fifth Dragoons were threading their way between the low-slung tanks and the formidable moving vans. Big blond sunburned lads of a Polish battalion, riding on a weird-looking truck, serenely contemplated the rout, not far different from those of the Bug and the Vistula. Possessed of an antitank gun and a case of ammunition, they felt ready to offer the Boches a modest bit of fireworks, deadly enough to warrant a certain anticipatory pleasure if nothing else. They nudged one another with their elbows as they pointed out pretty girls in the crowd.

Ardatov went into a café overflowing with rumors and came out at once.

"Moritz, they're going to fight on the Loire, we'd better be leaving, my boy."

Above the stagnant tumult the square tower of the church, its slate belfry surmounted by a Gallic rooster gleaming with light, preserved the calm of its age-old stones; and the June sky retained its sovereign purity.

From the heights of wounded Champagne, from the orchards of Normandy, from the plains of Beauce, from Île de France covered with dry bluish mists, from the gentle, bloody banks of the Somme, the Seine, and the Marne; to the mountains of Auvergne, to Provence still bathed in its tranquil joy of life, to the stern forests of Dordogne, to the deserted Landes, to the cafés of Bordeaux, Toulouse, Marseille; as far as the Pyrenees, as the azure shores of the Mediterranean, the roads of France were delivered up to this movement of human ants heading for escape, problematic safety, the unknown.

Neither the border nor the sea stopped it entirely. Facing the sea, foreigners driven from their last haven on this continent saw clearly the ruin that awaited them. Refugees hunted from country to country, Poles, Czechs, Germans, Austrians, Dutchmen, Belgians, Spaniards, Russians, Jews of a hundred nations, the last republicans of strangled republics, the last socialists of banned parties, the last revolutionaries of defeated revolutions, the last liberals of conservative democracies thrown overboard along with the proletarian revolutions, the last parliamentarians of discredited parliaments, the last idealists of an optimistic and scientific century—those who reached the sea speculated with ironic good humor on the minimal chance of a real escape: crossing the sea. The madmen, that is, the irrational daredevils with the spirit of Argonauts, dreamed of a sailboat with which to brave the sea as far as Africa, the British destroyers, Gibraltar. Those with common sense, the rational ones, if they had a little money, wired to New York, Lisbon, Shanghai, Buenos Aires, and even Tasmania, obtained the addresses of consulates. Those without money mailed letters like SOS calls from a sinking steamer, and then tranquilly viewing the waves, said to themselves, "Strange, in an hour, we shall perhaps be drowned, there is so little room in the lifeboats—such as they are!" And with nervous hands they strapped on their life belts as well as they could—but we must try not to lose our watches and our passports—for modern man is composed of a resistant body, an uncertain soul, and a passport loaded with deficient visas.

... Roads climbing up to the passes of the Pyrenees through which had passed hordes of defeated Republicans, authentically heroic divisions driving before them the remainder of flocks, international battalions, inquisitors still vigilant, governments still deliberating, German and Italian prisoners of war solidly guarded, political prisoners devoted to the revolution whom the revolution freed only when it was dying, wounded, blind, dying men, orphans, energetic old men who refused to stay behind to be shot—by these same roads, but in the opposite direction, motorcars now fled toward a strangely pacified Spain, carrying the elite of ill luck, provided with authentic passports, checkbooks, sensational documents to publish in New York, confidential missions of the highest importance. The poor people of Figueres marveled at the luxurious French cigarettes; in Manresa pretty girls offered themselves for a loaf of white bread from Carcassonne; the bureaucrats of Jaca stamped an official seal on a dubious situation for four tins of sardines. In the little overcrowded hotels of Navarre, of Aragon, of Catalonia, secret agents worked untiringly on their portable typewriters, writing out personal descriptions, confidential reports, notes on table conversations, instructions that would set elaborate traps between Madrid and Lisbon for important fugitives.

The cantonal police questioned suspects, searched the suitcases of Jewish families, mislaid watches and fountain pens, filled out papers for a Remington, for a silver fox—which will be returned to you, Señor, Señora, at the Portuguese border when you have completed the legal formalities. You may count on it, my word as a caballero.

An anarchist from Lérida, recognized by a drunken Falangist despite a flawless passport identifying him as a merchant from Toulouse, was put up against a farmyard wall and killed by a pistol shot between the eyes before he even knew what was happening—the hens and chicks scattered, clucking with fear, the skinny dog set up a lamentable howling at the sun, and the children came running to take the dead man's cuff links. Was he really the anarchist from Lérida? *Quién sabe?* Beneath a twisted fig tree the wife of the Toulouse merchant adjusted her makeup with a furious glance at the flat tire on the right rear wheel: Have you ever seen such roads? Madame would complain to the consul general about the inconceivable boorishness of that drunken Falangist, wait and see. On a white wall, burned up at the top, blood-red letters proclaimed FRANCO FRANCO FRANCO ARRIBA. The rest of the crumbling wall was used as a garbage dump. Blue flies made an intense buzzing above the filth. At the foot of this eloquent ruin, a young beggar woman with dazzling eyes and bared breasts was nursing her baby. The crickets sang. The air was sharp and warm. Spain washed in blood, kneaded in blood, yesterday's hell, today's promised land.

Even so, in ramshackle but fairly well-run hotels you could still dine (don't ask about the prices) on a good chicken and a tart little wine resembling Algerian vintages. You were sheltered, with a serene heart you could consider the prices on the Clipper, the sailing dates of ocean liners, the complications of transit, the terrible news, the government's flight to Morocco, Mandel's plot against Pétain at Bordeaux, the false departure of the *Massilia*, the intervention and sudden greatness of Laval, the battles at Menton, the two armistices, England's imminent debacle, the military genius of the Führer, the responsibility of various cabinets... Ah, on that subject, Madame...

10. THE MIRAGE OF THE LOIRE

"HERE we are at the Loire, Doctor," said Moritz Silber. "Did you sleep?"

Taking one road after another, they had bypassed all sorts of obstacles, only to encounter new ones. Army units, apparently intact, poured southward. Refugees from the North and East were now fleeing in turn from Paris. Refugees from Champagne carried with them either the noise of battles or the oppressive silence of creatures for whom words had lost all meaning. The roads were in such a state of chaos that one lost all sense of orientation, all hope, all reason . . . Nonetheless, a peace of expectation reigned over the Loire valley.

Green slopes tinted with lilacs descended toward a shallow valley where beyond the serene curve of the fields flowed the smooth, broad river, the color of a late afternoon sky, curving through rounded tufts of foliage like a great arc of tranquil light set down upon the earth. The very name of the Loire had a magic about it during those days. It signified safety. Once this soft band of water was passed, the menace became magically diminished, one felt oneself to be upon a different kind of French soil, mystically inviolable to invasion, certain of living, certain of being defended.

"They will not pass the Loire," said Martin Piéchaud, the Norman market man. Piéchaud gently shook the shoulder of his grandmother who was lying among the baggage, under the wheels of the baby carriage, asleep as usual, dozing through the final embers of her life. "Grandma, we are on the Loire! At last. We are saved, Grandma!"

José Ortiga smiled bitterly. What childish need people had to believe themselves saved! The Ebro, the Loire? Ortiga no longer believed in havens, in "natural defenses," in the "exhaustion of the enemy," in all the things that the papers spoke of when things were going very badly. The airplane mocks these ancient consolations, the airplane kills when it wants, where it wants, the airplane kills at random. Ortiga believed only in frantic attack, with hundreds of machines, tempests of motors unleashed beneath a low sky, tempests of anguish and fury in men's hearts. Men only save themselves by advancing, and only if they are resolved to perish. At the same time, for each of our little tiny selves, little tiny bits of luck are at play, and they work better when we are totally exasperated and free of illusions.

He said nothing. The old woman shook her head and several times lowered her parchment eyelids that resembled those of certain kinds of birds. In the end she made a grimace that might have been the skeleton of a smile, and repeated, "La Lou-ère, son, la Lou-ère—" For what she understood was not in the present, but in the depths of an unfathomable past, and this name brought back to her a flock of geese on a tangled, flowery river bank, tended by a young girl who had vanished three-quarters of a century ago.

"She's a native of the Loire country, from Tours," explained Marie Piéchaud, who was a woman of fifty with unkempt hair and the profile of a bandit. "She tended her sheep in this country as a girl." The tall, flat-chested girl with the equine chin, who was watching Angèle and Hilda with a sort of fear—strange young ladies, almost gay amid the disaster—added slowly, "They say it's a pretty river, the Loire, there are châteaux." But she made no move to look out, and continued peering down at the chickens trussed up at her feet and at her grandmother, who had relapsed into her previous immobility. Life is not for looking at pretty things, life is for work.

"They'll never pass the Loire!" said Martin Piéchaud again, the better to convince himself.

Ortiga shrugged his shoulders.

"What are you?" Piéchaud asked him, displeased that so husky a young fellow should not have been in the Army. "Ah, Spanish!" His face turned to stone as he reflected, "It was because of the Spaniards that all this trouble started. They wanted to turn everything upside down in their country, do away with business, confiscate savings, destroy the churches—well, they paid for it. After they'd destroyed their own house they took refuge in ours. We ran across them even at the fair at Elbeuf, competing with us with cheap goods they'd paid for God knows how. Well, so you know what it's like to be beaten," said Martin Piéchaud in a toneless voice.

Ortiga sensed his ill-concealed hostility, and it amused him. "Everyone gets his turn, Monsieur. You are a merchant?"

"Yes, lace, costume jewelry, articles for ladies."

"Well, I'm an anarchist."

The truck rounded a curve, and before them lay the broad, peaceful Loire, a washed-out blue verging on white.

"If those are your ideas," said Piéchaud in a conciliatory tone, "I respect them. As long as a man works."

"And fights."

"Right," said Piéchaud firmly.

They were filled with the blue sadness of the landscape.

They entered Nevers at dusk, passing through narrow little streets with shutters closed by panic, and deserted save for tardy vehicles. The cafés were alive with refugees. Stenographers from some ministry and clerks with haggard faces surrounded a truck inscribed in chalk: ARCHIVES NO. 3. A white-haired gentleman was saying over and over to them, "I beg of you, be calm. I have no orders. I have no orders!"

Outside the gas station was a sign: NO MORE GAS. Immobilized cars were lined up at the edge of the sidewalk. A radio gone mad droned out Viennese waltzes. "Hurry up and cross the bridge," someone advised Moritz Silber, "they're going to blow it up. You've arrived just at the right time. We've had a huge traffic jam."

The noble square tower of the cathedral rose above the graceful old houses, pale now. A military convoy was moving slowly across the main bridge, passing from a mournful, overturned world into a violet mist. Silber stopped the car outside a little café on the quay. A woman in an apron, her hair neatly dressed, pleasant in a commonplace way, stood on the threshold between the deep dusk hanging over the river and the desolate light of the café. Her tranquil expression would not have changed if she had been sighing and wringing her hands. Ardatov and Silber entered, following the woman who went in to wait on them. A few figures, grouped in near darkness around the tables in the rear, seemed bent beneath a great invisible burden: human forms crushed and dulled by fatigue. The waitress shrugged toward them.

"You ought to tell them to leave, messieurs. The bridge may be blown up in a little while. They come from the Yonne, they came on foot, they sit there like sick animals, it would break your heart. What will you have?"

From another direction a tall silhouette appeared, laid a heavy hand on Moritz Silber's shoulder, turned to Ardatov with questioning but utterly calm eyes, glowing even with a certain benevolence.

"Here you are after all. I'm always surprised when someone keeps his word. It's really nice of you."

Silber introduced them.

"Glad to meet you," said Ardatov.

"Glad to meet you," said the soldier. "Are you a physician? Isn't it a bit of a joke trying to cure people?"

"No, not at all. But usually they get well by themselves."

Having taken one another's measure, the old man and the young were pleased in some obscure way.

"There's nothing to be done for those people," said the soldier, lowering his voice. "They're drowned and done for." He was speaking of the human forms cowering in the back of the room. "I've tried. Some of their crowd were killed on the road and it broke their nerve. They have nothing more to lose."

And he went on: "This is the effect of a faulty education. In grade school, instead of learning grammar, they should have been taught to see blood without passing out."

The soldier, Laurent Justinien, slung the strap of his heavy backpack over his shoulder. The quayside streets, without their usual lights, faded into a vast bluish mist haunted by bats in twisting, grazing flight. Carts drawn by little phantom horses moved at intervals across the bridge. A swarm of cyclists passed. The cold stars were pointed;

evil little clouds moved among them. The proprietress of the little café, her hands folded over her apron, watched the truck drive off. Those who were not fleeing felt abandoned. The incredible menace was approaching them inexorably. But all France can't run away, can it? The houses remain, the land remains, you've got to have the courage to stay, if you have only the house, the land, a riverside horizon preserved since infancy. "Oh, I'm not afraid," said the woman in a trembling voice.

"Afraid? Christ, you'd have to be a moron to be afraid!" cried Laurent Justinien.

His words made them laugh and the laughter soothed him because his teeth were chattering at the very thought of fear. In the dim light inside the truck, the soldier made out gracious feminine presences and stowed himself beneath their invisible radiation. "It feels good in your Noah's ark." It's not blood that makes you scared, it's loneliness.

The truck crossed the bridge between the somber banks, the water, the icy stars, the clouds. At the end of the bridge, near little piles of sandbags laid out as if for a game with tin soldiers, slow moving sentries approached the truck. They were Home Guards.

"Better hurry. Get as far away as you can. Things are going to get hot around here."

Farther on, the highway to Moulins was filled with a human river which stagnated on and off for long anxious minutes. Panic already had taken hold of this marching multitude. Too many vehicles riddled with bullets, too many brains still filled with the nightmare of columns of refugees machine-gunned by enormous low-flying planes grazing the treetops, too many families carrying away a cold little body under a blanket—or a big body with torn flesh, consumed by fever. The mood was no longer that of a migration but of an inexorable catastrophe. In the silent night everybody seemed to hear the droning of distant planes that were surely flying toward this road, able to spot these trucks, prepared to let loose meteors of horror. The least glow of a headlight provoked hysterical rage—those bastards are going to give away our position, maybe they're fifth columnists, that's the third time they've lit up, they're giving signals. No one knew where the enemy was—perhaps he was close at hand, on this very road. It was rumored that German motorcyclists had passed through a column of refugees, that a Nazi tank had moved off the road to let some French ambulances pass, that parachutists had been seen landing on these plains.

"Let's take the first side road," Ardatov suggested. The truck turned into a road enclosed by black hedges on both sides, resembling a winding riverbed, and it was there that they had a moving encounter. It was heralded by the sound of marching men. "Halt, pull over!" About a hundred men, not drawn up in line but marching in order and at a steady pace, were resolutely bucking the current of flight, led by a little officer in spectacles with a schoolboy's frail chin. There was a muffled murmur of voices, like a living rain. The men were bent under the weight of machine guns. They could be heard saying, "I tell you that if we get reinforcements..." and Laurent Justinien growled, "Jokers. They think they're going to get reinforcements."

Justinien stepped over the sleeping grandmother, nearly crushing her thrashing, cackling poultry, and jumped out of the truck. He looked eagerly at these energetic men on their way to battle: alone, less than a hundred strong, carrying their weapons, their absurd gas masks, their backpacks, like night workers carrying their tools on the way to the job. Laurent Justinien and José Ortiga, shoulder to shoulder, exchanged burning looks.

"Doesn't it make you feel like following them?" muttered Justinien. "Christ!"

Ortiga's muscles hardened and it cost him an effort to answer. "No use getting killed to accomplish nothing."

"So you think it's necessary to accomplish something."

The troop had passed, swallowed by the calm, starry night.

"We'll have better occasions," said Ortiga. "It isn't over yet, it's just beginning."

"It's just beginning," thought Justinien, "and I can't go on. What am I?"

Ardatov and Piéchaud moved into sight, out of the opaque embankment. With sudden exaltation he called them to witness:

"If we tried to put some life into the—I won't say the Army, there is no more Army, there's nothing left but men—but say we tried to revive ourselves, what's left of the Army, men and more men, yourselves, any civilians who'd be willing to help us, and if we held on to the farms, to the little out-of-the-way bridges, to the brooks, the woods, each man with his hand grenade, his rifle, his knife? Say if we began to fight without orders, without officers, just passing the word around: we are defending ourselves, we are defending our territory! Tell me, don't you think there would be a change?"

"Everything would be changed," said Ardatov.

"Maybe we'd only need a few men to start with. It would spread like wildfire, wouldn't it?"

"I don't think so. It's too late."

Martin Piéchaud broke in with assurance, "We've got to wait for orders from the government. There must be a government somewhere."

Ortiga laughed loudly. Justinien became furious.

"We shouldn't wait for orders from anyone. We should be angry, mad. That can't be done on command, but it's sometimes easier than obeying orders. It's enough to . . . we ought to . . . Ah, damn, damn . . ."

From the depths of a thick silence came Ardatov's voice: "That will happen one day."

"I think they'll make peace," said Martin Piéchaud. "Why did France go to war? For Danzig? For England? For the Belgians who betrayed us? What I say is, every man for himself, we should have minded our business."

Ortiga's reply was like a quiet slap in the face. "You idiot!"

Sirius thrust its hard steely point into a wooly clump of trees cut out of the sky's black metal. The earth was fresh and firm, a savage firmness hovered in the night air. Under the insult Martin Piéchaud became again the lad of twenty who could knock an obstreperous fellow clean off his feet with a well-aimed punch in the solar plexus.

"What? What's that you say? You dirty Spaniard, you bandit, you arsonist, you scum of the roads! Say it again!"

Justinien came between them, lit up by sarcastic joy. "Shut up the both of you. I'll take it all on myself. I'm an idiot. I'm dirty, I'd like to be a Spaniard, maybe I'm a bandit, I have the tastes of an arsonist. —Are you happy now? Let's get going."

"Forgive this young man, Monsieur Piéchaud," said Ardatov. "It's his second war and his second defeat. We shall see many more."

The truck drove along toward Sirius, shaken by the ruts and bumps in the road. The hard blue star oscillated ahead of them. The passage of the men going to battle left a wake of comforting anger.

"May I sing?" Hilda suddenly asked the Piéchauds.

"Go ahead, nothing can wake Grandma."

Hilda began to sing, first in a soft voice, then aloud, one of those defiant songs young German workers used to sing in chorus under red banners. No one joined in. Her voice broke, tears came to her eyes. Then, without transition, she began the slow, sobbing, powerful funeral march of the revolutionaries—it had risen from the prisons of Russia and had hovered over so many funerals in Europe and Asia. Ortiga and Silber joined the song, three languages mingled in the triumphant lament. The truck rattled along the bumpy road.

Marie Piéchaud bent over toward Martin Piéchaud. "It's like church singing, Martin. Funny people, husband."

Martin answered into her ear, "I don't trust them."

"Does the singing annoy you?" Ortiga asked Laurent Justinien.

"No, it just gives me the blues. I like to be blue, sometimes. What's there better to do?"

For a long moment the song, the road, the broad moving sky became eternal. The grandmother slept, her breathing a monotonous *râle*. Laurent Justinien contemplated the void intensely, thrusting his angular head into space. He talked to himself out loud:

"What am I? Dead, living mad? All of them at once? I don't want to exist anymore, I'd like to fight, I'd like never to see again what I've seen. What would I like? When I remember what I was I'm sorry for myself and I laugh. I was nothing. A little shit, that's what I was, less than nothing."

Ortiga listened, perturbed, not knowing what to answer. He said in a friendly voice, "Laurent—"

"Quiet. I'm talking to myself. You don't know what I am. You don't know what you are."

Each buried himself in his own silence. The song died down. The truck halted at the edge of a meadow bristling with tall pointed grass, and these refugees without refuge had a bite to eat, quickly, talking little, for the midnight cold had crept into their bones. Martin Piéchaud passed some wine around, they drank from the bottle. Cigarettes glowed. Blankets were distributed. Laurent took his and went off to lie on the ground not far from a solitary tree, face to face with a fistful of stars as light as white ashes, strewn into the infinite. The funeral march rose up in him, he closed his eyes and fell asleep shivering, smiling.

The Piéchauds preferred to spend the night in the truck, close to what remained of their possessions. There at least they had a roof over their heads: to have slept under the open sky like gypsies would have been a social comedown for this family, inconceivably distressing. Man needs a roof, the family needs a hearth. With neither roof nor hearth man becomes a vagrant beast. Is it worthwhile living to become a wild beast? They were afraid of any tête-à-tête with the firmament, and men capable of confronting it filled them with vague fear. Martin, Marie, their daughter, pillowed themselves upon their most valued bundles. Martin, lying across the tailgate, grew calm and began to speculate on the price of goods, the unknown markets of the South. "It's sure that peace will be made. People have to live—" The grandmother's groans comforted him. "How strong she is, the old woman. We are good peasant stock, we are. Wars and invasions will pass."

A little before dawn the cold brought the grandmother wide awake, and she sat up to contemplate without surprise this fantastic world where nothing was as usual. This world was filled with a terrible cold, but it was not painful, it was just reality, unreality. The truck gaped into the colorless space. The glassy eyes of the old woman turned toward the void. She raised her fleshless hands, tried to see them, saw them as strange shapes, alien, somber, clouded. "La Lou-ère—" A Loire of other days, forgotten for thirty or forty years. "Julien—"

Julien, naked, plunged into the glittering water, the old woman uttered a cry of happy fright that turned into an imperceptible sigh. Her chin fell on her hands, she hunched over as cold as stone.

The sense of a presence made Simon Ardatov open his eyes—he was a light sleeper. Hilda was sitting beside him on the grass, her shoulders and hands covered by a shawl, her small curved forehead vaguely illumined. The grass had the greenish opacity of a heavy sea. The sky was no longer dark and not yet light.

"Ardatov, I didn't want to wake you . . . Ardatov, I have this feeling of deliverance. Nothing will begin again as it was. We'll never see anything more of what has ended. The whole past is collapsing at once. We were living in the past, I don't know if we'll live and I don't much care, but if we do live, it will be for a different future. It will be a long, long time, it will be a long nightmare, but the old unbreathable world is done with. All that's left is oceans of chaos to cross before we can begin life all over again . . . I'm sure I'm right, Ardatov."

"I'm sure of it too, Hilda."

She rose buoyantly. "Get some rest. I can't sleep."

He watched her move away—tense body, narrow shoulders, delicate head and neck—moving gaily toward the low-lying mists, through the shadows and the indistinct light of early dawn.

11. WE ARE BETRAYED

MORNING revealed the customary fields. No nightmare was possible here. A short, glistening rainfall brought out a segment of rainbow.

"I am amazed to feel so light," said Angèle, "when the misfortune's so great. It's almost as if misfortune no longer existed."

Hilda, stripped to the waist, had washed herself in the brook, was fixing her hair with upraised arms. "You're a kid. Take your joy whenever it comes. We don't know what it is, we don't know where it comes from. Once I felt like killing myself and then suddenly joy exploded inside me in spite of the death of my comrades, in spite of defeat, in spite of everything. I've felt all lit up inside in filthy prisons, in an ambulance, in the darkest misery. That didn't prevent me from suffering though...and I wonder if joy exists without suffering. Forget everything you've been taught, Angèle, let yourself live, you'll be stronger and better."

She hooked on her brassiere quickly for Moritz Silber was approaching. His gait was disjointed, his face ravaged.

"Hilda," he said. "You have nice shoulders. The grandmother kicked the bucket during the night, don't go near the truck. We'll be held up now."

"Kicked the bucket?" Angèle asked with big eyes. "What do you mean?"

"She has come to the end of her days. I hate the dead. You camp here, I've got to get them to the nearest village. They want a priest. And I'll try to find some gas."

Hilda took Angèle by the waist. "You see how it is: the most beautiful morning in the world, all the colors of the rainbow, you and I almost happy... and this old woman went off while we were sleeping, the world's dead for her. It's our turn to live, don't you understand? A little smile, come on. I tell you to smile, Angèle. Men I was in love with have been killed, I still love them, I'll love others... and when I've had enough I'll throw myself in front of a locomotive, do you understand?"

"I don't understand very well..." (But Angèle was smiling.)

"I only halfway understand myself, and maybe I'm wrong. For the old woman, it's neither tragic nor terrible, she died as you fall asleep, she'd been dying little by little for so many years. What's evil is the slaughter of the young, and the end of good minds. A man has thought, worked, learned to read souls, destinies, events, he is the only one who knows certain things, you feel better when you're with him than anywhere else, even when he doesn't say anything. He looks at you as he raises a glass of water to his mouth and then he falls gently, he barely opens his eyes and asks for camphor. I've seen that. And the young! Among all the corpses on the battlefields, how many were unique!"

"Everybody's unique..."

"Yes, everybody—everybody. But how many have brought unknown riches, the examples of their lives, inventions, works, into the world? There are Mozarts and Pasteurs in every heap of corpses in Poland or China or Flanders. There have been remarkable men, men to remake the world, and they've been turned into carrion. And a few of them were vaguely conscious of their worth. I think of their rage."

"And our joy has gone, Hilda."

"No, joy is impossible without anger. Do like me, take off your clothes and refresh yourself in the brook. It's good to shiver in the open air. I'll keep our friends from disturbing you."

Martin Piéchaud, the first to awaken at daybreak, clearly heard the old woman pass into silence. He shook Marie Piéchaud.

"Wife, I think she has passed on. She's frozen stiff. God rest her soul."

Marie Piéchaud crossed herself, saying nothing. Without a roof over her head, without sacraments, the lowest of the low die like this, it isn't just. Their daughter opened her eyes on a whitening sky, understood, was afraid to stir, thought that she ought to cry, remained dry-eyed. "I don't seem to be crying, Grandma, but I'm crying inside, Grandma. The young woman thought little, in images learned at school: when the soul departed, all that remained was a cold carcass that's quickly buried before it stinks...The soul takes flight like a dove, Grandma's soul is a strange dove, black and parched. A frightening dove. Ah, perhaps it's for the best, what good did it do her to go on living?"

The old woman's mouth hung open and was beginning to exhale a faint stench. Marie Piéchaud tied a clean handkerchief under her chin. It was hard to close her eyes because their lids had lost their elasticity.

"Well," muttered Marie Piéchaud finally, "she's at the end of her pains, she's worthy of Paradise ..." And in the back of her mind, she thought, "And what about us, what awaits us?"

Her traveling companions emerged from space. Ortiga asked, "What will you inherit?"

"Her courage," said Martin Piéchaud, "That's all she had, and she had plenty."

Martin Piéchaud had not noticed the insult. But Ortiga said to himself, "I'm a brute." He searched for words, a gesture to retrieve himself, but found nothing. "I'm a brute to have thought of inheritance," he said to himself. "You should have smashed my jaw, Monsieur Piéchaud."

Martin Piéchaud, seeing his dismay, explained, "We would like to inherit something, all right, and it would have been fair for the old woman, after so much toil, to have left us a few pennies. But that's not the case, and it's not her fault." He rubbed his large soiled hands.

"Well," said Ortiga, "if I can be of any help to you, call on me as a friend. I have a little money."

"We can cover the burial costs ourselves," Martin Piéchaud replied dully, yet with a note of injured pride. "But I thank you."

Ortiga helped him move the suitcases and bundles to one side in order to let the old woman rest stretched out, as was more fitting.

Laurent Justinien walked along the road for a while with Ardatov. "Is there a name for natural death, doctor?"

"No."

"Then there's a gap in the French language?"

"No, not at all. It's death, that's all, which doesn't exist . . . for only life exists."

Justinien seemed struck by this idea. "She went out like a light that's used up all its oil. But doctor, I can assure you that the death of the young exists. I've seen it, I've passed through it. Look at me, you must be able to see it in my eyes."

"Yes, I can see it, Monsieur Justinien."

Nervous hypertension, shock neurosis. They sat down under a beech tree. Justinien's pupils were dilated and shifting. He became aggressive. "You are old. You are approaching the end. What do you say about that? That it doesn't exist?"

"I don't often think about it," said Ardatov, "because it's useless to. There are no longer many things that I care about, and that's the beginning of the end, but I am interested in the things that last, that will last after me, after you. Nothing else counts really. We must discipline our thoughts."

"Invent a kind of mental first sergeant, eh?"

"No. You must say to yourself: I'm not a wreck. I want what I want, and I want things to change."

"You think I'm a wreck?"

"No. But perhaps you were what is ordinarily called a scoundrel. Is that right? You're the one to know, I can only suspect it."

"It's true."

A big bug covered with moist dust climbed a blade of grass close to the soldier's hobnailed boot. Justinien moved his foot aside to let the insect pass. He had grown simple again, his hands hung down, vigorous but lost.

"Now leave me by myself," said Ardatov. "Go and court Angèle and Hilda."

"I can only talk to whores."

"Go and tell the young women that."

Laurent Justinien felt like picking up his backpack—or leaving it there—and going off alone to the clump of trees over there, going anywhere, alone. "Old bore." He was sorry that he had not joined the men going up to the front in the night. Maybe they were fighting at this very moment, alone, without him, braver than he, more resolute, maybe they had already been destroyed without him, alone. Some of them no longer had any blood in their veins, they were cold as the earth and turning blue, while he retained his warm blood, and for what? He turned around toward Ardatov.

"Are you sending me away?"

"Why, you're crazy, Monsieur Justinien."

"I'm crazy?"

"A little. Like almost everyone else. Remember anyway that you can ride with us as far as you want."

The soldier held his fingers tensely clasped together; he raised his shoulders and his profile grew thin as he blurted out his confession. A child throwing a stone in the water to see the rings.

"I am a deserter and a murderer, Doctor. There you have it."

"Well, you don't have to bother us with your little personal troubles . . . as though there were no one else but you on this crazy planet. There'll be plenty of men and plenty of things to save from now on. If you'll let me give you a piece of advice, just think about these things without annoying the population."

Justinien often felt clouds ripping in his head. There were leaden ones and white ones and there were also sheets of smoke that covered his life with despair. And then it passed. "I find you something of a bore," he said.

"What difference does it make?" Ardatov replied. "You judge me as you can. And you're not master of your judgments, whether they are true or false. At the moment maybe I really do bore you. In that case forgive me, Monsieur Justinien. Suppose we go on to that farm? Maybe we'll find some milk?"

"Oh balls. I haven't said anything disagreeable, have I?"

"No, not at all. Shall we go?"

"Yes, let's go."

The Piéchauds remained at the village for the funeral. And nothing more was said about it. Silber and Ortiga brought back the truck. The news was fantastical. Paul Reynaud had sent a message to the president of the United States. Some officer said that there would be resistance in Brittany. A fragment of a radio broadcast declared that the government would keep up resistance even if it meant falling back to France's American possessions.

"In Guiana," Ortiga laughed, happy to have bought a Cantal cheese and two bottles of wine. "We're going to have a wonderful snack."

The truck bounced over the roads, making numerous detours to gain time. On one country road it picked up some dusty, footsore soldiers, still carrying half their equipment, their rifles and bags. Silent men, stunned by the heat, the marching, and the complete incoherence of things. In the afternoon Silber pulled up by a fresh green lawn. Hilda laid out napkins on the grass and the provisions were unwrapped. The soldiers' somber torpor dissipated.

"The joyful picnic in the park of the château!" one of them cried.

"What château?" asked Ardatov. "You know this place?"

The soldier The soldier pointed to the points of slate-covered towers above some fine old trees. "These are a-ri-sto-cra-tic lawns or I don't know what I'm talking about," he said. "Quiet comfort, where could you find better?"

Ardatov suggested moving to avoid any altercation with the owners. A Home Guard in a hunting jacket and sky-blue puttees brandished a carved cane whose knob was carved with nude dancing girls.

"I'd like to see the owner's mug close up!" Then: "France doesn't belong to their two hundred families anymore..."

"Since it belongs to the panzers," someone corrected.

But Ardatov was insisting that they move. The soldier, black-bearded to the eyes, proposed: "Why don't I go up to the castle as a delegate. I'll ring at the front door and ask if they haven't got a good dining room they can put at the disposal of refugees and soldiers of the defeated army... and maybe M. le Vicomte would like to contribute a few choice old bottles to raise our morale. I'm sure to get a good reception, don't you think?"

The cans of monkey meat were opened, the rosy Cantal reigned majestic on the white cloth—there would always be good moments in life. A man with the insignia of the anti-aircraft corps was lying next to Angèle in such a way as to get a good view of her knees.

"You're from Paris, M'selle?"

"I live in the Rue du Roi-de-Naples."

"And I'm from the Rue des Blancs-Manteaux!" The AA man was so pleased with having guessed right that he laughed aloud, spreading gaiety without rhyme or reason.

No one had noticed the approach of a solemn personage, smooth-shaven, thin-lipped, wearing a black vest with bright yellow stripes. The laughing AA man was the first to see him and he greeted him with renewed laughter.

"Take a look at him, M'selle, he has undertaker and valet de chambre written all over him!"

The personage maintained a disdainful gravity. Words filtered between his desiccated lips: "You are on private property. What's more, the place is posted. I must request you to go and camp elsewhere unless you wish to oblige me to telephone the gendarmerie."

"What did I tell you?" exclaimed the bearded soldier. "The château of M. le Vicomte!" He got up heavily and peered into the valet's eyes. He showed his teeth and swaggered, swinging his hips a bit.

"Go look after your chamber pots, friend, and M. le Vicomte's cows. I have a feeling that I never met your boss up at the front and you can tell him so. Or his gendarmes either. Now get your portrait of chronic constipation out of here or I'm liable to put some bumps on it. About face, forward march!"

The valet said no more about gendarmes until he was ten yards off. The bearded soldier made as if to run after him, and the valet took to his heels. He ran like a frightened penguin. The soldier staggered and stepped on a can of sardines.

"Too much trouble to hit a face like that—" He drank a whole glass of red wine. "That's the breed that betrayed us," he said. "Betrayed—you won't get that out of my head. Everyone knows it, and I'm saying it. Bazaine has made babies since 1870." This started off that same debate about treason that was going on in millions of other minds at the moment. The AA man said that no officer had ever been seen where he was stationed. "They were the first to run away, in cars. That's how it always is."

"Ours stayed till the end," said the Home Guard. "I think they were all killed. It's the high command that gave in. Everybody knows where the fifth column was. All those new tanks that ran off without a scratch in their armor, do you call that natural? And that munitions dump that was abandoned to the Fritzes ... when a hundred kilometers away we were short of ammunition in the middle of a battle ... and we were advancing. Does that look clear to you?"

"You'll see if they don't harness us under a corporative monarchy with Adolf's blessing. It's the Popular Front they were after."

"But what is a traitor?" Silber interrupted. "What does he look like? Who's seen one?"

"I haven't seen Mont Blanc either, but they say it's pretty big. In the old days, a traitor was some official and a kind of Bismarck handed him three hundred thousand pieces of silver at arm's length, with tongs."

"That kind doesn't create great catastrophes until they become as numerous as ants."

"Well they're as numerous as ants today. And nobody has to pay them, either, they're rich. This war is the rich man's treason. They don't give a hoot about their country, there's only one country that counts as soon as anybody begins to talk about nationalizing the factories. Better stock up on Italian shells, and what a great man this Mussolini is, the Latin Order, you know, and, say, Hitler's not a bad sort either. That's modern treason, it's been simmering long enough and now it's done to a turn—and we're the ones that are cooked."

Then the bearded soldier, a man of about forty, was speaking in a low voice, holding his glass firmly. There was darkness in his eyes.

"We Spaniards," said Ortiga, "we were betrayed first. By the same traitors. By the whole world. By our own stupidities—"

Silber said, "I'm Polish. A Polish Jew. It would take me three hours to explain to you how we were betrayed before any of you were. We had a republic of anti-Semitic colonels . . . You could live in it if you had to, but it wasn't really habitable. I went to Germany as a fur worker, first to Silesia, then to Berlin. I saw the economic crisis, people called it "the crisis," but it was the end of a world. Watery soup for the chronically unemployed, the streets filled with brownshirts and blackjacks. The German proletariat was betrayed, the unemployed sold themselves out, the youth was betrayed, the Communists voted with the Nazis, we were handed over with our hands and feet tied."

"Why didn't your German proletariat fight?" asked the anti-aircraft soldier. "They were afraid, eh? Well maybe fear is a form of treason."

"Maybe there's something in that. But why have *you* stopped fighting now? The German working class was as hemmed in as you are. No arms, no leadership, no capable organizations, no allies. The Nazis had everything: the police, finance, the employers, the Reichswehr. An old, deaf monarchist field marshal was president of Germany."

Ardatov lay with his hands clasped under his head, his eyes half-closed because the sky dazzled him. He said nothing, but listened, thinking of problems whose complexity defied simplification. On this battle enough light fell to make the situation obvious; these men, and the people, understood it well enough. But this tragedy was attached by a thousand threads to that of all of Europe, and it was buried not in obscurity but in the complexity of motives and facts that beget the clouding of minds. It takes a lifetime to know common neuroses, the structure of a great industry, the series of events of the past quarter century. Would a lifetime really be enough? Fidelity and betrayal mingle on multiple levels like rays of light decomposed by successive prisms. What deeper betrayal than the one that entered the soul of a victorious revolution, degrading the best through outrageous slander, initiating in the name of faith the gangrene of consciences? Out of fidelity, the innocent proclaimed themselves traitors. Motivated by another fidelity, the stronger ones subjected them to that fate and and so became fratricides themselves. The cause lay within the irresistible thrust of a new social structure, ill understood by those whom it was using, barely understood by those who saw it coming and who, unsure, stood up against it. Neither the ones nor the others could see the horizon from high enough, and I wouldn't have been any more clear-sighted than they. The true betrayal, the one expressed in deeds, results, the contradiction between promises and acts, came about through passion, through the passionate mission of men who believed, as long as it was possible, that they too were incarnating fidelity. The average man, the powerless man, could appear to be the guiltiest because he saw the crimes and lies without seeing their justification in himself; but the only choice he had was suicidal protest, bitter resignation, or willing blindness. Ardatov sought Hilda with his eyes, as though expecting her to speak. And Hilda said:

"We breathe treason, and I think there are no traitors. Real treason is much more difficult and rare than we think. A few wretches don't really count. There are old words, old ideas, old institutions that have lost their meaning. People without a compass who have no means of expressing themselves or disobeying. Much more weakness, stupidity, natural cowardice than bad faith. Working classes that no longer believe in themselves and are in any case bound hand and foot, ruling classes that have no future. When they fight all they do is discover new modes of suicide. The machines run all by themselves, great economic machines directed by small minds that go on thinking in terms of profits."

Some of the soldiers did not understand her, but it pleased them that a young woman with bony shoulders, with a bosom clear-cut as green fruit, with an open face, should say things that were doubtlessly intelligent. But Justinien, suffering once more from the breaking of his clouds, was irritated. Words. Learned phrases, as useful as leeches on a wooden leg. I'd like to see you in the smoking ruins of Saint-Junien, I'd like to see you looking at the man without a head who still had a letter in his hand, I'd like to see what you'd say to the kid with thirty pieces of shrapnel in his body and one eye gone and the medics torturing him—trying to save him, they said—trying to save a hopeless mass of flesh for two weeks of agony. The kid said to me, "I've never known a woman, Laurent, I hate to die without knowing what love is. They shouldn't send us into the front lines unless we've lived at least six months. I tell myself that it's for France, but I can see that France is all washed up. My life won't have done any good."

Justinien protested, looking at no one, "There're some people who talk pretty damn well. They've got their degrees, you can see that and it's all fine, but it doesn't keep them from talking beside the point. Machines running all by themselves, you say? I don't believe it. There's always somebody in command. The cannon doesn't fire without orders. The bombs fall because somebody drops them. You speak of classes? I don't go in for politics. Some workers are more stinking bourgeois than the Rothschilds, and I've known a lieutenant, the son of a millionaire, who was the swellest guy you'd want to know on the march ... and the proof is that he took a bullet in the spine. I say that there are the profiteers and the others, the munitions manufacturers and the wine merchants who sold us a vile relabeled wine at double the price and who are still selling it to the Boches with an appropriate increase. There are profiteers and suckers, not classes, and often they're the same people. It's a question of luck or energy, and men are all alike at bottom, all more swinish, worthless, treacherous, stupid than anything else. It's easier that way. One bunch sitting on their moneybags, the others on their bare asses.

"Obviously, we've been betrayed, there's no use discussing that, it's clear as day. But the idea of treason without traitors, you express it eloquently, Mademoiselle, but you'll never make me swallow that magic pill. Why and how we were betrayed, I don't know, I admit that, and it doesn't interest me. But there are some smart alecks rubbing their hands right now. If I ran into one it would give me pleasure to stick a knife into his guts, without any previous investigation or speech about automatic machines. They've made fools of us. I haven't much chance of meeting them personally, and I'm sorry. As for the war, those who have not fought it with their own hands and backbones can never know what it is."

The rest of the soldiers agreed. One of them spoke of the Hazebrouck sector: "We could have stopped them there."

Another: "And in the Somme Gap, you can take it from me!"

"No, it was too late. And what do we know, the communiqués were kidding the world and us, what could we know?"

They tossed in facts, the story of the bridge that wasn't blown up, and why we were taken in the flank, the story of the company forgotten in the woods, without orders to retreat, the story of the farm defended for two days after the general retreat by four men who held up a whole panzer division, the story of suspicious signals in the rear, the story of Captain Jauneau who wept with rage as he kept saying, "Ah, my friends, we've been sold out—"

"You're wrong, Grégoire, that wasn't Captain Jauneau, it was Dr. Lelong, he took command at Marles."

"At Marles, you're nuts. The doctor was no longer of this world at Marles—"

"It was at Auchy—"

"Ah, Dr. Lelong, I saw them pick up his pieces. He didn't last very long after the Stukas had gone by. I even said to the stretcher bearers: you'd need a shovel, you'd do better to look after the wounded . . . but they didn't know what they were doing by that time. And the wounded were under fire, one of the stretcher-bearers began to yell: 'Shovel yourself, you idiot, spy, parachutist.' So I ran away." The soldier tousled his hair. "It's certain we were betrayed."

They were calm and in rather good humor.

12. OPEN CITY

FÉLICIEN Mûrier lived through those days with the mysteriously ordered incoherence of a dream. The normal passage of time confused moments, dates, even images, in his memory; he was obliged to consult the calendar to discover the chronology of events, without really admitting it to himself. Broad daylight was like a white night beneath a strange low sky, pure yet opaque; a permanent midnight as during the white nights of St. Petersburg, where Dostoyevsky's characters press their foreheads to the windowpanes, contemplate the canals and deserted squares, then turn back to the empty room, recall that they have done evil, that they have descended to infamy, consider suicide, and suddenly decide to kill, to love, to give themselves to God, to flee beyond gambling, love, shame.

"What shall I flee beyond?" Mûrier asked himself. "We who are not possessed, we are riveted to ourselves."

The white midnight reigned over the enchanted city, intensified by its empty spaces, its silence, the blindness of its shopwindows and closed cafés, the boredom of the newspaper stands deserted at high noon like urinals at night. The streets were nothing but useless plane surfaces. A half-open bar was surprising like a reminiscence; a housewife going out shopping, God knows where, passed quickly by this absorbed walker, and cast a vague, questioning look at him. Where are you going, Monsieur, with that sleepwalker's step? Mûrier replied within himself, tranquilly: I don't know...The housewife had passed, he turned around toward the void, thinking foolishly. "Fourth dimension of terror, the four horses of the apocalypse—" He shrugged his shoulders, lit a cigarette, which irritated his lower lip, then another cigarette...What did I do after leaving that likable old coal dealer Charras? Went to see the two winos behind Notre Dame. Why there? Because of the memory of the morgue?

A family of Belgian or Dutch refugees, who had probably spent the night against the wrought-iron fence enclosing the square, were attaching bundles of rags to the saddles of their bicycles and installing an eighteen-month-old baby in a basket mounted on the handlebar; the baby was laughing and shaking a merry rattle. Young, sunburned, rosy-cheeked, both man and woman ignored the passerby, and when he turned around to convince himself that they actually belonged to outward reality, ready to believe that the rattle in the child's hand was a pure vision, they had gone—unless they had never existed to begin with.

On the Quai aux Fleurs, the flower-market women for whom the world simply kept on existing had set out their pots, their pails, and their displays in the usual places; a stout old woman, sitting in the midst of her fuchsias, her pansies, her ferns, was eating a sandwich and reading a novel. An ambulance passed on its way to the Hôtel-Dieu hospital. To think that children were being born at this moment. Mûrier sauntered along, charmed by the insane flower displays.

> The archer succumbs, the rock splits
> the flower is a cry triumphant—

From beneath the low round towers of the Conciergerie with their conical pointed roofs, a lady in black, holding a little girl by her hand, was advancing toward the flowers and passing from one stall to another with an urgent air. "Make a bouquet for Ubu Roi, Madame—or is it he who sends you?" No one was crossing the Pont-au-Change; the Châtelet, the Palais-de-Justice, the préfecture dozed beneath a gray veil; two motionless policemen guarding the closed portal of the préfecture, opposite the gilt-spiked fence of the Palais-de-Justice, appeared to be asleep standing up; if you approached, you would see empty eye sockets under the visors of their képis. The poet made a wide detour in order to avoid passing in front of them. Fatigue and that impulse to take cover that brings tired beasts back to their shelters led him toward his own neighborhood. In the Rue Dauphine, a belated rag picker was calmly examining the contents of the garbage pails. The whole street was infused with pale light, white midnight. Arriving beside the rag picker, Félicien Mûrier stopped and said fraternally, "Good pickings this morning, friend?"

The being did not react. He held in one hand a hook and in the other gently shook a piece of green muslin, trying to disengage it from the vegetable peelings and ashes. The muslin was still fresh and recalled the naked belly of a young girl. Absurd thought! Mûrier repeated his words more loudly. The being, guessing that he was being spoken to, disclosed the face of a young mummy covered with blotches around the mouth. The being smiled and explained by signs that he was deaf and dumb. His pink fingers made other incomprehensible gestures, he opened wide his eyes. Mûrier offered him cigarettes. The being explained by gestures that he did not smoke, that it would be bad for his lungs. A fantastic solitude descended on the two men. Mûrier helped him disengage the piece of green muslin and left him. —I'm bushed!

At his home on the Rue Jacob the maid came and told him that Madame had been worried, that Madame— "Ah leave me alone, let me sleep," he said. "Tell Madame I'm all right."

He entered his study as though falling slowly from a great height with the blissful certainty of finding soothing warm water at the end of his fall—Lethe. Yesterday's mail lay on his desk: publishers' envelopes, a long mauve envelope that he opened—"What makes you write to me, Madame Bovary?" A female admirer begged him for an autograph— "just two lines from your hand, Maître, and your signature." This lady also called him "my poet cherished among all poets"; on the back of the sheet he came on the words "ineffable affinities." He threw the sheet of mauve paper into the wastebasket. Who had put his own portrait cut from an American review on his desk: "*The famous French poet who* ..."? He tore the "*famous*" portrait into small pieces, forgetting that it was he himself who had cut it out for his file of press clippings, the "wastepaper of celebrity"—which does give pleasure though.

Without undressing he threw himself on the divan and buried his face in an old cushion. Madame, attracted by his snores, entered on tiptoe. Madame in a blue negligée, peroxide hair, with delicate features, bent over the man—the great man—whom she had not loved for ten years, who had not loved her for ten years, and wondered if he had been to see that vicious little slut who was making a fool of him; or if he had just gone out into the night with its shady phantoms, where he really did have to go for his "inspiration"—for to tell the truth, he had a screw loose. Madame read nothing in the heavy profile of this weary beast, but the sleeping man, turning over on his back, waved one hand at her, as if saying from the depths of sleep: go away.

A few hours later, while he was shaving, Madame entered the bathroom. Her makeup was complete, her heavy bust was sheathed in an afternoon dress. Raising her arms high to pat down a stray strand on the back of her neck, she announced that the café au lait and the buttered toast were ready, that so-and-so and so-and-so had telephoned, that Nathan had looked in . . . "But I told him you were out of town, you understand, this is hardly the moment for receiving Jews, he's crazy to be out wandering around the streets when Paris is capitulating . . . Yes, maybe you haven't heard about it, you live on a planet of your own, but I heard it on the radio. Paris is capitulating. I was glad to hear it."

His cheeks lathered, Félicien Mûrier saw himself in the mirror like a caricature of Renan, his nose too fleshy, his eyes too small and made uglier by triple lids.

"Ah, be still," he said wearily. "Be still, Clémence."

"You're angry about Nathan?"

". . . You showed Nathan the door? It's vile. You'll never understand anything."

The scene was brief. Clémence, lowering her voice on account of the maid, hissed between her beautiful teeth that she let him do whatever he liked and he knew it, because she respected his work, and for the honor of bearing his name.

"But there are some types of impudence you have no right to

commit—I can't permit you to be totally irresponsible—you go with anyone you please, whores, toughs, fairies—that's your taste—but as for Jews, that's not possible anymore, it's my duty to tell you that. Now that we are defeated, they're taboo, finished, all they can do is compromise you. You have a name to preserve, Félicien, a great name! You have your own safety, and mine, to defend!"

As he finished shaving his nausea became a stifled, breathless rage. "That's enough, Clémence, that's enough. I wish I were a Jew myself. I'm ashamed for you, you're vile."

"What's that? You dare to speak to me like that for the sake of a dirty Jewish bohemian who runs you down all over Paris?"

These words cooled his rage. He plunged his face into the cold water and straightened up, dripping.

"Eh…Well if he runs me down, maybe he's right. Anyway, he's an intelligent fellow."

Clémence retired, recomposing her face—on account of the maid.

Ten minutes later, while he was eating his buttered toast and looking in Péguy for that admirable passage on the Jewish people "awaiting the consolation of Israel" and on Christ: "He was a Jew, a simple Jew, a Jew like you, a Jew in your midst"—Clémence came back: "You're so rude to me that I shouldn't even speak to you, Félicien. But I do have one important thing to tell you. Major Lambert phoned and said we had nothing to fear, in spite of everything, that everything's all right."

"Oh yes, everything's all right. Shit!"

He breathed easier in the street late that afternoon, in the deserted streets of the white nights of defeat. Where could he find Nathan? He must make amends to him. The feminine soul is even viler than the masculine soul. In perfidy, in lies, in putrid conformism, women go further than we do—by intuition. You say that some women are saints? Show me one that stays a saint up to the age of forty, after twenty years of bourgeois life. There is young flesh, the alluring "mammalian with her hair in a bun," as Laforgue puts it; you lie down on her, you lose yourself, others take morphine, that's all: just instinct. He wanted so strongly to find Nathan that he ran into him on the

Boulevard Saint-Germain. Nathan was alone; far away a policeman could be seen, alone.

"I couldn't sleep last night," said Nathan. "This morning I looked for you. It's—it's unbelievable!"

Nathan: a little man of about fifty, sharply marked features, deep wrinkles, piercing eyes beneath thick lenses. As he spoke he swung his hat at arm's length. Bald, with gray tufts of hair over his temples. Caustic journalist, oversubtle critic, admired by thirty readers at the very most, still an habitué of the little dance halls near the Bastille, he was vaguely in favor of almost all ideas, and this often prevented him from expressing himself; for no sooner had he uttered a proposition than the contrary proposition presented itself seductively to his mind in the name of a higher equity. This faculty for destructive, comprehensive analysis diminished neither his curiosity nor his underlying fervor. Situated somewhere at the extreme left, between the humanists of the early twentieth century and the Russian Marxists, between isolated heretics and the inmates of the penitentiary of whom he spoke with compassionate humor: "for among them are failures from all branches of endeavor: high finance, grand passion, industrial imagination, spontaneous art; and the most successful examples of the debasement, the bestialization, the crushing of man by society—" His book reviews and his court reporting were no longer welcome in any paper; the Communists denounced him as a "Trotskyite" and the fashionable essayists said he still wrote with the outmoded sensibility of the immediate postwar period.

"It is the end of a civilization, Mûrier—of a civilization that was sick but which— I sent my wife and daughter down to Lyon, I was supposed to join them but I couldn't get started. Impossible. You probably think I'm out of my mind, but I'm perfectly sane. I can't leave. I want to see what happens. I want to be there. And besides, Lyon, Marseille, Nice, Pau—won't the Nazis be there soon?"

"My dear Nathan, it isn't sure, and you must try to survive."

"And why do you want me to survive if everything is washed up?"

Mûrier burst out laughing.

"That's one way of reasoning, of course. You're usually more of a dialectician—"

"That's just it. There's an infernal dialectic in all this and we were blind not to perceive its workings. Where are you heading, Mûrier?"

"I was looking for you."

"Really? I had stopped looking for you: I had lost all hope of meeting a man—especially among my colleagues—I've had the door closed in my face four times today. If you knew how happy I am to be a Jew!"

"I know it. But I met some fine men this morning—at the hour of the guillotine, as one of them said: a phantom bar, two winos, a coal dealer, a little German refugee girl who must have wanted to slap my face."

As by enchantment the boulevard came to life. First there passed an army truck camouflaged sand-yellow and pine-green. Then, in the opposite direction, a Buick containing two high officers in spectacles, képis covered with braid. They sat rigid as dummies, like painted toy soldiers from a department store.

"God Almighty," muttered Nathan. "Aren't we all decked out? Did you notice that both of them looked like Dreyfus?"

On the opposite sidewalk a well-dressed lady, carrying a book with her handbag, stopped, gracefully saluted by a partially bald young man with an unctuous smile; the young man remained hatless for several moments, no doubt until the lady bade him cover himself; he spoke to her with a half smile and he expressed himself no doubt like Marcel Proust writing to his intimates, in long sentences enriched with digressions and compliments, full of allusions like fine lingerie.

"God help me," said Nathan. "Look at them. True Faubourg Saint-Germain; see how the lady lifts her head, that charming movement of her fingers."

The man of the world saluted again, bowed, and the lady of elegance continued on her way in the emptiness, exactly as if a host of admiring eyes had been there to see. Charm suffices unto itself. Mûrier commented, "And you were saying that everything was washed up!"

The immense void re-formed in the wake of these vanished

apparitions. Nathan explained, "I've observed that traffic, which usually follows a continuous tide-like movement, has now begun to move in pulsations. I counted the passersby at the Danton Métro station; they came from different directions every three minutes, five or eight of them at once, neither more nor less. I continued my observations for thirty-five minutes. On an average, you can expect to see a car pass every four minutes." He drew an old watch from his vest pocket. "You'll see now, in two minutes someone else will pass."

Tranquilly, they waited, following the almost imperceptible movement of the hand on the little lower dial. And indeed, at the end of the second minute an old workman appeared at the corner of the Rue des Saints-Pères and stood there, hesitating to turn into the boulevard.

"Wait," said Nathan with intense interest, "I'm not satisfied. In view of the comparative unimportance of this spot, I judge that three persons are probable."

He had not finished speaking when a door opened behind them and out came a young woman carrying a baby wrapped in sky-blue blankets. "There you have your three persons," said Mûrier with amusement.

Extreme attention brought horizontal wrinkles into Nathan's forehead. "I don't think so," he said perplexed. "It seems to me that we need someone else. Mathematics does not coincide perfectly with reality. Reality hasn't the abstract rigidity of numbers. —Ah!" And he pointed a finger at a woman emerging from the Rue du Four. "And notice that all the ages of life are equitably represented."

"Mathematics," said Félicien Mûrier. "I call it pale magic. It's perhaps the only valid magic left in an age of enlightenment which we think is rational because, instead of exalting us, it tends to turn us into serial numbers ... A dizzying magic without warmth without color without error, whose secrets are given away in advance, that are entirely of our own invention but against which we can do nothing and which is perhaps nothing more than a fantastical way of avoiding problems. It's like an immaterial clockwork that we have constructed, and we are inside it and we will never get out. If we were to be killed at this moment, you and I, by a piece of loose cornice falling, that would be within the rule: in a town of so many inhabitants that accident must happen a certain number of times within a given span ... I asked a builder of calculating machines if he could conceive a machine capable of unforeseeable errors: 'That is something,' he answered me, 'that would be completely impossible for us ...'"

Children in fear of punishment often take refuge in daydreams; weak men, driven by the chain of inexorable circumstance toward a conclusion they fear, get drunk or close their eyes, refusing to believe in reality; for different reasons a man, accompanying the remains of the being the most dearly loved to the cemetery, may suddenly perceive that the weather is fine and begin to breathe cheerfully. Thus Nathan and Mûrier, wandering through the calm, distressed city by streets they did not choose, digressed from their true thoughts, which were not clear even to themselves. Nathan, more accustomed to introspection but eagerly seeking a way out of himself, asked, "Do you know, Mûrier, the story of the man condemned to death who worked out a complete proof of immortality while awaiting execution? It's by a Russian author."

Mûrier replied, "We spend our whole life at that game. Say, what have we come to the Bibliothèque Nationale for?"

They exchanged a look, so many ideas in their eyes that they laughed.

"Humanity began with cavemen—won't it end beneath an icy sky with the last librarians—who'll no longer know how to read because they'll have only learned how to burn books?"

They counted five passersby on the Rue Richelieu, which was only a colorless sketch of itself. The Square Louvois was inhabited. A miraculous little girl, blond, dressed in bright red, was running after her ball. Her expression was passive, almost grave, and it was impossible to guess what kind of eyes she had. Her little dress floated around her like a gentle flame. The guard, sitting on the middle bench, was stuffing his pipe. Some old women were knitting, peering down at their work. The curtains in the windows round about seemed never to have moved. Deathlike silence weighed on the trees.

"Let's get away from here," proposed Mûrier.

They hastened their steps. On the left-hand sidewalk a thin, scowling young man came toward them holding out a printed visiting card. A nondescript character, shabbily even if more or less correctly dressed. There was insolence about him, a stiffness, a kind of timidity. The card bore the address of a house of assignation, the proprietress of which had given herself a sort of floral and vegetal name like "Mme Liane des Lys."

"For euphony I would have preferred Mme Lia des Hortensias or Mme Dalila des Lilas," murmured Félicien Mûrier.

"I'm sorry, Monsieur," said the young man, "but I'm not familiar with those houses."

Nathan examined him, screwing up his eyes with concentration. "Where in the devil have I seen you before? Ah, I know. Weren't you the automaton?"

These were no customers for Mme Liane. The nondescript young man left them without a word, sucked up by the silence, the horizontal planes, the vertical planes, the oblique failing light. Nathan spoke with enthusiasm:

"That was him, Mûrier, I swear. A Parisian that neither of us could invent. It would take a drunken Hoffmann to invent him. And this Hoffmann took the shape of a feebleminded old restaurant owner. If Paris were emptied of all human substance, this marionette would still be living here in a cement cell under the Eiffel Tower. The automaton of the Boulevard Montmartre. He used to trouble me. He was dressed like a Second Empire dandy, gray spats, top hat, cream-colored gloves—a dandy in royal rags, pure *Beggar's Opera*. He moved through the crowds in little jerky jumps, as if he were dancing or slowly running... A waxen face, a dead smile imprinted in rouge, rigid eyes that looked like glass, and he never blinked. That was his masterpiece. He made you think of a wax figure in the Musée Grevin, moved by some absurd, complicated mechanism—those long jumpy strides he took, keeping his body perfectly stiff and pausing between steps. He frightened the women—but your serious people paid no attention to him. Man of wax or man of flesh, what was it to them? A sandwich man accompanied him, advertising the bargain prices of a restaurant that I wouldn't have set foot in for anything in the world. I followed him several times and I couldn't make him out. Finally I saw him blink just a little—human weakness triumphed over discipline, to me it was a revelation. And I also saw little drops of sweat seep through the makeup on his forehead. —I was as happy as a detective who had solved the mystery of the corpse in the trunk, the day I caught him turning into a doorway in the Rue Vivienne. Suddenly he was nothing but a plain, thoroughly exhausted mortal. He stopped and closed his eyes for a minute or two, then he went into the kitchen of a bistro. At last I had the certainty, you understand. I imagined the novel about a delirious little woman, a circus rider maybe, in love with this automaton, and heartbroken when she discovered that nothing about him was really mechanical. Etcetera."

"How did you say he walked?" asked Mûrier, preoccupied.

"Like this, watch."

Nathan took his hat in his left hand and tried to immobilize his bulging forehead surrounded by gray bushes, his sniffing nose, his tattered eyelids, his twitching mouth, but they were pulled every which way by his nervousness. He bent forward, leaned on his right leg, described an absurd gesture with his arm, as though to seize a nonexistent speck in the air, and goose-stepped forward for several yards. Mûrier, his hands in his pockets, a dead cigarette butt between his lips, watched him with almost painful attention. Nathan pivoted and returned, a jumping jack in an absurd gray suit and shining eyeglasses, grotesque as a captive crane.

"The hardest part of it," said Nathan, "is to keep your eyelids still. But I'll get it ..."

"My poor friend," murmured Mûrier. "I'd like to smash someone's face in or get drunk or jump into the Seine from the top of the Eiffel Tower, slowly like falling asleep. Oh God, oh God, oh God!"

"So would I," said Nathan. "But I'd rather become a kind of assassin, a just assassin."

On the Grands Boulevards the closed cafés made them think of blindfolded heads. A taxi was cruising. "It's not possible, it must be the only one."

They drove to the gloomy canal section between the basin of La Villette, the slaughterhouses, and the industrial section of Pantin. It was Nathan's idea. He felt full of decision.

"My friend," he said. "I'm not afraid of anything anymore. I'll never be afraid again, I think. Don't worry, I know where I am taking you. You'll like it."

And Mûrier, less forlorn, for his sadness was turning into dull fury, assented, "Oh, yes, I'm sure I'll like it."

They left the cab in a petrified spot along the deserted canal. The vast dusk was impregnated with a note of green. The Canal de l'Ourq was a hard line cutting through a fragment of a forlorn city. The dead surface of the water reflected only the colorless nakedness of the sky. On the deck of a barge tied up at the quay, a stout redheaded woman was serving coffee to a bunch of river men. The comings and goings of the tin coffeepot over the cups were the sole movement visible in a landscape of stone, congealed water, sky, and tranquil death. Alluring letters across the lower floor of a square building proclaimed HOTEL, BAR, but the iron shutters blinded this haven of small pleasures, lovemaking, alcoholic slumbers ... All that was finished, washed up. The night fell quickly. The first stars appeared, feeble, separated from one another by great spaces of nothingness. Mûrier and Nathan, standing at the foot of a schematic wall, felt that it would be strange walking through this ordinary world that had lost its soul. The barge men, the redheaded woman, the coffeepot with the gentle movement vanished.

"It would be nice to see a sparrow in the air," said Félicien Mûrier.

Wild music, muffled but violent, burst forth from within the barge. The radio was blaring out a military march. "Radio Stuttgart no doubt." The brief clamor of an army on the march floated across the water.

The working-class suburb resembled a prison city. The factories had harsh façades of red brick or dirty plaster. A tall chimney rose at an acute angle above the long, low wall of a factory compound. At the end of the street were the low corrugated-iron roofs of warehouse sheds. Two-story houses, all identical, disclosed curtains of faded tulle drawn on identical interiors. Behind a windowpane, a mending-woman's pink cardboard sign showed a black stocking meticulously drawn by a lunatic hand. The chance visitor was grateful for the intimate touch. Everything was neat, orderly, low, the indifferent sky seemed very high. The only natural denizens of this place could have been silent convicts marching in feeble cadence.

Farther on was the Avenue Jean-Jaurès, broad and wretched. Nathan knocked on the iron shutters of Saturnin Chaume's hardware store. No doubt worried faces were peering through the curtains of the neighboring houses. A little gate opened, still held in place by a safety chain; the ferret's profile of Saturnin Chaume, the shopkeeper, looked out furtively. He had prominent eyelids of a sickly red color, an anemic mustache, a pointed chin, a timorous yet benevolent look.

"It's me, Nathan, Saturnin my old friend, you can open."

"Come in quickly. I'm glad to see you today, Nathan."

Passing through the shop, they found themselves in a dining room feebly lighted by two candles. The Chaumes were at dinner. Two tall young girls went on eating their soup, watching the newcomers from under their hypocritically lowered foreheads. Mme Chaume, bony, faded, with regular features, came forward with a forced smile. Her husband and Nathan had been fast friends since the bitter days of Joffre's trenches and wooden crosses; they had drunk the same water poisoned by decaying corpses in a shell hole at Sissonne; they had nearly died of the same dysentery; they had slept on the same manure pile at Rethel; and they had celebrated the final victory together at Metz in brothels shaken from cellar to attic by the lungs and buttocks of the victorious survivors. Fifteen years ago, twelve years ago, ten years ago, they had met in this same dining room to enjoy a succulent *gigot*, and Saturnin Chaume, pouring the wine, had addressed the ritual question to his brother-in-arms, Nathan, "the well-known writer": "Well, old man, do you still believe in something? Do you still have hope?" And ardently Nathan had said yes, had spoken of Bolshevism, of rationalization, of Stresemann, of the treaties of Rapallo and Locarno, of the Chinese Revolution, of Trotsky, of the Five-Year Plan. To be sure, he had come to speak less and less of these things.

His latest enthusiasms had been the demonstrations at the Bastille, Léon Blum, Madrid. During the last two years Saturnin Chaume had been charitable enough not to put the question. Men are hopeless, and you know it as well as I do, I wouldn't want you to knock yourself out trying to look hopeful.

Nathan introduced Mûrier. "A friend, a really great poet."

The two young girls shuddered with emotion. The older one sometimes listened with rapture to ballad singers on the Rond-Point de la Villette: the blind accordion player, the man with the tremolo, the girl with the auburn hair selling pink cards on which were printed stirring promises of love, kisses, moonlight, sorrow, and mimosa. Jacqueline Chaume, thirteen, swallowed her soup the wrong way, for a poet was the ineffable being who had written those words that take you by the throat and strangle you deliciously. Never having tried to imagine what one was like, she was not surprised to see him so sad—and ugly; sorrow makes you ugly, everyone knows that.

Saturnin Chaume noticed the button of the Legion of Honor and it produced a certain effect. And I always thought that only bankers, generals, ministers were decorated. A poet is probably worth more than all those zebras. A funny trade—but if it manages to support its man better than hardware and the rest...?

"You'll both of you have a bit of stew?"

Mûrier ate like anyone else, that is to say, he ate more than anyone else, and his thoughts, his anxiety unfolded within him. He made up jingles to chase away his lucidity:

> Ursula if the danger falls asleep
> your hair loses its gold
> 'tis no longer a world upside down
> 'tis our thirst in the desert.

The others saw him silently, carefully, spreading Camembert on a piece of bread.

> the thirst of roots beneath the sand

Mme Chaume sent the girls to bed. "Tomorrow," she said, "will be a day like other days." And she took her head between her hands and contemplated her cold coffee. Her elongated face became monastic.

"Will it really be a day like other days?"

She had spoken for herself. Saturnin Chaume tried to break the queasy mood. The two candles were too much like church, "Well, old man," he said to Nathan, "this time we're really falling into the bottom of the ditch, eh?"

"No," Nathan replied with passion. "No, no, and no! There is no ditch deep enough for France and Europe. No, I say."

"You'll end up exasperating me," cried Chaume. "I would like to admire you but I can't. The human beast is hopeless."

"Speak softer," said Mme Chaume. "The children might hear you. Maybe Monsieur Nathan is right."

The roar of motorcycles passing at top speed through the street was so unreal that it took them several seconds to understand. "There they are," said Mme Chaume.

Mûrier listened to the humming of his interior voice:

> straighten the back of your neck beneath the amphora
> Ursula I am afraid of meteors

Infuriating, this worthless song without rhyme or reason. "Why yes, there they are," he said with a broad smile. If the others had been watching him they would have thought him mad, but they were not watching him. The upstairs bedroom had two windows on the street, covered by large white curtains embroidered with swans:

> my black swan my lovely swan
> 'tis thee the swords have chosen

The bed, the mirrored cupboard emerged little by little from the attenuated darkness. Standing behind the curtains, the two Chaumes, Nathan, and Mûrier contemplated the dark, dead street bathed in the indistinct phosphorescence of a starry night. Mûrier wanted to talk loudly, cry out—cry out what? The lamentable bits of doggerel that he could not expel from his mind?

> motors, motors, crush our hearts
> I am Sesame Sesame without a soul

—he found the words "heart" and "soul" intolerable in a poem:

> I am Sesame, open, oh tomb

Nathan cautiously lit a cigarette between his knees.

"Hush," said Mme Chaume. "Hide your cigarette, Monsieur Nathan."

Nathan gave a stifled, hysterical laugh—a slow-moving motorcycle appeared on the avenue without a sound. The helmeted enemy leaned over the handlebars, of a piece with his machine. He was all dark watchfulness. Around his neck he wore a strange necklace of cartridges. A swastika inside a vague whitish circle clung to his arm like a great spider. When he had passed, another appeared without a sound, watchful, slow, bent over, the spider more clearly discernible; and then another, and several more. They rose out of the bluish shadows or the opaque ashes of the night and moved slowly over the asphalt in a swarm, like enormous insects on the surface of a stagnant pool. One of them turned around, flashing a blue light.

"Ah!" Nathan was the first to regain his composure—or at least he thought so. He pressed Mûrier's arm.

"Wouldn't it be wonderful to have a machine gun hidden up here?"

Mme Chaume went, "Sh-sh."

Saturnin Chaume laughed softly like a clucking hen. "You make me laugh, Nathan."

Nathan was overcome with embarrassment, irritation, uncertainty. "Maybe I talk nonsense, but is it certain?"

After the motorcycles there came empty waiting. The avenue

seemed to glow feebly. The muffled roar of a subterranean hurricane shook the ground and the windowpanes. The first fast tank passed, a shadow, thunderous yet mute. Those that followed seemed to move slowly. Massive black beetles, rounded, conical, low, unliving, moving straight and inexorably along the ground. Each exactly resembled the last, as if the same picture were being flashed again and again on a dark screen. This multiplicity of the same metallic monster, this absolute monotony, was crushing. The continuous clatter was that of a fantastic power drill boring through rock. When at last a truck appeared, filled with men standing in a rectangle, it brought relief. The eyes grown accustomed to the night distinguished faces, plain ordinary hands resting on the edge of the truck.

"The Fritzes," said Mme Chaume softly. She added, "Maybe they're no worse than anyone else. Can we believe everything we read in the papers?"

"We are under the machine," said Nathan. "They are in it. That's the whole difference."

Félicien Mûrier saw beside him the pale profile of Nathan. With a braided beard, he would have been an Assyrian thinker. Broad, furrowed forehead, deep eyes, aquiline nose expressed the man with a talent for torment, inward energy, exaltation, vision, sensuality.

"Now," thought Mûrier, "they can spit in your face, turn you away from their doors, take your books and pile them on the dump. Soon no doubt, they will be able to kill you with impunity on the public square—and the children will come home and say: they smashed a dirty Jew's head in. And for you there will not be the consolation of Israel. Spinoza would be no more than a moth-eaten refugee, a poor hunted bastard." He bent down to Nathan and in a tone he tried to make as ordinary as possible said, "Nathan, old man, I want you never to doubt my friendship."

"Of course not," said Nathan absently.

The trucks bristling with helmets and rifles rumbled like a storm. Félicien Mûrier realized that the presence of Nathan and these simple people—the Chaumes, sitting on their marriage bed, holding hands, listening to the muffled thunder of the street—that their presence filled him with anguish:

Ursula let us bleed together
let us love the earth when the sky trembles

13. INMATES

THE INVISIBLE tempest descended on the village of La Saulte without troubling the luminous calm of the June days. Nothing changed in this fertile land cut into long parcels and traversed by hidden paths hospitable to lovers. An inconceivable and serene peace continued to reign over the countryside as though war, blood, defeat, the armistice fruitlessly solicited had been no more than phantom misfortunes invented by the radio. At the top of the steep hill proudly called The Mount, the ruins of the Tour des Captives, overgrown with wild eglantine and surrounded by wasps' nests, recalled only an extinct legend. Protestant women, imprisoned there during the religious wars, had let themselves die of hunger.

"Ah, those were courageous women, Monsieur, and barbarous times," Christophe Lagneau, mayor of La Saulte, would say to visitors. At seventy he stood perfectly erect, his head seemed carved out of a solid root impregnated with earth. He went on to speak of the concentration camp. "See that brick building at the foot of the Tower, it used to be the Pointel mill—the Pointel sons went bankrupt in the crash, they retired to Saint-Jean-de-Luz nearly ruined. Well, that's the camp, the 'Center' as they call it. The gendarmes brought in a raft of tramps of all nationalities, including Boches, of course. Some of them don't look too bad, but there's probably more chaff than wheat in the lot." An old Huguenot, Christophe Lagneau concluded, "Man cannot live in impiety and go unpunished."

Covered with fine red tiles, surrounded by orchards and spacious farmyards full of poultry and little pink pigs, the houses of La Saulte were scattered at the foot of The Mount. Halfway up the hill, removed from the other houses, just beneath the Captives' Tower, the abandoned mill stood inside brick walls topped with broken bottles; tall colored windows, cracked and covered with spiderwebs, looked out into space. The natives had viewed among the "undesirables," "suspects," "enemy aliens," "foreign refugees" climbing up this Internment and Screening Center: dignified, well-dressed gentlemen carrying pretty suitcases, bearded jailbirds with ragged suits discolored by disinfectants, disquieting intellectuals...

Christophe Lagneau and Gendarme Sergeant Durant, the latter holding his bicycle by the handlebars, entered the office of the camp commandant. Prudently, Sergeant Durant brought his bicycle in with him—after all, a bicycle had become a means of salvation. In the rectangular courtyard some sixty men were gathered into several groups holding councils of war. Speaking in German, Czech, Polish, Yiddish, Armenian, and doubtless several other languages, they commented upon rumors, conjectures, news reports, projects, and ideas of varying merit. Half of them looked like pirates of bygone days, like the convicts of today. The others, shaved, wearing neckties, stubbornly preserved the look of riders in the Métro who had fallen into evil company by mistake, or of sportsmen sightseeing among the buccaneers. Like the fifteen Nazis, gathered on the right and among whom a number of young men were loudly snickering. Sergeant Durant ignored their rather obvious insolence and said darkly to the mayor, "I wouldn't like to fall into their hands, Monsieur Christophe. —We were too good in '18. We should have tightened the screw till they squealed. Now they're on top again."

"Yes," said Christophe Lagneau. "We were not just enough. Without justice force is bound to perish."

"Old windbag!" —The office of the camp commandant, whitewashed but yellow with tobacco fumes, contained nothing but a desk with spotted blotters, duty rosters, and a dossier. A large black heart, enclosing the name of Amélie, had been charred into the woodwork with a hot poker. The window opened on hard green foliage haunted by white butterflies. A colored Michelin road map of France, MICHELIN TIRES DRINK— Here the paper had been torn across the blue of the Mediterranean, but beneath it a wit had written: *Crap*. "Rules of the Internment Center," three frayed typewritten pages: "The inmates have the right—" Large question marks had been inserted after the word *right*. A portrait of General Gamelin: a sad man on the threshold of old age, more professor than soldier—in any case, no warrior— a civilized fellow who seemed to look into your eyes and ask: What should I do, Monsieur? What should I do? Beside him on a calendar an Arlésienne maiden was smiling, so pleased at being beautiful for the benefit of EXTRA-SUPERIOR OLIVE OIL, GOLD MEDAL, 1897, that happiness had deprived her convex smile of all humanity.

Second Lieutenant Cyprien struggled all alone among these senseless posters. Stubborn forehead, resplendent mustache, and alert eyes, he was a bovine type, a man neither good nor bad, jovial and shrewd; in easier times he had defined military service in the following terms: "Piss people off as little as possible, don't let anything get to you, and keep your paperwork in order. In the army, you see, it's not like in cattle dealing: nothing counts but the paperwork."

He hung up the telephone receiver. Neither the *sous-préfecture* nor the préfecture nor the military district answered. The gendarmerie promised one truck for the evacuation of inmates: four at least were needed! "Ah, here you are at last, Sergeant! What about my trucks? Where are they? Are you trying to put me on? You know that the Boches are only forty kilometers away?"

"You mean thirty, Lieutenant. The gendarmerie itself has to evacuate. Oh, yes, we have the truck requisitioned from the Jonas farm, but old man Jonas won't let it go out. Do the best you can, Monsieur Cyprien. But if I were in your shoes—"

The lieutenant brought his first down on the table. The inkwell turned over, a trickle of black liquid ran down on the floor.

"You're not in my shoes, that's plain. You're responsible for nothing but your own skin, Sergeant. After all, I can't hand the anti-Nazis over to the Boches. And I can't give the Boches back their spies, their Fifth Column, that gang of bastards that laugh in my face whenever I show myself in the yard. Have you seen them?"

As though in answer, the cadenced singing of a chorus arose in the courtyard.

"That's the third time since roll call that they've sung their 'Deutschland Über Alles'!"

"You ought to make them stop," said the old mayor, Christophe Lagneau, severely. "Those are Satanic songs."

"Satanic, sure. But what can I accomplish with my guards, all well past middle-age? If the truck doesn't come, I'll be the prisoner of those jokers."

Lagneau sat down slowly on the bench, joined his hands on the knob of his cane and murmured, "Will God permit it?" reflected a moment—or lost the thread of his thoughts—and continued, "Marthe Andrieu and Juliette Ponceau say they saw the Boches crossing the railroad bridge in violation of the prefectoral regulations."

From another corner of the yard rose another song, less cadenced but rasping and violent: the "Internationale."

"I'm getting out of here," said Sergeant Durant, grown very red. "Lieutenant, you'll get the Jonas truck in an hour—or you won't get it at all."

He dashed out dragging his bicycle without saying goodbye. If the Fritzes were crossing the railroad bridge, well, the département was done for!

The yard offered the spectacle of a calm riot. The broken-down, miserable, indifferent were lying in the center, the in-between space, in the depths of their own silence; some were delousing themselves. At the far ends two railing, resolute groups were singing—the Nazis their anthem, the Internationalists theirs. The latter group, more disparate and more numerous, were stamping their feet; a few swarthy men were raising clenched fists. At the gate of the enclosure a middle-aged sentry stood listening.

The fields were beginning to sizzle under the heat—a stifling day, infuriating in its calm and simplicity. What in the devil was he to do? Lt. Cyprien unbuttoned his jacket. The old Huguenot Christophe Lagneau replied:

"Pray."

He bowed his head over his joined hands, and Cyprien saw that the old man's lips were moving. He almost screamed, "I can't even do that! I'm a free thinker. I'd give the Bible and the holy tabernacle for a couple of trucks. Oh God, oh God!"

Internee Gottfried Schmitt, forty, Austrian, Christian Socialist, writer, political refugee, entered quietly and firmly. Bald with massive head and bright eyes, he was dressed in a short suede jacket. He leaned both fists on the desk.

"You surely realize, Lieutenant, that if we fall into their hands, my comrades and I, we shall be shot—or decapitated."

Outside, the "Horst Wessel Lied," though clearly dominated by the "Internationale," had not abandoned the field: it was the assault of a seething torrent on an isolated rock. Christophe Lagneau murmured a psalm. Cyprien and Schmitt distinctly heard these words uttered by the old man in a solemn tone: "The Lord of hosts is with us. He breaketh the bow, and cutteth the spear in sunder—"

It was all madness. "Will you be still, Monsieur Lagneau?"

"No, I shall not be still."

The sun must have been a flaming ball overhead. The telephone rang hysterically. "At last! The truck! I'll load the Nazis on it—let them yell—and drop them at the Military District. Do what you like with them, Colonel! Ah!" Cyprien sighed with relief and looked Gottfried Schmitt straight in the eyes. He spoke with sympathy.

"I know it, Schmitt, you will be shot." I'm getting senile—Cyprien broke off.

"Schmitt, I have no orders, I have no right—"

"There are no more orders, lieutenant, and no more right. We're going to make a break."

Lieutenant Cyprien beamed. "Why, that's a fine idea, Schmitt!"

"But we need our papers."

"They're in the cupboard at the back of the storage shed. Take these safe-conducts and this stamp—I haven't seen a thing, I've heard nothing, Schmitt. Get out through the kitchen before the evening roll call. I've said nothing. Fine weather we're having, Monsieur Schmitt?"

"Fine weather, Lieutenant."

Gottfried Schmitt bowed his head. As he was withdrawing Engineer Gottlieb Scholl, delegate of the Nazi internees, entered. The two internees nearly collided in the doorway but both had the same movement of recoil.

"Let me out," said Schmitt brutally.

Engineer Scholl, corpulent and bourgeois, avoided all contact with this wretch, but muttered audibly in a contemptuous tone, "Not for long, you lousy traitor."

Schmitt passed, indifferent. These were men molded by a collective insanity. They had lost Christianity, humanism, the scientific spirit, they had mutilated the German soul of which Goethe, Schiller, Beethoven, Bach were the expression. Their consciousness had become an armed unconsciousness. They had no control over themselves. They would pass from crime to crime, from catastrophe to catastrophe. The only power they have over me is to kill me.

Schmitt walked with his idling step, his hands in his pockets, toward the internationalists. His hands in his pockets: to the initiates, that meant "Everything is in order. Get ready." The "Internationale" rose to new heights, then died down.

Stripped to the waist, the Spaniard Ignacio Ruiz Vasquez, cried out in a resolute voice, "Hey! Soup detail!"

The Marxist Seelig, with his slanting pince-nez, was waiting for Schmitt in the doorway of Room B. "I've arranged everything. Perfect cooperation. Watch out for the Communists, the cell is deliberating."

The cell was indeed deliberating while peeling potatoes for the evening meal in the kitchen yard between the latrines, the storeroom, and the cooks' dormitory. Over the piles of potatoes five preoccupied men were carrying on two conversations at once: the one overt on the subject of bridge, growing loud when any non-party member came within earshot; the other, nervous and muffled, concerning the decision to be taken immediately, a decision meaning life or death.

Should they put their confidence in the Molotov-Ribbentrop pact?

Jellineck, the sickly Pole with the red mane, expressed doubts. Franz Kraut, Silesian metallurgist, who had once been wounded in the face by Nazi strong-arm men, had preserved an embittered respect for them. "I think they will respect us," he said. "We are not alone in the world."

Bela Szanyi, student at the Sverdlov University in Moscow, a small-time secret agent, who had fought at University City in Madrid, raised his dry young oblong face to express sententiously an opinion neat and hollow yet formulated with craft, for it obliged the representative of the Executive Bureau to express himself: "There are two things to consider," he said, carving a pinkish tuber, "the intentions of the party and the percentage of risks in special cases."

Ambrosio, whose name and real nationality were known to no one, spat into his goatee before summing up: "The safest policy would be to clear out."

Doctor Mumm, delegate of the Executive Bureau, usually as mute as his name, shook his placid puffy head with its oriental profile. "The Culbertson style," he declared in clarion tones, because the soup detail of centrist, social-democratic, Trotskyite, democratic, and liberal rabble was passing close by—"the Culbertson style is in a sense the diplomatic style of bridge. I prefer the classical style." Then softly, "Pacts, hum, hum, are never anything but compromises, and compromises are always a little dubious. In a way Hitler's victories are dangerous to us."

He was displeased, because of the responsibilities involved, at having to formulate a clear position, but his rank in the "apparatus" made it incumbent upon him. The latest instructions of the Executive Bureau did no more than comment on the directive message of the Special Bureau of the Comintern for Western Europe, and this document did not foresee such an overwhelming victory for Germany. The circular insisted only on the necessity of preserving underground cadres and initiate intelligence work among the troops.

Jellineck proposed, "Those expecting American visas should leave— and those who are under death sentence in the Reich. That's my opinion."

On the motion of Dr. Theodor Mumm, it was decided that (1) no decision in principle would be taken; (2) individual decisions taken would be submitted later to the competent bodies for ratification; (3) the comrades who chose to escape would receive a thousand francs and a blank identity card and would go to Toulouse where they would report to the Regional Bureau; (4) the expulsion of Willi Bart, pronounced by the Superior Control Commission, having become final, no member of the party would in future speak to "this undisciplined and demoralized element." No one inquired into the reasons for this ostracism—it was enough that the SCC had judged. The corpulent Mumm, swaying his hips, which were clad in gray gabardine, went personally to inform Willi Bart, who was waiting in the latrine. The announcement was brief but delivered in two tones of voice, the one slow and rather loud, the other hushed, hurried.

"Final expulsion." (Quietly, quickly: "*Willi, it is in-dis-pen-sa-ble.*") "It will be published in the organs of the party." (Quietly, quickly: "*You will keep contact with Boniface. The money is under your mattress.*") "The party formally repudiates your activity." ("*Boniface won't drop you whatever happens.*") "Do you understand?"

The narrow, anemic face of Willi Bart rose over the stinking boards and he could be seen nodding sadly. An evasive look filtered through the weary lashes of his small glassy eyes. He left the latrine with lowered head, passed beside his ex-comrades without a glance, entered the large yard, drifted around it, alone, forlorn. Ten years of militant youth had fallen into the abyss of "political death." A loyal comrade, he had fallen into the rubbish heap along with the scum of humanity, the traitors, the saboteurs, those who had sold themselves to the enemy. What roomful would receive him? What men, different from those he loved, what strangers would consent to share their bread with him, here or elsewhere? The thousand-franc notes he found in the handle of a shaving brush under his mattress attested to the absolute loyalty of Boniface but in no way relieved his despair—so great that he staggered like a sick man taken with dizziness. Yet there was no time to lose. The Gestapo would spare him no torture were he identified. He went into Room B, where his entrance created a sensation. Standing before Gottfried Schmitt, he was direct: "Herr Schmitt, I am a German revolutionary. A rank-and-filer without importance. Condemned to death at Karlsruhe. I have been expelled from my party for disciplinary and ideological reasons. From now on I am absolutely alone. Will you please ask your friends if they will let me join them in their escape."

"What escape?" Schmitt countered angrily. But the expression of distress on Willi Bart's face was so sincere that Schmitt was moved.

"Our escape. Don't turn me away…"

"Leave me now. I'll raise the question."

Willi Bart turned around and moved slowly and straight ahead across his desert.

Kurt Seelig, himself expelled from the party—but twelve years earlier—was opposed to admitting him, "What can we expect of a man who has followed them up to now?"

Ignazio Ruiz Vasquez hesitated. "They fought well in our country. The rank-and-filers are often made of good stuff."

"He's no rank-and-filer," insisted Seelig. "Look at his shifty eyes."

Gottfried Schmitt concluded the debate, "We can't reject a man who has been thrust out by his people for no crime."

"For no crime!" said Seelig, indignantly. "What do you know about it?"

Others were in favor of a circumspect tolerance. Willi Bart ate his five o'clock soup with these fraternal, distrustful heretics. The last preparations for departure were made with the utmost care.

Esteban entered Hall B. His gaudy shoes squeaked. He was beardless, his features were vague with a touch of the feminine, but there was much youthful vigor in his muscled build. He came and sat down beside Willi Bart. "Willie, I want to play a game of chess with you."

"This is hardly the time. What's the matter with you?"

"It's the only time we'll ever have for this game. Take out the board."

Sitting side by side on the same straw tick, they set up the pieces. Esteban leaned forward. He had the look of a pretty girl sulking.

"You're not supposed to talk to me, Esteban."

"To hell with that. I'll be censured. I'll be glad to be censured so

I can say what I have to say to you. Move a pawn, they're looking at us. I forbid you to pronounce my name. Listen, Willi. I don't know what you did, but I know that the party is right and that you are absolutely no good. I loved you more than a brother. Do you remember the barrage at Brunete? Do you remember that Trotskyite viper of a girl we liquidated at Valencia? She was only a little vermin, but she had only one face and that was her own. But you, you're double, you're triple, a false witness, a counterfeit coin, sold or rotten. I spit on you. You stink like a corpse. You are a corpse. That's all."

"Check and mate," Esteban concluded, upsetting the chessboard on the brown blanket. And he went away, his shoes squeaking, a little red light in his eyes. He went up to Béla Szanyi, secretary of the cell, and said, "I wish to be censured. I have violated discipline. I spoke to Bart. It was to express my disgust. You understand: I loved him like a brother."

"So impulsive," said the secretary. "I won't raise the question in the bureau. I'll only inform the organizer of the executive committee."

Willi Bart, having no reply to make, made no reply. Pale, his anemic skin stretched over thin bones, he picked up the chessmen with his long fingers. The man who rises after a terrible fall, astonished to be alive, feels this physical disarray. Esteban was rectitude itself, but he's a big kid. What admirable men we had. Esteban was fair-minded. If only he could understand someday. But he will never know. I shall always be a stinking corpse to him. Boniface never confides in anyone. Boniface is nothing but secrecy, work, utility, silence ... Boniface signified the most potent, most efficient, most devoted organization, the organization that expelled no one, but that planted an unfailing dagger in the hearts of traitors (or of the weak); it was the organization that destroyed its agents' real identities, that sent men on difficult missions, luxurious missions, demoralizing missions—to China, Brazil, the United States, everywhere! The organization that compelled you to live in palaces and at the same time risk the worst imprisonment; that repudiated its agents but never abandoned them. It was an immense honor to belong to Boniface, but it was a secret honor, sometimes covered by glaring dishonor. The agent lived for his party but no longer saw the party; the party no longer saw him; he feigned, if his mission demanded it, to hate the party.

This last afternoon the usual circle formed around Kurt Seelig, the theoretician who, in order to economize his strength, spent the greater part of the day lying down with his hands behind his head, for he breathed better in that position. Reddish hair covered his lofty head. Concentric wrinkles surrounded his thin nose with its fluttering nostrils. His eyes were deep-set, diminished by heavily wrinkled lids. The tendons and veins stood out on his long neck. "I have just the neck for the gallows," he said. "You remind me," Vasquez said to him affectionately, "of a plucked bird, one of those turkey cocks full of philosophy. Anyone can see that you're tough and full of tough philosophy. If they hanged you, you'd probably rip the rope with your neck and unhook yourself. They'd think you were dead, you'd twitch your nose a little and say: 'Not yet, gentlemen!' And then of course you'd ask for the latest Wall Street quotations and you'd begin to compose an *Analytic Treatise on Hanging*. You'll be killed at least three times: by the annoyances of prison life, by the refutations of imbeciles, and by the three bullets in your thinking box—a single one would never be enough."

Seelig appreciated this flattery for—though he did not show it—he had as much need of human warmth as of lucid statistics. He worked amid the noise of the barrack room, probably on a study of the concentration of capital, the decline of finance capital, the rise of industrial technique "which is beginning to supplant money as the dominant force in production." In any case, he had a notebook full of minute handwriting on these subjects, he knew all the new coal-tar derivatives employed in the synthetics industries, and he was well versed in the interconnections between the great financial structures of the world. The rare numbers of the *Economist* that reached him gave him almost as much satisfaction as the infrequent letters from his wife with whom he had not lived for four years; on the day when this heavenly manna was accorded him he could be seen walking in the yard, comically wagging his baggy, clownish trousers. Strings served him as suspenders. He spoke a learned French, full of Anglicisms,

Germanisms, Russianisms. His good sense was spiced with humor so that it was not always possible to tell whether he was making fun of others, of himself, or of others and himself—or if, simply, he looked upon things from a very elevated point of view. Since the first week of the war he had been "exploring" concentration camps (after having passed through various Republican prisons in Spain): first the Wagram Stadium, then Gurs, then a camp for Spaniards in Hérault (this had been a mistake), finally this camp for the unlikely rectification of numerous mistakes.

"I present problems to the képis and their attitude toward problems is one of aversion and irritation. The képis only like solutions and in our time there are no solutions! 'Now what really is your nationality?' What they need is a course in thirty lessons on the concept of nationality, the recent history of Central Europe, the role of ideas in this history, the crisis of socialism, all this in relation to the deplorable survival of the old police states and the system of passports. I am of German-Polish blood, Messieurs, born in Posen, consequently I was a Prussian in spite of myself, until the resurrection of Poland, after which I became a Pole out of horror of the Prussian spirit; then I became a Soviet citizen out of love of liberty and Marxist conviction, then a stateless refugee in Paris, still out of love of liberty and Marxist conviction. Naturalized a Spaniard by the revolution—is that clear enough?—I feel myself to be merely European, German-Latin by education. 'But in the département of the Seine you had no papers, only an expulsion order deferred for successive periods of two weeks.' Could I help it? All the trouble came from the frequent change of ministries, from the disorder in the préfecture where my papers were lost, from the incompetence of the inspectors. The képis have a hard time following these demonstrations. At length, in the interests of clarity, the one with the most silver braid, upon whom the École Normale has conferred tortoiseshell glasses and a Cartesian love of logical concepts, raises the political question: 'Are you a Communist?' According to the manifesto of Karl Marx, assuredly: but that is exactly why I was expelled from the CP, etc. 'Ah, good, you are a Trotskyite?' In the general sense of the word, that is possible, but that is an inaccurate sense; in the exact sense given to the word by the Trotskyist Party, if there is such a party, I am not. 'In short, you consider yourself a socialist?' And I am one, but no affiliation is possible, for in my eyes the SP has ceased to be anything but a liberal party. 'Let us get this over with, Monsieur. Your loyalty toward France—' I have fully proved it by all my preceding remarks."

This last day, this last hour before the break, Kurt Seelig held forth. He said:

"The communal civilization of the great epochs of the Middle Ages constructed cathedrals and monasteries. The cathedrals expressed the spiritual impulse of the people, channeled by theological thought and imagination; the monasteries signified the conflict between asceticism, this attempt to dominate elemental man—if necessary by mutilating him—and the turbulent instincts of a barbarian society. The theocracy wisely exploited this conflict: the monasteries flourished ... Baroque is the style of an aristocratic and bourgeois society enriched by mercantilism (then spreading over two hemispheres) under the efficient administration of absolute monarchies intelligently advised by the Jesuits. It is a style full of motion because life has become more and more dynamic—ornate, because the rich love adornment—often voluptuous and nobly ordered. The grace of living has been discovered. Versailles perpetuates in brick, cut stone, ballrooms, and fountains the geometrical, decorative, and well-polished order conceived by great administrators who already have some big bankers behind them ... Remark that the French Revolution did not create a style of its own. It was a breech in history rather than a creative period. It opened the way to future creation: the essential thing was to destroy. The Goddess of Reason borrowed the balance of her edifices from the Ancients. The nineteenth century produced shapeless factories as ugly as the new slavery they instituted. And, moreover, rising capitalism, with a universal and encyclopedic bad taste picked up the leftovers of past styles, as though its architecture were demonstrating to the generations that everything since Nineveh, *everything* was its natural booty. This parvenu ambition is not without grandeur; capitalism was making no mistake when it laid its hand on the globe, past, present, and future. The only thing it lacked was real soul and intelligence, the intelligence that goes beyond techniques. Among its creations I appreciate only the Eiffel Tower, because of its purely symbolic uselessness—or usefulness. Towering above cathedrals built long ago by poor people who believed in paradise and hell, this steel frame proclaims the power of metals that suffice unto themselves, that dominate without reason and without faith. Then, at the beginning of the twentieth century, there began an era of moderately intelligent creations: great railroad stations wonderfully equipped, sumptuous banks, cinemas. The skyscrapers of New York raise business to a prodigious height over the movement of crowds traveling underground in squeaking, hurtling, suffocating subway trains. It would take a Dante to extract a real vision of this world from these commonplaces.

"Well, now the century is collapsing, it couldn't last: in the end the strongboxes burst of their own accord under the corrupting influence of paper that claimed to be gold. The mystification breaks down the very molecules of the best steels. I have wondered what architecture, perhaps still in embryo, best defines our epoch. The giant factories, of course, Krupp, Le Creusot, Magnitogorsk, Detroit: note that they only amplify, by rationalizing, the industrial style of yesterday and that, by virtue of an excessive rationalization, they become grotesquely irrational—inhuman, uninhabitable, vulnerable, they are monstrous cities built for machines, the market, money, and not for men. The Brialmont forts, the Maginot, Siegfried, Metaxas lines? These impressive concrete, electrified molehills are made for death and not for life, they are an ingenious perfection of the Great Wall of China, and it has just been seen that they are useless. The true style of the present era is that of the concentration camp. We are living in this atrocious hole here because we are in a gentle country characterized by a negligent humanism that was a generation behind the times or perhaps two generations ahead of the times—that remains to be seen. The concentration camps of Russia and Germany are masterpieces of organization of a type hitherto unknown in history. The White Sea Camp embraces a country vaster than Belgium or Holland together, with fisheries, industries, laboratories, aerodromes, model prisons, schools, recreation and execution centers. In the Third Reich, Dachau and Oranienburg were conceived in accordance with the scientific principles governing the storage conditioning and destruction of human beings, that is to say, the strictest economy in the pursuit of these aims on a large scale. They combine irreproachable methods of isolation with collective life, they inspire a sentiment of fatality without—provisionally—destroying a minimum of hope. The water closets are hygienic and if open latrines are more widely in use, it is for the moral effect. The classification of victims has been perfected to such an extent as to baffle the administration itself, just as higher mathematics baffles arithmetic teachers. The torture chambers are equipped like operating rooms; the cremating oven is not far away, and urns for the ashes, of suitable size for mailing, are provided by mass production. Barbed wire of modest appearance is traversed by high-tension currents; projectors placed by geometricians surround the human herd with terrifying beams of light. Note that concentration camps are being imposed little by little upon the whole of Europe. Italy is fortunate in having its islands; the Spanish Republic adopted defective improvisations because in all fields it lacked a sense of organization. The Third Republic, likewise improvising without the least genius for evil, has nevertheless succeeded in lodging a whole army at Argelès. But the war, necessitating the storage of prisoners, will bring about new progress in this field.

"The real problem deserves to be formulated with detachment, without superfluous indignation. Are industrial societies going to become immense rationalized prisons? It seems that they are headed toward this paranoiac perfection. But it is not unlikely that war, by becoming more universal and of longer duration, will release sentiments, ideas, necessities, techniques, capable of orienting societies toward other modes of existence. We know more or less what we should desire but we do not know what will be. The economic premises are not very encouraging, but they are expressed in figures, and figures are only a skillful juggling of reality. (I am speaking as an economist.) The most human premises are contradictory. Present-day man tends to consent to various types of captivity, but it seems likely that his own vital drive will never adapt itself completely to captivity. His present neuroses will probably lead to cures or to opposite neuroses. In any case, you and I sleeping on this straw, nourished on these unbreakable beans, guarded by these puerile barricades, we are the precursors of a future world, the miscarriage of which will be exceedingly complicated..."

"There must certainly be such a thing as a vital drive since we aren't dead yet," said Vasquez joyfully.

These words were spoken in a strange corner of the barracks, resembling the hold of an old ship long foundered. On a sort of shelf affixed to the wall, a brilliant fleet of little metal caravels was being fitted out for discoveries on an ideal sea. Captain Ignazio Ruiz Vasquez had graduated from the Royal School of Engineering at the head of his class. In the battle of Guadalajara he had set a trap for the Italian tanks that had won the admiration of experts. Now he occupied his leisure making these radiant ships out of tin cans. The sails of his vessels were swelled by hope—that is to say, wind. Corporal Cointre sold them at the town market to schoolboys, dreamy girls, traveling salesmen, a retired pilot. As he listened to Kurt Seelig, Ignazio Ruiz Vasquez finished cutting out the proud forms of an imaginary brigantine. Using a nail, he traced a pathetic face on the lofty prow. Then he lifted the silvery two-master in the palm of his hand, smiled wryly and said, "In order to appease the inclement gods, I christen this lost ship with the name of the faithless beloved, *Maria-Gracia*. I have completed this work out of a useless sense of duty. Seelig, you are eloquent but the time has come to throw general ideas overboard. They will always rise to the surface. Now we must set sail."

Lacing his hobnailed boots, Gottfried Schmitt had the nose and forehead of Beethoven's death mask, but the curve of his mouth was ironic. Kurt Seelig finished dressing. He tied a yellow tie with red stripes around his patched shirt collar. Seeing that Vasquez was ready to burst out laughing, he asked, "Am I ridiculous?"

"A little," said Vasquez.

Schmitt intervened gently: "No Kurt, you are never ridiculous. Let him laugh."

Seelig folded his raincoat faded by the rains of Bohemia, Austria, Germany, Spain, Île de France. "The ridiculous arises from contrasts. I must often be ridiculous."

Vasquez—bluish jowls and chin, arched forehead, angular nose, eyes somber, gentle, laughing, malicious—having put an old jacket on over his khaki shirt, had the proud look of a loyal adventurer equal to the boldest deeds.

"I'm taking command," he said. "*Maria-Gracia*, my pretty brigantine, sail the dangerous seas we love, and if you sink, sink straight down, without remorse, and see to it that the water is deep. Well, it's time to send out the first group, watch the yard."

He left the barracks, whistling, "Granada, Granada, garden of our loves." A signal. Shadows moved in the corner of the hold. He went and tapped Willi Bart on the shoulder.

"Be ready in fifteen minutes. You're going to team up with us. As little as possible, of course. Confidence is low, amigo."

The Internment and Screening Center affected still to be living in its everyday apathy, as though, like certain madmen, it had a certain mental picture of itself to live up to. A dull-witted pretense of order dissimulated secret activities. A wisp of white smoke rose from the office chimney; Lt. Cyprien was burning papers. He even burned the portrait of the supreme commander, General Gamelin. Through an idyllic countryside, the requisitioned truck carried away the Nazis in a compact group, well dressed, haughty, and scornful, escorted by five old soldiers. There remained only one sentry at the entrance of the camp, the two watchtowers on the wall were deserted. Through the kitchen windows, M. Chibot, the steward, nicknamed "Turnip Face" because of his bilious pallor, and Corporal Cointre were evacuating cases of provisions. "This is something the Boches won't get anyway," gasped Cointre, who was covered with sweat.

The five o'clock soup was thin, but the men who stood in the mess line had a festive look. They had all put on their Sunday best for an unexpected holiday or funeral. Liberty, dear liberty (song), thou art also abandonment, peril, penury, the promise of captivity. The rectangular yard was almost empty.

Only an Alsatian with a patriarchal beard sat there, reading the Bible as he had always done; he was an intractable fellow who understood little of this perverse world, but carved handsome canes, washed clothes conscientiously, never grew angry, and lived in fear of blows though in his secret heart he desired martyrdom. The servants of the Beast approached, he awaited them in peace, protected by the Lord, inadequately protected. His beard curled like wool.

Cane-Stalk, the Annamite, was cleaning mess gear. The word passed around, and one by one the men resolutely departed—for form's sake making two trips, the first in shirt sleeves carrying their satchels and bundles, the second with an air of nonchalance. In the kitchen yard, Ignazio Ruiz Vasquez, wearing a chocolate-colored jacket and a cap with a broken visor, gave them a sign and they vanished between the latrine and the logs piled up against a low wall topped with a tangle of barbed wire that had been deftly cut through. Each man took one running step, lifted himself by the wrists, landed on the hard roots, brushed the dust from his trousers, and ran up the steep path leading to the Captives' Tower. From that moment on the seconds struck in their breasts. Weighted down with anxiety, they gasped, joyful without real joy.

The world opened out along the dry bed of a brook between tall mulberry trees. Would there be a last train at the station? Or a last gendarme in search of the Fifth Column, taking orders from some real Fifth Column? Vasquez was last to leave, at the heels of Willi Bart. Farewell, prison. A civilization had to collapse before we could scale this wall and head for the unknown. The world was new just the same, always new, as long as you had good nerves. We will have good nerves!

Vasquez scratched his hands on a thorny branch. The slight pain made him laugh. He wanted to have a big wound seething with blood, after a tussle from which he would emerge with singing veins, happy to be bleeding, sure of being alive, victorious—like the Valencian matador who had been gored in the thigh and stood in the middle of the arena, saluting the crowd with tears of joy running down his yellow face.

Willi Bart, a leather briefcase in his hand, climbed with agility

ahead of him, as solitary as a wild beast. In the distance, on the road
to La Saulte, they perceived a Dr. Theodor Mumm, corpulent, clad
in light-gray gabardine, expertly impersonating a Levantine merchant.
They saw him climbing into a car driven by a lady. For Willi Bart this
was the reassuring and obscurely frightening image of Boniface. A
supple schemer, this fat man, but what a worker, and what confidence
he enjoyed. We have all the useful men: the crafty, the sly cowards,
the naive, the pure of heart, the hard-hearted. We have everything,
and here I am alone with this secret, without honor, without name,
without any faith I can declare.

"Why did they throw you out of the party?" Vasquez asked brutally.

"Disagreement on tactics—ideology."

"Fine tactics, the tactics of shrewd maneuvers and zigzags ... The
ideology of the vacuum cleaner, sucking in all the old fifth. I congratulate you."

Willi turned on the Spaniard a face white with anger.

"I'm desperate!"

"You'll never be a man. The revolution is freedom."

It would be easy to answer: It is obedience above all. And besides,
what revolution are you talking about? Ours, the only true revolution,
is not yours, you incorrigible petty bourgeois. And what is freedom?
Did you ever see it except in the shape of a painted whore? Perhaps
there will be no freedom until a century or two after us. —But these
replies would not have been prudent. Willi Bart leaped forward.

Lt. Cyprien omitted the evening roll call that day. Some thirty internees abandoned by the world and by themselves were left in camp:
Dutch teamsters whose language no one understood, dubious Ro-
manians with whom the lieutenant had no idea what to do, Spaniards
tired of everything—might as well die here as anywhere else—Alsatian autonomists (apparently), nondescripts without papers, a filthy,
terrified mumbling Turkish or Bulgarian exhibitionist who was no
longer punished since it did no good; the Jew Shmulevitch, a tearful
wreck; Cane-Stalk, the Annamite with the eyes of a sick girl.

And four soldiers of the older age classes were left, wearing comical uniforms—khaki, the slate-blue of Verdun days, tan corduroy, British puttees: Jacquinet, a Breton fisherman dulled by nostalgia for the sea; Tolle, a peasant from the Vendée driven to drink by nostalgia for the earth; Feutre, a waiter in a Calais café, who had given up washing since his wife's letters had stopped coming; and Corporal Cointre. Lt. Cyprien gathered them together in his devastated office.

"My boys—"

(He was the youngest of them all.)

"My friends— Look, an immense calamity has descended on France. If the Jonas truck gets back on time the Internment Center will be liquidated tonight. Otherwise I shall hand it over to the mayor of La Saulte and we will withdraw—in accordance with the commandant's instructions—in good order."

Corporal Cointre sprang to attention and stammered, "Sir, I have my farm twenty miles from here—my wife and my cattle. I'd rather run the risk of being taken prisoner than leave here, Lieutenant, begging your pardon. The war is over. At your orders, sir."

Cyprien replied simply, "Well, put on civilian clothes, Cointre. The rest of you, battle dress at seven o'clock sharp. We'll get out as best we can."

He had a headache. "If we have to fight, we'll fight."

I don't know what I'm saying anymore. I'm talking like a hick. Well, we didn't deserve this. Why are men so afraid of being killed? Wives, kids, that's what holds us.

"Fall out!"

Feutre, the waiter, said, "I'd like to kill a few of them before the armistice is signed, Lieutenant."

"So would I, my friend."

No one had thought of the Jew Shmulevitch—either to bid him goodbye or to say: Come, pull yourself together, get out of here, I'll help you over the wall! Immersed in his bitter insignificance, he escaped notice; shut up in himself, obsessed by himself, sick of himself.

Comic and unclean, he bunked in the most obscure corner of Room B. In his comings and goings he left behind him only a vague image like those droll dream characters that are unaccountably lost among other, clearer images. A round hat, turned green by the rains of misery, hung draped around his ears; his beard was like a frayed rope, his long black overcoat resembled a caftan. He was devoured by vermin, and this gave him pleasure by humiliating him. Stoop-shouldered and bowlegged, with remarkably pointed knees, he wore flat carpet slippers that never quite left the ground when he walked. Shmulevitch aroused no more laughter or pity than a mutilated insect.

How could he forgive himself for having abandoned Warsaw, his burning hovel, his children lost in the smoke, his sobbing wife? Like a sick dog, frightened at sensing that the house is deserted, leaves his corner, Shmulevitch arose when the barrack had emptied. With dragging slippers he headed for the little wall of deliverance bristling with metal thorns. He looked at the path by which, despite his stiffened joints, it was possible for him to get away—without a centime, alone, contemptible, wretched, incredibly wretched, filled with remorse. Get away—where? Hideous, rocky path, an evil shadow clung to its bushes. Shmulevitch turned away, shuddering. He was appeased only when he reached the shed and was surrounded by things completely dead: old tires, harnesses, planks, cat skins, ropes, ropes.

He was bowed down by a glacial serenity. He folded his hands and wept and laughed without knowing why. At length he picked up a thick rope, scraped his hands in tying a slipknot, slid the rough knot several times, was satisfied that his work was well done, stood up precariously on a tire to fasten his rope to a hook and then contemplated this mechanism of eternal repose. Pity seized him, a burning pity, tremulous, mingled with sacred horror, with convulsive happiness. He passed the noose around his neck, made a false move, slipped. The tire rolled away, leaving him hanging, hanging askew, for his beard had caught in the rope—his last bit of ill luck. Strangulation was delayed—but what matter a few minutes of agony more or less—at the beginning of deliverance? It is good to suffer.

…When night fell, the local forester, armed with a carbine of an ancient model—a good old weapon just the same, it could still plug a wild duck on the wing and a hare on the run—leaned against the door of the Center. The mayor, Christophe Lagneau, accompanied by a spaniel with wagging tail and large affectionate eyes, moved along the wall of the old mill. With the tip of his cane the mayor pushed aside little stones. Arrived at the corner, he sat down on a rock and faced the vast darkened landscape of his life. A white mist arose from the valleys. He was chilled through. Past seventy, a man is almost always cold. He feels himself turning to dust again. That is the Law. The flares of an unknown army, rising up on the horizon like great colored stars and falling with an evil slowness, neither astonished nor worried him. For Christophe Lagneau shared the calm of the universe.

14. "PATIENCE, PATIENCE..."

THE CLASSIFICATION of people according to their resemblance to various animals was one of Félicien Mûrier's familiar pastimes. There were simians, felines, and bovines; others revealed an affinity of character with rabbits, sheep, asses, and even zoophytes. These last, it may be guessed, had floating, vegetative natures, whose very destiny it was to be ensnared: tenacious victims, dangerous by virtue of their passive, engulfing obstinacy. The Japanese artist who compared women to cats saw clearly, but he lacked imagination.

A certain colleague, a virtuoso at denigration and harmless pin-pricks, who walked in little hops, his small head inclined over extended paunch, Mûrier couldn't call any name but "The Flea." He sought out the common type of scorpion, hostile but harmless, living under warm rocks in the manner of the humble wood louse, unaware that legend attributes to the scorpion a deadly poison and an astonishing aptitude for suicide. And he also affected the human type of the great vesperal butterfly sometimes named Death's Head. "People," he thought, "find in me resemblances only with rodents. They are blind. I recognize myself only in this nocturnal butterfly, sumptuous and somber, stupidly attracted by the light, which he will never be able to understand and who bears on his fragile wings a mysterious symbolic design."

Mûrier classified his two visitors in a flash—the one among the felines, the other among the large, formidable ruminants of the bison type, a strong, stubborn, belligerent species that lives in herds, does not lack intelligence after its fashion, but is completely without genius. The bison, though he bore the rank of major in the Wehrmacht, had on a grayish brown suit and had entered bareheaded; he had a bulging forehead, white hair, a rather sanguine complexion, deeply molded features; his eyes were somewhere between faded blue and icy green. He held his head with an aging vigor. Ex-sportsman no doubt, hunter, traveler, a tough customer to do business with, learned perhaps in the manner of specialists, inclined perhaps toward those contemplations—or inner battles—in the course of which a man is overpowered by emotion but is not disarmed and coolly notes an imperfection in the deltoid of the right shoulder of Donatello's shepherd. You could conceive of this visitor listening to Beethoven, overwhelmed by a hurricane as methodical as a battle; or facing a woman with that comprehensive, shrewd, gentle, and almost violent look that causes her to drop her last secret defenses and reply in silence, "Yes, that is how I am, here I am." He might just as well have been pictured computing the resistance of metals in an armature or questioning with pitiless objectivity a defendant convicted in advance. —And you will be the defendant, my old bison, Félicien Mûrier said to himself, aware that he did so without much assurance.

The other man, the young lieutenant with the discreetly shiny buttons, had an almost pointed chin protruding over his high collar, an aquiline nose, blond hair plastered carefully over a high narrow forehead; his eyes were aggressive and cold, without innocence, incapable of error. Neither a man of the world nor a parvenu, neither a bon vivant nor a technician—though by dint of discipline or respect of instinct, capable of being to a moderate degree all these things at once. A fanatic? No spiritual drive, no burning faith under an aspect created by perfect training. In short, a young beast full of controlled vigor. His lucidity did not necessarily imply what the Latins, the Russians, and Goethe called consciousness.

The letter of introduction, signed by a contemptible academician, recommended Major Erich-Friedrich Acker, Doctor of Philology, Privat-Dozent—whatever that was—at the University of Bonn, author of a remarkable study on *The Tendencies Toward Abstraction in Modern Art*; and Lieutenant of Engineers Gerhardt Koppel, now attached to a staff section, "whose essay on Rainer Maria Rilke is one of the most penetrating known to me; no one will refute better than this brilliant young mind the deliquescent Rilkean love of death . . ." The academician wrote even his most trifling notes for the eyes of posterity; he omitted in any case to say whether these two gentlemen were Nazis. Well, that remained to be seen.

Seated facing Félicien Mûrier's desk, they smiled amiably, Major Acker with lips slightly parted and benevolent eyes, Lieutenant Koppel with his chin and white cheeks: a thin smile, deferential and mute, as precise as a bite.

"Rilke," said Félicien Mûrier in a muffled voice. "You have written on Rilke, Monsieur Koppel. I like Rilke very much because of his prescience and his compassion. We French are very far from Rilke. We are too absorbed in the instant to be prescient; and we have never needed compassion. We had an equilibrium—"

"We had. Have we still?" The arched shoulders and outstretched head of Lieutenant Gerhardt Koppel stood out against the old tapestry with an unpleasant clarity. The ideas, the words of Félicien Mûrier were in harmony—it struck him—with the faded tapestry. The lieutenant, sharpening his stylized smile, replied, "My little book on Rilke is filled with errors which I deplore. It dates from a period in which Germany had not yet found herself."

"I understand," said Mûrier, who was studying attentively the intricately carved handle of his Chinese paper-cutter. "To disown oneself is perhaps a great sign of strength. And then one can proceed to disown others."

This young feline soldier was beginning to be repulsive to him. Mûrier shook his head.

"Forgive me, Monsieur, for thinking aloud—it is a custom of our country—but you seem to me very young to be repudiating your first works. Ordinarily, one clings to them." (I am being tactless, but what good is tact with this breed?)

"It is not a question of age, Monsieur, but of Weltanschauung, vision of the world—the French translation of the Germanic word is inevitably inadequate. The vision of a powerful race, that is what counts, and not my modest personal efforts."

"I understand. But we French are still very individualistic. We are inclined to believe that the phenomenon of consciousness, in its highest manifestations, is essentially individual. I prefer the word *consciousness* to the word *vision*. You perceive the nuance..."

The good fencer parries a direct thrust without effort. Koppel's inflection was courteous, as if in apology for the answer he was obliged to make:

"The great misfortune of the individualist nations is precisely their failure to comprehend the superhuman will that expresses itself in the collective thought of a race."

Major Erich Friedrich Acker, the philologist, intervened quietly. "Let me tell you, Maître, the Superhuman, the Übermensch of Nietzsche is the organized collectivity—pure race, united people, one leader—the leader being at once the symbol, the guide, the incarnation. This real superman attains such greatness that through the accomplishment of the human, he renders superfluous any aspiration to the supernatural. He abolishes Christian mysticism. And he calls forth a new lyricism; it is on this point, Maître, that an understanding becomes necessary between the true poets and the builders of the new order."

"Damned if this philosophical heavy artillery doesn't knock me cold," thought Mûrier. He remembered the tanks driving through the night toward the heart of Paris. A house that had collapsed in the Avenue de Versailles. The photographs of ravaged Rotterdam. The incredible image of a Bavarian lawyer led through the streets of Munich, head shaven, feet bare, on his chest, a sign: I AM AN UNCLEAN JEW. Nathan's magnetized stare.

"Those are great ideas," he said. "Still, the Freudian analysis of the concept of the Führer—"

Koppel turned slightly red and even raised his (white-gloved) hand to interrupt: "Freud was only a Jew, profoundly perverse, nourished on the scum of European decadence."

"I beg your pardon, Freud is alive. He is in England."

"But European decadence is finished. England will fall within six months."

Mûrier was regaining his self-confidence. The white, bony, deeply indented mask of the young officer seemed to him almost insignificant. And what a standardized imbecile!

"You are a soldier, Lieutenant, an excellent soldier I have no doubt. You will not be offended if I say that the judgments of warriors on psychologists do not seem to me the most pertinent."

"And what judgment might be superior to that of warriors?"

"Warriors have authority only as long as they are victorious. Well, you know the law: He who lives by the sword..."

"...will perish by the sword. It is a noble way of perishing. And there is always a victor and he is the judge. War constitutes the sum of human activities, it is the balance-sheet of a nation's capacities."

"We do not deny," said Acker, the philologist, in a conciliatory tone, "that there are relatively precious values still to be found in declining civilizations. But they are corrupted values that must be selected and purified before they can be put into the service of a vital force. You quote the Gospel, Maître: remember that the chaff must be separated from the wheat."

Mûrier withdrew into himself, ceasing perhaps to hear them. They noticed it. Clémence brought in whisky on a red lacquer tray—in order to show off her forearms, irreproachable in shape and texture. She felt left out in the cold. Mûrier replied under his breath to the young lieutenant. "As you please, you handsome military brute. After all you are only a figure of polished quartz."

"Messieurs," he said finally, "the object of your kind visit...?" For one cannot show the door to the officers of an armored host intoxicated with fanfares by saying, "Gentlemen, you bore me. You have the most efficient panzer divisions in the world. You are trampling on my country. You are past masters in the technique of destruction and massacre. But you are only barbarians. It is not impossible that you will destroy our civilization, but I defy you to understand anything about it." Out loud, Mûrier continued, "Monsieur Koppel, you are a practitioner of dynamite, of gelignite."

"No. Those explosives are obsolete today. Modern chemistry does better."

"I have no doubt of that," Mûrier continued, affecting the most hypocritically insolent patience. "For me, a mere man of letters, these malignant compounds are worth nothing—nothing!—beside simple verses such as these by Paul Valéry:

> "Patience, patience,
> Patience in the azure sky,
> Each atom of silence
> Is the chance of a ripe fruit."

In a stifled voice Clémence proposed whisky and soda . . . no soda? She exposed to their gaze her "Venetian" throat, her "caryatid's" arms. Félicien was raving mad! He was compromising himself, he was compromising her with his insolence. He was holding forth as if he were sitting in a café. Mûrier, sensing this judgment—the judgment of women without wit is no better than that of warriors—felt only a mournful exasperation.

And Lieutenant Gerhardt Koppel of the field staff of the Ninth Motorized Division, formerly a demolitions expert, now attached to the Bureau of Cultural Affairs, said to himself that intellectuals of this caliber, vain voluptuaries, cowardly and sophisticated, more harmful than useful—human beings of softened fiber, with hardened arteries and brains obscured by putrid old ideas—could be driven into line only by the most elementary methods: twenty percent of them behind barbed wire, sweeping the yard at six a.m., pushing the wheelbarrow at seven a.m.—and the other 80 percent would soften, become converted, develop so admirable an understanding of the inevitable course of history, begin to expatiate so learnedly on the true doctrine, that you might end by doubting yourself, doubting racial thought, doubting everything, if the hard, exalted, luminous and raucous words of the Führer—man of another essence—did not expel all doubts as TNT pulverized all obstacles.

Today, however, the directive was to recruit these debased rhetoricians of the world's last Alexandria, men who were stupid enough to believe their own rhyming couplets. To this kind of mission, Koppel would greatly have preferred elevating research into problems of a very different nature. Given the probable capacity for resistance of a certain concrete pillbox, the crossfire of certain machine-gun nests, what charge should be employed, at what angle should it be placed? Reduce the foreseeable cost of the operation to the sacrifice of two lads of our own race, just two. Gerhardt drank his whisky neat. It was up to the major to speak first, in accordance with age, seniority, his experience with this kind of people … *This* is what they call a great poet!

Major Acker, sincerely saddened, for he loved Paris, France, Europe, the museums, good literature, old architecture, men molded, even to their souls, by this accumulation of work and riches, knew nonetheless that the old stones had to crumble, that the dominant race had to bring organization into chaos, that worn-out cultures succumbed to new powers. Could we live as things were? Acker calmly dissipated the brief silence, which in a few seconds had grown tense.

"Monsieur Félicien Mûrier, it would grieve me if we have importuned you, believe me. For years I have wanted to meet you, for me it is a real honor. I love the verses you have just quoted as much as you do, I know them by heart. Germany has had infinite patience, I might say, a geological patience. I possess your finest editions, they were my friends in time of peace—in the time of a peace without equality, of a dictated peace. It was a peace without fraternity, without conciliation, but I know that you were one of those who did think of conciliation. You are suffering, I have lived through the same moments as you; I was a soldier at Verdun, I lived in Mainz during the occupation—for eight years I lived near here, in the Rue du Vieux-Colombier. The French Army is defeated, it was as heroic as ours. French culture is not defeated, it is invincible, it is complementary to ours. Frontiers and regimes change, civilization renews its framework, great works remain. Your work is durable, Maître, it is not finished. Whether this war be short or long, we shall rebuild or, rather, we shall build Europe. The new unified Europe has need of men like you. Monsieur Mûrier, the Franks who were the first Kings of France spoke the same language as our ancestors—and the word *frank* signified: the hard, the implacable—as you are well aware.

"I am only a reserve officer, an academician. I have come to do you homage. I honor in you a great country, the brother of my own. There is no quarrel between you and me, there is only mourning and a great common duty: to build Europe. The museums will reopen, the press will be reborn, the French reviews will appear again. We ask you only to continue your work. Write, publish, have confidence in us."

"Are you perfectly sure that I am neither Jewish, nor Jew-contaminated, nor an anarchist?" asked Mûrier in a confidential tone.

"Be what you are, my dear great poet. And then, listen: We are the European revolution."

Everything he said could be true—when truth itself had become an insult and a lie.

"And what about censorship?" Mûrier asked brutally. "Are you going to establish a censorship?"

"You had it before, Monsieur Mûrier. Wartime censorship."

"We had our own. It left writers alone. Are you going to outlaw 'degenerate art'? Are you going to purge the bookstores?"

"You will agree, Monsieur Mûrier, that there are many bad books. In our country we eliminated the art forms that were demoralizing us. The France of tomorrow will encourage the art forms befitting its genius. Can it be indulgent toward those that have weakened it? Are there not subtle poisons against which a people must defend itself? Do not be stubborn. We are holding out a hand to you."

Whereupon Lieutenant Koppel, irritated by all this talk, made a blunder.

"Monsieur Félicien Mûrier, censorship is only discipline. It imposes the most fruitful constraints. You know better than I that the poet's labor consists of censorship, selection, a constraint upon the soul for the sake of a noble, powerful language ..."

"Ah, not at all!" Félicien Mûrier burst out. "I don't remember what stupid dictator called writers the 'engineers of souls.' That pedant of the Department of Highways and Bridges imagined that the secret man, the nocturnal man, the unknowable man could be put together and taken apart like a turbine. I need no censorship. Nor any discipline. What I have been seeking is escape, escape, do you understand? It is the undiscoverable, the—I have never known what I was seeking! For all I know I might suddenly feel like shouting things that would make you shudder. I might feel like prophesying calamities or singing the praises of harlots or cursing all armies and ... How do I know?"

"Führers," he had been about to say. He restrained himself in time, but the sacrilegious word hovered in the air. The two visitors rose together, Acker having begun to move a thousandth of a second before Koppel, who would not otherwise have stirred.

"Think it over, Maître," said Acker. "We are holding out a hand to you ..."

But so saying, he did not hold out his own, though he would have liked to. The presence of his subordinate deterred him.

"I'll think it over."

A thousandth of a second perhaps before his superior, the supple lieutenant clicked his heels, extended his right hand so that his gloved fingertips were at the level of his forehead—"Heil Hitler!"

Major Acker's Roman salute was less crisp, his ritual invocation of the leader less rhythmic. He seemed to follow the junior officer. Félicien Mûrier's arms were of lead. "Goodbye, Messieurs."

From the window he watched the gray automobile driving off. Clémence said between her teeth, "With fools like you, Félicien, we're in a fine fix."

Mûrier did not grow angry.

"They are the fools. Defeated and happy, is that what they expect us to be? That little lieutenant, clever like a trained dog—a hunting dog, a watchdog, of course—this old Nazi, one-third believer, one-third dupe, one-third charlatan, and with a very heavy heart, I'm willing to bet—"

With the blunt point of a blue pencil, he scribbled on the back of an envelope:

> It is you who weep, I who lie
> Ursula I am ashamed of these torments

Weariness and fear penetrated his flesh. They are the masters. What was to prevent them from kidnapping him tonight? And he had this vision, astonishingly precise: standing outside himself, he saw himself, fleshy, clad in the overcoat of his midnight ramblings, his hat on his head, rather stout, rather old, rather weak, rounded back, hands in pockets, Félicien Mûrier, descending a broad staircase of dull stone, and these two officers following three steps behind, one on the right, the other on the left, with big pistols in their belts. Cowardice raised a tide of nausea within him, but he went down calmly. At the bottom of the steep stairs lay dark glimmering water. Was it day or night?

> Rose-window glimmering fear
> shine in the depths of my fervor

He turned around belligerently toward his wife.

"And what else? What were you implying a moment ago? Perhaps I'm a coward?"

15. SMALL DESTINIES

AUGUSTIN Charras slept for nearly fifteen hours, a deep, heavy sleep. In his dreams he saw clear fragments of his past life. Waking for brief anguished moments, he mulled them over. A man exists in spite of himself, like a draft horse drawing his loads until the very day the knackers slaughter him—he exists because he cannot help existing. The horses condemned to underground existence in the tunnels of a mine had so aroused Augustin Charras long ago that, preferring to earn less as long as he was out in the daylight where he would no longer see beasts that were even more enslaved than men, he had left the mines in the North for the forests of the Vosges and become a lumberjack for three francs a day. It was also sad to cut down great trees; their leaves were full of nests, they asked only to live; but it was necessary to destroy and kill in order to live, and here at least he was breathing fresh air. And according to the naturalists, the deep sigh of falling trees expressed no real suffering.

Charras lost this exaggerated, unreasoning sensibility of his when he went to war. Bent beneath his helmet, he struggled up a bare hill. Pitiful stumps of trees studded the chalky ground in which grass, thistles, wildflowers would never grow again. He was missing that lost earth gorged with the dead, but under his eyes the earth grew green, revived, and he saw Angèle, his wife, running down the path. She said, "Husband, Dreamer has got lost again, that animal is crazy, she is, didn't you hear her bell?" Dreamer, their black-spotted white cow, looked at them through the enormous black globes of her eyes. Dark windows opening on rage.

Angèle, his wife, was untrue to him with buddies who were gayer and slicker than he, who knew how to turn a pretty phrase, but there was so much animal innocence in Angèle's clear amber eyes, in her well-rounded shoulders, in her hairy armpits, in her way of singing when she washed clothes, that he couldn't beat her. Angèle spoke and her face merged into the countryside, yet remained clear before him: it was an emanation of the countryside like splotches of sunlight on a bush. "What can I do, my poor Augustin, I don't love anyone but you, we are tied together like two trees with their roots intertwined. But when I'm on the trail to La Chevrette, when I smell the resin and the damp earth, I feel myself melting, I laugh all over for no reason and think I'm going to cry. Then if I meet one of your friends and he begins to look at me with burning eyes and say things I don't understand, what can I do—it's as if I were naked in the middle of the woods, and I'm not ashamed in front of the birds. I'd like to be different for you, Augustin." Charras, his face carved in hard wood, weighed these words, and didn't know what to do, whether to kill this one or that one, whether to undo Angèle's braids and twist them around her neck, or to go away—they say lumberjacks get good pay in America. "Try to behave yourself, wife."

His fists were those of a tree-smasher, he held them out under the luminous rain and Martial, the gravedigger, dug his spade into a corner of the cemetery. Angèle, cold and unrecognizable, slept under this earth: she had died in childbirth. "Martial, Martial, aren't you afraid of hurting her?" "Naw," said the other. But where did he get a face like a big black cat?

The diver rises to the surface, surprised to see the sky. Charras, from the depths of sleep, of dreams, of the past, rose to the surface of the real world. Through the window, from his bed on which he had thrown himself all dressed, his shoes on his feet, he saw the dark wall of the little courtyard with a fringe of sunlight at the top. "It's a nice day." He realized that he had slept numberless hours to escape his solitude. "Ah, miserable war!" The temptation to close his eyes and tell himself that Angèle, that pure child, would be there next morning to make his coffee—this childish temptation made him angry with himself: how stupid can a man be!

Yet how could he look steadily and calmly on the immense perspective of devastation? How could he take it all in? A pallid Paris grown unlike itself, the forests of the Marne, the wounded of 1914, the tank battles he had read about in the newspapers, the air-raid warnings in the calm, starry nights, the gossip in the air-raid shelter at the Saint-Paul Métro station, dawn on the banks of an unchanging Seine, his swift farewell to Angèle in a truck at the Porte d'Italie—all this was muddled with fog. Few thoughts, and those hard and unfriendly, shone amid the confusion. "It serves you right, Charras, it serves everybody right, we are a nation of idiots, we didn't know what to do with our lives, we let ourselves be swindled by the capitalists, the Boches, the Socialists, the Radicals, the Communists, we believed every soft-soap artist in the world. Here you are, well past sixty, Charras, Croix de Guerre from the other war, a hard worker all your life, no more of a fool than anyone else, and your daughter is a refugee on the roads, and Paris isn't Paris anymore. The Boches, the Gestapo are coming in, they'll make you sweat for them. 'We'll sit on the French Republic,' they'll all sing. And what will you say? You have nothing to say, Augustin. The Spaniards at least fought like mad for two years. True, it didn't help them much, the whole world left them in the lurch..."

Charras had a horror of his cavern. He looked out on the street and the morning was like other mornings. Widow Prugnier was arranging her vegetable stand. A servant girl with red arms was sweeping the sidewalk in front of the Marquise bar.

"Good morning, Monsieur Augustin," said Mme Prugnier. "Well, the medicine's been swallowed. It feels better now, doesn't it? M. Dupin heard that the English have won a big victory in the North. M. Dupin saw the Fritzes, they're equipped like kings, he says; ah, it's not like our army, you'd have thought they were outfitted at the flea market. They are correct, not insolent at all, they pay for everything they buy, they are establishing order, and God knows we needed it (sigh). M. Carpe, the deputy precinct captain, came to investigate the death of poor M. Tartre. He says the war is almost over. My dirty foreigners on the sixth floor have all beat it, I guess their conscience wasn't clear—and their rent was overdue, you can imagine! And I almost forgot" (she lowered her voice) "there's someone hidden in the house, someone I can't help being suspicious of, given the crime."

Charras nibbled at the fringes of his mustache. His look was not amiable.

"There's nothing more nourishing than suspicions, Madame."

Now exactly what did he mean by that?

Charras departed, walking at random. Paris all clean, in mournful Sunday clothes, was coming out of its semi-lethargy. On the Place de la Concorde, with its noble expanses, movement was concentrated around a group of gray-green trucks. A huge red flag with a swastika in a white circle floated over the Palais Bourbon. Blond soldiers in sober green uniforms trimmed with white, wearing rawhide belts, were having their pictures taken at the foot of the obelisk. In the distance Charras could see a great coming and going of uniforms around the Hôtel de Crillon—a military spectacle without a public. Little officers, booted, straight-backed, polished, flung complicated salutes at astounding personages with gleaming coat-linings and képis tilted up like roosters' crests. Each salute released a series of mechanical movements—right foot thrust forward, elbow raised, other arm close to the side, head rigid. And the marionettes froze to attention while a fat man in fiery red cavalry breeches slowly disengaged his elephantine posterior from a touring car. "They are drunk with militarism. I'd like to be here ten years from now and see the price they pay for this little spree."

Charras had no desire to linger in the region of conquering might. Two massive policemen accompanied by a green-clad noncom with a silver eagle over his right breast, wearing a red armband and a helmet like an upside-down stew pot, contemplated Charras. "They think I'm going to compromise them by pissing on the sidewalk. I'm not that crazy." At the end of the Champs-Élysées, the Arc de Triomphe was shrouded by a light haze. "Triumphs are exaggerated farces," thought Charras. Peaceful soldiers of the Wehrmacht, wearing caps with visors, passed him by and their looks were blue, cold, friendly. "They're putting on the nice-guy act. Better be on our guard.

These fellows are ordinary soldiers. They're just carrying out orders." In the Rue de Rivoli a crippled newsdealer, whose face seemed to have been kneaded of soft clay and then punched flat, was selling *La Victoire*, edited by Gustave Hervé. "That's quite a title," said Charras. "Have you got *The Boot in the Ass*, the journal of current events?"

"No," said the cripple amicably. "What a circulation that would have. But *Paris-soir* will be out soon." Charras bought the paper to help the cripple's business—then rolled it in a ball and threw it away.

At Anselme Flotte's in front of the siphons, customers were discussing the headlines: Pétain's request for an armistice, the liberation of the prisoners of war in two weeks, the imminent demobilization, the end of the war. Some of the drinkers couldn't get over their consternation. "I don't get it. Couldn't we fight in the Massif Central? Couldn't we hold out somewhere? The Americans are bound to come in sooner or later." Anselme paid close attention to the words, intonations, and looks around him, in order to make sure of offending no one by his remarks—which would bear the mark of authority, for he saw things clearly, he already had German marks in his till, a solid currency. And the responsibility of running a business obliges a man to think straight. He said sententiously, "What I say is that our honor is saved, and that's the main thing. France lived up to her commitments, she fought for Poland, for Danzig, for the English, she did what she could with the armament she had, it was clay against iron, and that's the long and short of it. And when you've lost a game, you've got to pay up and go back to work."

A little man who looked like an old department-store clerk became so excited that he spilled part of the green mixture he was drinking on the counter. "What about the English? They're going on with the war!"

Anselme Flotte observed the general consternation. His reply was crushing: "Oh yes, the English. Oh là là! There's nobody more egotistical than those people. In the first place they played us for fools. In the second place they're lucky enough to have the Channel at their service. In the third place what about the punishment they're going to take from the German planes and all the rest of it! I give them three months and they'll be on their knees. Suppose we hadn't been there in 1914! They've never been soldiers, not the English. Financiers, plutocrats, yes, and lousy with Jews. Other people have to fight their battles. No, thank you. I'm going to tell you how I feel. I'm relieved and I make no bones about it. You need order on a continent. We couldn't put our house in order, well, the Boches will do it for us. The profiteers, the demagogues, the kikes from all over Europe, the smart alecks—God knows we had plenty of them, luckily most of them have cleared out of Paris, they knew what was good for them—well, Adolf will show them what's what, he knows just how to do it. The Nazis aren't dumber or meaner than anyone else, just take a look at them. What I say is: let's make peace, and quickly, let's pay the damages and get back to work for real. We need discipline and that's what we had forgotten. Not me, I was working my fingers to the bone, you can believe me."

Mme Sage, the herbalist, who had come in to telephone, agreed with a sigh. "I've opened up again," she said. "I can't live without my clientele."

M. Dupin, who worked for the PLM, stood there pale, with worry in his eyes. He opened his mouth to answer and for an instant was like a carp pulled out of the water, gasping for breath; he had his own problem. Shut your mouth, Dupin. Charras remarked calmly, "You're keeping right up with the times, Monsieur Flotte." And he always would, this poisonous fox. Nothing mattered to him as long as his bar was running, as long as the springs in his transient hotel rooms squeaked with the weight of business every hour or so—and that wouldn't be lacking now that a victorious army was here with their pockets full of paper marks! Charras approached M. Dupin and in tacit agreement they moved aside to speak without being heard.

"You look sick, Monsieur Dupin? It's a hard pill to swallow, eh?"

"It made me cry," said M. Dupin, "but that isn't all, if only you knew!" He hesitated at the brink of confidence. Nothing is so hard as to keep a secret without moral support or advice. "Listen, Monsieur Augustin. My boy Julien has come home. He demobilized himself, he says, there was nothing else to do. He fought near Château Thierry, there were three hundred survivors, no more, from his whole regiment. The corpses were floating in the Marne along with the dead fish, it seems the shells bursting in the water killed the gudgeon. His best friend had his head blown off while he was lighting a cigarette. Julien had bent down to scrape the mud off his shoe with a knife, so he wasn't hurt. His friend remained standing for a moment, without a head, there was a red hole where his neck had been, and he still had a Gauloise in his fingers, it was still smoking. Julien said: 'I wasn't frightened at all, first I began to look around me for the head, as though I could pick it up and put it back in place, but I didn't see it, the body fell and I ran away; after a while I sat down to think . . .' The shells were bursting all around him. He was covered with dirt, a rain of earth and pebbles, he fell asleep under it, he says. When he woke up, there was no more battle, no more regiment, only quietness and moonlight. He walked along the road all alone, toward the rear. The Boches had occupied the rear, he passed among them like one of them, they were asleep. He's been here for three days, he may be a battlefield deserter. That isn't so bad, because the war is going to be over. But get this, M. Augustin, a soldier was seen loitering around here the night when Monsieur Tartre was killed. And that was the night Julien came home. So that grocer woman and Flotte—how do they manage to see everything?—suspect him. Maybe they sent word to the police; a cop came up to our place, I just had time to shut the boy up in the toilet. If the cop had needed to urinate—what then? It was Fardier, he asked me if we hadn't noticed anything the day of the crime. He looked at the floor of the dining room as though he expected to find bloodstains, and he said: 'It seems a deserter did it . . . I spend whole hours here to watch the boss and to please him by ordering drinks, he likes that.'"

Charras said, "I can put your boy up in my place. All he has to do is jump over the wall in the court during the night."

"You are a man," said Dupin ardently.

"What can they be scheming about?" Anselme Flotte wondered. The radio was repeating a message from Marshal Pétain to the nation.

Charras smoked his pipe for a long while, leaning against the black

door of his shop, while the twilight became shadow, uncertain darkness, hesitant night. The girls, in a hurry to get their work done before
curfew, had stationed themselves at the approaches of the hotel. At
nightfall three soldiers in tall képis appeared at the end of Rue du
Roi-de-Naples. They were swinging their arms and looking into
doorways with attentive indifference. The shortest, who was also the
youngest and the blondest, walked stiffly and at times stepped off the
sidewalk for no reason at all and stared at the resplendent tips of his
handsome boots. They sighted the girls from afar and smiled in an-
ticipation.

"The Boches," whispered Émilie to Fernande.

The blond and the brunette pinched each other's fingertips to
comfort themselves. "What do I care?" said Fernande resolutely.

Émilie frowned. "They killed Charlie."

Fernande spoke seriously: "I'm sure it wasn't those three. Don't be
stubborn. Charlie killed some of theirs too."

Émilie beamed. "That's true."

She stood there with her pointed breasts, her parted lips, her slanting eyes, and watched the men, resembling those who had killed
Charlie, draw near. "He was a better man than any of them, my man
was. For his one wooden cross, there are three on the other side."

Throwing dignity to the winds, Raymonde la Soufflée ran up to
the soldiers.

"Aren't you ashamed of yourself?"

The three stopped in front of the girls. The one who put his hand
on Émilie's shoulders smiled into her eyes and several times repeated
lighthearted words which she was glad not to understand. Émilie,
though retaining her professional charm, felt like hurling insults into
their faces. To gain time, she suggested having a drink at the bar.
"*Trinken*," translated the little blond, stiff and already drunk. La
Soufflée held him firmly by the arm, like a prey, because when men
got a good look at her they tended to run away. The three pushed the
girls into the door of the bar, holding them around the waist. As they
went in, they raised their arms: "Heil Hitler!" They had only a single
voice, loud and guttural, the voice of duty. Not one of the customers

budged. The ground shifted under Anselme, he blushed, shook off his embarrassment, slowly raised his fat arm, extended his pink, moist hand in a servile salute to the strong and stammered, "Welcome, soldiers!" And to calm himself: "What'll I serve them, Émilie?"

The bright, wan little face of the girl with the peroxide curls was deformed by a mirthless laugh that revealed her bluish teeth. There was poison in her eyes.

"I couldn't give a damn, *patron*," she said.

Anselme pointed to one bottle after another, and the three said *Ja, Ja.* They clinked glasses with the girls. Anselme raised the prices on them. He avoided the eyes of the other drinkers. The three couples left and went into the hotel, the long tinkling of the bell could be heard. A stout old man who needed a shave looked up from his game of *manille* and said without apparent anger, "Flotte, I'm going to tell you what you are. You're a swine."

Flotte was expecting this moment, this insult. He didn't know who would throw it at him, but he knew that it would stick. His limbs were soft.

He asked stupidly, "Why?" And the ripe mass of his cheeks shook like jelly. The question was too much for the insulter: "And he asks why. You're a turd, Flotte. Show us again how you saluted them. Show us how you wiped Adolf's ass."

No one offered to defend Anselme Flotte, and he knew that it was a time for blows; vainly, he invoked the fury that hardens muscles. Issuing from behind his counter, his rampart, he took three feeble steps forward.

"Come and get your licking, Flotte!" cried the stout old man. "I'm gonna settle your account!"

Flotte took one step more, tried to look menacing, but his body had gone abominably soft, his eyelids twitched, he felt that he would allow the man to slap him, that he would be ridiculous, but there was no strength in him. The fat old man raised his shoulder and wound up for a roundhouse—then he sat down with all his weight, he too overcome by feebleness, and wiped his face on his sleeve.

"Get back behind your counter, Flotte. I can't knock down all the bootlickers of Paris. Serve me an old brandy and make it quick. Anyway, you know I'm right."

Flotte filled the little glass. And said, "I should ask you politely to leave my place. But I don't bear grudges."

"You can't expect shit to smell like violets," muttered the stout old man, pretending to be busy with his cards. "I'm cutting. Diamonds!"

M. Dupin raised his voice and said, "Oh, after all a salute is only a salute. They're stronger. It's no reason for Frenchmen to brawl among themselves."

Flotte rinsed his glasses with desperate energy.

The blond soldier, half drunk, was first to emerge from the hotel, driven by self-disgust. The large mirror in the ceiling had got terribly on his nerves. La Soufflée, like a pink cuttlefish, had taken all his marks before spreading out her enormous viscosity for him to lie down on. She had bad teeth, she reminded him of the hideous creature who had abandoned herself to the soldiers in the ruins of a convent in Poland, between two fragments of whitewashed wall, hiding her sores under her rags—until one day a *Feldwebel* had charitably blown out her brains from behind as she was beaming at a can of beans with salt pork . . . The soldier sobered up and blinked in the dim light. He saw Charras, his pipe between his teeth, his arms folded.

"*Guten Abend, mein Herr, bon-soir-mon-sieur.*"

He was only a colorless little man of about twenty-five, a corporal. Not much of anything. Surely not one of those responsible for the war.

"Me no enemy. Soldier. France more nice than Poland. Paris *wunderbar*. Eiffel *Turm*, *sehr schön*, wonderful."

Charras muttered, "Imbecile."

"*Was*? What? I saying: Me no enemy, me soldier. Me no Nazi. Me from Hanover." In his effort to express himself with words learned from a pocket manual, he was like a schoolboy reciting a fable.

"Me assistant bookkeeper department store Hanover, big department store."

Charras, a step above him, a head taller and thirty-five years older, seemed severe to him. The evening was growing cool, the solitude more somber.

"War not fault of German, war fault of England."

"You're a poor devil," replied Charras. "You don't understand a damn thing."

"Poor, *armer*, devil, *Teufel*—"

The Hanoverian, pleased with the success of his mental translation, remembered how he himself had often said that the soldiers of the most glorious armies were nothing but poor devils. *Richtig!* The diffused light of drunkenness rose again to his brain. At this stage it induced melancholy tenderness toward himself and others. If he held his shoulders too stiff, it was because he wanted to cry, because he needed friendship. He translated the second sentence to himself. *Und ich verstehe nichts, nichts.* And God knows it is hard to understand why I wasn't killed on the bridge at Warsaw, why I didn't break anything when I fell five yards trying to scale a wall at Namur, why we fired so trigger-happy into the doors of empty houses, why we threw grenades at cows grazing by the roadside, why we smashed the piano in an abandoned living room with our rifle butts, why we gave tinned rations to prisoners and didn't even worry about being punished. If you can't understand, obey. March. *Ich marschiere.* I march.

"Ich hatt' einen Kameraden—"

It was a sad song. I had a comrade who wanted to understand too much and always wanted to do things better than the next man. He carved heads of Oriental dancing girls out of wood with his penknife. One day he wanted to do things too well. He was sent out on a mission. He took the shortest way, the most dangerous way. He got lost (or the captain read the map wrong), he returned too late, and they shot him. He fell crying *Heil Deutschland!* He was a Swabian but what was his name? The pale features of the Hanoverian lit up when he said to Charras, as if he had just told him the whole story, "His girl's name was Gerda."

He gave Charras the salute due to noncoms. That's how life is. We are the strongest people in the world. Who is Gerda? I'm getting a headache. Well, I hope the others get through with their whores someday. Mine was filthy, filthy. What can I think of to keep from thinking of her? Better think of nothing. One, two, three. One-two-three. *Ein-zwei-drei.*

Another soldier came rolling out of the hotel like a marble rolling toward its hole. The hole was the vast darkness. Well, it's not too soon. Hans must think it's his wedding night. He wants tenderness, divine eyes, the dregs of the soul and the moon, all for four marks. He's going to make us overstay our passes. I'll go and knock on his door. At the hotel office, where the keys hung, the Hanoverian encountered the maternal firmness of Mme Alexandrine Flotte.

"That isn't done, soldier."

Das macht man nicht. Warum?

"It isn't done, Monsieur."

Ach, verboten! If it's forbidden, it's forbidden. The drunken corporal saluted stiffly and went out like a mannequin. Why did I go back to that sickening place?

The most commonplace soldier in the world, with the most commonplace name in the mightiest army in the world—no one remembered his features, the sound of his voice, his insignificant gestures—finally emerged, buttoning his tunic. He had such a look of exaltation on his face that one of his comrades asked him if he had been drinking again. He rebuffed their curiosity.

"Leave me be. Let the sergeant yell, fuck the sergeant!"

"They are beasts," thought Charras, "poor famished beasts. Ours are the same, poor fellows. Man and woman, it's disgusting, but more than that, it's terrible."

Hans Müller, the insignificant, the exalted, didn't want to go home. Expectancy made his heart beat like a holiday bell. "Leave me be if you know what's good for you. *Ach!*"

Slender and graceful as a trained snake, her hair piled heavily over her forehead, her nostrils thin, Émilie emerged into the deep night. Hans Müller ran to her, took her elbows in his hard hands, peered into her face to recapture her slanting and singularly vast eyes, so malicious and radiant, her big mouth as firm as her breasts and her belly. She was not frightened, she laughed silently, malevolently, to herself, obscurely oppressed by the memory of Charlie. A hot breath murmured into her cheek.

"*Mädchen, Mädchen, du bist*—" Hans Müller would have blushed to say: *Ich liebe dich*, I love you, but he would never forget her, never, nowhere; if he were to die soon, as so many others had died in a hole in the earth, he must be able to call up her image exactly when he closed his eyes.

"I'll be back," he said. "Wait for me. *Ich komme wieder*."

Émilie did not understand the German words, but she understood much more; amiably she said yes, yes with her chin, her teeth, her eyelids, yes, yes. Afterward, Hans Müller walked resolutely between his two friends—the insignificant Hans Müller without any story worth knowing had become more alive than they.

Charras closed his shop, lighted the lamp, fried two slices of lard. Angèle's bed was white, the piano black, black—silence. "They are men." Charras felt a sense of satisfaction: the trees must be happy on a night like this when they were all breathing deeply and the stars were pouring down their inexpressible cold gentleness. He opened the door leading to the yard, noisily poured some water into a pail, whistled—signals agreed upon with M. Dupin: the boy can come. On the fifth floor of the next house a window closed without too much sound. I heard you. Wait. Charras waited by the lamp, his fingers intertwined, his head bowed, thinking nothing. Sometimes waiting is good, it feels like living.

And silently the door opened. Dupin's son entered.

"Good evening, Monsieur Charras, it's very kind of you."

Insignificant, as well, Julien-Marie Dupin, postal clerk at Ribemont, Aisne, married for eighteen months, no news of his wife—it seems the whole town had been destroyed, but some said that nothing had happened. Julien-Marie Dupin, survivor amazed at surviving, a hero all in all without suspecting it, believing himself a deserter, obsessed with remorse, with fear of court-martial, visions of being shot— What have I done, good Lord above. At the same time he was delighted to be alive and delighted with the taste of adventure.

"Well, my boy," said Charras, "I can tell you one thing: you did the right thing when you saved your skin. Here you're at home. As long as the neighborhood gossips don't suspect anything. Speak low."

Two men, one old, one young, in a safe hideout, by the fire, with storm and danger outside—it's a fine and pleasant thing!

"Have you had supper, boy? A bit of wine or coffee?"

The two men began a secret life, compounded of whisperings and winks immediately understood, of inconceivable intimacy. "We won't speak of the war, the war's over," Charras proposed. They talked until late into the night about life's vicissitudes, about the little house at Ribemont, nearly covered by the leaves of an oak, about trout fishing and poaching. All life was in the past. Julien-Marie Dupin took out pictures of his wife, Armandine; Charras produced a picture of Angèle. "It would be funny if they met on the roads!" And why was it impossible? They wished it and almost believed it would happen.

Days and nights passed. Julien lay on Angèle's bed and spent the day reading *The Three Musketeers* in a series of illustrated installments; alone, he could not resist his fears, he was sure that Armandine was dead—but what had happened? The presence of Charras dissipated his nightmare. Charras opened his shop for only a few hours a day—summer was the dead season for this kind of business; he seldom showed himself at the Marquise, and then only to avoid having anyone notice a conspicuous change in his habits. Anselme Flotte observed that since Angèle's departure Augustin Charras had a livelier look, an air of restrained satisfaction, and spent more time at home, where he couldn't possibly have anything to do. M. Dupin, who bought neither wood nor coal, went into the shop every day. Mme Jérôme Prugnier made the same observations, combining them deep down in her mind with the fact that when she pressed her ear to the wall of her bedroom, she could distinguish vague murmurs next door that went on until two in the morning—it was annoying, there must have been a fissure in the masonry.

Those first days of the occupation were quiet, the Germans paid well, business was good. The soldier Hans Müller came back to see Émilie as often as he could, once or twice a week, bringing her presents, an old silver bracelet looted in Galicia, the finest silk stockings he could buy at Les Trois Quartiers. "The kid's sweet on me," Émilie observed without pride, but with a sharp light flickering across the stony blue of her eyes. "He's very nice, not vicious at all." M. Bœuf began to respect Émilie, so much so that she bluntly refused to go upstairs with him. "M. Bœuf, you know I'm a good-natured girl, but bizness is bizness, I've decided to drop the extras. I may get married to a German, you understand?"

"I congratulate you, Émilie," said M. Bœuf, intimidated. "Will you invite me to the wedding?"

Émilie was politely insolent: "We'll see. It's up to him to decide that."

Mme Alexandrine Flotte offered Émilie a rake-off of 50 percent on the room rent she brought in. "You're such a hard worker, Émilie, and so proper, I have real affection for you, my girl." Émilie was getting to be somebody.

And one starry night at the end of July the bicycle patrol, consisting of two policemen and an M.P. noncom of the Wehrmacht, made out in the darkness a figure stretched flat in the middle of the street. *Halt!* The noncom's blue flashlight moved from the tips of the boots to the collar insignia. The body of the soldier Hans Müller, grown forever cold, was lying arms outstretched, face lit in a smile, eyes open, on a flat cushion of red-black blood. Anselme and Alexandrine Flotte, dragged out into the street in their nightclothes, recognized Émilie's lover in the blue beam and were seized with violent nausea. The noncom questioned them mercilessly in one of the transient rooms. Seated heavily on the bed amid the pale mirrors, this colossus with his concave face, his enormous hand hanging down over the pink bedspread, close to his revolver, scrutinized Alexandrine in her dressing gown and Anselme perpetually trying to hitch up his old corduroy trousers under his nightshirt. The formidable back of the pink colossus was reflected in the rear mirror; the ceiling mirror suspended his hunched back, his shaven skull of polished stone.

Boiling with fury, he kept repeating the same questions and the same insults.

"Swine. Swine. What Émilie? Émilie who? Where is Émilie?"

The Flottes knew nothing. They were faint with terror. Alexandrine burst into tears.

"My good Monsieur, we are innocent."

The colossus snickered, but the only sound issuing from his throat was the squeak of a eunuch.

"Swine. Nobody is innocent. You'll be shot, the whole lot of you."

The springs squeaked beneath his bulk. He had neither lashes nor eyebrows, his hand rested on his revolver, which had a bluish barrel. He shut Alexandrine up in the room, stationed a policeman at the door, and pushed Anselme out in front of him. Anselme moved like a pitiful beast being led to slaughter. From floor to floor, from room to room, the revolver in his back.

On the third floor, the sight of a couple more or less naked increased the fury of the colossus. He thrust his gun against the hairy chest of the man, a sickly, pasty creature who couldn't find his glasses. *"Schweine! Dokumente!"* He tore the blankets off the woman, fat and ugly, her hair undone, and her faded nudity, porcine to be sure, was exposed to the light.

"Émilie? Émilie?"

"No," Anselme said in despair, "it's La Crampe, I mean Mélanie. Mélanie Lembourbier."

"You'll all be shot. Cover yourself, pig. Shameless bitch!"

The creature did not have the strength to obey. Without looking at the papers, the noncom pushed Anselme out. In the narrow corridor he shoved the icy barrel of his revolver into his stomach. "Assassin!" And suddenly, in the same low tone of rage on the verge of paroxysm: "Cognac!"

Anselme Flotte, his spine and shoulder blades bruised by blows, went to get his best cognac. The colossus drank a large glassful and seemed to calm himself.

Deputy Chief Carpe, Fardier, and another German M.P. noncom arrived at about two in the morning. The second noncom, less formidable in appearance, proved to be more so in reality. His hands were remarkably white and well manicured, his triangular face was cut in two by a large aquiline nose; the general impression was of an insect. He looked no one straight in the eye, but gave you a three-quarters look, his left eye darting its somber point over the crest of his nose. He spoke with the absurd voice of an old woman, from a hollow chest covered with ribbons, in fluent French with an Alsatian accent. First he inquired, rather courteously, of Anselme Flotte: "You are the guilty party?"

"Lord!" cried Flotte and clutched at his throat.

"You deny it, Monsieur?"

"If you are guilty, Flotte, you'd do best to confess right away," M. Carpe advised. "We know how to make criminals talk."

Flotte found commiseration only in the spent eyes of Officer Landois. Fardier said in a servile aside, "Anyway, if he's not an accomplice he'll have to prove it. There's nothing shadier than this hotel."

About three o'clock in the morning the insect noncom with the effeminate hands loaded the seven persons found sleeping in the hotel, plus the Flottes and a worker with a cough by the name of Émilienne, into an open truck. They were made to sit on the floor, helmeted soldiers stood over them with revolvers. The truck grumbled a moment, then vanished into the mortally unknown night.

The investigation, conducted by Magistrate Billain-Sec assisted by Lieutenant Wichter of the Geheime Staatspolizei, yielded no information. It did bring about the arrest of M. Bœuf, inspector of the vice squad, denounced by Anselme Flotte as having been the lover of Émilie from Nantes.

"What?" said Lt. Wichter with amazement, "you had sexual relations with the prostitutes you were supervising and you don't know the criminal's address?"

Even so M. Bœuf was not incriminated but, even though he had recently joined Jacques Doriot's party, was held at the disposal of the military authorities. The Parti Populaire Français immediately announced his expulsion. The innocence of the arrested persons soon became obvious. Magistrate Billain-Sec and Lt. Wichter agreed that the affair had no political character. At the end of an excellent luncheon to which he treated Lt. Wichter, Magistrate Billain-Sec bravely suggested that he sign ten no-cause orders.

"Hum," said Lt. Wichter, an obese, rather conciliatory fellow, formerly a salesman of pharmaceuticals, and established for years at Billancourt; he never lost sight of the probable opinions of his superiors. "Hum, that would give us two unpunished crimes in the same place in too short a time . . ."

He directly found a reasonable solution. "Sign your no-cause orders, Monsieur Billain-Sec, we'll let the women go, and I'll keep the men as hostages. How would that be?"

"A wise solution," agreed M. Billain-Sec, satisfied that he had done his duty. "The population of this neighborhood, you know, are about the least praiseworthy in all Paris."

While finishing their Port Salut and burgundy, they talked of other matters.

The same day the center of interest shifted to a deposition made in the presence of M. Carpe by Widow Jérôme Prugnier, "whose trustworthiness and perspicacity are beyond all praise" (noted by M. Carpe). A soldier, probably a deserter, probably the son of M. Dupin of the PLM, probably the murderer of M. Tartre, and quite possibly the murderer of M. Hans Müller, was hiding in the lodgings of Augustin Charras, dealer in coal and wood, known moreover as an anarchist, antifascist, or worse.

Anselme Flotte, brought in for further questioning, sighed with relief when he heard his neighbor's name. The tone of Messrs. Billain-Sec and Wichter clearly announced the end of this dreadful affair. He represented Augustin Charras as the prototype of the undesirable, hypocritical citizen, sympathizing with the Reds in Spain and with the English—in short a man capable of any crime. M. Flotte's memory revived, he recounted his observations, his suspicions. Sure of getting off with a whole skin, he spoke freely, giving proof of a rare sagacity. He saw the countenances of the two magistrates darken. The obese Wichter, despite his civilian clothes, threw out his chest as though in full uniform. Drawing a notebook from his pocket, he classified Anselme Flotte under hostages of Category A (those especially suspect or dangerous). M. Billain-Sec, growing a little grayer in the face than usual, said in a tone of reproach, "You had suspicions, Flotte, you even had precise evidence, yet you kept silent. You who seemed to understand the need for loyal collaboration so well. You, an honorable businessman. I was going to sign your release, now it's impossible."

Flotte made an imploring gesture. Such a flood of arguments rose through the muck of his despair that he could say nothing.

"Take the prisoner away," sighed the obese Wichter.

That evening Officer Landois met Augustin Charras, who was on his way home with his can of milk. There was no one else in the street except two little boys playing marbles.

"Monsieur Charras," said Landois tersely. "That old hag"—he indicated the Widow Prugnier's grocery store out of the corner of his eye—"has denounced *both of you*. I have no advice to give you."

Someone was coming out of the grocery store. Landois made off.

The first blow of the ax only cuts the bark. Charras had only a second of dismay. He took a breath. Then he called one of the little boys.

"Hey, Baptiste, here's a can with milk in it, you're in luck, it's for you."

The names of M. Bœuf, discharged police inspector, M. Dupin, employee of the PLM, and M. Anselme Flotte, hotelkeeper, figured later in a list of hostages shot in consequence of an act of sabotage committed by persons unknown in the freight station of the North Railroad, not far, it is believed, from the Chapel of Saint-Denis. According to one rumor, perhaps no more than a legend, Bœuf, Dupin, and Flotte died along with a group of young people who sang the "Marseillaise" and the "Internationale" in their last moments.

16. CHANCES

FÉLICIEN Mûrier discovered that "the imaginary laws of impure lyricism"—"that direct apperception of reality stripped of rational clutter"—were insufficient to guide him among the puppets and their puppet ideas. He was witnessing a sinister carnival without humor, unless it was black humor, the ultimate carnival, as serious as a catafalque. Disappearance of faces. And the shriveled masks spoke freshly learned languages.

"We are going to start up the review again, old man, it will make a tremendous splash. Oberleutnant von G. was just telling me. Accepting the established situation as a given, we must work toward a new Renaissance. They have in mind a European Academy, a great congress of writers."

Mûrier was circumspect, listened more than he talked.

"You will be translated immediately into German, Italian, Hungarian, Spanish, Czech, Romanian, Turkish, perhaps into Russian. Planning and eugenics applied to the works of the intellect. These Germans are really brilliant."

What could Oberleutnant von G., and Major General Z., and the amiable ambassador, the learned advisor from the board of directors of the Beaux Arts, and the charming Major Erich-Friedrich Acker, and that other diabetic, automaton, polyglot official who in his Munich office maintained files of suspects so complete that they even recorded the opinions of Bolivian and Iraqi professors—what could all these important personages, directed by circulars from the Ministry of Propaganda, what could all these flexible, incisive personalities, some like keen scalpels, some like heavy oiled shears, do to prevent a gagged literature from dying or to call forth a single authentic poem?

"But they've got the cash, old man, they are the masters of the continent—just as Pericles was master of Athens!"

The allusion to Pericles, launched by a young novelist, made the rounds of the literary circles, applauded by some, liquidated for others by a humorist who wrote this commercial advertisement: "For your shoes! Incomparable Black Eagle shoe polish and our Pericles buffing brush." Pursued by certain gentlemen of Spartan cast, the humorist, it is believed, crossed the line into the Unoccupied Zone. Teachers at the lycées were embarrassed at having to mention the wise tyrant praised by Thucydides.

Catastrophes that cultivated men would have thought inconceivable only a short time before now seemed natural and even irrevocable to them. What they now felt—or so they said—was less sorrow than manly and philosophic resignation.

"Childbirth is always painful," said the editor of a paper that had been leftist under Léon Blum's cabinet. "What are we to do, my dear Mûrier? The Third Republic was stricken with total paralysis, the great hereditary disease; think of the Panama scandal, think of the Dreyfus case—about which France understood nothing, its history remains to be written!—the Masonic scandals, the Stavisky scandals! Poor Marianne was limping with both legs, her Phrygian cap, stolen from the September cutthroats, had become a nightcap. It was sitting all crooked on her gray hair. Old demagogic republics must die like old procuresses, Monsieur. Marianne was rejuvenated in 1918 thanks to the Americans, the Russians, the English, the Italians, the Portuguese, she got away with a victory just before the menopause. At that time we had a great military leader who was clear-sighted, the man of Verdun, who drove Poincaré to despair. The Popular Front was the final bit of senile delirium before the end."

This gentleman and many others spoke of a return to the earth, of old peasant France, of intendants-general, of salvation through the old monarchy made corporative and social and integrated with the New Order!—of repentance, of the hegemony of the cohesive and warlike, industrial and hierarchic nations. Mûrier was looking into his interlocutor's spectacles for signs of broken bottles. Answer: "Nonetheless, you were flattered to have lunch with Daladier's cabinet chief? Doesn't it make you blush to spout all this rubbish?" —But that would have been imprudent. "And don't you think," the poet asked, "there is such a thing as the demagogy of the panzers? Between you and me, I prefer the demagogy of paid vacations and free publishers."

A Nazi orator proclaimed in Berlin that "the New Reich will last a thousand years!" The air became charged with absurdity, futility, baseness, cynicism. If such were the byproducts of power, what was power worth? "Maître, the Parisian styles continue, our mannequins are all the rage. When it comes to dresses and hats, there hasn't been any European war." The theaters were reopening. Outside the Folies Bergère and other nude shows, huge buses poured forth battalions of gray-green soldiers—survivors of the battles of Poland, the Meuse, Flanders, the Somme, destined for other battles from which most of them would not return—but tonight they thought, as they beheld the pyramids of flesh, the plumes and the smiles, that they were plumbing the very depths of joy.

The invasion of the British Isles was foreshadowed by the burning of London. *Paris-soir* wrote: "England is short of gasoline, England expected to win the battle of iron but has lost it." The Tripartite Pact created "the Berlin-Rome-Tokyo bronze Axis for a new order, for a future of justice and peace" (speech of Count Ciano). Dr. Funk, Reich Minister of Economics, who had been seen on the Champs-Élysées, was preparing "the reconstruction of Europe—" In the Free Zone, the National Revolution seemed ready, if Hitler permitted, to branch out into a monarchist restoration. In Paris, *L'Oeuvre* commented: "Restoration? In Vichy it is the name of a chic café across the street from the Casino. Nothing more." Revolution signified reaction, national meant treason, and restoration—a little chic café. Trade unionists who had formerly been revolutionary published *France at Work*, passed by the military censorship, approved by the Geheime Staatspolizei; a group of old anarchists, grown excessively sad and wise, praised Proudhon and denounced that evil Jew Karl Marx. The underground *L'Humanité* demonstrated the responsibility of the Anglo-Saxon plutocracies. A worried essayist wrote: "We are conquered, all we have left is wisdom." Maybe he thought so. Drieu La Rochelle worked on a "Defense of Laughter." Louis-Ferdinand Céline, lyrical and half-mad, lewd, scatological, and prophetic, foamed at the mouth for a thousand pages on the Jews, the Jew-infected, the sodomized, and the Negroids—in a word, the greatest writer of the century. Montherlant lauded the censorship: "Thanks to the censorship we shall at last cease to be regarded as a drunken helot or a naughty child." At last! Alphonse de Châteaubriant traced the portrait of the Führer: "His eyes are the deep blue of the waters of the Königsee when the lake, all around Sankt Bartholomäus, reflects the deep furrowed valleys of Tyrol ... His body vibrates but never for a second departs from its basic rhythm ... The nape of his neck is warm ... He is immensely good ..." Count Wolf Metternich, delegated as protector of the arts in Belgium and France, attached to the Wehrmacht high command, reopened the Louvre in the presence of Field Marshal von Rundstedt and Infantry General Streccius. The Jew Bergson was about to die in utter neglect. A Commission to Deprive Undesirables of French Citizenship was set up. Other commissions studied the application of the Nuremberg racial laws. An old scholar hid the documents of the age of shame in the cellars of the Musée de l'Homme.

Paris preserved unity only in its proud architecture: never would the waters or the skies of the Seine commit treason. Several cities, several different and mutually hostile lives were superimposed, one upon the other. There were the military staffs, the pleasures of the military staffs, the whisperings of governmental intrigues, the surveillances, the subterranean rivers of millions—marks and francs, merchandise, selected flesh, selected consciences, half consciences, quarter, eighth, and hundredth consciences. In the total blackout, music, fine wines, and amorous looks; Napoleonic soirées, where discreet field marshals suddenly appeared, surrounded by décolletés; where champagne bubbles mingled with state secrets; where men soon to be shot displayed great wit. Only a madman, Madame, could doubt in our continental victory. There were swastika flags, parades, uniforms; the member of the Fascist Grand Council at Maxim's; the aces of the Luftwaffe supping at Fouquet's with pretty girls from the Bal Tabarin; and the dead Métro stations and the living Métro stations, the resigned queues outside the grocery stores, the rackets in butter, cheese, chicken, cloth, paintings, jewels, authorizations from the military commandant, genealogical researches, cleansed birth records, falsifications of the past, falsifications of blood, great and petty circumventions of the law.

There were espionage, counterespionage, commissions, subcommissions, inspections, secret police in factories, banks, offices, railroad stations, trade unions, newspapers, prisons, apartment houses, brothels; raids on Masonic lodges, the archdiocese, the préfecture; all this produced reports, memoranda, dossiers, classifications, stool pigeons, arrests, flights, disappearances, sudden careers—and registrations, inventories, requisitions, confiscations, planning, Order. There were perilous clandestine traffickings, messages to prisoners, liberations at a price, mail to the other Zone at ten francs a letter. Horse cabs reappeared, woodburning autos appeared, bicycles were registered, great projects for urbanization were in the wind. Trains rolled eastward, loaded with machinery and raw materials, luxury articles, Normandy apples, potatoes, furloughed soldiers invigorated by Paris nights—and in the somber blue light of camouflaged railroad stations, trains full of severe casualties were arriving, disgorged their loads of the badly burned men, blind men, men with their genitals torn, men with their lungs crushed, men with tubes hanging out of their bellies.

And Félicien Mûrier, who had always felt the life of Paris in his veins and his nerves "from the Claridge to the squares of La Chapelle, from the flea market to the institute," passed in front of the Café de Flore but did not enter. "How sick I am of those faces, those scribes and Pharisees!" He remembered a dealer in wood and coal whom he had met on the dawn of the saddest day: Chabas, Chavas, or Cherras, Augustin. Now that fellow had the look of a man—a man like millions of others no doubt, lucid and silent.

Along the quays Mûrier entered that other Paris, strangely famil-iar, over which a fine autumn day spread a cloak of white mourning. On the threshold of the Hôtel Marquise a young man in a beret was smoking, his eyes said nothing. Outside Widow Prugnier's grocery store stood a sign: NO EGGS, NO SUGAR, NO SOAP, NO— But a colored poster pasted on the inside of the windowpane showed fatherly Wehrmacht soldiers surrounded by happy children. The door of Augustin Charras's shop was closed. Mûrier knocked gently, as though calling on a friend. The emptiness echoed behind the door. Now things began to happen quickly.

"This way, Monsieur," said the young man in the beret. "This way."

He had an anonymous but clinging look, pimply cheeks, and a flat mouth. "M. Charras is waiting for you," he said, leading Félicien Mûrier into the vestibule of the hotel. Bells began to ring violently, pursuing one another, playing leapfrog from one floor to the next, and out jumped figures in civilian clothes and pistol belts; several faces, noc-turnal in broad daylight, looked at the poet with dull coldness.

"What's going on here?" Félicien Mûrier asked heavily. "See here, I'm looking for M. Augustin Charras."

This statement sent someone running to the telephone. Two burly men looked him over from top to toe; in an instant he felt himself frisked, searched, imprisoned between their mechanical paws. "No resistance, eh, or I'll make jam out of your face. State Police."

Lord, here I am right in the middle of a murder film. Someone spoke German on the telephone: "*Ja, Herr Leutnant, gleich, Herr Leutnant, Jawohl, Herr Leutnant—*" A rat in a trap. Mûrier smiled stupidly at the farce while they slipped the handcuffs on him.

"See here, Messieurs, you're out of your minds." The answer was an imperative "Silence!" It was grotesque.

For a long moment he stood leaning against the wall between the toilet stinking of carbolic acid and the storeroom under the stairway, into which an enormous gray motorcycle thrust its giant handlebars like monstrous horns. A few feet away a young bruiser sat in a chair, contemplating his revolver. The rat's in his trap, toss it into a bucket of water. Ratface. It's funny. The outward world was growing perceptibly paler. The handcuffs were not uncomfortable but they provoked an itch behind his ears.

He broke the enormous menacing silence to say in his bantering tone, "Look here, young man, couldn't you take off these burglar's bracelets? I'd like to scratch behind my ear and have a butt. There's no harm in that, is there? And besides, that silly gun of yours is beginning to get on my nerves."

These simple words affected the bruiser with the revolver like a bomb going off in his chair. He leapt to his feet. A flash of frightened anger passed over his expressionless face. "Quiet. State police. You are under arrest."

"Oh, no," Mûrier replied calmly, "if there is still a shadow of law in Paris, you may be sure that I am not under arrest but that you soon will be, my boy."

The bruiser seemed about to leap at him, but nothing happened. Mûrier slouched over, a cold gloom penetrated his bones. A couple of young ruffians like piano movers picked him up and loaded him into a car, which brought him to the neighborhood police station. M. Carpe, acting captain, thrust into the room his gawky frame, his pince-nez, his black bow tie.

"You are the Gaullist? Last name, first name, identity?"

"I am Félicien Mûrier."

Someone guffawed. "Good name for a cocoon."*

"Profession, residence? Kike?"

"Man of letters—Rue Jacob. Anyhow this is a ridiculous misunderstanding. I demand that you immediately call the permanent secretary of the academy on the phone, he'll tell you who I am—or the Préfecture de Police."

"The old 'connections' story," M. Carpe answered soberly. "For the last eighteen years I've been hearing it twice a week. Come on now! You are associated with the bandit Charras?"

"No."

---

*Mûrier: mulberry tree, on whose branches silkworms build their cocoons.

"You have the impudence to deny it. You'll get over that. Lock him up."

A policeman vigorously shoved Mûrier into an empty cell. The poet felt nothing but a nauseous curiosity. A calm detachment from himself gave him two personalities. This fat man, handcuffed, rather ugly, slipping from one compartment to the next in a complicated rattrap—can that be me? It flashed through his mind that his manifest innocence made him invulnerable. What an absurdity! Innocence no longer existed, the laws no longer existed. And what am I innocent of? How am I to guess? The innocent are the guilty. There you have it. These reflections did not frighten him, for if there is no more innocence, there is no more crime, everything is just fine. The cell, ordinarily reserved for drunkards and whores, occasionally for a jealous murderer, a bicycle thief, a rude wino, contained only a bench and a slop jar; its only light came from the corridor through the wicket in the door; it exhaled a moderate but persistent stench of old urine, mold, and cold cigarette smoke. Less somber than it seemed at first glance, it did not give a sensation of absolute solitude. Why? Mûrier deciphered inscriptions on the wall as monotonously delirious as the unmentionable dream haunting the backstreets of Paris or the Boulevard Sébastopol between midnight and three o'clock in the morning. There were couplets, realistic yet stylized by obsession, visions of sodomy, hearts with daggers through them, a guillotine, profiles and eyes of women, and suddenly a transatlantic liner with three stacks giving off smoke which spelled out in a fine hand: "My desperrate love is on her way to Buenos Ayres." The word "desperate" seemed enriched by the two r's. The names written under the confidences and notices arranged themselves according to poetic harmony: Florelle, Gazelle, Bebert, l'Albert, Céline, Frangine, l'Astuce, la Luce and Dessalée and la Dragée, Hector from Les Batignolles and Monique-Fesses-Folles. Black constellation! Carnal specters, short but powerful, these beings had Herculean torsos, muscular thighs, enormous sex organs, little faces tinted with burst blood vessels, obscene tongues. The twilight penetrated the cell; with the dusk came a sense of forlornness—because these creatures all had felt it. Mûrier lay down on the bench, which was like the block of a guillotine, but he was facing the blade.

> Good evening widow, here's my head,
> —my heavy head without a halo—
> I am Félicien the Innocent,
> Take oh take my blood.

Officer Landois entered, preceded by a violent clanking of bolts. He brought bread, sausage, a half pint of red wine. He removed the prisoner's handcuffs. Before Mûrier had said a word he cried out in an angry voice, "You can shove your complaints up your ass! You're not at the Majestic here!"

And pressing his mouth to Mûrier's ear: "Augustin Charras has taken a powder. He's in the Free Zone. What can I do for you?"

"Notify my wife."

"That has been done."

Their two faces beamed with complicity. Landois slammed the door as he left. Mûrier knew one of the great joys of his life. Night fell, and he was left in the mutilated shadows; an abject yellow light, coming from the wicket, clung to the dirty wall, bringing out the Atlantic steamer and the long breasts of a Negress drawn with delirious concentration. Several prostitutes were locked into the neighboring cell. Every hour a policeman went *psst* at them through the wicket and they exchanged strange crotch jokes with him. Mûrier, falling into the torpor which precedes sleep, thought he could see them: they were not women but headless creatures consisting of broad spreading pelvises planted on long legs sheathed in black silk. They had one eye with a mad insolent stare, half-concealed in their pubic hair. "Ah, they are flumales."

Night spread over Paris. That this filthy prison should be only a few yards from a street where people were taking their evening strolls became hard to believe. Mûrier placed it in the midst of unknown catacombs, full of larvae, decomposed flesh, creeping fears, and disgusting pleasures. The shadowy Seine with its sudden reflections of moonlight passed over it, sweeping along its dead animals, its bluish corpses, its rotten vegetables, its undersized gudgeon. The Métro passed overhead, carrying its human cargoes—inconceivable. At what Alpine heights above him were the benches of the outer boulevards in the shade of moth-eaten trees, the bars, the enigmatic urinals, the numbered, partitioned houses and their commonplace histories, the cafés, the editorial offices, the rotary presses turning out great sheets of print covered with nonsense, lies, baseness—and a few rays of wit like pearly shells beneath the muck, pure fire under the dung. How to conceive the unlimited, multiple extravagance of reality? Mûrier, divided between fright, lyrical semilucidity and the calm of a reassuring despair, sank into an asphyxiating reverie. How could one ever rise from this underworld into what is believed to be "real life"? He was at the bottom of the sea. The men in the lost submarine listen to the fantastic sounds of the depths and discover the sole and ultimate reality, shapeless and nameless, destructive and chaotic, to which they already belong and which reigns in its immensity beneath the sea, beneath the countrysides, beneath the cities, beneath the delirium once taken for reality.

Bolts clanked, a flashlight beamed like a giant searchlight, belts and képis moved slowly through the oceanic mud pierced by the lunatic light. M. Carpe's pointed nose, the reflections of his glasses could be distinguished in the middle of this incoherent vision, and Félicien Mûrier heard himself grumble, "What now? The firing squad already, sons of bitches?"

But M. Carpe, acting precinct captain, was offering profuse apologies. "M. le Préfet himself has instructed me—" And so forth.

"This joint of yours is full of fleas," said Félicien Mûrier, sitting down again.

"Believe me, I infinitely regret it," said M. Carpe. "The budget allocated for the disinfection of these premises—" And so forth.

The poet reflected that some places could be disinfected only by dynamite.

"All right, all right, I'll go home. Why not? But I would like to have you give a good shampoo to those stupid young men who have been so imprudently equipped with armbands and firearms."

The stupid young men filled the narrow corridor. Passing by the cell where the whores were, Mûrier saw a pair of green eyes in the wicket. He halted and his respectful escort halted.

"Good evening, my charming ladies. Be of good cheer. May I request you, Monsieur le Commissaire, to send these delightful ladies some cigarettes, sandwiches, and good hot coffee at my expense?"

"Of course, Monsieur Félicien Mûrier."

And Green Eyes exclaimed, "Thanks, chubby, you've got a heart of gold. English cigarettes, OK . . . ?"

Outside the police station an automobile was vaguely discernible in the feeble violet light of a lamp under stars even feebler. Two gentlemen courteously requested Félicien Mûrier to accompany them to the 17th or 317th Bureau for a brief but indispensable interview. "As long as there are no fleas in your Bureau." The gentlemen made no reply. The auto slipped through the streets of a city dead for a thousand years, turned off into side streets, slipped elegantly around the statue of a general surrounded by somber figures that no doubt represented glory; and stopped in front of an indistinct housefront. The sudden illumination of a hotel lobby dazzled Mûrier, the mirrors in the elevator showed him his rumpled tie, his soiled collar, his puffed pale face, his hairy double chin "like pork rind." The 17th or 327th Bureau was a little Louis Quinze salon furnished with a sofa and a desk covered with beveled glass. Watercolors hung on the walls. A little portrait of Hitler stood on the mantelpiece between a candlestick and several books published by the Éditions de la Pléiade. Mûrier sat down on the sofa. Major Acker entered in uniform. Not until he was seated behind the desk did he greet the poet with a nod.

"Monsieur Mûrier, I deplore the necessity of questioning you. Though I cannot conceal from you that this affair may be extremely serious. Please believe me, it was my admiration for the great writer you are that led me to undertake this preliminary investigation which is not in my department."

Mûrier opened his hands with their dirt-encrusted nails.

"We seem to be acting in a bad play, Monsieur Acker. Here I knock on the door of a coal dealer, I'm collared, thrown into a foul hole of vermin, dragged up here at an hour when honest people are home in bed—or rather when poets used to roam the streets before a powerful army came here to prevent them ... It's completely idiotic and I can only expect apologies from Père Ubu himself. Do you know, Monsieur Acker, that you have aged in these few weeks? The hard trade of victory—"

But as he watched the officer's nervous fingers, the pockets under his eyes, his sad, faraway look, Félicien Mûrier realized that he was struggling in the void and that it might be dangerous. His cigarette went out, and he chewed on it without relighting it. Well, then it was dangerous—what of it?

"I don't want to play with your life, Monsieur Mûrier. Martial law is what it is. You may not believe me, but I attach importance to your life. I must ask you to answer me clearly, frankly if you can, weighing your words if your defense makes it necessary. In this case, take time to think. What are your relations with one Augustin Charras?"

"Why—nonexistent."

Acker turned a petrified stare upon Mûrier.

Mûrier told Acker about the dawn of June 14 on the banks of the Seine, not far from the Pont Sully, his encounters at Le Joyeux Matin bistro, the words he had exchanged with the courageous old man Augustin Charras. "And that's the whole story. I won't deny it, Monsieur Acker, those copy-pissers, my literary colleagues, rather nauseate me at this moment. They're often much too stupid and cowardly, you know that better than I do. I wanted to see other faces, good plebeian jowls, valiant and simple. I have no idea what this Charras may have done, but I would have enjoyed drinking a bottle of wine with him."

Acker listened and watched the speaker. With the shrewdness not of a magistrate, but of a man who had studied the psychoanalysts, finding significance in lapses, intonation, the position of fingers, facial expression.

"What you say is probably true, Monsieur Mûrier. I am relieved."

Acker might have added, "Besides, you've been shadowed several times and nothing out of the ordinary has been noticed. But our police can't do more than their best."

"Only you indicate a state of mind which I cannot approve."

"But I don't suppose that's the issue, is it?"

Acker came and sat down beside the poet. They were about the same age, with the same corpulence, the same essential interests in life.

"Why yes, as a matter of fact, that is the main issue, even if we two should deplore it. I am going to set you at provisional liberty. You will sign a promise not to leave Paris without our authorization. My report will be favorable to you, but I haven't the final decision in these matters. My department is that of cultural affairs, my dear Monsieur. The examination is over, I am speaking to you as a colleague, a modest colleague—we are two intellectuals."

"The conqueror and the conquered."

"Precisely, and that depended neither on you nor on me. Will you rally to victory or persevere in defeat? We are the masters of the future. History cannot be turned backward. Defeats are balance sheets that can't be corrected. Whether you agree or not—you and a few others—a France different from the one that has just succumbed will be born, magnetized by our will, incorporated into our continental organization. Those among you who take the road of resistance will provoke plenty of trouble but they will be crushed. I understand them, I respect them, but I can't do anything about it. Let the dead bury the dead, you know who said that. And Nietzsche: 'The dying must be helped to die.' All they will accomplish is to retard the recovery of your country, the reconstruction of our common country of Europe. Such, Maître, is the inexorable language of facts. Perhaps I might prefer it if the facts were somewhat different—less inexorable. But you and I can only understand and adapt ourselves to historic circumstances."

"You mean naked force?"

"Naked force if that term appeals to you. What is more real than that? If you associate yourself with impulsive fellows misled by noble, blind sentiments, you will kill a dozen poor soldiers on our side and you'll be shot, my dear poet, because—poet or baker, great mind or mediocre—you are subject to the general law. War is also natural law. The skull of a Beethoven offers no more resistance to a bullet than that of the humblest laborer. Our duty is to be objective, realistic. I might perhaps have preferred to live in the time of Goethe—or half a century from now, because there will be no room for new Goethes before then. These are absurdly subjective prejudices. The new Europe will make average men and great men of a new and unknown type. A firm beginning in the organization of the intellectual realm will provide for that. At first the organization will no doubt be excessive and clumsy—that's only human. I esteem you too highly to conceal the truth from you. You were in danger just now of a bullet in the neck, twelve bullets in the chest, the rope, or the guillotine, I don't know exactly which. And it would have grieved me."

"My preferences, subjective as you say, lie in the direction of the guillotine," Mûrier replied dreamily. "We have reinvented it after the Scotch, it removed the head of Chénier, Marie Roland, Lavoisier, Marie-Antoinette, Lucile and Camille Desmoulins—fine, thoughtful heads. It is an elementary machine, neat and Jacobin. Traditional and revolutionary. I favor the guillotine, Monsieur Acker."

If he was posing, it was involuntarily. Acker noticed that the poet's double chin trembled with nervousness. He seized the moment to say: "Be on your guard against literary masochism, Maître. You wouldn't have your choice. What you have told me is true? You give me your word of honor?"

"A hundred times. No, I wouldn't have my choice, that's true. Well, so much the worse. Masochism? By no means. It even seems to me that it would give me great pleasure to see several heads fall into the basket before my own."

Acker took a few steps on the carpet. Mûrier's reactions were making him feel ill at ease. "I belong to the old Europe too. If the roles were inverted, I . . . Monsieur Mûrier, you are incoherent, forgive me. You convince me of your innocence and you offer me your head as if I were Samson! I speak good sense to you and you talk nonsense. There are millions of Frenchmen like that, emotional, irrational, peaceful, and always ready to fall into hysteria. It is the cowards, the practical, supple fellows who get the better of you. You will need an inflexible master to save you, in spite of yourselves, from useless sufferings."

"You think so?" Mûrier gestured with his fleshy nose. His little eyes sparkled. "Incoherent, perhaps I am ... But I find you inconsistent. If the cowards win out, you have more to lose than I. How many millions of them are there in your superb imperial machinery? They'll desert you at the first sign of trouble, they'll survive you and bury you. You make a long face. You know as well as I do that the famous march of history isn't over. We had a Napoleon who won a lot of victories, from Madrid to Moscow. But France got over all the pomp and fanfares—which you are discovering a hundred and twenty years after us. I was a coward like everyone else, Monsieur Acker, that is to say, a peaceful fellow. I am no longer. If that's a crime—and it is—put that in your favorable report. You loot Paris, you set us up a government of timid little tadpoles, you bring ignominy and desolation upon us, and you expect all this to be understood, accepted as final, and blessed as though the creation of the world had ended at this moment."

Major Acker wrote.

"Sign here. Thank you. I'll have you taken home to avoid the patrols. I deplore your passion, Maître, I respect your misguided patriotism. In eighteen months, when England has been brought to reason, Europe pacified, you will come to us."

He did not believe it, but he knew the price of great names, the directives of the Propaganda Ministry, the importance of neutral opinion. "Let the Gestapo do its work, I'll do mine." Yet anxiety haunted certain compartments of his brain. We see a civilization ending, we do not know what is coming. He doubted the invasion of the British Isles, he weighed the complexity of the Russian problem, feared a conflict with the United States, remembered the victorious years of the other war and the black days that followed; he had in his bones an intuition of the tragedy that turns triumphs into defeats. Victories run down, nerves wear out. He often told himself that the old generation of Germans to which he belonged could serve honestly but could not change itself. Devoured in its soul by critical thought and dying humanism.

"You are free, Maître. I think that in spite of everything that divides us we can shake hands."

Mûrier, relapsing into his apparent nonchalance, but in reality tired, murmured, "Yes. We understand each other better than it seems. You are complex, multiple."

Major Erich-Friedrich Acker seemed to recede, though he did not budge, like a person seen through the wrong end of field glasses. He did not proffer his hand. His presence was opaque, his face hard and blurred. Mûrier thrust his hands into his pants pockets and hunched over a little. The objects in the room and this intellectual in uniform appeared to him through a deforming mist. He shook his head: Ah là là là—and followed a slender, long-necked aide decorated with the Iron Cross down the cream-colored corridor. Ah là là.

Clémence Mûrier held back tears of exasperation when she saw him. "You'll be the death of me yet, Félicien. You are irresponsible!"

He wanted only to eat, to get rid of his fleas, and sleep. Clémence's scene passed off on an oblique plane, somewhere between the absurd and the inevitable, in that commonplace region where nothing is more unreal than the tangible.

"I knew that miserable Jew would be your ruin—that Gaullist, he'd be only too glad to ruin you."

Mûrier, bending down by the open refrigerator, asked, "Isn't there any more cheese? What did you say about Nathan?"

"We were able to get you off this time. But your Nathan, you'll never see him again, he's at La Santé, at Vincennes, at La Petite Roquette, I don't know where, with an eye knocked out."

A bucket of ice water in the face would not have snapped Mûrier out of his torpor more quickly. The refrigerator became grotesque, his hunger vanished.

"Clémence, please forgive me. Poor Nathan had nothing to do with it. Leave me alone. I've got to get some sleep, I've got to get some sleep right away."

"And I've got to flee, and I've got to fight back, and I've got to . . ." he thought.

Two days later, between two and three in the morning, Félicien Mûrier crossed the demarcation line that separated occupied from unoccupied France. For several hours he waited, hidden in a large dark barn with a group of silent strangers, for the peasant woman to give the signal to go.

"The ground is hard," the woman said. "You'll hear the patrol pass. Last Tuesday they came in: there was nobody here, I was in luck! Don't speak, don't move."

His limbs were stiff with cold. This time the damp tunnel through the underground world led to hope—or despair. Over him he no longer had the stirring density of Paris, but a country sky, low and heavy, swollen with rain. Mûrier could not see his companions, they were only an animal presence. A young man thrashed around on the straw, the little bluish dial of his watch shone like an eye. He became aware of Mûrier.

"We have a good night," he said. "On starry nights the crossing is more dangerous. We'll make it." Dear musical constellations, you are danger!

"Listen."

The silence was broken by the clatter of swollen metallic insects on the road.

"They've passed!"

A woman, very young no doubt, burst into a shivering laugh. The farm boy opened a door on the clouds. "Follow me one by one. Put out your cigarettes. Don't make any noise."

Feeling the fresh air, Mûrier stood up straight. He went out fourth, next to last, in front of him a tall young girl in a beret danced up and down over the clods of earth, drunk with joy. "Oh little girl, big black will-o'-the-wisp—" Mûrier carried only a briefcase full of manuscripts, photographs, a razor, a shirt. The stranger from the barn in Limbo followed him.

Word was passed along the Indian file: "Watch out for the brook. Step on the three stones, three stones. It's deep."

The black will-o'-the-wisp turned around to pass this on to Mûrier, and he thought he could see her blue teeth.

"What's your name, Mademoiselle?"

"Francine."

"A pretty name. Permit me to call you Ariane for the moment."

They exchanged unseen smiles. Ariane-Francine held out her hand to the elderly gentleman to guide him across the black brook, which hissed like an angry snake.

"There's a steep hill to climb, hold on to the bushes, put your feet down flat, don't dislodge any pebbles."

Mûrier was out of breath. The stranger at the end of the file said, "Up there we're safe." The first in line sent some stones rolling down. Their sound spread terror, but the night closed over it like deep water. Keep going. At the top of the slope a clump of trees spread protecting branches over a clearing. The five travelers gathered in a semicircle and the farm boy explained to them: "You are in the Free Zone. Follow the path through the brush for three-quarters of an hour. The Jardelle girl is waiting for you at the crossing. You'll have to separate."

"Ariane, black will-o'-the-wisp," the poet called softly. The girl took his arm familiarly.

"What did you say? Well, you've got imagination. I weigh one hundred and ten, you know. Some will-o'-the-wisp!"

"It makes you dizzy to feel free," said Mûrier.

The stranger from the barn revealed a fine death's-head in tortoiseshell glasses.

"A free land? Some freedom, you'll see."

They walked together with a lively step, stumbling over roots. Two shadows ahead of them distrusted themselves and the universe: they moved apart and vanished beneath the first drops of rain. A little girl in wooden shoes detached herself from the shapeless trees; she was serious and in a hurry.

"Here you are. Separate. I'll take Mademoiselle with me. Follow at a distance."

Taking leave of the young woman, Mûrier held her long cold fingers for a moment with emotion. "Bon voyage, Mademoiselle Francine-Ariane. I have never seen you, I never will see you, yet we have gone a stretch of road together that I'll never forget."

"Ah, everything gets forgotten," she said. "Believe me. And how do we know?"

There was distress and laughter in her low voice. The rain was falling.

"If we hadn't forgotten the other war," said the stranger, "the world wouldn't be where it is. The power of forgetfulness is terrible. It is the true name of unconsciousness."

The young girl was already vanishing in the darkness of oblivion. The rain came down like a pale curtain. The stranger continued, "Our generation will not forget again. We're just beginning to awaken to reality, to harden ourselves. Ah, the things we'll do one day are inconceivable. My name is Lucien Thivrier, I am a teacher. I recognized you at the station, Monsieur Félicien Mûrier, you were hiding your face in your muffler, attracting attention. When you are hiding, you must leave your face free, it's safer. I have the greatest admiration for you. You are not a bourgeois poet. I wouldn't have let them arrest you. I have my little seven-shooter."

Without fear of appearing cowardly, Mûrier made a cowardly reply: "But then both of us would have been killed?"

"Isn't that better?"

"Yes . . . And thank you."

Mûrier raised himself erect and the rain gently whipped his face. For years he had not walked with this firm step on the damp, invisible, solid earth.

"If you wish, Monsieur Mûrier, I'll lead you. I'm at home in this region. We'll have a cup of hot coffee with a signalman I know, he listens to the BBC and he'll tell us the news. We'll sleep a couple of hours and take the first bus."

17. ANTON CHERNIAK

No one in the world knows what a man can suffer opening a window. But Cherniak knew. As long as the closed shutters protected him from daylight and the warmth of his sheets, favorable to the unconscious, recalled the warmth of the womb, life seemed suspended. The semidarkness was so comforting that occasionally, repulsing the hostile light that filtered through the defenses, he lit a candle, took a book, preferably a medieval romance, read a page, and even felt the desire to write something intelligent. Then he closed the *Loves of Lancelot of the Lake*, quickly blew out the candle, rolled up into a ball, and tried to dive back into limbo, pulling the sheets over his eyes. But a moment inexorably arrived each day when the window had to be opened, when one had to return to life—why? An average life consisted of sixty years, or about twenty-two thousand days. Crushing arithmetic! And supposing only three hundred, two hundred, one hundred days remained to him before—(*before what?*)—That was even worse. Not so many mornings would pass *before*—Cherniak opened the window with a determined gesture, with sad resolve, the way a man loads his revolver—dreaded and alluring. In the yard little red chicks were moving about under a merciless shower of light.

Véronique was clanking the squeaky pulley at the well; then carrying the pail of water toward the house, her left arm half-extended, her head raised in a friendly smile to the lodger's window. "Should I bring you your breakfast, Monsieur Karel?" The massive coil of her hair seemed to press her head back as though it were a savage ornament of black bronze. With her hazel eyes and round pink cheeks, she resembled a little Bohemian peasant girl. All she had on was a blue blouse and short black petticoat covered with specks of straw, she was barefoot, and her feet would make a moist slapping sound on the stairs. Her bare arms would still be full of light.

"Yes, yes," said Cherniak quickly.

The yard was separated from the orchard only by a low board fence of an attractive ashy gray. Hills rose up beyond the orchards; beyond the graceful broad hills lay the sea.

Véronique brought in a tray with two slices of gray-brown bread and a cup of black coffee.

"There's nothing to be had at the market," she said, just to be saying something. "No more butter, no more anything. And the women are beginning to scratch each other's eyes out for the potatoes. I put a piece of my sugar in your coffee, Monsieur Karel."

He thanked her. The strange look—full of fear and of mad gaiety underneath the fear—that poured over her from the weary brown eyes of this solitary, sickly, unhappy man was to Véronique like the big raindrops that fall on your neck at the beginning of a storm. You run away but you'd like to get wringing wet, your breasts, your belly, and all.

"And there's this paper that's come for you from the gendarmerie. I hope it's nothing bad."

"Oh no, nothing but a summons from the foreigners' section at the préfecture: '...is requested to report...with identification papers... at the... Screening Depot for investigation and regularization...'" Cherniak swallowed his spittle.

"It's trouble, Nique."

The girl came closer.

"Bad trouble?"

Bitterly, with trembling lips, he asked, "What difference can it make to you, Nique?"

The servant girl came even closer, touched.

"I just wouldn't like you to have any bad troubles."

She thought foolishly: You aren't bad, no, you're not. You wouldn't hurt a fly, you wouldn't. You, you aren't like the others. There must have been some women who made you suffer, yes, that must be it. I'm sure you didn't make them suffer. You're so comfortable in this room. I only hope they don't make you leave it, with this damned war. Reluctantly she whispered, "Is it bad?"

"No worse than lung cancer," he said derisively, because he didn't want her to understand and because he felt like slapping her—on her pretty full-blown cheeks, smooth and pink, covered with down like ripe peaches.

"Real trouble, then?"

The frank glance in the amber-flecked pupils seized on the bad news. Véronique bent her head. Her blood-infused lips were swollen into the pout of an upset child. Her nipples stood out under her blouse, the smell of her armpits wafted.

"My God," she said. "so much unhappiness on every side..."

A reddish ray of light tinged the bronze coil of her hair and her large wide-open mouth was smiling broadly, red, white, and compact, with the voluptuous innocence of certain tropical flowers. Her raised upper lip revealed a fringe of violet gum.

"Lung cancer, kick in the face, straw mattresses at Gurs, a bullet in the groin," thought Cherniak mechanically, accustomed to turn out strictly equivalent comparisons in series. "I shall never see these tropical flowers again." He felt hot, so hot that he began to pant. His muscles, forgotten, acted of their own accord, he took Véronique in his arms and his mouth sought a thirst-quenching freshness in the hollow of her arm. But once in contact with this firm, smooth, moist body, he perceived the coldness of his own lips, the inner trembling of his being, frozen in spite of the hot madness running through him. I'm all washed up, Nique, Véronique.

"Everything will come out all right, Monsieur Karel," the servant girl murmured, her eyes half-closed under his convulsive embrace.

Fortunately a man's hands sometimes follow their own path; and when this man's hands touched the woman's thighs and breasts the vigor of living came back to him from afar, from beyond the deserts of desolation.

Véronique, lucid in her enchanted confusion, said, so softly that he could hardly hear her, "Push the bolt, Monsieur Karel."

United, they moved like a swaying pendulum across the room to the door, from the door to the bed. "Your mouth is cold." You feel faint, she thought vaguely, and then strength comes back to you, you don't know how, you're like a mother who would like to devour her little baby. You open, all of you entirely. "Let me warm your mouth." They rolled on the blankets. How feeble I am. Finished, finished, jump in the ocean, Cherniak, you're disgusting. But abandoned beneath him, her eyes half-closed, breathing so deeply that her breasts and belly created a comforting swell, Véronique magically caressed his temples with her rough palms. The intense blue line of the Mediterranean stretching across the hills lifted Cherniak up, the sea-taste of a drop of blood on Véronique's lips raised a painful virility in him. He moaned. The young woman received him in peace, resisting and defeated. Then, raising himself on his elbows, his face changed by radiant frenzy, he asked himself: What remains of the man when the beast is finished?

Véronique opened her eyes. "No trouble that lasts forever!" she said gravely.

Jumping to her feet, glowing with a confused happiness, she smoothed down her black petticoat with both hands.

"You won't think ill of me, Monsieur Karel . . . Karel? You could love me a little, couldn't you?"

He caressed her from her round shoulders to her ears and to the line of her hair, like a master. "Be still, Nique."

"Your troubles will straighten themselves out, won't they, Monsieur Karel? . . . Karel? Would you like me to ask Mme Gilles to speak to the mayor about you? Mme Gilles is already looking after my prisoner."

"Don't worry about me, Nique, sweet Nique."

Véronique's cool footsteps died away down the old wooden stairs. Cherniak admired Nique's bare feet, broad, with big detached toes and noble nails; their sculptural curves were gilded with dust. They stood firmly on the ground, proudly they carried Nique—short, broad, and muscular like the statues of Aristide Maillol. To hell with statuary: Nique alive!

The nervous shock, the organic illumination, the recovered power of contentment brought back a simple lucidity, a resolute calm, ordinary but precise movements. I am cured. He shaved without cutting himself by the pocket mirror he had filched one night of melancholy drunkenness from the compact of a homely prostitute on Rue Broca. He tossed it out of the window onto a little pile of stones and nettles, the little disk gleamed in the air, then broke into a thousand fragments on the gravel. Our desires are accomplished by chance.

The absurd Lilliputian locomotive—ataxic, asthmatic, whistling, sizzling, spitting, straight out of an illustrated magazine from the Second Empire—was already hauling its three little piss-green cars toward the quarries, the distillery, the vineyards by the sea; it was panting along at its tired top speed when Cherniak caught it on the run. He jumped on the running board and sat down on it to look at the landscape, which he detested, which he found pleasant. His mind wandered. "Sweet Nique, Véronique—" She came in without knowing what he was doing, without knowing what she wanted, her veins singing, she gave him back his strength, she gave him the signal. The recompense and the signal . . .

At the thought of meeting Jacob Kaaden, Cherniak resumed his usual expression, morose, aggressively discouraged. Kaaden, the barbarian, the primitive trade unionist, collector of dead texts and fossilized hopes, Comrade Fallacious, in a word, all the more detestable in that he was necessary —Kaaden was working legally for a socialist wine grower, and maintaining liaison between the Aid Committee and the comrades in the department, several of whom were in hiding. The little money received from New York or Marseille passed through his hands. He attended to the complicated business of obtaining visas, and corresponded with the concentration camps under various names; in a fisherman's café he had met a blond young Gaullist who was negotiating—somewhere in Wonderland—for the purchase of a sailing vessel on board of which he planned to make contact with a problematical British patrol on the high seas. Cherniak had asked for a berth on this phantom ship, ghoulishly delighted at the prospect of jumping overboard if a coast guard should stop them. "It's only the first mouthful that counts," said Paul Claudel, after which you become that indefinable being or that unthinkable thing, a drowned man.

Kaaden in a leather apron was standing in the gateway of the farmyard, holding an enormous pair of blacksmith's pincers. With his bony nose, angular chin, and red hair—Cherniak thought—he was the ideal proletarian for a naive artist, the schematic corporal in a Germanic socialist army. (That is how Cherniak saw him.) The stone arch of the gateway sliced sharply across the sky. The long metallic tentacles of an agricultural machine, looking like a prehistoric insect, proclaimed the absurdity of technology. The two comrades sat down on a stone in the shade. The nearby field was radiant.

"You look well, Cherniak."

"So it seems. It's easy to say, anyway."

"You do look well, Cherniak. I'm not making it up. Drop your constipated mannerisms for a moment. The bombing of London has been a failure, that's a big point. Goering's blunder makes a negotiated peace impossible. You see, the lords can send their children to Canada but the people have to stay."

"You're still sustaining yourself on international politics, Jacob, you have a strong stomach. Where will we be when it begins to produce the humanitarian flowers and bureaucratic mushrooms of the future society?"

Kaaden did not lose patience with this neurotic. He watched a gray lizard describing commas in the scorched grass.

"We will be there, you and I—or many others will be there without us."

"What about the boat?"

"Fallen through again. But we have something less adventurous in view at Sète—a coasting steamer bound for Valencia. Three thousand francs. And the captain undertakes to get you ashore."

"And into prison in Spain free of charge, eh? *Muchas gracias*. What about the visas?"

"The State Department is studying the lists, it may take another month or two. Your chances are better than mine, they have a preference for pen pushers. Honduras, doubtful and too expensive. Mexico, reserved for real or fake Spaniards. San Domingo reserved for Jews with pull in New York. Siam, not expensive, a hundred francs, a bargain, but discredited: no transits. Exit visas going up, the prices have tripled at Vichy—beyond the means of the Committee."

"I can understand that," said Cherniak bitterly.

"An armistice commission has arrived at Montpellier, it's combing the lists of foreigners."

Cherniak fished in his pocket and brought out a piece of paper rolled in a ball: his summons. Kaaden frowned, bared his teeth and went: hum, hum.

"They've put the finger on you, old man. That's not good." And nonchalantly: "They killed a Spaniard in that screening depot three weeks ago. But some get out alive. I can call on Abbé Munier. He'll do whatever he can for you. And I advise a change of air. We can hide you here for a little while: you can play the farmhand, stir up the manure, feed the horses, it will remind you of the *Georgics*. I'll give you one of the farmers' draft cards and you can slip off to Marseille."

"Without safe-conduct?"

"Nothing we can do about that. You'll take little backwoods bus lines and a roundabout route. It'll take you a week. I can get you a voting card too. But do you look like a voter from Hérault by the name of Hyppolite-Césaire Nicaise? I'll come and get your suitcase tomorrow."

Kaaden juggled his blacksmith's tongs, which left thick stains of soot on his hands. Cherniak looked around at the dead earth cleft by drought.

"Good," he said. "I'll go and have a look at the sea. I've got time before the train gets back. That implement of yours exasperates me."

Kaaden tossed the black tongs into the thistles.

"Take a good look at the sea. Every time I go there it winds me up. Go to the end of the cliffs at Les Riches, they make a cape, an enormous tooth of warm granite, broken off at the end. You'll see the waves coming in for an endless, inevitable battle, a battle without anger, without the possibility of discouragement. It's the energy of

the world, free, self-sufficient, happy to exist. You'll see great yellow
fish sliding along, happy to exist. You'll see naked energy—"

"That's enough," said Cherniak irritably. "Naked energy...OK.
See you tomorrow."

The word "naked" touched a pleasantly raw fiber inside him.
Cherniak entered into the incandescence of the South. Parched fields
slanted toward the beaches. A stony path sloped gently down toward
the Dent des Roches. The overheated air sent transparent flames
creeping along the ground, and the incandescent white stones dazzled
him. Cherniak felt the breath of a furnace; he lost all substance and
heaviness and shriveled like a paper doll sucked up by fire. He hopped
along on tiptoe, a slight dizziness kept him from thinking, made his
arms flutter, shook the tufts of his hair as though he were dancing.
"Well, Dionysiac jumping jack, where is your shadow? Have you lost
your shadow?" He laughed from the bottom of his soul. The shadow,
reduced to nothing, bobbed about beneath him. "Trample the rest
of it."

Solitude, rocks, a few bristling bushes, and the igneous white
beach, all were absorbed into sizzling, sparkling heat. "Naked absurdity. The French have invented the perfect word for the clouds or the
sky: *la nue*—homonym for *la nue*, the female nude. The solar fire in
the zenith reigned abstractly. "No more memories, wonder of wonders.
Memories, a heavy shadow. Véronique—*nue*." His laughter disturbed
nothing in the crystalline space. The soft monotonous roar of the sea
rose up to him.

Made up of harsh and black violet rocks licked by invisible tongues
of flame, which turned them reddish in places, the Dent des Roches
slanted out toward the Golfe du Lion. What paranoiac had invented
geometry? Cosmic shapes defied it. Everything rational was false. The
summit of the cliffs offered a pleasant narrow path that went over
two fantastic rock slides whose base was surrounded by seething
foam; only a few yards beyond the miniature maelstroms the fiery
water abandoned itself to a rolling lethargy. On the horizon, beyond
the sea and shining sky, a faint sand bar went on melting away.

Cherniak moved with an impalpable, almost incorporeal step

toward this world's end. The breath of the celestial furnace carried him away. Consciousness of another reality came to him fleetingly. "To hell with visas! Europe gone rotten. America drunk on dollars, electricity, egotism." The summons of the Foreigners Affairs Department was an odious wad of paper—he flipped it into the air and it lost itself in a tranquil spout of spray traversed by rainbows.

The Dent des Roches ended in a sharp, vertical promontory, tall as the Himalayas—over a hundred feet. The impact of the waves, the underwater cannonades, the explosions of foam created only a delicate liquid lace at the base of the wild, flaming granite spur. Karel Cherniak sat down at the edge of the abyss, his legs dangling over the immeasurable vastness. The comic ugliness of his goose shit–colored shoes, bought on the Place de la République, distracted him with their humiliation. Folding his legs under him, he unlaced them with disgust, let them fall. His darned socks, soiled and sweaty, holes at the heels and toes, sickened him even more; he took them off and threw them over his shoulder in order to avoid offending the shifting lace of the waves. I shouldn't have thrown away my shoes. Do I always have to do these foul nonsensical things? His bare feet in the limitless light were even more lamentable. He turned away from them to the glassy arc of the horizon. His eyes filled with tears, although at the same time irrepressible laughter burst out in his brain. Simply, with a spontaneous movement of his wrists, Cherniak gave the rock under him a shove, leaned out toward the vague abyss, caught a stifled breath, slipped imperceptibly from the earth, his two arms thrust forward like atrophied wings.

18. FRENCH NATIONAL RAILWAY

HAVING arrived at a station in the danger zone, Augustin Charras and Julien Dupin had no idea what to do. Julien was full of fear, and went to the urinal every ten minutes. Charras felt a fatherly irritation.

"The heebie-jeebies, I've had 'em a few times, Julien—for instance at Neuve-Chapelle, in 1915, at zero hour when they were passing the hooch around in the trench. Up to then the fear had been asleep in my stomach, rolled up in a ball; but now it seemed to get up and bark loudly enough to burst my eardrums. I saw the earth, green and black with rotten flesh, I saw myself lying on it with my guts out, trying to collect them under my jacket. And I flew into a fury at my guts and at my carcass that was trembling all around them. I was disgusted with myself, boy. And that's the cure. Get disgusted with yourself, you'll see how it picks you up."

"If they collar us," Julien replied humbly, "will they hang us?"

"In the first place, it's not absolutely sure. And if they did, you'd hear some yell out of me. It would be a small satisfaction but a real one. You've got to get up a rage before you swallow the last pill."

They were at the station buffet; field-gray soldiers on furlough, seated a few feet away, were gravely examining pictures of naked women. An old railroad hand—worn to the very soul from sitting in the yellow light of bistros, from inspecting tracks in the rain, from filling out administrative forms, from checking signals, from cursing into the fog to make things run—gave them a lugubrious smile.

"You look like two pieces of unclaimed baggage," he said to them familiarly. "I can see by your faces that you're trying to pass the line. Don't waste your time saying no. Mustn't look like a funeral, young

man, I've seen plenty of guys caught just by the look on their face."
He concluded, "If you'll trust me, I'll cross you over right under
Himmler's nose. OK?"

Julien turned pale. To say yes might be fatal. Charras looked the
man over with penetrating sympathy. He assented with his eyelids
and his lips.

"Your price?"

"Don't be foolish. We're Frenchmen. My price is the pleasure of
putting one over on them. When I've brought five hundred across
and they send me to the Konz-Lag, maybe one of the five hundred
will even the score."

"I wish it could be me," said Charras.

In a blue smock and railroad cap, Charras looked the part of
second engineer on the giant locomotive. At the control station Julien
went along the train, absurdly tapping the hub of the wheels with a
hammer. It was all he could do to keep from passing water in his
pants, but when he nearly bumped into a German noncom getting
out of a third-class carriage, he cursed with such natural ill-humor
that the soldier gave a friendly grunt. Then Julien sat down in plain
view, on a pile of crates on a freight car. His life hung by a hair but it
wasn't too unpleasant, because he didn't know it. The dawn was
dismal white, the freshly sprinkled cinders of the roadbed gave off a
mineral smell, there was a jangling of bumpers as cars were coupled
together, sparrows hopped up and down on the platform. A paunchy
noncom of the German security police stepped up to two women
whose travel permits demanded a thorough examination. The engineer
said to Charras, "The ones whose papers are in order get pestered the
most. It seems like they were never completely in order. It would take
a five-legged calf to meet all the requirements nowadays."

"Is he tough?" Charras inquired.

"Oh, he's not so bad. At first he was a little too zealous. Until one
foggy night he was standing between the tracks and a bottle hit him
square in the glasses; since then he takes things easier. He's bearable.
Wait, I'll heat him up for you."

The engine, from deep in its shining viscera, suddenly spat

clouds of burning steam. The tasseled turkey cock led away the two ladies.

"He's going to make them miss the train just for the pleasure of talking and tying up red tape. That's the only fun he gets out of life. He used to sell soup and beer in Bavaria."

The train started off across colorless plains. The trees were bent low. The engine growled rhythmically, like a colossal beast drunk with its own power. The engineer wiped his face.

"The other France," he said, pointing with his elbow. "Now there's nothing to be afraid of but our own Nazis. They pulled a fast one on us. They got even with us for occupying the factories!"

Charras replied, "Politics and I have never been bedfellows. We should have been strong and carried things through or else not started in putting a scare into the moneybags. The moneybags have jumpy nerves, like ladies with their migraines. We didn't know what we wanted: paid vacations, the forty-hour week, nationalization of the factories, intervention in Spain, a real uprising—or a nice friendly revolution, nonintervention, a breathing spell, an Exposition. We should have become hard. It's a time for hard men."

"We couldn't, old man. It's not man who makes life, it's life that makes man. And we wanted life for man, the pleasure of living, you know what I mean. That way of looking at things doesn't turn out fighters. We had convenient illusions, we took the avalanche for a good joke, the bosses' bombs for slightly excessive little gewgaws, the Maginot Line for a miraculous invention, Munich for a triumph of peace. All in all, we ate ourselves silly. I'd just bought a motorbike and a set of furniture on the installment plan, no one felt like having his face smashed in for a general strike—let alone for Czechoslovakia. We had no good reason to imitate revolutions that turn into dictatorships and grind out trials and firing squads in mass production and betrayals to make your hair stand on end ... We didn't know that everything hangs together, that a little massacre in Berlin or Barcelona leads to bigger massacres on the Somme. Massacres are mighty contagious. We are undertaking our advanced studies now, old man, if it isn't too late."

"The war will last ten years," said Charras. "It will travel around the world. Humanity is sick, as if from epilepsy. Since she can't drop dead all at once, Humanity, she'll have to get well one day...What we need to do now is become men who are hard, who are careful, who are patient, and who will never ever forgive any of them."

The telegraph wires cut an undulating line through the landscape with their rising and falling waves. Past the smooth flanks of the engine, the two men saw the curve of the rails, narrow in the distance, growing wider as they approached. The air was damp, at the stations nerve-shattering sirens were blowing. The day was ending. Trains coming in the other direction burst upon them with a roar of calamity. The headlights cast their dry beams on the immutable, broadening rails. Charras and the engineer spoke little. They were covered with grime, sometimes they were too hot, but when they leaned out to escape the oil fumes the cold pinched their faces. The engineer unburdened himself in disjointed phrases.

"What a life! These fine Creusot locomotives, one fine day they jump the track as if they couldn't bear to go on—as if they'd had enough of this crummy world. Between you and me, the oil we burn is shit; they weigh it, check it, save it—well, I throw it in the ditch whenever I get a chance. They make more of a stink about it than if you ran over a man. They send the good engines up north on some pretext; and when I know that the one I'm driving will never be seen again I attend to it, I do a little engineering in reverse, a bolt here, a little sand there, a nut loosened somewhere else—it gives me a toothache to think of it, but that's just too bad. Locomotives are no whores. I give it twenty-four hours before total paralysis sets in...Last month, in the East, some of the boys did a job on the tracks, and a train full of requisitioned armaments quietly lay down in a ravine...I saw it. New machinery all over the hillside, the cars all in a heap, the French agents took a little punishment for their helpful spirit, the German detail was squashed like flies on a wall...Are you listening? You're not saying anything? You don't like it. Go ahead and tell me if you don't. Do you think I like it?"

"That human beings should come to such a pass," said Charras. "That's what turns me to stone."

At dawn, in a sleeping station at Corrèze, they took each other's names down in their notebooks, moistening the same pencil with their tongues.

"I hope we get together someday," said Charras. "Someday, years from now, if we come out alive. You're young, let me give you a piece of advice. Don't expose yourself any more than you have to. We've got to preserve ourselves."

The engineer winked. "I'm not as dumb as all that. I do everything out in the open. I belong to the Rassemblement National, Monsieur. I read *L'Oeuvre* the way a priest reads his missal. I know by heart twenty-five of Doriot's old saws about plutocracy, judeocracy, masonocracy, imbecilocracy, the New Order, the European Revolution—as they call their international counterrevolution. I keep up with things, and I'm not the only one. We've thought up a gag that can't miss—to make hash out of their propaganda: we push it just a little too far, an excess of goodwill, see? The people gape at you, the ones in the know scratch the right side of their ass. Suppose Déat announces the disintegration of the British Empire, all you have to do is repeat what he says, only simplify a little: Why, your perfidious Albion is all washed up, I'm telling you there's no such thing, no need to invade the British Isles, that's why they didn't even attempt it—Hitler only had to give the signal, England was down and out, her navy is nothing but a bluff, but Hitler is human, the blockade was enough for him. No need for an invasion—that hit the mark. After that, you recite the old refrain about the proud, defeated nation working honorably hand in hand with the generous conqueror: don't forget his generosity. If the newspapers start saying that the Parisians are having a fine time, with potatoes coming in from Westphalia, you add that lard is expected from Nuremberg, ham from Hanover, and that life will be perfect this winter without Léon Blum. I'm giving you the formula, it may come in handy this side of the demarcation line. The marshal is more alert than he was at twenty, Mossieu. He has the Boches scared out of their wits. Three hundred thousand prisoners are coming home at the end of the month, Mossieu. That'll stop the idiots of the Legion. You can end up by saying that we ought to declare war on England and mobilize under the Francist banner with enthusiasm. With the youth this line is irresistible. And if you're speaking to women lined up outside a grocery store, you explain to them that the rations are entirely sufficient for the maintenance of French health, that they are even a little excessive in fats, in fact a Nazi scientist has proved it. You add that Adolf is a vegetarian and that his health is only the better for it. Then you run away quick because the housekeepers might make it hot for you. They've a little more sense than the Legion."

The three-minute stop was over and they were still laughing. Charras jumped out of the engine. The station stood indistinct in a vast countryside. Julien Dupin crawled out of his freight car and heaved a deep sigh.

"We are saved."

"Anyone who thinks he is saved today," thought Charras, "is lost." But he affected good humor. They washed at the pump, changed clothes, and looked around them at the cold rusty earth under the damp dawning light. One hill was pink; another, half-hidden by the fog, was copper at the summit. To stretch their legs, they went down the most deserted road in the world. The barking of dogs, the crowing of cocks, floated in space. Charras stopped on the slope. Stretches of valley and field mingled with the wooded crests. High in the heavens golden beaches descended to an ocean of pink light. Azure blue of a wondrous lightness spread through the sky. Charras suddenly looked grave and muttered something in his mustache.

"What? What's that you say?"

Augustin looked down upon his companion with so much hardness in his pale face that the young man felt ill at ease.

"I said, peace on earth, my boy."

Some betray, others close their eyes. Still others pretend to betray, they lie and betray the betrayal. They bleed, they swallow down their envenomed fury and laugh. Those who look after magnificent locomotives derail trains; peaceful men kill too, all crushed under the

same train—murderers, innocents, or poor slobs, Boches or Franzo-
sen, who would rather have stayed home. Bombs fall on cities. France
is cut in two, in a hundred pieces. No one knows what will become
of him. The harvest of these fields will be looted. Men who should
be breathing in this dawn, who should be emerging from their houses
whistling and going to work over these roads, are rotting in the stalags:
hunger twists their bowels, gloom spins in their brains. Their women
shed tears and sleep around. And the earth is beautiful, somber, illuminated, damp, rusty, peaceful—nothing affects her, she is stronger than all, wiser than all. One would really like to understand what
she is. Oh, God!

Charras gazed fiercely at the countryside, which he had not seen
for years. How can a man live without seeing the earth? Is that living?
The earth gave him back a cold strength—beyond hope and fear.

"Monsieur Augustin," said Julien. "It's near train time."

"To hell with it."

A weakling this boy was, the earth did not speak to him. He was
all worry and lamentation, he was afraid to report to a demobilization
office, he was afraid not to report, he would always be afraid of missing the train, he would never understand walking aimlessly, resolutely,
over unknown roads. He was cut out to be a civil servant; in times
like these, cut out to be a victim.

"One train or another, Julien, what does it matter to us? It's beautiful out!"

The nameless countryside, the unknown earth, frightened Julien.
On their way back to the station, he spoke: "Don't you think, Monsieur Augustin, that I'll be able to go back north soon? Things must
be beginning to settle down. I'm entitled to have my job back."

"That's an idea you'd better get rid of, my boy. No one will go back
to the fold. Not you, not anyone else. There's no more fold. No one
can guess when things will settle down or even whether they'll do so
in our lifetime. You're not a soldier or a civil servant anymore, or a
voter or a citizen—or anything else either. You have nothing but
yourself and the land that you don't know and that doesn't know you.
Do you know what we are? We're a couple of dead men that the firing

squad barely missed. I congratulate you, you can congratulate me. What a joy it is!

Domestic comfort and Sunday games of *boules* continued in the towns of the South. The refugees were not liked. Why didn't they agree to be repatriated? Did they prefer, rather, to eat other people's bread, send prices skyrocketing, apply for rations, steal bicycles on the road? The Legion paraded on the squares, solemn masses were intoned, and the Rue Jean-Jacques Rousseau had its name changed because the author of *The Social Contract* had sown the worst illusions. Did he really believe in the underlying goodness of man? Our generation is better informed on that score. The Rue Jean-Jaurès had its name changed too. "Why he did more to destroy France than a hundred armored divisions." —"But, Monsieur, there were no armored divisions in the days when Jaurès was demanding social justice. Would we have been so weak if we had established a just society, if Europe..." —"In any case, Monsieur, schoolteachers who maintain the cult of Jaurès deserve to be fired or sent to a concentration camp, I say."

The Rue Pierre-Curie, the Avenue Émile-Zola, the Cours Anatole-France all had their names changed—we've had quite enough of the alien (alien by marriage), the Great Fecal, and Anatole-*Un*france, let's hear no more about them. Some gentlemen in black looked on while the bust of the Republic was being moved out of the banquet room in City Hall. "Put her in the attic," said one of them quietly to the movers—"take care not to break her." Who knows? Nothing is finished. We might need old Marianne again.

These events were no more important than the Luftwaffe's victories, the changes in the stable government of Vichy, the battles in Ethiopia... Reality began with ration cards, lines of housewives outside the shops, the price of carrots, the nutritive qualities of the squirrel, the sparrow hawk, the crow, the fat carp poached in the castle pond. Reality began with the recantations of Freemasons, Socialists, Communists, Radical civil servants—amid mental reservations, of course, and with an effort to persuade themselves that a new historic epoch was beginning during which it would be best to lie low—sincerely if possible. Reality, tightening like the silk cords the Mongols use for strangling, appeared with the postcard marked STALAG 214, said to be near Königsberg. "Where is Königsberg?" —"Why, it's in East Prussia, not far from Danzig, it used to be mentioned in the newspapers. It was at Königsberg that a philosopher named Kant, Immanuel . . ." —"Oh, no, don't talk to me about philosophers, particularly Boche philosophers." The boy's alive, will he still be alive in a month? They have half of our young men in their stalags, will they ever give them back, winners or losers, what do you think, Madame?" —"The Vatican is interceding in favor of the prisoners, my good woman, a minister for prisoners of war is being appointed at Vichy, he's a veteran of the other war himself, he's blind, he has a good heart. It is even said, Madame, that he has become deaf and dumb, in that job it was the only way to preserve his heart."

Printed postcard forms brought news from the occupied zone. *I am fine, Aunt Elodie is sick*—would that mean in prison? *We expect to celebrate St. Vitus Day waltzing at Uncle Buffet's.* Do you get that? They're dancing the St. Vitus dance in front of the bare buffet. Their nerves are shot. The postman brought back reply cards all blue-penciled: *Inadmissible. Content strictly limited to family matters . . .* Have you tasted soybean sausage, Monsieur? It isn't very attractive, you'd think it was a turd, but they assure us that it contains vegetable oils—and the Manchus, if the rumor is to be believed, have lived on nothing else for centuries. —Lucky Manchus! Get me a pound anyway, since you're on such good terms with the butcher woman.

The newspapers contained missing-persons columns for the benefit of dispersed families. These ads had only recently been for the benefit of lost soldiers looking for their units. Mme Pierre Durand of Valenciennes was now seeking news of her children—Yves, ten, and Céline, thirteen, lost in June on the road from Guéret to Limoges—reward. Corporal Mathieu of Beauvais gave his address and requested news of his wife Elise, née Vandoeuvre, a refugee at Tours . . . Fill in the complications yourself. The Refugee Bureau filed millions of cards of this sort; the movies showed young girls diligently studying heaps of these notices and the tearful grandmother who, thanks to our tutelary administration, had found her grandchildren. Ah, the movies! A plump smiling star, oh so well fed, draped in a white cape, presented a pennant to young soldiers in white gloves and berets as the drums rolled. Palm trees in the Pacific moonlight, the young woman from Hollywood, in moonlit silk, fainting in the arms of the gallant gentleman, the close-up of the handsome, tuxedoed murderer, face impassive, among the dancers; the happy Negro musicians, the detectives, the old bankers...The climax of the script. But the only thing that moved the audience was the sight of a turkey being carved on the screen—oh, ah, ah, oooh...The radio announcer reminded his audience that Jeanne d'Arc had saved France and that the marshal had made the gift of his person to the country; the ration of "national coffee" would be reduced after the first of the month, unused sugar coupons would be valid until the tenth. M. Philippe Henriot in *Gringoire* extolled the abolition of divorce, which would restore the happiness of family life. M. Henri Béraud wrote that English is not a language but at most a dialect...The Armistice Commission demanded an inventory of the department's stocks. All tires were requisitioned.

Charras lost his taste for life. His whole day centered around the arrival of the mail. As he stood in line, he envied the little lame woman going away with a letter. For a moment he closed his eyes, saying, "If I count up to twenty-seven before the line moves..." At "twenty-three," the brown-jacketed discharged soldier ahead of him took a step forward. Charras studied the features of the woman at the window, he concentrated so much attention on the young woman's hands that a cramp developed in his own neck muscles. The woman saw this old man as a momentary image superimposed on many others. She held a yellow envelope.

"Barthélemy Charras?"

The old man swallowed a big blob of saliva.

"No, Augustin, Augustin, Mademoiselle."

There would never be a letter. "Angèle," he called, "Angèle." But men who have lived know the uselessness of distress, the crushing power of resignation. It was wisest to say that there would never be anything. What is one lost daughter in a lost nation? Charras went away a little older than he had come, careful not to bump into people he could not see clearly. He sat down on a bench on the promenade, under the hard-leaved magnolias, stuffed his pipe, forgot to light it. Try to stop thinking of anything, Augustin. Hard, it is true, not to think of anything. It is not we who think, but thought that lives all by itself inside us.

Julien found him there, in the nippy cool of the evening, like an abandoned stump. Julien understood at once and tried to distract the old man.

"We loaded eleven cars: boxes of biscuits direct from the factory, sacks of grain, sewing machines in transit—destination Paris, they say, they expect us to swallow their fairy tales. My back is broken, Monsieur Augustin."

Charras half emerged from his desolation. He inquired, "Isn't there any way of putting a box of biscuits aside?"

"Can't be done. Those zebras watch sharp; they help themselves. They're worse than the Fritzes."

Charras grew sententious. "The eunuchs that serve Judas are worse than Judas. That's well known."

They went home. Here and there, at street crossings, arc lamps shone, punctuating the provincial loneliness. Their lodging was near the slaughterhouse, in a neighborhood full of puddles and the stench of decaying meat. They would dine at the hotel, on tough stew and half a liter of white wine, among workmen and refugees who were beginning to look like tramps. They would go to bed, each in his tiny compartment, and the human odors, the snores, the sniffles, the whispers, the steps on the stairs, the bedbugs would surround them with bestiality even in sleep... Julien asked, "If you were twenty-eight years old today, Monsieur Augustin, what would you do?"

"When you have three quarters of your life behind you, is it possible to know what you would do if the great force and the great farce of life could begin again?"

"You might not know," thought Charras, "if you would even be willing to begin again, given your experience . . ." But, too simple to give in to discouragement, he told himself that after all, if living is not worth the trouble, what would you have to lose? He thought out loud:

"I have always thought that a man belongs to himself alone. Take care of yourself, I would tell myself, take care of yourself! Governments, laws, elections, call-up notices, beautiful banknotes, newspapers, all that is made against you, by people stronger than you who want your pennies, the work of your hands, your skin, your wife if she's pretty, your little bitty conscience, which they themselves have stuffed with saws like 'Work enriches man' (yes, it enriches the other man, who doesn't lift a finger), and 'Be kind to animals,' 'A good deed is never lost.' But what ought to be posted is: 'Respect the human animal' and 'Beware of journalists' and 'Think of the fabulous quantity of kicks in the ass that go undelivered.' I'm beginning to believe that I was half wrong. I don't know any longer if my life is my own, if yours is your own. A man alone is nothing more than an insect in a field, not needed anymore: there are too many hands on the earth, machines get along better without you and me. No one can look out for himself anymore or save himself. Don't try to hide yourself in a hole, you'll only succeed in croaking there. People can only save themselves by the millions, each playing his little tiny chance with the others. You can only save yourself by risking yourself. If the working class lays its head on the chopping block, don't think you'll be spared as an exception or forgotten. No one counts, but no one is forgotten. There is no personal Providence watching over you. If France is in bad trouble, you'll get run over too. We can only count on ourselves, but all together . . ."

Julien was not good at understanding general ideas.

"So, what would you advise me to do, Monsieur Augustin?"

"Nothing at all. Advise yourself. Try to have courage. If you don't have any, try anyway."

The next day the waiting ended. Two letters came to General Delivery for Charras, Augustin. One, from Angèle, called him to Marseille:

"You will find work, Father. The Mediterranean is so beautiful it's a real joy." The other, typed and unsigned and likewise postmarked Marseille, informed him of the execution, published in Paris, of the hostages Anselme Flotte, hotelkeeper; Bœuf, dismissed police inspector; Dupin, agent of the PLM. Charras received the two blows at once, the inconceivable joy and the horror. Struck on two sides, the tree did not waver. But in the cold of the evening, under the magnolias, Julien saw him white, immobile, a head of marble.

"No mail?" Julien asked, knowing there was mail.

"Yes. Angèle is well. They've shot your father."

The young man sat down on the bench, legs outstretched, hands in pockets, and stared at the high fence of the *sous-préfecture*, lit by a round lantern. A trembling rose from his knees to his jaws, nausea bored into the hollow of his chest. Having little imagination, it was hard for him to see the connections between things but his flesh understood. "If they had caught me, I'm the one they would have shot." He saw his father winding up the alarm clock before undressing for bed. He felt like vomiting.

Charras, his spent pipe between his teeth, murmured, "There are no more innocents. There are no more neutrals. No more peace or war, justice or truth. No more mystifications. Things are getting ferociously interesting."

19. THE SOWER

FROM HIS balcony window Laurent Justinien could see the whole of the Old Port. In the foreground the rectangular basin, cluttered with boats so close together they formed continuous lines crisscrossed with little masts. On the far side, along the Quai Rive-Neuve, a big black steamship, the *Île de Beauté*, which formerly did pleasure runs between Marseille and Bastia, lay rusting. A group of shiny destroyers, big dangerous toys, cautiously maneuvered their way under the lofty cross-harbor footbridge, advancing gracefully through the confusion of yachts and barges, and dropped anchor in front of the big cafés on the Quai des Belges. Some officers came ashore, so pleasing to behold that they dispelled the memory of the lost war. Admiring them through his field glasses, Justinien unconsciously recaptured the exaltation of those childhood moments when he had set up squares of lead soldiers on the table; first of all the Marines in white leggings, who had returned home from Tonkin by way of the Indian Ocean, the Red Sea, Port Said, and the Empire of Ali Baba. And his colonials had gloriously changed the outcome of a Battle of Waterloo while the "Little Corporal" in gray cardboard looked on from the heights of a Mont Saint-Jean represented by the *Petit Larousse Illustré*. And then this memory from his tenth year rose up in full clarity, radiating solitude.

Justinien lowered his field glasses and closed his eyes. At first he felt like railing against himself, his best inner defense. "The pretty play wars of illustrated French History... Ah, how they bullshitted us from the time we were in diapers..." But, unskilled in the art of self-deception, he sensed that this railing rang false, fell into insignificance, and that he was submerging into the dull horror of solitude.

Nothing but the insipid futility of everything, nothing but this garish city vibrating, for no reason, with lives innumerable, queues of women outside the shops, couples, brats, black men, yellow men, cops, whores, racketeers, scum—plenty of scum, and in a way I'm part of it. He opened his eyes with a sarcastic laugh and saw the rocky hill, tinted pinkish-gray at this moment, upon which Notre Dame de la Garde stood like a reliquary, with its tall tower like a lifted arm. Superstition, of course, shops selling religious medals. A lot of good they'd be under a dive-bomber attack. There's been nothing left to believe in for quite a while.

"I can't stand being alone anymore, this week I'll have to take up with some bad-tempered little tart. There's nothing like it for chasing the blues. We'll go to the movies together, we'll make scenes, she'll be too stupid to come in out of the rain or she'll be mean and goofy all in one—that's what they call love life. If he talked that way in front of Angèle, her pure dark eyes would turn dull with reprobation as if they were saying "You are unclean"; in front of Hilda, her cold gray eyes would become inexpressive. Angèle, Hilda, he mainly avoided them. What could they understand about a man who has rolled the gutters of Paris, who knows everything about the rottenness of bipeds, who knows there is nothing to believe in anymore, nothing to do? "Innocence," he once told them, "I haven't seen much of it since I was eight years old . . . Younger than eight, you're not innocent, just a squirt . . . It just a tricky commodity that procuresses sell on the market . . . A more refined one which you lose as easily as a bad tooth. Then you see life as it is, and you laugh under your breath . . ."

Bitter and uneasy, he watched the people passing under his window: a white-bearded old man in a fur coat, obviously a run-down patrician, holding the arm of a woman stiff and distant, somewhat younger than himself—Italian political refugees, friends of Dr. Ardatov. They think they know how the earth turns and they don't understand that there's no place left for them on this ugly spinning ball. He saw two tall Negroes with pretty, crinkled round heads, one of them carrying a guitar with green ribbons. They were Senegalese or Niam-Niams, laughing and thieving, serious as archbishops. Thoroughly alive, they munched the pleasure of living in poverty like a ripe watermelon, but when one of them is picked up with his head bashed in by a bottle the story is of no interest, *Le Petit Marseillais* gives it a scant three lines. A nigger killed by a drunk—who cares, the liveliest life isn't worth much. Some little boys ran by, the leader squeezing a frightened cat against his chest—they were about to give the animal a definitive bath—nasty little brats, the stuff that murderers are made of, though it wasn't their fault—but whose fault was it? The fault of the cat that let himself be caught. He saw well-dressed gentlemen in soft hats, talking with mechanical gestures, surely discussing some shady deal. Vermin, vermin that we are from first to last!

Justinien moved away from the window, conscious of a malaise that he had been trying to repress since getting up. About once a week this malaise took him by surprise. It rose up unexpectedly after a bad dream forgotten except for disconnected snatches: an endless corridor leading to a cemetery, the face of a corpse looking on with wakeful eyes as an autopsy was performed on him. The purple interior of a Dupont bar on an immense Place Clichy, rocking like a ship on the ocean, and on the black carpet of the gaming table a hand cut off at the wrist was dealing out cards, each of the cards became a portrait, a scorpion crawled toward the ash tray. A madman's dream, nothing more. Are *you* sure you're not insane? Today's the *day*, well and good, I can only obey.

He silently double-locked the door, checked the clip in his Browning, hauled the leather suitcase from under the bed, opened it, emptied the contents out on the bedspread: gold and silver wristwatches with tiny jewels shining against the black silk, men's leather watches with square dials, the Lip watches prized by country people, glittering trinkets. Having consulted his own old steel timepiece, Justinien began to wind up all these watches one after the other, fixing the hands at the exact minute—mustn't cheat with time. Then he put them back in the suitcase. The first watch always caused him a little trouble, his nervous fingers thrust the hands a little ahead of the correct moment—mustn't cheat with time, Laurent, time is the only honest thing in the whole of creation, everything passes, friend, everything passes in its time. —He knew which were slow, which fast; he felt rancor toward the slow ones, for nothing can be retarded, but toward the fast ones his feeling was of affectionate understanding, for who would not gladly get ahead of the time. Each week, with unaccountable certainty, he selected a watch to take along when he went out. This time it was one inclined to a nonchalant slowness, with a pentagonal dial, Roman numerals, a light-colored leather strap for a vigorous wrist. Meaning: long life, plenty of nerve and luck, drowning in the end. Not a bad fortune. Having closed the suitcase and put it back under the bed, Justinien recovered his zest for life.

He descended to the ground floor and sat down on the terrace of the Poisson d'Or, which had only two round tables and four dingy metal chairs. Inside the obscure little bar a primitive visionary, handling light like a paste, had painted a group of powerful frescoes representing a Marseille carnival intermingled with fish, flowers, and obscene fruits. It was a carnival without masks, the faces of the crowd were uglier and warmer, more brutal and more touching than real faces or real masks.

"Jesus!" Justinien had exclaimed on his first visit to the café. "Who was the Pierrot that put that up for you?"

"He was more of a madman than anything else, he must be dead. My guess is he died at Saint-Laurent-du-Maroni."

"Well," Justinien commented, "I'm telling you that he was lucky just the same!"

For an instant the proprietor's mug emerged from the surrounding fog and he said with the smile of a dead haddock, "I've always thought so too."

Since that day Justinien had come to the terrace almost regularly for his "national coffee" with saccharine. He crossed his legs, put his elbows on the table, held his Gauloise between thumb and forefinger, and relaxed. Today, though the weather was gray and cool and the city had lost its gilt, taking on the pallor of a Paris suburb, he felt good. Ginette's bosom wobbled under her red wool sweater as she waited on him. She accepted his order for a brandied cherry and brought it out in a cup, since it was neither the day nor the hour for spirituous liquors. She had a muscular neck and her almond-shaped eyes made her look half-Chinese. Ginette was aware that this friendly customer knew something of her private life because of the proximity of their rooms.

"How's your love life, Ginette?"

"Fine, and I mean it. Just because he beats me, you mustn't think he's not good to me."

"He's a good guy," said Justinien with conviction. "You only have to look at him. He has character."

"Hasn't he?" said Ginette with enthusiasm.

Justinien hesitated before going about his business, because he had something important to do and wished for time. Rapidly, but without losing his breath, he climbed the iron staircase leading to the high footwalk of the trans-harbor bridge that hung in the void between the harbor mouth and the city horizons. Up there, according to a sign fastened to the gate at the entrance, the air was healthful, rich in ozone. On reaching the bridge, Justinien, magnificently alone in the limpidity of the air, between the sky, the sea, the port, the city, walked slowly toward the other bank. Some prisoners were taking the air in one of the courtyards of Fort Saint-Jean, which from its cliff dominated the harbor mouth. I'm free, boys, and yet I'd like to be in your place—and I'd like you to be in mine! It's stupid, but that's how it is. His eyes only grazed them. He came to a bench and deposited on it the wristwatch bringing vigor and luck and drowning in the end. From that moment his true deliverance began. After that his absurd fancies disturbed him only at odd moments, there was nothing but real life that has its good sides. He moved on with a swifter step.

In the oily back room of a little café near the Noailles Station, frequented by vendors from the nearby market, he met Ace of Diamonds, alias Monsieur Léonard, smooth, close-mouthed, and impeccably dressed. His felt hat was so light a gray that it looked white, the sumptuous rings on his fingers were turned so as to double for brass knuckles. M. Léonard's large moon face was full of his own lofty dignity, his plum-like eyes concealed circumspection behind affected good humor. His mustache, reduced to a simple line between his thick nostrils and his prominent lips, was the key to a physiognomy both personal and conventional. Without that line of hair, M. Léonard would have passed for an insurance agent; with it, he smelled of police, white-slaving (in better times), dope traffic, and other indefinable businesses. He had rounded gestures, a concise way of speaking tinted with detachment, and a natural insolence.

Ace of Diamonds procured the rarest merchandise for his customers: fine materials, Brazilian coffee, French olive oil, sugar, fine soaps—even Italian sausage. He bought dollars at 120 and sold them at 200, no arguments or risk with me. He was on good terms with the préfecture and, it was believed, with the Armistice Commission at Aix. The inspectors exchanged winks with him. He negotiated residence permits at 1,500 francs for reputable foreigners. "You understand, shady deals don't interest me, if I'm willing to do it for you, it's because—" Because what? He let the end of the sentence drift off into vagueness and sent a lump of spittle to the floor between his shiny little shoes, so burnished that they seemed to have an unsoilable splash of materialized sun at their tips. Justinien intrigued him. Now you, *mon bon*, are a tough customer, but you're off your nut.

"A Pernod?" M. Léonard suggested, thus indicating his power. I defy the laws!

Justinien accepted. With M. Léonard, Justinien spoke little.

"Your health is good?"

"Flourishing, Monsieur Léonard!"

Ace of Diamonds said, "I have the identity papers for your friend, Monsieur Maurice Silver. But the price will be two thousand."

"Why?"

The price had been agreed upon. It wasn't right to raise it.

"At present, my friend, every little thing counts. If I had seen the pictures, I would have told you in advance. Your friend is of the Semitic type. It's not your fault or mine." (Soft laughter.) "Or his. Let well enough alone. He hasn't a thing to worry about for three months or more—he's a Lithuanian, a good Christian, etc. It's worth the price."

"I don't like to be swindled," said Justinien darkly.

Not a polite way to talk. But the strong man doesn't let himself be ruffled by a word, he is indulgent.

"Take it or leave it."

They meditated, savoring the coolness of the illegal alcohol. A thirteen-year-old flower girl, charming and faded, put white carnations in their buttonholes. A swarthy one-legged man squatted on the bar. Holding a kind of metal stopper between his teeth, he tapped it with two little hammers and the result was the languorous strains of "O Sole Mio."

"I'm in a hurry," said M. Léonard. "Don't forget that your client is already involved. He has deposited his photos and all the rest."

"There's no doubt about that," replied Justinien. "But a price is a price. You're not the only man in the business."

"And a Semite is a Semite," said M. Léonard with an air of detachment.

He looked at his gold wristwatch fastened by a massive chain. Justinien blinked strangely.

"Monsieur Léonard, I'm going to tell you a little story. I used to be in business. Once a wholesale commission man tried to pull a fast one on me. He died. Acute apoplexy. I believe in fate."

Ace of Diamonds showed no sign of agitation. He scorned even to look at the other man—but from under his fleshy lids, he studied Justinien's profile in the mirror: youthful, bony, a stubborn forehead, an aquiline nose. A blue vein stood out on his temple. Deep-set, tormented eyes. A nutcase, an uncomfortable type. With reasonable people you know the rules of the game in advance.

"Stories," muttered M. Léonard with so much contempt that his words seemed to float in the realm of sleep. "Let's get this thing over with. Seventeen hundred and fifty and I'm losing by it. Just as a favor to you."

Distracted, Justinien let a few seconds go by before replying. The one-legged musician was gone, an old woman came begging for charity—please, please, Monsieur—with the tenacious, hideous voice of a creature that might have lived in the sewers for a long time. Some dried-out Annamites were speaking softly in their hissing tongue.

The thirteen-year-old flower girl stood in the doorway bending slightly forward, looking attentively at the street. She had long well-shaped legs, round buttocks, brown hair; the flowers she carried were a snowy spot in her arms. —Oh for a drink of snow! Outside the drugstore across the street hung a poster: QUICKILL, THE AMAZING MODERN INSTANT-ACTING RAT POISON.

"Quickill, Quickill," murmured Justinien, preoccupied. "Ah rats, rats, there's lots of rats in this world, Monsieur Léonard."

He had a peculiar look. M. Léonard was on his guard; nonchalantly he stretched his hand toward the right-hand pocket of his jacket. The art of bringing down your man consists in firing suddenly, without change of position, through the pocket, but high enough so that the flap will hide the burn in the material. Under these conditions you've got to aim low, so much the worse for the other fellow. M. Léonard was covered with a hot sweat. That'll teach me to do business with nutcases.

Laurent Justinien moved his hand to his inside pocket. Watch out. The flower girl turned around, came in, moved toward the ladies' room, but she saw only Ace of Diamonds, the moist half smile of his resolute terror.

"How hot you look, Monsieur Ace," she said playfully, and her young mouth was like a red gash. I'm cooked, thought M. Léonard. That crackpot will fire first.

Justinien pulled out a black-bordered death notice containing a sheaf of banknotes. He stripped off several bills.

"Seventeen hundred and fifty."

The fifty were missing; M. Léonard preferred not to notice.

"Here's your paper. Will you have another Pernod?"

"No. By the way, Monsieur Léonard, change your watch strap quick, it'll bring you bad luck."

"I have my lucky star," said Ace of Diamonds unsmiling.

Justinien was aware of the immobility of his eyelids, the hardening of his eyeballs, and he was afraid of himself. Why hate this plump hypocrite, no worse than anyone else? But I don't hate him, I— A cold energy flowed into his muscles and made them brittle: it was only the need to smash something. Luckily the little flower girl returned from the ladies' room, her carnations white on her arm, her eyes wide. Justinien stroked her thigh and she bent toward him.

"Another flower, Monsieur?"

"No. Will you give me a date for this evening, M'selle?"

The hoarse voice seemed familiar to her.

"No, I can't tonight," she said. "I am— Anyway, I've got my period. But I can introduce you to my sister, she's much prettier than I am."

"No, we'll make it another day."

His cold energy died down and Justinien took a breath. In the street he bit at the stem of his carnation and was almost gay.

Toward the end of the afternoon, having left the precious envelope at Moritz Silber's place, he went home tired, threw himself on the bed without even removing his raincoat, and tried to sleep. His head was empty and vaguely painful. If I could only sleep I would be cured. Cured of what? If I'm not cured, I'll go mad. Outside, the city, covered by a white, late-autumn sky, must be bitter. The cold of the city penetrated the limbs of the reclining man. The thought of closing the window frightened him. The sounds of the docks kept him in contact with life. Separated from these sounds, he would plunge into an intolerable solitude. No presence would subsist in him, not even his own. To doubt his own existence would not have been unpleasant to him—not to exist would be good—but to feel himself a hollow mold full of emptiness and lifelessness, to compare himself to a wax statue that knows it is of wax, exposed to the incoherence of nothingness... He sometimes imagined that his head was full of holes like a sieve, and that the four winds were blowing through it; and, in the winds, like motes of dust in a beam of light, floated memories, images, desires, ideas torn into little pieces... Then he imagined his head, detached from his body, larger than life, floating on the surface of a liquid mirror, deformed, sniggering, full of holes. Maybe I caught a volley of bullets in the skull. Yes, that's simple. Can you be dead and alive at the same time? Maybe I'm underground and I'm delirious and I believe I'm alive... So get up and do your delirious job, ghost-Laurent. Go have a drink, go buy some Gauloises! Walking sometimes dissipates anxiety, not completely though, for once, out on the Cannebière, among the passersby, he had felt stripped of everything, nonexistent. Can they really see me? Go up to a man, ask him: "Monsieur, excuse me, can you really hear me? Please touch my forehead, do you feel the air passing through the holes? They are bullets, I'm not sure how many, that hit me during a fight on the Marne. I think I'm still alive, but I'm not sure of anything, it's beyond the imagination, Monsieur, what do you think?" Justinien threw a long, convulsive look at the man, so loaded that the man turned around, vaguely troubled, and Justinien thought, "Ah, he saw me, but did he see the holes in my temples?" and the routine of common sense half sobered him, he stumbled on the flat sidewalk—what's got hold of me, in the name of God? The bad moment passed away, without any reason, Justinien found the trees beautiful.

That day, he had struggled like this several times. Lying down, he hoped that two capsules of Veganine would calm him down. Then he would go and see his comrades, Silber, Hilda, Angèle. For several days he had been avoiding them, fearing to give himself away in their presence, especially with the young women. They would think he was sick, he would feel ridiculous if he confessed the nightmares that no one in the world could ever understand.

He thought he had dozed off because silence invaded him, the sounds of the city had died down, dispelled by a sad beatific calm. This had lasted only a few seconds, or perhaps for hours: time exists only for real creatures and they don't know what it is. Then in the depth of the calm there arose a slight sound that gnawed imperceptibly at terrestrial time, the sound of the substance called seconds. Innumerable as snow crystals, the seconds shoved, rode, lashed, penetrated one another, they were agile, they jumped in all directions, not one subsisted or ended, they fell like drops of fine rain, like grains of sand when the wind raises eddies on the dunes...

Justinien opened his eyes. The familiar spot on the ceiling represented the dial of a clock on which the hours were slowly intermingling, not a single one was in place, the hours were in disorder, revealed in unknown numbers, unknown fires. Distinctly Justinien heard the watches in the leather suitcase running, under the bed, under the mattress, under the flesh and bone of his skull. Everything became clear. The chorus of watches spread imperceptibly, victoriously through the silence, with an immense haste. Tick-tick-tick-tick-tick ... Every second followed its own path, nothing could stop it. Seconds are not made by those little cogwheels adjusted by watchmakers, seconds would exist without men, they would fill up the universe, they would perhaps be stars, they would never be captives, even if the watches in the solitude of the suitcase were. The escaping seconds overwhelmed him, they invaded the room, they brushed against his hands and face, they spread through the open window out into city evening, tick-tick-tick-tick-tick. Justinien lived only through them, perceiving time, multiple, active in his fingertips, under his nails, at the end of his eyelashes, at the point of his teeth, on the edge of his dry lips. Maybe he fell asleep, it was the same thing as sleeping, only even stronger, for you can't escape from time: there were seconds like prolonged, deliciously sonorous gongs being struck, seconds like thundering explosions, seconds swinging bronze bells, seconds waving enormous hands with spread fingers, seconds raising graceful hands, white hands turning purple, streaming vermilion blood, a downpour of seconds raining on the asphalt of a road, on rails, on shining water, drops of rain, drops of blood ... Tick-tick-tick-tick-tick ...

He didn't want to turn on the electricity for fear of frightening time. The key refused to work in the lock of the suitcase—because of the seconds exploding tumultuously around the hands of Laurent Justinien. He tossed the suitcase on the carpet. He did what he did with the precision of a sleepwalker. With one swift stroke of his trench knife he split the leather—and, strange, the imprisoned seconds immediately dispersed, he still heard them, but farther off, and the suitcase seemed full of silence. He filled the pockets of his raincoat, his jacket, his trousers with watches. No sooner were they in the pockets than the disordered chorus of the seconds imprisoned in the watchcases resumed. Julien descended the stairs, walking strangely on his heels, surrounded—he alone—by the infinite, secret sound of time, punctuated by radiant gong tones and the crackle of singing machine guns.

The night was falling fast over the quay. Ginette was bringing in the chairs and tables from the terrace of the Poisson d'Or. There was no one about: on the last round table Justinien set a wristwatch studded with jewels. He precipitately turned the corner of a street, Rue de la Prison. He was escaping from an unfathomable prison. He climbed the backstreets of the Old Port. Don't you know that seconds (no, they don't know!) are eternity? Justinien saw eternity in the shape of a somber city, a labyrinth of wells; a few icy stars shivered overhead; whitish shadows floated in the vertical planes of the walls; children, little girls, whores, old women, soldiers, Negroes, cats appeared, moved about and vanished, swallowed up by eternity. Everything vanishes. Justinien followed his furtive course with a light, sure step, carried on by time—vanishing. As he passed by the housefronts, he deposited watches on windowsills, on fences, among the sorry greens of a miserable grocery, at the edge of the darkness surrounding the cruel circle of white fire traced by an acetylene lamp. He rid himself of the watches one after another, choosing a destiny for each. The fury of time began to be appeased when one of Justinien's heavy pockets was at last empty. He smiled at the narrow streets, at their swarming creatures, at the fetid garbage, at the sounds from the bars darkened by the partial blackout. Voices and music issued from doors closed by bead curtains. In the red-light district an unaccustomed crowd stagnated at the edge of eternity, over black puddles and gleaming sidewalks. Big African soldiers, beturbaned and deep-eyed, came and went gloomily, in search of women, light, and noise; the houses remained dark, sordid, and silent, and they encountered only a few decomposed creatures cowering in doorways like dead women at the edge of the tomb. Near them, for them, Justinien put where he could elegant little watches chosen by his fingertips, preferably ornamented with jewels, false or real—everything is false, everything is real. His pockets empty at last, he descended a narrow street studded with brutal lamps throwing light on wretched-looking foodstuffs. And he stopped on the quay, at the water's edge, free, refreshed, saved. The sea breeze washed his face. The present remained.

Black curtains covered the windows of the big café. From the outside you could get no idea of the sumptuous aquarium within. Justinien pushed the door open and faced the bright light, the bright red leather, the tobacco smoke, the hubbub of voices, the slow motion of faces and hands. Alone, in a corner seat, Dr. Ardatov was reading *La Gazette de Lausanne.*

"Good evening, Monsieur Justinien, what have you been up to? Sit down."

The doctor's attentive eyes had often troubled Justinien, but now he was not troubled. For a moment he watched the dancing flame of his match, then extinguished it with a snap of his wrist.

"I was sick, wasn't I, Doctor?" he inquired calmly.

And Ardatov calmly replied, "I think so."

"Was I insane?"

"No, hardly. Obsessions, insomnia, violent impulses, anguish. All quite common, they don't constitute insanity."

"And am I cured now, doctor?"

"You are cured."

"And what should I do?"

"Live."

"You think it's possible to live?"

Old Ardatov, to signal his affirmation, merely nodded his head.

"I'd like to do something," said Justinien. "Something dirty and dangerous—something useful."

20. THE VIPER

MORITZ Silber made the rounds of grocery stores in the Marseille suburbs, selling an ersatz soap that neither lathered nor cleansed but which more or less allowed for a family of stateless refugees to make ends meet. Silber also had a clientele of friends in too precarious a position to show themselves in the center of town. He kept them informed of the latest news from the travel agencies, the black market rate on the dollar, the price of visas, the requirements of the various consulates...

He lived in a small back room in a poor middle-class street near the Saint Charles Station, among tall, narrow, rather forbidding houses. The ground-floor windows in this neighborhood were protected by gratings, the doors seem to be always shut tight, the curtains drawn on all floors, the sidewalk clean. A stray dog would sense the disapproval of the very stones; he would feel that his skin had been promised to an ogress for a hearth rug—and never would he find a bone to gnaw on. These buildings exhaled the coldness of economy, hypocrisy, closed-off egotism.

Madame Concepcion's house was lower than the others and painted pink. Her triangular courtyard was full of potted plants, so that in his room, which gave onto the courtyard, Silber could imagine living in the middle of an inanimate brushwood. Madame Concepcion, formerly a "Midwife, First Class," had stopped practicing after the serious trouble she had got into—on account of her kind heart—terminating in a two-year visit to her native Alicante. "Ah, what a beautiful country, if you only knew!" Returning from this fairy tale with a serial number on her laundry, Mme Concepcion continued, out of sheer kindness, to render services to pious-looking ladies, to prostitutes, to worried ingenues and cynical matrons... Spanish, French by marriage, a widow, she was a person of good sense, rather obese, with a massive head poised over white chins like a thick, white collar of flesh. Over an imposing mass of hair, she tied flowered kerchiefs in the Spanish peasant style. A delicate, charming profile was lost in her broad flabby face. She quickly guessed that this refugee, M. Silber, had been in prison—in Poland—and was afraid of going to prison again. She spoke to him like a mother: "I know what it's like. My late husband did two years at Montpellier for smuggling—as if everybody, beginning with the customs officers, didn't smuggle. But it's the little fish that suffer for the big ones, eh? In my house you'll sleep in peace. The cops don't pester me. You couldn't count all the little favors I've done for their wives. I only hope you don't get picked up in the street, young man."

The pomegranate-colored living room was decorated with stuffed lizards, photographs, a pair of painted terra-cottas representing a snake charmer and a Kabyle shepherd, an enclosed case of medical books, and some rancid artificial orange blossoms under a glass dome. "That's for effect, young man. The looser a woman is, the more she likes to see orange blossoms under glass, like soft cheese."

Sometimes, when Moritz retired early, Mme Concepcion brought him a glass of mulled wine in bed. "I can't tell you," she said, "how sorry I feel for the young people nowadays. How many fine young people have been killed in my country, and what for? I'm convinced of one thing: it's better not to be born. If all women knew it as I do, there'd be an end of suffering in this world, *Dios mio!*" Between the violet-tinted tips of her plump fingers she held a cigar from which the smoke rose straight up. She had the smile of one of Goya's old women. The skinny young man lying between the sheets inspired a kind of tenderness in her.

"Go to America, Monsieur Silber, and get rich—walk all over them, wring their necks—there's nothing but money that counts—and the meaner you are the more you take in. Ah yes! You think I'm talking nonsense? That's the gospel truth: either you've got to be a crook or you might as well never be born ..." Squat, flabby, powerful, she filled the tiny, flower-papered room with fleshy opacity. As she was leaving, she turned abruptly. "Women aren't worth much, and don't forget it: victims, whores, lechers, liars, and crybabies ... But men! They're really disgusting. I'd roast them all from first to last over a slow fire. I wish there was such a thing as hell!"

"There is a hell," Silber replied, mentally.

The door closed. The spiced wine made for sound sleeping. Savoring his beatitude, Silber unfolded his identity certificate: SILVER, MAURICE, Lithuanian, born in Kaunas, religion Catholic, valid until— His feet did a dance beneath the sheets.

Usually he avoided the main thoroughfares; the poor streets enjoyed a tolerance based on meager profits, mutual aid, and adroit knife-play in the dark hours. Police buses parked near the squares, which, in spite of history on the march, remained centers of gaiety, and the raiding parties spread their dragnets on the open spaces, the sidewalks, the cafés. The police buses filled up with a human jumble. Two plain-clothesmen who looked like pimps sat in the rear, discussing the war in Africa, one betting on the Italians, the other on the English. The ocean-blue streets fled by, the prisoners looked around at each other like cautious drowned men. They said nothing. The (Jewish) director of an art theatre in Berlin; the (Jewish) correspondent of Amsterdam's (defunct) leading daily; the noncom in the Polish Army who had escaped from a concentration camp; the pretty little Catalan girl, who had also escaped—but for love; the aging, crotchety German intellectual woman with an expired residence permit; the Tunisian with no papers at all, who laughed maliciously in the knowledge that he would be beaten; the Viennese (Jewish) psychologist whom this absurd arrest might kill, because his papers would never be in order, because his American visa would expire in a week; the lame, painted widow of a an old-time German playwright, looking like a figure in a danse macabre; the Italian Freemason who had come to Marseille without a safe-conduct and was wanted by the Armistice Commission; the gigolo in silk shirt and rings who claimed to be a Spaniard, a supporter of Franco, "under the protection of my consulate," but was most likely Romanian, or Syrian, or Turkish, or Egyptian, or Maltese, or Smyrniot. These people and a throng of others—the persecuted, ruined elite of many countries, the scum of the ports, of the gin mills, the brothels, the spies' nests, and the universal dislocation—were corralled in the dusty halls of the Évêché. Their faces revealed every nuance of mute panic, despair, polite fury, outraged pride. Inspectors moved through this human flock like sheepdogs. Other inspectors, more important, sat arrogant and sweating at little desks under glaring lamps, examining papers and settling cases with the insouciance of a Chinese headsman.

"This international rabble, this nest of Jews, if I was running things, Monsieur, I'll tell you what I'd do, I'd put the lot of them on board some leaky old tub. Why yes, ladies and gentlemen, you're going to England, take my compliments to de Gaulle. And one fine moonlight night I'd sink the lot of them in the middle of the ocean, like plague-ridden rats, yes, friend, like rats!"

"Come on, you. You're a Belgian? Suspended sentence of deportation? You will report to the préfecture tomorrow"—this meant the internment bureau—"that's all, get going. —Next! Russian? What kind of Russian? Nansen passports aren't valid anymore, Madame, to hell with Abbé Siccard, he can come and see you in the cooler if he has time, ah, and if you think you can make scenes here, you've got another think coming. You can bawl all you like in the cooler, you should have got your papers in order, take her away. —Next! What? What's that you say? Born in Danzig, volunteer in the French Army, wounded on the Somme? Service record doesn't count here, what counts is the stamp of the Service of Foreigners. Jew of course?"

The man, leaning on a long crutch, acquiesced politely.

"Good. You will tell your story at the Screening Depot."

A Negro in a pink shirt and threadbare jacket lamented hypocritically, "But it's impossible leave France—no boats run—me from Protectorate, French protection."

"Shut your trap, you, Jaspar—say, where is he? Jaspar, give this fellow a good black eye, I don't want to see him again. Get going, Ben Alouf. —Next!"

A frail little old man, pale and breathless, former head cardiologist in a Viennese hospital. He was unable to speak French and held out some pink papers and several letters of recommendation in longhand, addressed to a former minister now under house arrest. "Fervent Catholic, illustrious scholar, president of the congress of ... friend of France ..." Monseigneur Illegible had written.

"All that's very fine, Monsieur, but your status isn't regular. Translate that to him, you. He'll have a chance to explain at the Screening Depot, let him sit down in the Assistant Chief's Office. —Next!"

A lady had fainted, they were sponging her face with a handkerchief soaked in spirits of ammonia. A well-dressed Dutchwoman, arrested with her whole family, was demanding sandwiches for the children. A bearded young American, born in Hungary, kept stamping frantically and shouting in cadence, "*Kon-sul amé-ri-cain! Kon-sul amé-ri-cain!*" No way to shut him up, you couldn't hit an American, in the end they dragged him off somewhere. Some went out to the toilet and hurriedly tore certain pages out of their address books. Others made little balls of paper and chewed them thoroughly before spitting them out.

When Moritz Silber passed through this Gehenna he had the good luck to reach the examiner's desk with his dubious papers and forged safe-conduct just as the sanguinary inspector had finished his shift. He was succeeded by a mournful, tubercular soul of about fifty, nearsighted and discreetly indulgent, who discharged his duties as quickly as possible in order to improve the air supply, and regretted the peaceful days before police had come to be synonymous with persecution. He held only the most impossible cases, and then reluctantly—such as the well-dressed feebleminded gentleman who presented two different identities at the same time; or the aged Serbian lady who had come to Marseille in 1892 with a diplomatic passport and had never heard of the Registration of Foreigners— The mournful, tubercular inspector wrote out a blue slip for Silber and sent him to the correct bureau.

Silber had spent seven hours breathing the foul air and speculating on the possibilities: prosecution for forgery, and for the use of forged papers and for infraction of the law relating to foreigners; two years in prison—a beating, of course, internment at Gurs, if he weren't dead and buried by that time, if he weren't handed over to the Nazis, if… He left the Évêché at dawn, giddy with good luck, with hunger, thirst, and a depressing joy. The naked square was as white as a transparent winding sheet. On the pink wall of the church, twenty feet up, a trail of brown blood could be seen, left by an unknown body hurled against the stones. The iron benches were still twisted every which way from a fantastic explosion. The streets slept. Two bicycle policemen rode up and stopped him.

"Your papers…"

"I've just come from the Évêché, I've just been checked." Fear sullied him to the marrow.

"You were in a spot," said one of the cyclists amiably. "Better not be out so early in the morning."

Now he was a Lithuanian, equipped with an authentic identity certificate. He idled on the Cannebière and the Quai des Belges, almost seeking encounters with the plainclothes men, like the primitive warrior made invulnerable by magic who wants the test of bullets for the pleasure of scoffing at them. The police at this tranquil afternoon hour were enjoying siestas at home or playing cards in the bars, often side by side with refugees whom they observed half-professionally, though asking no questions—for enough is enough, there are hours on duty and hours when duty is forgotten—we're not watchdogs after all! On the half-deserted quay, outside a shop displaying fresh sea urchins of a brown undersea color, Silber met Dr. Ardatov and Tullio Gaétani.

"Maurice," said Gaétani, "you're in luck, I can see it by your eyes. But you ought to put on a clean shirt when you go to meet your unknown charmer. Tell me her name."

Silber's joy burst forth, lending beauty to his humiliated features.

"Her name is Préfectance! I'm all kitted out."

At once he realized his lack of tact.

"What about you?"

"More or less."

Gaétani made a floating gesture.

"We keep afloat. Now all you need is thirty-six visas and a seat on the Clipper."

The word *visa* could make asthmatics breathe again, relieve sufferers from heart trouble, cure neuroses, dispel the temptation of suicide; it reigned over condemned horizons as a mirage reigns over a desert strewn with bones—but this word also wrought devastation, giving rise to diseases of the personality hitherto unknown to psychiatry. After the thirtieth day spent waiting in the antechamber of a consulate, a white-haired woman clutches her handbag and dashes across the Place Saint-Ferréol like a lunatic in a catatonic state, preserving just enough of her wits to ask for a dose of veronal sufficient to assure sleep without waking. The only difficulty is that you don't know the dose and the doctors often succeed in reviving you, and everything begins again, but with weakened kidneys. She meets someone, she speaks out of habit, smiling even, though rather hysterically, she is advised to try Paraguay, you cable New York, I'll give you the address, you undertake to devote yourself to agriculture and invest some capital. Hope unreasonably returns, just as an exhausted heart begins to beat again after certain injections. Somebody knows the price of various dubious visas, somebody has precious bits of information about aid committees, the Quakers, the Unitarians, the American Aid, the Joint Distribution Committee, the special channels of the Communists, the influence of the White Russians, the religious orders, various moribund political parties or the League of Nations, the possibilities of relatives lost sight of eighteen years past but now become rich, naturalized, and established in Brooklyn, Buenos Aires, Montevideo, Shanghai.

"I haven't much faith in that American visa of yours," said Tullio Gaétani to Moritz Silber. "You haven't an uncle with a business in Chicago, you're not a famous pianist or a well-known journalist, or a ladies' hairdresser, no party will claim you, you are nothing but a buck private of the extreme left, all very compromising. Now your Ecuadorian visa has more serious possibilities. Do you know where the Republic of Ecuador is?"

"Out in the sun, latitude zero."

"I've been there. Spectral mountains under an incandescent sky. The Indios move about at an altitude of eight thousand feet, taking little short steps. They are stoop-shouldered and covered with red and brown blankets and big hats. Their donkeys are the most patient and most desolate in the world. Men and beasts out of prehistory. They believe in the gods of the Incas, in the copper-colored Virgin, in Christ the King, in the Serpent Creator, in the Omnipotence of the Colonel. The earth burns, the heavens are aflame, and man can scarcely breathe. The wild plants have thorns like long steel needles. You move in the crushing silence of the celestial fire or of enormous icy stars that seem close enough to touch. I see you there, Maurice, with your box of glove samples, meditating as you look down into the crater of a volcano extinct for six thousand years. I can also see the thin red snake likewise meditating as it watches you from under the burning stones. It is called the *coralito* and its bite is often fatal; but it has never been known to bite a Jew in distress. It is free, you are free. You'll discover that no one needs any gloves."

"And I'll find a gold nugget!"

"Better not. The snake will tell the colonel, and the colonel will have you hung by the ankles under big leafless trees covered with purple flowers."

"I'll risk it."

Silber outlined the steps to be taken. As a rule Ecuador did not accept applications for immigration visas, but some providential connections were at work and the visa might arrive in about a month, cable expenses paid. On what passport should he take it? The préfecture might grant a stateless travel paper, the American Aid Committee would support the application, which would have to be filed at the same time as the application for an exit visa, with a certificate of unfitness for military service (cost, three hundred francs), a certificate of residence, a letter (promised) from Abbé N. Would the Spanish transit visa be granted to a Lithuanian? Spain theoretically recognized the existence of an independent Lithuania that no longer existed. The Portuguese visa was contingent upon the Spanish visa and on a certificate from a steamship agency in Lisbon attesting that the price of a tourist-class passage from Lisbon to New York or Havana had been paid. The United States would probably not grant a transit visa. Cuba would demand a deposit of $500, this would be reimbursed on his departure from Cuba—but meanwhile where was he to get money? "The Jewish HICEM would consent to pay for one-third of the passage, I know Dr. S., Little R., and Miss B.; Mayer will bond me for another third, the Americans will pay a third if you put in a word for me, Gaétani. The danger is that in view of three thousand seven hundred applications, the Ecuadorian visa might expire while I'm waiting for a place on the boat. Or if it doesn't, one of the transit visas might expire; or the Spanish border might be temporarily closed on account of rumors of invasions; or Vichy might decide to suspend all exit visas; meanwhile my residence permit is sure to expire, the newspapers will carry another announcement that foreigners whose labor is not indispensable to the nation will be interned. And another thing: one of these days the panzer divisions may head for the Mediterranean, followed by special detachments of the Gestapo. In any case, I'm going to take out Siamese and Chinese visas, you can get them without the slightest difficulty for a few dollars; and I'm going to apply for a visa for San Salvador; and Mexico. Some Spanish friends will recommend me. If the *Halcyon* returns to port, if the *Halcyon* leaves again for Dakar and Brazil, I'll try to get Brazilian and Uruguayan transit visas, it's not entirely impossible—"

Gaétani said, "I remember the days when we carried a map of the Métro around with us. Today it's the planisphere. Our vision is broadening."

"There are enchanted isles again," said Ardatov. "A Dutchman proposes to get me a visa for Curaçao and the Windward Islands."

These safety planks across the abysses of perdition seemed perpetually on the point of breaking but you had had the time—about ten seconds—in which to jump to the next plank. At the very moment of despair a letter arrived bearing stamps from the other world; someone brought up the possibility of reaching Africa in the hold of a freighter; it seemed the HICEM was going to charter a steamer, a Mexican ship was expected, the American Red Cross was taking some steps. The Swiss newspapers ran the story of some Bohemian Jews embarked on a ship sailing down the Danube, rejected by Hungary, rejected by Romania, rejected by Bulgaria, dying of hunger on the gentle blue waters, landing secretly in a forest, tracked by the police. A ship overcrowded with refugees was wandering through the Black Sea, the Golden Horn, the Aegean, the Mediterranean. It had been turned back at the ports of Greece and Turkey—because the visas, granted in principle, had not been granted formally—because there was disease on board, because health officers raised questions of quarantine—because international law had not foreseen the condemnation of a whole people—because the chancelleries, very busy with more important matters, acted slowly—because the governments were discussing the problem of stateless persons, the question of the Jewish National Home, the Balfour Declaration of 1917, the Arab question, the nationalist terrorism of two peoples. (No one knows what became of the human cargo of this phantom ship. It is even possible that they were saved. Later, another steamer, the *Struma*, put out from Romania and after having been turned away from Istanbul and Palestine, sank somewhere at sea, blown up by desperadoes. The number, perhaps exact, of the refugees without refuge who sank with it is known: 769.)

Moritz Silber would doubtless have embarked for Ecuador, well resolved not to go any farther than Havana or Montevideo, if M. Sulpice-Prudent Vibert, former proprietor of the bar Au Clairon de Sidi-Brahim, had not had profound reasons—of which he himself was unaware—for nourishing several confused but widely ramified hatreds. The sketchiest outline of his development suffices to make this understandable. Returning from Macedonia in 1919 at the age of twenty-two with a serious wound in the groin, M. Vibert at first professed hatred of war and even adopted the motto of the German pacifist veterans: *Nie wieder Krieg!*—No more war! He joined the movement represented by Henri Barbusse. During the Riffian insurrection, he became so enthusiastic over the anti-imperialist courage of Abd el-Krim that he considered enlisting in the army of the Moroccan warrior, and to this end entered into correspondence with a Communist leader, a former metalworker, then Mayor of Saint-Denis, by the name of Jacques Doriot. "Big Jacques" had a loud voice and was not afraid of blows. He inspired confidence, for he was neither an ordinary politician nor an incompetent, nor an intellectual adroit in handling doctrinaire formulas; he was a real man of action. In 1934 when "big Jacques," against the will of his own party, came out for working-class unity, it was clear that he alone was on the right path; a little later when he began to denounce the turpitude of the Comintern, with which, having been one of its leaders, he must have been thoroughly familiar, Sulpice-Prudent Vibert had the sense of a revelation. He had suspected it all along. What could France expect from Cossacks, muzhiks, unintelligible Marxist doctrinaires?

At this point Vibert, out of curiosity, read an old pamphlet entitled *The Twelve Hereditary Flaws of the Jew* and was very much impressed. He fell ill with a disease of the spinal cord and recovered, but was no longer capable of sexual desire. Dr. Rosenblatt finally said, "There's nothing we can do about it, my friend, you can only hope for a miracle. Nature sometimes performs miracles." While the hypocrite was pronouncing this sentence, Vibert recognized his Semitic profile, a profile which must not be confused with that of the Bourbons, of Léon Daudet, or of the father of anti-Semitism, Edouard Drumont. Vibert, enlightened by a terrible suspicion, wondered if he might not kill Dr. Rosenblatt; but why risk a lifetime in Guiana for the malodorous skin of such a villain? Four thousand francs' worth of treatments at the hands of Dr. Durand left him without hope—so great was the harm done him by the Hebrew quack. Vibert sought compensation in gambling, he dreamed of another potency, wealth. He lost on the stock exchange, at the races, at cards, at roulette in Monte Carlo. The casinos were nests of corruption where the Jews and their friends grew rich, aided by international prostitution. These women available to all, their outrageous gaiety, their vices—which he studied in special works—inspired him with nervous horror and at the same time attracted him. He went on trips in order to be alone with them in the hotels of unknown cities, he insulted them in a soft voice and tried to beat them. At Montélimar the manager of a transient hotel knocked out two of his teeth. The fear of scandal cured him of these adventures but he took pleasure in reading stories about stranglers and rippers. These madmen avenged human purity.

"Big Jacques" meanwhile continued his tribune's career and went on denouncing the Reds. Vibert joined the PPF, put on a beret, and bought a set of weighted blackjacks. The desire for action spurred him on. With his own eyes he saw the immense plot of Jewish finance, Bolshevism, popular fronts, the disintegration of morals, the falling birth rate.

The two windows and the tightly closed door of Mme Conception's house were situated across the way from his living room; he detested the "Spanish witch," the "vile angel-maker" because she lived amid confidences and the open wounds of vulvas. He vainly denounced her in anonymous letters, in the name of the French birth rate. Hidden behind his curtains, he watched young women, tall young girls, respectable ladies ringing the doorbell across the street—whores, scum, scum! In these moments of icy fury, he thrust out his chest and his chin, defying in his solitude the forces of decomposition. Would ten thousand heads suffice for the national rebirth? Or would that many be needed in Marseille alone? He was a member of the Legion, he had volunteered for special missions requiring dedication. The acquisition of a white armband, a revolver, and special instructions gave him a new dignity; he was transfigured. He helped guard the approaches to the Hôtel du Louvre, now the residence of high German officers, the conquerors of disintegrating republics. Yes, they treated France severely, that was certain, but M. Vibert had no doubt that half of France deserved it, and that the clean, healthy half would benefit. Europe needed a Leader and it recognized this Leader in an austere corporal of the First Great War, whom neither women nor Jews, Marxists nor pacifists had ever been able to seduce.

Vibert was tall and slender and he wore a close-belted raincoat like Hitler's. With his aquiline nose, dry hollow cheeks, and indiscernible lips, he resembled a plucked night bird. His opaque eyes were extremely mobile. Crafty in the performance of duty, he was infallible at picking out the unauthorized prostitute, the bad Frenchman, the refugee in distress, the colleague inclined to goldbricking. The denizens of the bars knew him and called him Monsieur Vipère—Mister Viper. He was not offended.

He detected the presence of a Jewish lodger in Mme Concepcion's house. He observed Moritz Silber's look of assurance and thought, "You're making out. We'll see about that..." He never made a false move. "The viper strikes only at the right moment," he said to himself with pride. He is an elegant, intelligent, reserved animal, prompt to attack, much more dangerous than he looks, an animal people affect to despise because they fear him. Without armband or revolver, he followed Moritz Silber and overheard him talking in a foreign tongue with a shopkeeper in the Rue Paradis: a Yid. As soon as Silber was alone, M. Vibert accosted him:

"Your papers."

The street began to move, the sidewalk shifted under Moritz Silber's feet as he presented his pretty identity certificate.

"You will come with me to the police annex."

Silber rebelled feebly: "But my papers are perfectly in order."

"In that case you have nothing to fear."

It couldn't possibly be serious. Yet this officer's malignant look and purring tone warned Silber that... A car stopped, the haberdashery display remained in its place, people passed: nothing changes when a man vanishes. They entered the guard room, which had been freshly painted a light gray. The windows faced a high wall and the room was rather dark. Benches and tables were placed obliquely on the red tile floor. The air was close and full of lazy yawns. Men in civilian clothes, with armbands, broad black belts, berets, moved about with slow boredom. One was cleaning his pipe. Another was examining some stamps through a magnifying glass.

Vibert frisked his "client." "No weapons?" With a smile, he pulled a publication printed in Hebrew characters from one pocket and tossed it on the table. No one paid any attention to them. Vibert sat down on the edge of the table, with one leg dangling.

"What is your race?"

Silber felt himself crumple completely, growing sordidly ugly and old.

"Lithuanian. I am a Catholic."

Ecuador and life were surely worth this disavowal.

M. Vibert took his time about answering. "I am going to book you for false statements."

He paused again. Then: "Are you circumcised? Take down your pants, if you please."

These words caused all heads to turn. The stamp-collecting agent rushed over to them.

"I protest," said Silber lamentably. His limbs had gone soft and his eyes were clouding over. "You have no right—"

M. Vibert's leg unbent so fast that it was scarcely visible. The kick struck Moritz Silber in the groin. The pain was frightful, like an unspeakable flame plunging deep into his sexual organs, spreading through his bowels and kidneys. Silber bent double and groaned. With his hands on his hips, M. Vibert looked down on him.

"Now that was a kick!" said the stamp collector.

Silber drew himself up painfully. He was panting and he held his hands over his fly. A ring of faces surrounded him. His pain was transformed into an oppressive heat. To gain a few seconds, only a few seconds. He drew himself erect and smiled madly. He spoke with difficulty. "I have the honor ... the im-mense honor ... to b-be a Jew, a Jew."

M. Vibert's indiscernible lips sank a little deeper into the slit of his jaws, for he in turn was beginning to smile. The persistent hot pain made Moritz Silber double up again. He huddled grotesquely. A violent impulse, originating in his thighs, in his heart, in a burning point at the back of his neck, hurled him forward. His head struck M. Vibert like a battering ram in the pit of his stomach; he gouged him with his knee, clutched his throat, hammered at his face. M. Vibert lost consciousness. The oblique tables moved, a bench fell with a crash, an Afghan stamp of the issue of 1893 was trampled underfoot, heavy bodies fell in a heap on Moritz Silber who, insensible to the blows and the weight, continued to gouge, strangle, and hammer until a leather belt, fastened around his neck, cut off his breath.

When he came to himself he was sitting on the tile floor, leaning against a window ledge. His left eye was enormously swollen and closed. A hairy hand threw water in his face.

Silber cried out, "Jew! Jew! Miserable thugs!" He was all savage determination.

21. TRAILS

IT WAS Angèle who investigated the disappearance of Maurice Silber.

"I am his fiancée," she said to Mme Conception.

"Ah, how pretty you are, my little one. Well, be brave. The police came yesterday morning, but I had been warned, don't worry. I left only a few odds and ends in his room, I removed everything else."

Papers, books, underwear, a pair of sport breeches still showing the marks of his knees, lay on the dresser in Mme Concepcion's bedroom. These effects were like a dead man's remains, devastated by an immeasurable absence. Angèle looked at them with a kind of inertia, for she lived this instant on two different planes. Calm to the point of cold rigidity, she retained every word that was spoken, registered in her mind the four books, the package of letters, the newspaper clippings, the clean socks. The other, inward Angèle, likewise calm, contemplated this disappearance, this total, indecipherable, unthinkable, impalpable end. The horrified voice of Mme Concepcion poured forth intelligent, precise phrases, unconsciously calculated to kindle hatred, to stoke it and raise it slowly to white heat—the hatred of this tall, pale child dressed in beige might be nothing, but who knows, who knows?

From Angèle's thick black hair, gathered into a coil over her slender neck, a sense of strength emanated. There are frail, kindly women who have the tenacious strength of the plants capable of dislocating walls. They are held in check, repressed, but they rise up invisibly, they intrigue, they magnetize; without knowing it, they inject a savage fire into men's blood—and the drama ripens and bursts . . .

"It was that Sulpice Vibert, Monsieur Vipère, who did everything, I'm sure of it, I know all the details, I have friends everywhere, you know, it was a friend of mine who gave Monsieur Maurice a drink of water…I feel like I'm your mother, ah, I know what life is, I know men, take it from me, they're all vile, but not him, I'll admit, not your fiancé, really, he was a fine young man, and so discreet, if you knew how he respected you. There aren't two like him in the whole of Marseille, this cesspool of the five continents. The Viper, this Vibert, followed him and asked him for his papers in the Rue de la République, next to the Lloyd Star, and then—and then, I can't help telling you what a vile creature this Vibert is, but your friend made a fine mess of him."

The story of the police annex unfolded in the mirror inclined over Moritz Silber's effects with the precision of a film, and strange to say, it was true. "Monsieur Maurice is being held in secret, he won't be able to see a lawyer for some time, terrible charges have been drawn up against him, assault and battery against policemen while in performance of their duties, forgery, use of forged documents, infraction of the law relating to foreigners, Gaullism, and God knows what else. Vibert is leading the dance, there's no worse scum than that man, if any man deserves to be killed, it's him. I know what sin is, but I'm saying it to you, and I'd say it before God himself at the Last Judgment."

Mme Concepcion took Angèle by the hand, led her into the little room where she held her intimate consultations. They stood next to the curtain.

"There you can see his windows, on the second floor. He used to stand behind those closed shutters and watch Monsieur Maurice coming and going. That's his den, little one, take a good look at those hypocritical shutters, would you think they could hide such a ferocious beast? Ah, what crimes he has committed in his life. He's coming home from the hospital on Thursday."

And, in passing, she gave a detailed description of M. Vibert's person.

"You keep Maurice's things for the present, Madame," said Angèle finally, "I'll just take his letters and papers. And I'll give you some money to help him with."

Mme Concepcion's fat, shapeless hands folded over the medal of the Virgin that she wore in the hollow of her bosom over a knot of lace.

"Oh no, my child, I won't accept a cent. I've worked my fingers to the bone for thirty years. What for, if I didn't have the means to help your friend? You can't refuse me that."

Angèle thanked her dryly, for she was beginning to feel physically ill at ease. Mme Concepcion, in looking at her, in touching her, felt that she could see more than the visible. This young girl whose short coat fell straight from her shoulders, this child with chaste narrow hips and the merest beginnings of breasts gave the experienced woman a distant presentiment of a world unknown to her, a world of concentrated, organized energies such as men set in motion for the conquest of money or love. Mme Concepcion had the sharp eyes of a fat reptile, surrounded by crinkled skin. She moved odiously close to Angèle.

"Tell me, child, tell me, my lovely, your friend will be avenged, won't he?"

Angèle evaded her eyes, narrowed her shoulders, drew herself in, and she too had a vague sensation of a dread shadow rising. She had to summon up all her willpower to answer, "I don't know, Madame, vengeance is so useless."

Mme Concepcion's repulsive mouth exhaled a hot animal breath.

"Don't doubt it for a moment, child, I know better than you. The other day, my lovely, just outside Monsieur Maurice's door, I saw a black tarantula crawling out from under the flowerpots. Have you ever seen one? They are big spiders, bigger than my thumb"—Mme Concepcion showed her fleshy thumb with its short scarlet nail—"They are black and hairy and beautiful, because when ugliness and wickedness are as deep as existence, when they come down from eternity, they have a perfection of their own. I watched this beast and I said to myself: How beautiful you can be, with your long strangler's claws, your fine corset of dusky velvet, your hairy belly, your ferocious jaws. The Creator must have dropped a big drop of living poison, that's how you were born—and the Creator let you live because you were perfect. But I'm going to take my revenge on you, filthy insect; I've known too many victims and I have a debt to pay. And just imagine, the spider understood me, my pretty, he was paralyzed, befuddled by his destiny, he looked around stupidly for a way out, but for him there was no way, my eyes hypnotized him. I was so sure he wouldn't go away that I went into the kitchen for the hammer. It gave me pleasure to swing the hammer on the black beast, and I laughed as though I'd had a drink too many—I crushed the velvet tarantula with one blow, crack! That's what you've got to do from time to time in this world, or the air would be unbreathable..."

Angèle took the streetcar home. A discouraged dusk was falling over the Boulevard Chave. The jangle of the trolley's bells grew louder as it passed the prison. On both sides of the tracks were village streets lined with bare trees. The wall of a cemetery was like a prison wall surmounted by arrogant, meaningless crosses. How disconcerting that a living man should suddenly become as inaccessible as a dead one! And how incomprehensible that this living man should be violated, trampled underfoot, condemned, thrown into a black hole to die, just because he wanted to live! "But everything that is happening is like that. All France...The other countries..." Angèle made her way through a plowed field, a gray garden. The Charrases lived in an abandoned farmhouse outside the city. Several roads and paths led to it, and this was convenient. A spy would be easily detected in this place.

That evening Augustin Charras had invited his friends over for onion soup. Dr. Ardatov sat perched on a high stool, awkwardly grating cheese. Hilda was setting the table, buzzing about like a bee. Angèle did not make her report until Justinien and Ortiga had come in from the yard with armfuls of dry kindling and broken branches. Angèle told the whole story, omitting only the episode of the tarantula—though she herself was haunted by Mme Concepcion's story. Her report was followed by a dead silence. Dr. Ardatov reported that a lawyer from the Aid Committee was looking into the case, but so far had only obtained a vague promise of improved living conditions

for Moritz. Escape would be possible only after he reached the concentration camp—in six months or two years. By that time the Nazis
would probably occupy the whole of France.

Ortiga concluded, "He's done for, that's clear."

No one contradicted him.

"Well," said Augustin Charras, "the soup is ready."

He forced a false good humor. "Now tell me what you think of it."

A dismal soup. Justinien created a little gaiety by describing Ace
of Diamonds's panic.

"At the idea that I might think he was guilty, his phiz went from
purple to green. In the end, he gave me half a pound of coffee." Real
aromatic coffee beans.

"Good Lord!" cried Charras. There was no coffee mill. A corner
of the table was cleared and Hilda, smiling desolately, crushed the
beans with a bottle. "One more lost," she thought furiously. "Well,
let's make coffee..."

Angèle, alarmed at seeing José Ortiga and Laurent Justinien going
out alone, slipped away and joined them in the starless garden. Despite
the shawl tied around her neck, she was shivering.

"I'm not in the way?" she asked. "The coffee is done." The two men
were silent, heavy heads filled with night. Tense with emotion, Angèle
feigned playfulness. "What are you plotting?"

"No, you're not in the way," said Ortiga brusquely, taking her
around the waist. "You can even settle the question. We are agreed
on one point: that this Monsieur Vibert has to be liquidated. Of
course the one who does it will be risking his skin a little. I say that
it's up to me: I'm Maurice's oldest friend. That ought to count."

Laurent took the young girl's head in his big bony hand and turned
it toward him. Angèle felt herself held in a twofold embrace, but she
was alone and free, her body cold, her soul frozen. She saw the black
spider on a sunlit flagstone and an enormous hammer hovering
over it.

Even her lips were cold as she murmured, "No, you mustn't...you
frighten me."

Laurent's strong hand glided over her hair and playfully seized her neck. "Don't be afraid, Angèle. See the world as it is. It's a time for killing. We are in the midst of a fight."

"Yes, Angèle, it's a time for killing," repeated Ortiga, pressing her close to him. "What can we do about it? We will get ourselves killed, fighting for different times. And you too."

"Yes, me too," said Angèle with fervor. Laurent laughed.

"You see that we're right. So decide. Him or me. I'm stronger. I have a sure hand. I've not yet done anything worthwhile on this earth. I've lived only for myself. You know that I wasn't worth much."

A bat grazed their three heads in its drunken flight. Angèle swallowed down a weight in her throat.

"Is Maurice really lost?"

"Eight or nine chances out of ten," replied Ortiga. "Decide, Angelita." There was an ardent tenderness in his voice.

"Laurent," she said very softly, looking into the emptiness, astonished to hear herself speaking. Laurent's large caressing hand did not tremble but a warmth rose into it. Laurent's face became distinct. He sent into Angèle's eyes a look so filled with emotion that she felt it like an indefinable thrust.

"You can't begin a life in times like these," said Ortiga, alluding to something unexpressed that all three of them had understood. Angèle heard herself reply, "We must always begin and always go on, there will always be..."

She did not know why she spoke like this. She had a vague sense of desirable, menacing words in the air.

"Be still... Let me go... Come and drink your coffee."

And again everything was as simple as if nothing serious had been said.

Ortiga went to get another armful of dead branches for the fire. Laurent and Angèle went back into the big kitchen. Hilda drew Angèle toward the fire.

"Come, you might help me a little after all. What's the matter with you? You look as if you were dreaming. Pass me the kettle."

The two old men, Ardatov and Charras, were discussing the situ-

ation. Charras would explore the neighborhood of the prison, Ardatov would see his American friends.

Laurent caught sight of a book lying on the table among the
breadcrumbs. The title appealed to him: *The Will to Power*—the only
will that saves. He read in the middle of a page:

"We covet others, in fact we covet everything that exists outside
ourselves, just as man desires food. Often it is a question of fruits that
are just ripe for us in this particular year. Should one have only the
egotism of the brigand or the thief? Why not that of the gardener?
The pleasure of cultivating others as one cultivates a garden!

"Lasting love is possible—even happy love, because we are never
done with possessing, with conquering a human being. Unceasingly,
depths, unexplored regions of the soul are revealed and the infinite
covetousness of love extends to those regions too. But love ceases as
soon as we sense the *limits* of a being…"

Laurent interrupted Dr. Ardatov. "What is this book, Doctor?"

"Philosophy. Nietzsche, a German author."

The word "German" recalled to Laurent only the thundering
descent of the Stukas, plunging out of the sky above terrified men—
their din, their crazy wings, the fire of their machine guns. (Afterward,
he turned toward his comrade lying beside him with his nose in the
grass, his body shaken with convulsive shudders. "Lureau, eh, Lureau!
Are you hit?" And the little Norman, who was such a joker, answered
plaintively, "In the balls … and in the heart … get out of here …" He
was already turning cold.)

"They have written fine things…"

"In their country as in any other," said Ardatov, "the men who
think and the men who kill are not the same. And in their country,
as everywhere else, when the men who kill are the masters they begin
by killing and gagging the men who think."

Laurent said to himself—his lips could be seen moving, "That's
true. I'm a man of murder. I've never known how to think." He showed
his teeth in a snarl.

"But most men," Ardatov continued, "are made neither for murder nor thought. They are just made for life. They would prefer thought if they had the choice. They haven't the choice."

"Just for life—but we haven't the choice. That's right, Doctor, we all have a rope around our necks."

"All of us."

Charras, intervened, quietly at first, then with impatience.

"Drink your coffee, Laurent, and leave philosophy alone. We didn't want these wars, none of us. We weren't consulted. Nor were the German people, poor slobs. If we could change the world, it would be cleaned up quick. I fought in one war, you fought in another, but I swear to you we are innocent. Innocent, by God! And to put an end to it, I'm telling you that I'm ready to fight again, and that I'll keep my conscience clean, whatever I do! When I hear you mouthing off, Laurent, I feel like balling you out. You think about yourself too much. You drive yourself crazy. For nothing. Look straight ahead of you."

Laurent was smiling.

"You're right, lumberjack. You're right, coalman. The charcoal burner's logic. I shouldn't mess with books: they'd make me lose my mind."

Hilda was questioning Angèle: "Which one told you he loved you?" Angèle burned her fingertips shifting some softly glowing coals in the stove.

"No." The fire from below lit her forehead, over which her bunched hair formed a dark, trembling crown. "One of them almost did. I don't know which."

Hilda put back the hot cast-iron covers back on the stove, likewise burning her fingers. And with a desolate air that smoothed her features, she said, "Now you're getting close to the real fire, Angèle."

Moritz Silber was condemned several weeks later to eighteen months in prison: instead of Ecuador, the bottomless pit. In a leather-bound loose-leaf notebook, M. Vibert kept a methodic record of the clients he had "fixed." He entered SILBERSTEIN, alias SILVER, MORITZ, JEW, as number 67. In high spirits, he strolled around the quayside cafés, frequented—contrary to all prudence—by "irregular" foreign refugees. He was watching a young artist, stoop-shouldered and old-looking, who when alone sketched elongated faces of women emerging from tree trunks. They had crystals instead of eyes and their hair resembled smoke. "Nuts or not, friend, I'm going to get you. You're ripe for the cooler." That evening, M. Vibert saw the artist surrounded by a group of people and postponed his pleasure until the morrow. He felt lazy and his throat itched—let's go to bed, Sulpice.

A light mist floated in the streets. As he passed them, the wrought-iron window gratings looked like filigree in the darkness. The closed doors were perpendicular paving stones. The sidewalk was hard and slippery under the walker's heels. He walked stiffly erect, his beret down over one eye, his overcoat collar turned up, his waist squeezed in his leather belt, the holster of his revolver within easy reach. Now and then he coughed a little. His jaws were clenched, his head empty. "I'll make myself a bit of tisane." While the linden tea cooled on his bed table, he would read *Gringoire*. Which led him to think about the upcoming promotion of acting inspectors. The thickening fog became like a muddled mirror, and in this mirror M. Vibert's silhouette was distantly reflected.

A silhouette strangely resembling his own came toward him with a light sound of steps in the rhythm of his own. M. Vibert yawned, drawn toward sleep; the Legionnaire's silhouette was only three steps away. He feared the annoyance of meeting a colleague, M. Chausse or M. Lisque.

"Ah, Monsieur Vibert!" exclaimed the silhouette in an unknown voice.

"Eh," said M. Vibert hesitantly, "I don't . . ."

A thudding lightning blow crushed the words in his mouth, his breath, his teeth, and folded his knees. He opened wide his eyes, more stupefied than frightened. The disjointed silhouette raised an enormous arm elongated by a black thing, curved, supple, animated. The blackjack struck M. Vibert vertically, full in the face, between the eyes. M. Vibert reached for his revolver, for the cup of linden tea on his bed table, and reality ended for him definitively, without suffering.

22. THE INQUISITORS

THE BUCHAREST restaurant, situated at the end of a blind alley in the Old Port, was known only to its habitués, although it advertised its existence to passersby with a cutout of a chef in a white toque, placed at the alley's intersection with the through street. Originally this personage was dressed all in white, properly, but with the passage of time dirt had covered him with such a lamentable gray he could hardly be distinguished from the wall. He still bore his sign: GOOD AND NOT EXPENSIVE! He would bear it till the end of time. Empty-bellied sailors sometimes strayed into this blind alley after black plunges into voluptuous hells full of weary flesh, confetti, guitars, drunken embraces, brotherly fistfights, and sentimental refrains. Today most of these sailors were aboard black ships sailing shadowy seas, in constant dread of torpedoes; some of them no doubt were at the bottom of the salt sea. There were only a few buildings in the alley, and these were narrow and tall, characterized by hard, tenacious sadness. Across the alley hung the washing of the underworld: gaudy slips, kimonos with gold stripes, blue G-strings, brassieres the color of a ripe mango, wide, green oriental pantaloons. Mended sheets floated in the breeze like banners of misery and disease. The opposite wall was five stories high, as dark at the top as at the bottom. At its foot lay a heap of refuse so lamentable that junk dealers disdained it—there is the rich garbage of prosperous streets and the nameless garbage of back alleys. Stray animals engaged in frequent battles in this place. The black cat arched his back and bared his fangs, an alcoholic gleam darted from his yellow eyes—the pink mangy dog panted and his bloody tongue hung out. The dog did not bark; he fought better without noise, without glory. Sitting at his counter, M. Nikodemi observed these battles through the grimy windowpanes. "Animals and men!" he would say. "You've only got to throw them a bone. That dog's name is Pluto, he has only one eye, but he has the temperament of an assassin, he'd have had a career if he'd been born human." Nightwalkers were in the habit of urinating against the wall; at dawn maniacs wrote their confessions on the dummy-chef's paunch. However, the Pirate, that is to say, M. Nikodemi, still served a tolerable meal for fifteen francs; and if you had no meat or fat coupons, the Pirate found it quite natural, he had always known that interesting people can't have everything.

The zinc-covered bar was narrow, the oilcloth covering the tables bore a design showing Persian falconers hunting amid woods and lakes. The ensemble gave the effect of a mess hall on board a Red Sea steamer. The sauces steamed in a tiny kitchen behind a glass partition, skinned rabbits hung on the walls like red specters. The "cabinet" WC was crowded with mattresses and bathrobes, and it was there that young ladies retired to refurbish their charm in front of what was left of a mirror. Sometimes a pair of lovers supped at the Bucharest—he with slick pomaded hair, she giggling and a little mussed. The cataract sound of the toilet flushing lengthily was audible from one moment to the next. Let us be fair: the beans in gravy had real fat on them, the rabbit stew was rabbit stew, the Turkish coffee had not yet gone "National"—it remained Turkish and saccharine-free. And since the plainclothes men held M. Nikodemi in respect (whether on account of adroitly conceived murders in days gone by or because of protection money regularly paid, nobody needs to know) it was almost certain that nobody would come in here to check worrisome identities.

The source of the Pirate's evident strength was his prudent silence. He had an intelligent forehead, a tiny thin nose, shiny little eyes that looked like unbreakable glass marbles. Ordinarily he wore a striped red and white jersey under his jacket. He spoke little, but wisely, often in aphorisms: "It's unwise to be overcautious when your skin's at stake. A man without dignity is like a louse without legs. The war will end with a plague and the plague with a revolution." Refugees of the Left and Far Left dined at the Bucharest. Also Jewish moving-picture men driven out of their profession, and intellectuals who would have remained famous if only they had had an orchestra, a hospital, a magazine, or a party to direct. But having only their brains overloaded with memories and superfluous knowledge, they were less competent at living than the pimps and Sudanese longshoremen, the pretty streetwalkers, the unemployed seamen, the Balkan racketeers at the next table. Toward the end of meals a Salvation Army Lass came in and set down on the tables a little illustrated leaflet entitled *The Way of the Savior*; it showed a group of shipwrecked men, adrift on a raft, suddenly illumined by a divine light—but whether they were picked up by a freighter or eaten by the sharks, the caption did not reveal. Most of the diners conceived of salvation only in terms of American visas or other contrivances, the secret of which they confided to nobody.

José Ortiga was dining at the Bucharest one night with Hilda. Greetings were exchanged from table to table. Ortiga spoke gaily but Hilda was somber. A smell of a prison mess hall, the bitter taste of stale beans came back to her, the feel of a torrid little courtyard where the women washed their clothes in the daylight hours and discussed interrogations, executions, the probable murder of comrades in another jail. Through a barred window, an imprisoned nun watched the movement in the antifascist section of the prison. Hilda became interested in a nest of mice she had discovered under the beams at the foot of the wall; the little beasties seemed to know her ... Suddenly Hilda remembered something, on account of the mice, because the man looked gray to her with his colorless sharp profile, his sad eyes: the man sitting with Kurt Seelig and Ignacio-Ruiz Vasquez at the table near the kitchen wicket. Hilda pointed him out to her companion with a nod of the head, and José Ortiga saw the young woman's forlorn look. "Do you know him, José?"

"Vaguely. He's an Austrian or Czech comrade, his name is Willi Bart, he escaped from La Saulte with Kurt."

"I've lost my appetite, Pepe. His name certainly isn't either Willi or Bart. And he certainly isn't either Austrian or Czech."

Hilda's lips were pressed in a deep frown which the entrance of Laurent Justinien did not relieve. She glanced frequently at the anemic Willi Bart, but his back was turned and she could only get partial glimpses of his face. Justinien affectionately took her hand in his two bony, cool hands.

"What's the matter, Hildette? Life's not a fairy tale anymore?"

"Oh yes. But I've just been thinking of mice and executioners."

This was the beginning of suspicion. At first, investigation revealed nothing, then some information came in from new sources. One day, toward noon, when the Bucharest was still empty, Ignacio-Ruiz Vasquez and Willi Bart pushed the door open. The Pirate came toward them with blood in his eye.

"Captain," he said to Vasquez, "excuse me. I have two words to say to this gentleman in your presence."

The Greek thrust his bumpy forehead at Willi Bart, his voice changed pitch and was full of mockery.

"Mossieu, the clientele of my establishment is ab-so-lute-ly honorable. There is no room here for people of your type. A word to the wise . . . I am entirely at your service, captain."

Without effort Willi Bart preserved a kind of impassivity—seemingly weak, in reality maintained by a nervous discipline so tense that it woke him up in the middle of the night. If he grew pale, it was only slightly. If he didn't smile, he almost did. If he was astonished, it was hardly visible. He said simply, "You insult me without knowing me."

"Go and get hanged somewhere else."

"I honor your scruples, Monsieur Nikodemi," said Vasquez, "but this must be a misunderstanding. Come, Willi, we'll go to the Chinese restaurant."

And standing by the grimy wooden chef, Vasquez affected a stupefied candor. What's this all about, Willi?"

"I don't understand a thing," replied Willi, coolly playing the same candor. "The Pirate must have taken me for someone else."

"For someone else?" Vasquez insisted mischievously.

Willi realized at this moment that no misunderstanding was possible. Nor any retreat. At Toulouse, at Perpignan, they would find him; and the visas would arrive here. What could they know? In any case, he must put on a good front.

"You understand, Ignacio, that I don't give a damn about that hash-house keeper. But if the comrades nourish the slightest doubts about me..."

"Nourish the slightest doubts..." Vasquez repeated teasingly. "You speak good French, Willi. Only, if there are doubts, they're certainly not the slightest. In our days, doubts are as heavy as a cargo of peanuts in the hold."

Willi spoke of a jury of honor.

"Oh, yes, honor, that's a big word," said Vasquez. "But if you insist on it—"

Hilda recognized Willi from having seen him in a Valencia prison where he had sometimes attended interrogations. Italian volunteers reported having met him in prisons of the International Brigades where they had been awaiting summary execution. But they refused to testify formally, stating merely that one of these nights they would settle their old impersonal accounts with him. "Nothing serious will ever get done," they added, "until we stop the intellectuals from forming commissions and drawing up resolutions." Even as it stood, their deposition seemed valid, but nothing more was discovered and it was difficult to disentangle the web of confusions. Kurt Seelig set his analytic mind to work and drove everyone crazy with his subtle distinctions. "There is the possible, the plausible, the probable, the proved, the proved minimum, the hypothesis. We are not judges, and consequently I don't accept any counterfeit arguments, even if they look authentic at first sight." What was more natural than that Willi Bart should not be the man's real name? He could not legitimately be condemned for working in the prisons of his party, unless it could be shown that he had administered torture or framed evidence. Once expelled from his party, this past was removed from him, he deserved neither special confidence nor ostracism. "There are thousands like him who will be expelled someday, and many of them have done dirty work out of devotion; which should weigh more heavily, the dirty work or the devotion?" Shipwrecked men had to help each other, even when there was no special sympathy between them.

The Commission of Inquiry was self-constituted, but with the approval of some fifty comrades: its members were Simon Ardatov, Kurt Seelig, Tullio Gaétani, Jacob Kaaden, who had just arrived from Sète, and Vasquez in an advisory capacity. It met one Sunday morning in a little wooden house encrusted in the cliffs of the Corniche, forty feet over the seething foam. The house belonged to an Italian businessman, reputed to be a Fascist and consequently in good with the police, the Legion, the Italian officers, "the whole mess of skunks," as he put it. "Hence, security…"

The mistral was blowing in fitful squalls, raising explosions of spray. The sea water fell in showers reaching to the road and rebounding like hail from the galvanized iron roof. There was a comic little Neapolitan sitting room decorated with views of Vesuvius framed in seashells. The furniture consisted of a round table and several green plush armchairs. M. Gatti, the businessman, had left two bottles of Chianti for this "political gathering," but there were no glasses, the good wine had to be served in cups and a tin can.

Ardatov, the eldest, declined the chairmanship because he detested chairmanships, Kurt Seelig accepted it because it was a long time since he had felt himself invested with any authority. Willi Bart would have preferred to sit with his back to the window and his face away from the light, but for that very reason, Seelig offered him an armchair facing the dripping panes and their blurred view of the cold metal sea. Let's have a good look at your face, friend. Ardatov, in his squared-off jacket, looked like a physician attending an uninteresting consultation. Gaétani, delighted with the good wine, fought down a great desire to talk too much. Seelig, with his lofty forehead and glittering spectacles, wearing a red-and-gold necktie, looked like a professor in a Punch-and-Judy show and maintained a formal silence. Jacob Kaaden was all hardness, from his chin to the roots of his hair, from his fingertips to his impersonal gaze. Vasquez affected a dry cordiality.

And Willi Bart, beneath the pinkish pallor of his long, clean-shaven face, was calm. In his heart he rather despised these men. Confused minds, eclectic doctrinaires, petty bourgeois whom history had passed by—enemies of the party. Bakunin—who had been one of them— would have said that such men might serve—badly—before revolutions, but that, after, they had to be put out of the way. Yet since he had been living among them he had begun to feel a growing sympathy with them, the beginning of corruption, he reproached himself. He had lost contact with Boniface, that weakened him—but, as he realized with irritation, it relieved him too. And now he was in danger. Once burned, Vasquez and others like him would be capable of killing him. But no one in the world could know what no one in the world should know: Boniface is infallible. Brave, accustomed to hidden perils, Willi composed his manner; he was perturbed but self-assured.

Ardatov decided to give him time to worry. He postponed the debate by asking Kaaden if Cherniak's suicide had been confirmed.

"The sea confirms nothing," said Kaaden with a stubborn look. "The fishermen say that bodies are sometimes cast ashore as far as ten miles away. It may take three to five weeks, depending on the weather. Sometimes a body gets caught in the rocks underwater and the crabs and lobsters eat it up. I found his socks, I had given them to him, so no doubt is possible. Funny idea to take your socks off before jumping. He was completely demoralized. He wasn't a Marxist for two cents."

"He felt too much alone," said Ardatov.

"I did everything I could for him, but he was so weak that he detested me. The gendarmes seized his papers, a few rough drafts of poems, nothing serious. They classified him as a 'fugitive': well, let them chase him."

"God rest his soul," said Vasquez with a solemn smile. "Who'll have some more Chianti?"

"It's a pity," Kurt Seelig muttered, "his American visa had just come through. A wasted visa. Well, let's get on with it. The session is opened...Willi Bart, what did you do in Spain? I warn you that you have a perfect right to lie. The commission is sufficiently informed."

Willi Bart replied softly, "Lies are sometimes useful in politics, I don't need them today."

His remark provoked a small storm. Tullio Gaétani set his cup down sharply on the table and exclaimed, "*We* believe in the politics of truth!"

"The politics of efficacy would be more to the point," said Willi.

Kurt Seelig's belligerent goatee wagged. "Let's get on. Answer my question."

The names of battles, battalions, air fields, prisons, rivers that were battles, monasteries that were prisons filled the circumspect narrative of Willi Bart: liaison agent in an International Brigade, political commissar of a battalion, wounded in the head at University City, wounded a second time in the fruitless Battle of Brunete, sent to Paris on a mission, assigned to counterespionage in Albacete and Tarragona, appointed interpreter to General Diego....

"Who was this General Diego? Do you know?"

"No one ever knew. Maybe a Hungarian, or a Yugoslav."

Willi Bart was interrupted by brief, dangerously competent questions:

"Did you participate in house searches in Madrid?"

"Yes, four of them. I searched the house of three Falangists and a Left Socialist." Bart answered quickly and without apparent reflection.

"Did you serve in the postal censorship?"

"Yes, for twelve days, in the secret section. I intercepted one of your letters, Comrade Seelig, on the agrarian question."

He gave a clear account of his activities at the Convent of Santa Ursula; he was drawing up reports on matters connected with military operations. Just as he was beginning to feel safe and regain his inward assurance, he stumbled on an Italian name.

"That witness," said Tullio Gaétani, who was bluffing, "is prepared to testify next Sunday."

"It would be useless," said Willi Bart distinctly.

Something crumpled inside him, a spot of color came into his pale cheeks, his subdued eyes sparkled with anxiety. He could get up and leave, probably no one would prevent him. He could disappear this very evening, before an accident should occur. Five faces surrounded him with icy sternness. Framed in the window the sea swell was white with foam.

"Ah, so that's at the bottom of all this."

His blue tie with the white polka dots was new, he had on a freshly ironed shirt, his beige jacket was pressed, he looked like a department-store clerk—and his hands, clasped over one knee, were a little bigger than might have been expected. He raised himself up firmly, sadly.

"You are sentimentalists."

Kurt Seelig tapped the table lightly with his chairman's pencil.

"Willi Bart, I must ask you to refrain from any remarks concerning the members of the Commission. Continue. You have the floor."

The anemic young man, turned out like a department-store clerk, smiled, but without irony, without good humor, without confusion. A smile like that is not often seen, the tranquil smile of a man flayed alive.

"That I've occasionally served as executioner, is that what bothers you?"

Vasquez's profile seemed drawn in charcoal, his voice was dark. "*Que dice? Fué verdugo?*"

Seelig whispered, "Silence."

"*Verdugo, sí, compañero Vasquez*. Why not? Somebody has to do it. If none of you has ever done it, it's because others did it in your place. The theoreticians, the orators, the organizers, the staffs, they all do their jobs. But there are bound to be a good many things that they leave to others. I recognize the necessity of this hierarchic division of labor. The verdicts were delivered by men more qualified than I, men in whom I had, and had to have, confidence. They were intellectuals and old comrades like several among you. But they didn't have time—or the desire perhaps—to handle the revolver themselves. They were the head and I was the hand. I executed"—the ill-chosen word stood out from the others as though of a different essence—"the orders of the party. Everything done for the party—I thought—is clean, well done, useful, and necessary. Was it necessary to shoot the agents of fascism? Do you doubt it?"

Ardatov asked, "Did you volunteer for the work?"

"I don't know what that means. I have always been voluntarily disciplined. What had to be done had to be done."

Ardatov went on to ask, "Did you experience satisfaction in fulfilling this function?"

Seelig intervened, "That question is purely psychological. I authorize you not to answer."

"It doesn't embarrass me," said Willi Bart. "It is physically painful to take a man out behind a wall and shoot him. So painful that it becomes difficult to take quick and correct aim, even at close quarters. But it is a satisfaction to destroy the enemy. It is a satisfaction to accomplish a painful task and spare others who are useful in a different way."

Jacob Kaaden: "Did you execute any of our people?"

"I don't think so. If I had been ordered to, I would have done so. We were liquidating enemy agents. It wasn't my business to judge."

Seelig: "And you never had any doubts?"

"I might have, but I couldn't afford to."

"Have you any doubts now about all you have seen and done?"

This was the time to lie without hesitation. Willi Bart said, "Yes."

Having made sure that no one had any further questions, Seelig asked Willi Bart to withdraw. Vasquez went out with him into the bathers' dressing room. The swinging door opened out on the sea and the wind, the interior was wet and smelled of salt. The two comrades leaned against the door frame and silently watched the whitecaps moving in toward the coast. Their faces were sprinkled with salt spray.

Seelig said, "I don't think we'll get any more out of him and we don't know any more than we did before."

Kaaden clenched a resolute fist. "He's a bloody scoundrel, there's no job too dirty for him."

Tullio Gaétani moved his thick lips and his thin weary face was full of wrinkles. "If it were that simple . . . juridically."

Seelig resumed, "He inspires me with no confidence whatever. But juridically, as you say, Comrade Gaétani, we have no evidence against him."

"But there's never any evidence in such cases," Kaaden explained.

Seelig: "His explanations were complete, his arguments unassailable. Juridically, neither sentiments nor intuitions can count."

"Right," said Gaétani, "and we cannot permit ourselves to be unjust."

"Shit!" said Kaaden.

"The commission did not hear you," said Seelig with a half smile. "What is your opinion, Ardatov?"

"We are on the eve of new beginnings. We will run across many men of this type. We will see worse, and they will hold out their hands to us. We cannot repulse them. Our epoch is one of fratricide in obscurity. For the masses without a compass, revolutions, counter-revolutions, humanity, truth, intoxication are all mixed together. They do not know themselves. They are caught in the gears, their very souls are caught. If this young man is what he seems, I believe that the commission can only pronounce an acquittal, provisional at least..."

This solution prevailed by a majority of three to one.

"You are priceless," Vasquez laughed. "Put yourselves in their place, Willi, what would you decide?"

"I have no idea," said Willi. He stood erect, cold, and uncommunicative.

"I'm the one who voted against you," said Kaaden, refusing his hand.

But the others, even Vasquez, did not refuse theirs. Willi Bart went out first, alone, the belt of his raincoat buckled tight, his beret pulled down over his head, all of him leaning into the wind. A heavy liquid gust fell dully on the house roof. "Oof! They don't know anything. I'm saved."

Tullio Gaétani and Simon Ardatov decided to walk along the deserted Corniche, in the colorless light of the sea. Gaétani said, "Everything used to be so much simpler! Against us, there was reaction; and we stood for progress, liberty, the republic, socialism. It was as clear as a Kantian antimony, as the battle between Good and Evil. We should have distrusted such logical contrasts but nobody did distrust them ... Do you remember the big demonstrations with their red banners, and the stupid prefects who ordered the police to charge them and then sent letters of explanation to the papers? Do you remember the radical magazines with a picture on the cover of an athlete breaking his chains, and behind him the sun rising with straight lines for rays, one line long, one line short, representing the dawning day, black on blue? Do you remember the discussions until three o'clock in the morning on the emancipation of women? And now she emancipates herself by making shell casings. We wrote good books, we created ideological fireworks based on mountains of statistics, observations, scientific findings, and we did not suspect that we were passing through the prodigious gates of hell ... Until history descended on us with rains of shrapnel, with dictatorships, propaganda, castor oil, socialist inquisitions, liberating revolutions transformed into tyrannies, abject tyrannies affirming by decree the genius of rational organization, an anti-socialist national socialism, a Bolshevism that exterminated the Bolsheviks. I understand how people could lose their heads and come to believe in chaos, in the perverse nature of man. I say: complexity, maelstrom, and man is in it, weak with his weak little mind, a prisoner of the machines he has built, crushed by the facility of destroying and being destroyed: thirty years of work are needed to make a man and a millionth of a second to destroy a hundred or more of them, without seeing them, by opening a valve in the belly of a bomber. It takes centuries and generations to build a cathedral and a single bomb pulverizes it by mistake in thirty seconds ... Don't you miss the good old days, Simon?"

Ardatov had the taste of the sea spray on his lips. He wanted to quote Spinoza, but the exact words escaped him—a passage that says that the function of intelligence is not to deplore but to understand. Yet this would be true only if we were disembodied minds, or if we really knew what intelligence was. And Spinoza's disciples underwent torture for the truth.

"It was a naive century," he said. "The construction of beautiful locomotives, the invention of the telephone, the phonograph, canned foods, the safety razor, inspired man with an unlimited confidence in himself; and rightly so, for these were real accomplishments. Perhaps it's no more difficult to invent a human order, though it's more difficult to bring it about. We were not insane. I agree that we lacked a sense of complexity, that we borrowed an infantile determinism from mechanics and a blind optimism from the prosperous bourgeoisie. Our apparent error was to be neither devious nor skeptical. We anticipated too much, we thought in terms of diagrams, and our diagrams were muddled by the daubs and splotches of reality. From the point of view of Sirius, we were right and events were wrong. Our mistakes were honorable. And even from a point of view less absurdly exalted, we were not so wrong. There is more falsification of ideas now than real confusion, and it is our own discoveries that are falsified. I feel humiliated only for the people who despair because we have been defeated. What is more natural and inevitable than to be beaten, to fail a hundred times, a thousand times, before succeeding? How many times does a child fall before he learns to walk? How many unknown navigators were lost at sea before a Columbus, guided by a magnificent error, could discover new continents? He followed an immense and correct intuition, he groped his way, he was right. If his nerves had weakened like those of his crew, twelve hours or twenty minutes before the discovery, he would have sailed back over the pitiful safe route of true defeat and into oblivion. Others would have succeeded at a later date, can we doubt it? Everything depends on having strong nerves. And lucidity."

"You speak words of gold, Simon. Are your nerves that good?"

"Growing old helps," said Ardatov. "I am no longer able to change."

23. JUSTINIEN

EVERY now and then the city's last rotisserie lit its fireplace. The sumptuous flames of wood logs licked the last hen, the last rooster in creation. A crowd of thirty passersby gathered in the street, captivated by the spectacle of times past. So there are still fortunate people who will soon enjoy a fine dinner? Either foreign diplomats or the accomplices of many crimes... Among the spectators, the boldest women and the brashest of the men actually went inside, affecting an interest in the colorless ragout or the buffets. Then, after a while, they planted themselves by the fire and breathed in the delicious aroma of chicken.

Laurent Justinien did like the others and entered to admire the fire, the great revolving spit, the golden fat streaming over the marvelous birds. "A million human beings are hungry in this city," he thought. "And a few thousand profiteers stuff their bellies. Once upon a time I would have thought that just fine... Have I changed as much as all that?" He had just lunched next door, standing at the counter. He had had two pieces of pizza, meager but warm, and the girl had taken only one of his bread coupons. He still had a lean and hungry look, although he could have eaten couscous every day in the Algerian restaurants. But since the city and France were hungry, it seemed right to him to be hungry and to live on a cold inner anger. It restored a certain self-esteem. This was no time to be working the angles just to fill my belly, no thank you. And another change had come over him, he was getting cautious, avoiding useless danger, as though the life he had almost thrown away had become surprisingly precious. In this connection, the sermons of Dr. Ardatov pleased him, though he sometimes found them exasperating. "Courage consists in endurance:

in continuing the fight even when it seems impossible, even when it means running away like a rabbit. Neither gesture nor pose, nor bravado nor big words, nothing but utility." The first time he had heard such words, Justinien rebelled against them:

"A man has to keep his face up even if he's filling his pants."

"Your face is no more important to me than the seat of your pants. If you risk your skin for your personal pleasure, we can't work together. If you are working with me, you'll need common sense, not the fine manners of an aristocrat or of a neighborhood tough. I want to be able to count on you, alive and healthy, not glorious and dead."

Why, in the pleasant atmosphere of the rotisserie, did these words come back to Laurent Justinien? Scarcely turning his head, he studied the profiles around him suspiciously. A well-dressed young woman stood hypnotized by the impossible feast; a little old rentier was watering at the mouth and smiling as though gone mad; a tall old man, dumbstruck, pouted like a punished child; the nostrils of a blond girl student were quivering... Justinien turned around quickly and saw Ace of Diamonds standing there with averted eyes.

"Why, if it isn't Monsieur Léonard? How's your health?"

Justinien held out only two fingers.

"Splendid, and yours?" said Ace of Diamonds too amiably. "I haven't seen you for a long time. I thought you had left town."

Justinien lied stupidly (and was immediately aware of it): "I've been spending some time over in Cassis."

M. Léonard replied with a broad affected smile, "What a coincidence! I was there too."

Justinien understood his obvious irony. So you weren't in Marseille when M. Vibert got smashed up? You don't know a thing about it, you have an excellent alibi, eh? You expect me to swallow that? You don't know me, friend.

Laurent Justinien's eyelashes flickered and Ace of Diamonds saw it, for he was observing him through a fantastic enlarging lens. His last doubts vanished. The reward available to anyone facilitating the arrest of the "terrorist" was worth a little inconvenience. And—apparently—no danger was involved. Not for M. Léonard in any case:

if the police get shot full of holes, that's how they earned their retirement pensions. With his camel's hair coat and his hat down over one eye, Ace of Diamonds offered the passable likeness of a gentleman— well, not quite a gentleman—a detective. His contracted pupils followed the blond student who was leaving. And:

"It's a shame I didn't meet you in Cassis. I didn't go out much. I was busy with romantic love. A real honeymoon at high temperature." (With gusto.) "You're going to have dinner with me, Monsieur Laurent, I won't let you go. A real feed you won't forget. And if you're not afraid of pretty legs..."

In the middle of the crowd on the sidewalk, Justinien picked out a thickset, mangy little man, with his neck craned toward the rotisserie. Pudgy face, greasy tie. The man looked away. Justinien slipped the safety catch of the Browning in his coat pocket, and answered curtly, "Impossible today, thank you. I'm sorry. I've got to go now. By the way, if you're interested I've got half a dozen automatics to sell and quite a collection of magazines for them. Moderate prices, wholesale... or retail."

Justinien mangled the softening fingers in his grip. He rushed to the door, staring brutally at the thickset gentleman with the furtive eyes. As he crossed the sidewalk he stepped heavily on the man's foot, sent him staggering with a poke of his elbow in the ribs, smiled wickedly, and muttered, "*Pardon*, M'sieur." He jumped into a moving streetcar. The pudgy face ran along the sidewalk, trying to catch the second car. The camel's hair coat hastily crossed the street... Tailed.

Justinien snickered. Now let's see if they have my address. That would be bad. No witnesses; no alibi either. No witnesses? Who knows? I suppose they'll have no scruples about digging up a few? Ace of Diamonds has plenty of scum on tap. Capital punishment, forced labor for life, benefit of the doubt unlikely. I'll play the hand, Messieurs, the capital hand. Justinien dropped off the moving car and bumped into a line of women waiting outside a food store.

"Clumsy lout! Can't you look where you're going?"

"Beg your pardon, Madame, I'm a doctor, there's a very sick man waiting for me."

The very sick man is myself—no, the world. With his hand on his Browning, he turned into an alley, took ten steps, and stopped short, ready to fight. No one except a housemaid carrying a basket. He breathed easier.

He made a detour through the Old Port. Near his hotel several men were loitering about, any one of whom might be suspicious—especially the man sitting on the terrace of the Poisson d'Or in spite of the cold breeze, reading a paper. There's a hole in the page—an old trick.

Chance, the worst enemy a man can have, played against Laurent Justinien. As a rule, he carried his money with him, in a little silk bag tied around his waist. That day he had stupidly left the little bag hidden in his mattress. He had set a trap for himself, and that seemed a bad omen. Convinced that he was lost, he calmly climbed the stairs, entered, thrust his hand into the wool batting, and took the little bag. He took off his raincoat, which he folded over his arm, and his hat, so as to change his looks a little when he went down. These are your last moments, Laurent. He stopped a few seconds for breath at the edge of the stairwell. He wanted to think of all the things that were ending: the world, France, life, love—no, not love, no! But he could summon up neither thoughts nor images. Down below, blood and death. The last minute dwindled away miserably: the last drag. The last drag of existence.

Ginette climbed the stairs, as supple as a cat, without even making the old wooden steps squeak. She was breathless and wide-eyed with fright.

"The cops are after you. You can get out through the attic, turn left and you'll come out on the roof of the butcher shop. Hurry. And don't make any noise."

A ladder led to a trapdoor, which Ginette opened.

"Quick, up and out!"

"You're swell, Ginette!"

Delighted, Julien hoisted himself up toward the sky. The slopes of the roof slid downward toward the abyss. Squatting on the attic window, Justinien put on his raincoat and smoothed his hair. From his perch he could see only the harbor basin, the Quai Rive Neuve on the other side, the hill of Notre Dame. The roof was like a steep-sloping beach of no precise dimensions: it was terribly narrow and terribly vast. Justinien lay against it, clinging to the crest. Hard spasms ran through his muscles. "Oh Lord, I don't want to end up splattered all over the sidewalk, I have better things to do." His electrified wrists carried him toward a double chimney providing a niche where he stopped for a few moments, incapable of thinking. "If I start thinking, I'll fall." But he felt within him the presence of a thought as clear and limitless as the sky. "Something better to do, something big..."

Leaping down to the crest of the neighboring roof, three feet below, was not difficult; there began the realm of pure vertigo. A straight path four inches wide led between two nearly vertical inclines sloping down to destruction. Should I crawl on my belly like a slug? Standing erect, with his back to the masonry and his arms extended to balance himself, Justinien rejected this reasonable idea and put one foot forward like a tightrope walker... "You'll make it, Laurent, I know it," murmured an unhoped-for voice in his ear, and he answered, "I'll make it..."

He ran over the vertiginous path, touching it only with the tips of his shoes, drunk with air and vision. The city was unforgettable. A short climb, which broke off the tips of his fingernails, brought him to the third roof, which was terraced. Here Justinien saw, to his horror, that instead of going left toward the butcher shop, he had turned right. "You'll make it, Laurent, you'll make it..."

Now he observed that the spacious terrace was inhabited. On the terrace stood a green carnival booth that seemed to have been set down by a hurricane. No stairway, the stairway must be inside the booth. The whole affair was a closed trap in the middle of the sky. Justinien approached the window and looked inside. He saw a thin, disheveled woman in a pink kimono, moving about between a little cast-iron stove and the unmade bed. Justinien tapped gently on the windowpane with his fingertips, which he had torn climbing the wall. He pushed through the door.

"Don't be afraid, Madame, good evening, Madame."

The woman in the pink kimono retreated toward a dingy wall covered with postcards and pictures of movie stars. The little iron bed disclosed soiled sheets.

"Oof!" said Justinien cheerfully. "Not easy getting to your place by the rooftops, but you can't say it's disagreeable. I beg your pardon for disturbing you like this. The cops are on my trail. How do you get down from here, dear lady?"

"Well, you sure gave me a scare," said the woman.

She was dark-haired, with a sinewy neck, hard shoulders, harsh face. Rather beautiful in an irritating way. Her eyes were arrogant, she had character; ten years of little bars, ten years of lovemaking without joy or ill humor.

"If my man came in what a fuss *he*'d make."

"I'd explain the situation to him politely. He must know what's what."

"Yes, that he does."

Justinien spoke in a playful tone. The woman put a cigarette between her dry lips, he held out a light.

"What bothers me is that I haven't got my makeup on. The stairs are this way, you'd better cut your visit short." She blew smoke out of her dark nostrils and looked at him intensely. Assassin? Racketeer? Burglar? Gaullist? He might be any of them, but in a clean way. She liked him.

"Trouble?" she said vaguely, for it didn't do to ask questions.

"War," said Justinien. "War on skunks."

"Well, you've got your hands full. This way."

He entered the darkness of the stairway.

"Thanks, angel," he said, and felt a humiliating anger toward himself—because Angèle has "angel" in it.

On the fifth-floor landing he met a very old woman in a glittering silk turban, carrying a green bird perched on a petrified finger. The corridor on the ground floor was like the exit of a tunnel. It opened out on an alley full of movement. Mobile Guards and Legionnaire police were running toward the quay.

And then it happened. Ace of Diamonds came slowly down the

opposite sidewalk, looking up, watching the roofs. The whole of his moon face was exposed to Laurent Justinien's Browning. Justinien's hand was steady, he was sure of his aim, but he was in no hurry to pull the trigger. An invisible hand was placed on his wrist, an inner voice said to him: Think, you have the time, you have a whole second. Why kill this bastard? The world is full of these well-fed parasites nowadays, they swarm over it like worms on rotten meat. One replaces the next, we have better things to worry about than them. This one doesn't concern you anymore, Laurent; he'll never escape his own baseness. One day we shall disinfect—and radically. We shall save the world. Everything can be saved, Laurent. You have saved yourself, you see that it's possible. Don't shoot, Laurent, you are saved if you don't shoot. It's not your skin that's at stake now, it's—Justinien could not have said what, but he knew. —It's no longer the time for killing, Laurent, it's the time to fight, to fight murder too, and the men who murder. Cease to be a man of murder, you are a man of deliverance now… Let that bastard pass, save your nerves from the wretched temptation…

Ace of Diamonds passed. A woman came up the same sidewalk holding a little boy by the hand. "Mama, Mama," the little boy kept saying in an excited voice. Justinien stepped out of the doorway. Fugitive thoughts ran through his head, he was looking for something inside himself under a serene, reassuring inner light. Keep running, you hounds. The sky did me good. I couldn't have fallen, I had too much drive… God, how beautiful the city was, from up there! Beyond imagining—and yet, what a filthy city. The red cliffs, the sea, the freedom of the sea. Justinien remembered, like a stranger, another self that had walked through these backstreets wondering if he were going mad, if he deserved to live, if his hidden wounds would ever heal; a self afraid of his own hands, afraid to think, afraid to look in a mirror, afraid to confront certain eyes, the only eyes that could save him. "I can say that I've recovered from a bad sickness—the sickness of the world."

24. SOLITUDES

OVER THE last twenty years Félicien Mûrier had left Paris only for brief visits to Deauville, Cabourg, or Nice, where people of his acquaintance played insipid comedies for each other. Every once in a while he took the express for Budapest, Vienna, Warsaw, to attend literary banquets. Amazing, how stupid intelligent men can be under those circumstances. Sometimes he accepted an invitation to the country, to the house of some rich patron of letters. He would walk alone down the park paths and grow bored at the sight of a river less imaginative than the Marne; he would speak to blushing farm girls who took him for a portly doctor or a priest in civilian clothes; desirable creatures, intermediary between the animal and vegetable world, unfortunately gifted with speech. Oh, the country is all right for Jean-Jacques and neurasthenic creatures physiologically a century behind the times. Lamartine overdid it, and it made him murky. The "lake" was only a pond—and to pour out effusions in such a soporific purr is to proclaim that you never had anything in your gut. Either Lamartine didn't know how to make love or he was a consummate hypocrite, buttoned up in the boudoir, ruminating on his elegiac moonlight on the toilet seat. (Did they have them in those days? Not that it matters...) Insects and birds were of no interest to Félicien Mûrier, except for the Parisian sparrows, whose ways recall both the bourgeoisie and the lumpenproletariat and who were despoiled by the automobile, which deprived them of horse manure.

Mûrier would return from the country stupidly refreshed—I'd turn into a ruminant if I stayed there—and eager to return to real human life, so powerfully condensed in the illumination of cafés on a rain-soaked square, in the stone silence of buildings, in the pathetic faces of the slums, in strange, exciting, everyday shopwindows. Have you observed the erotic charm of the dummies in the windows of ladies' lingerie shops? There must be perverts whom the sight of these bare bodies, these pink wooden faces with blue eyes, transport into trances, walking through the streets as though in Mohammed's paradise—how do they avoid getting run over by buses? Their ecstasies are filled with a roar of motors, their voluptuous reveries are interrupted by stoplights... Have you observed those two narrow shopwindows framed in black at the end of the Rue de Ménilmontant? One displays funeral wreaths—for what disinherited coffins? The other shows off pâté de foie gras from Normandy, truly delicious. Inside, both the funereal and the edible merchandise are sold over a single counter. A lady in black receives you with a discreet smile. How is she to know whether you have come for a jar of pâté or a wreath appropriate for the obsequies of a tubercular demi-virgin?

It is man who makes the human, cosmic, metaphysical, pataphysical drama—man and not trees. I appear to be talking nonsense, but tell the truth now: which do you prefer—the Place Pigalle at eight in the evening or the Forest of Fontainebleau? His stubborn, ironic, and ideal but imaginary companion replied: Verhaeren said all that before you: *Tentacular Cities* and *Hallucinated Countrysides*... Oh, Verhaeren, why he's as boring as Père Hugo, a poetic technique that raises cacophony to hyperbolic heights: *les sourds hoquets des canons lourds* ("the muffled hiccups of the heavy cannon")—or *les lourds hoquets des canons sourds* ("the heavy hiccups of the muffled cannon"). Good God! An ignoramus and a Fleming to boot—ah, poor language of Ronsard!—pushing his plow straight through the lyricism of the century... And impressive just the same, yes impressive! *Le monde est fait avec des astres et des hommes*... ("The world is made of stars and men..."). I'd like to have written that. He perceived that this proud aphorism also contained the word *désastre* (disaster). For us disasters are more real than stars... Won't I be boring in fifty years? Nathan affirms I am already. A little journal with a psychiatric name,

Schizo, *Delirium*, or *Oedipus*, had written, "Mûrier, more stultifying than Valéry..." (These young men cultivated an unoriginal, feebly imagined senility of expression.) Félicien Mûrier's thoughts were diverted to the subject of insult, that deep need to put down others, which gives power to certain men; to incomprehension, for abuse would no longer be possible if one thought about the other person in order to understand him; to solitude, for we are surrounded by such total incomprehension that it's as if incompatible human species were living side by side, mistakenly wearing the same jackets; to work pursued blindfolded without really knowing why...but no, I do know, I do know, there is something I want to shout, even if I were chained among deaf people!...That most of them are deaf goes without saying, and that itself is only half the problem: aren't you yourself dumb? You who want to shout?

"I have dumped it all...A dream come true, old man. Publishers, magazines, cafés, invitations, dear friends, and Clémence, the bedroom, the workroom which killed dead the desire to work, the mail, the bills, the page proofs, the flattering dedications...At bottom, that should be a welcome deliverance. But Paris, Paris! They may stay there for another half century, and I have ten years ahead of me, fifteen at most, a rather problematical fifteen on account of heart disease that haunts fat people starting at age..."

From the train he contemplated passable landscapes, absurd stations, women travelers agreeable to pursue mentally—and he was seized with nostalgia for the banks of the Seine, for the Sébasto, for the aquarium reflecting the red of the leather upholstery in the basement of the Dupont bar on the Boulevard Saint-Michel. And the narrow streets where the gangsters used to hang out between the Hôtel de Ville and Rue Rambuteau, now full of empty spaces where houses had been torn down, the dangerous Rue de Venise, Rue Aubry-le-Boucher, where you follow the trail of ancient crimes and walk on the edge of the underground world...How happy I was in the holding cell of that police station, underneath Paris, underneath the whole life of Paris! What a memory! What a poem! A poem I will never write, I haven't the breath for it, it is inexpressible, unthinkable. I did not go down deeply enough into that reality. Words need to ripen within you to finally find expression, and you would have to invent new words, reforge known words, pull authentic images out of yourself with forceps: then the subworld would become faintly expressible, a glimmer would shine out of it, what glimmer? Mûrier began to feel himself practically insignificant. Colleagues, vile fraternity, my colleagues, we never expressed what is truly essential. We were unaware that everything was decomposing around us, that life can, should, have that taste of danger, of distress, of frenzy, of seriousness pushed to the limit of horror. Nonetheless, I have written some excellent pages about it, prophetic pages, Monsieur, worthy of being collected in a book, but they were only essays for a big weekly that no one will miss, and I was playing with foreboding like a child playing with bombs: in truth paying more attention to the feel of the five hundred francs for the copy and the flattering comments ("Félicien Mûrier reminds one of Kierkegaard...") than to the dynamite and the cyanide, to the sun that was setting, and to death. We were getting the benefits of a comfortable sunset; we were building country homes in the Chevreuse Valley under it. Suddenly, we have been totally devaluated, old counterfeit coins, honest false witnesses who didn't suspect that that they were accepting rhetoric in the place of thought. Begin again? Do something different? What?

He went through this crisis in a third-class carriage at nightfall, somewhere between Montauban and Toulouse. He lowered the window and leaned out to breathe in the air and the smoke, took a fountain pen and a mechanical pencil out of his pocket, got ready to throw them out without being noticed ... You still have the need for symbolic gestures, and you will only run to buy yourself another pen in Toulouse ... Don't act like an idiot. He put the pen and the pencil back in their places, sat back in the corner of the compartment, ran his hand over his face, especially his nose, as he did when he woke up in the morning. The people on the opposite bench could see lines of soot on the fleshy nose of the decorated gentleman who was looking at them mournfully.

In Toulouse the weather was mild. A light rain had just stopped,

life was flowing back into the boulevards. The streets had the animation of an overcrowded anthill, still incongruously lighthearted. The
bright bars illuminated the crude appeal of drink, women, idleness.
Mûrier lost his way, though he knew the city well. He was reminded
of Warsaw in '29 or '30. He had wandered around in the melting snow
and lost his way somewhere near Napoleon Square; he had arrived
late, all muddy and tired, at the literary banquet, but meanwhile he
had made a rendezvous for the night with a slender Polish girl swathed
in furs, a disquieting silhouette on a white sidewalk. Now Warsaw
was half-destroyed, tears of blood over Warsaw, and we understood
nothing when *Paris-soir* ran the headline WARSAW STILL RESIST-
ING. The girl is worn out by now, if by chance she survives, the armies
have passed over her, she was the coat-check girl in a café with Gypsy
music. What end for lovely tired bodies and polluted mouths in a
city under bombardment?

He recognized his friend's house, raised his hand to push the bell,
hesitated. The man who lived there, an engineer and industrialist,
surrounded by a sick wife and three athletic, musical daughters, would
shower him with friendly attentions. This rich man nourished a su-
perstitious admiration for famous intellectuals (not for the nonfamous)
as if they were the guardians of secrets he would never be worthy of
knowing. A poem was to him a piece of magic. "I have been punished
too much for having devoted my life to material goods." The wine
would be old, the phonograph records beyond reproach, the intimate
conversation (cigars and liqueurs) after the retirement of the three
marriageable Graces, would be easy, elevated, rich, since everything
was rich in the house, even the well-chosen witticisms, the humor,
the opinions on books that deserved no better than a basket in the
attic. If they discussed such books, it would be with quotations from
Edmond Jaloux and Thibaudet, Freud, Charcot, Gide, Emerson.
Politics would be avoided, since this friend considered himself a
disciple of Maurras, and like Maurras he was a Catholic without faith,
for the sake of spiritual order. He would ask what was happening in
Paris. And Mûrier would have to answer that nothing was happening
but that all was lost, that Paris was as beautiful as ever, commonplace

and unique, and that we were complete idiots, you and I and everybody, and Maurras most of all. My breath would poison the aroma of the cigars. And if this man, a sensitive fellow, whose lips trembled when he listened to Beethoven, should suddenly grow emotional over the fate of France, and admit that he felt like putting a bullet in his brain, we would be capable of weeping together like calves, old intellectual calves, we would be ridiculous, we'd deserve to be slapped in the face, both of us, in the mahogany smoking room. Mûrier departed in haste, afraid of running into his friend.

For a moment he followed some young men who were talking Yiddish and carrying books under their arms. For fear that they would take him for a detective, he turned abruptly to the right. The street he took, narrow and dark, was like the gallery of a prison. Toward the end, shone a tawny glow. The light, a bar naturally, grew more distinct. Mûrier's padding steps, *floc, floc, floc*, drew a square-faced, redheaded girl out into the light, her hands in the pockets of her red suit. She opened her mouth and took a long look at Mûrier. He went in, and felt himself sink into a pit full of glaring lights. He was served a rather copious meal, which dissipated his bitterness. The people at the bar seemed cut out of wrapping paper, hovering between the gelatinous light and the aerial night behind the door. The girl in the red suit moved among them. From time to time her insolent gaze rested on Mûrier; she had a large mouth, an air of laughing without really laughing.

At a sign from the mournful diner, she approached him.

"Do we take a room, old-timer? It's clean, you'd think you were in a family hotel. Funny family!"

She had a drawling, poised voice, vulgar, well-manicured hands; she seemed wrapped in the scarlet cloth and her lofty hairdo was tinted with fire. Mûrier followed her up a well-swept wooden staircase into an impoverished old middle-class room ("like the one Vincent Van Gogh died in").

The woman looked him over familiarly. "I can guess that you have traveled. You're not in the merchant marine? Captain of an ocean-going ship?"

He took off his heavy overcoat. He would gladly have taken off the burden of living, always the same.

"A long voyage," he said, and the young woman understood that he was a little crazy, perhaps with grief.

She opened her jacket under which a white, coarsely knitted sweater revealed vigorous breasts with blood-orange nipples.

"Well, what journeys will we take tonight? You look like you had your troubles. Don't think of them, old-timer. Do like me." The intimacy of her manner was comradely rather than professional.

"Most of all, I'm sleepy," he said. She pressed close to him, her head bent back, her eyes contracted and red.

"You'll sleep as much as you like . . ." And speaking from far off: "The time of joy is over, but that's no reason to deprive yourself of a pleasant moment."

It was an hour later, in bed, that Mûrier, restored to indifference and lucidity, asked her name. "Florelle, that's my nom de guerre."

"But wait a second, wait a second, where have I run into that name? You don't happen to know a certain police station in Paris, near the Rue du Roi-de-Naples?"

"Sure I know it! Now I bet you'll ask me if I know the Hôtel Marquise and that fat pig of an Anselme?"

The redheaded girl studied her memories.

"Say, you haven't been with me in Paris, have you? You know, I forget quickly, you're all alike: the fat ones are fat, and the thin ones are thin."

"That's true. Be still."

He felt a nauseous tenderness for this creature of the underworld. And what an intertwining of threads! "Anselme Flotte the hotel man? I heard they shot him."

"Shot, you think, darling?"

They were cold together, then suddenly warm, and they came together, unseeing. Florelle said softly, "I have a feeling that . . . that you've had a close call, yourself."

"It's possible . . . I'm not sure."

"Just what I said: the days of joy are over. But it's neat we met like this, even if it doesn't mean anything."

Mûrier got up early in the morning, leaving the girl asleep and money on the dresser. This city was awaking, the Garonne, between old buildings of tarnished brick, was a river of innocence. Mûrier had a shave and shampoo; the barber's hands smelled of garlic. He was lazily pleased to find no public baths open, to keep his contact with the underworld on his flesh. Nothing held him anywhere, but a kind of courage came back to him. He wanted never to write again, or to see anybody. Alone. The old life must all crumble into dust. We shall live again later. Someone will live again later. He decided to take another train, to head for more sun and more forgetfulness. To go, without knowing where, to live without knowing how long, to allow the void and something unknown, new and dangerous, to ripen within him. I'll stop—or I'll be stopped. All France has come to that, with a moribund old man at its head.

Mûrier had just seen the recent portrait of the marshal in the window of a stationery store. He stopped to contemplate it, as though he had never seen it before. For a long time things float before your eyes, suddenly you discover them in their reality. The picture of a man, in reality, a man unknown to the universe. His képi, his white mustache, his handsome face, his name on posters, in syndicated dispatches sent all over the world, his name on millions of lips with the taste of doubt, of admiration, of contempt, of falsehood. The taste of the end. At the bottom of all the noise and pictures, somewhere an old man like most well-preserved old men. Drawing to his end and conscious of it (this consciousness must be exceedingly vivid). Not a Tolstoy still preoccupied by mystic grandeur and the love of mankind—not a great sage—not old Hugo playing the Olympian. No, a soldier, a technician of the general staffs of other days, eternally chewing the old cud: Napoleon, Moltke, the promotion schedules, mutual denigration. A phantom chief of state, himself humiliated, desperate, congealed. It is difficult to be great in defeat, in this incomprehensible defeat; difficult to seem great when you are buried in excrement up to your neck. Weeping, it was said, when he received indignant letters from rabbis; promising in his plaintive voice to spare the civil servants belonging to the Left parties from persecution. Saying brusquely to an archbishop, "But don't you know, Monsignor, that I am a prisoner bearing my cross?" Complaining that news was concealed from him—news that might bring about his death or suddenly lead him to make some gesture like a real living man. Perturbed to see the newspapers comparing him to the Maid of Orleans, that proud young girl who saved France—while I, an old man with a rope around my neck, am dragging my country to perdition (could he, after all, think otherwise?). Gravely nodding a head of funereal marble as he listened to enemy generals, enemy ambassadors with oily smiles, politicians who had sold out to the enemy, double and triple agents. His trembling hand signing decrees, laws, commandments of misery and shame—"with honor"—for if he didn't, things would be even worse. (Really worse?) The doctors had to give him injections before and after. "If he were not there," people kept saying, "it would be chaos, treason in chaos." Pro-English at the bottom of his heart, it was said—but detesting Queen Victoria. How much truth was there in what people said?

A man at the edge of the tomb, living one day after another between desire and fear of death. Four hours of lucidity a day—or only three? Fatigue mingled with torpor, an incessant desire to sleep, a restless drowsiness filled with dread of waking. And what would they want tomorrow? The blood of a hundred hostages or of a hundred million more every week, or the fleet, or the airfields of Morocco? Spasmodic accesses of pride and decision—I won't sign, I am the Leader! Oh well, I'll sign, what else can we do, I'll take responsibility for this as for everything else. I will assume the heaviest burden. Fear and dislike of the well-fed puppets who bring in papers, the temptation to cry out: Go to the devil, let me end my days in peace, you know perfectly well that these palinodes are useless! (To end *in peace*, what a crushing thought!) Instead of a human consciousness confronting the end of life, the repetition of oppressive words: *Duty, France, Leader.* And after me? After me that abject scoundrel in the white tie. Big words like the words on the posters, flat, hard, stereotyped in big black capitals, and under them paper, and behind them a wall.

This particular portrait showed the aged man in uniform overcoat and képi with Oak Leaves, face pale, eyes blank, leaning on a cane and bending down to pat a dog full of vitality. "He's absolutely alone," thought Mûrier. "Tyrants, and the false tyrants pulled by strings, are the most solitary of men. That's their punishment." This idea, though just, seemed to him literary: every idea capable of providing the subject for a magazine article began to repel him. We have debased everything by thinking in terms of printed matter and newspaper clippings.

The train for Avignon was three hours late. Mûrier went for a walk. A bookseller whom he asked for his own works asked him to spell the name—what's that you say, Mugnier? Oh yes, Mûrier, like the silkworm. "No, Monsieur, I have nothing in stock . . . No, I don't remember ever having sold his works either."

"But he's very well thought of in Paris," said the poet, not without irony. "What poets do you sell?"

"We have a provincial public here and a few literary people who order their books direct from the publishers. I am asked mostly for Musset, Hugo, Lamartine. High school students ask for the Pléiade, Vigny . . . sometimes Villon."

In the poetry section, Mûrier saw Baudelaire, Albert Samain, Valéry, Paul Claudel, Rimbaud. "Verlaine's *Parallèlement* passes for an erotic work, it has been a moderate success."

"You sell Claudel and Rimbaud?"

"Why, yes, Monsieur, the city is partly Catholic, and Rimbaud remains a favorite with students and artists."

Mûrier pointed to *Toi et Moi*. "And this druggist, M. Geraldy, who writes with rose bath soap?"

"A regular seller. A few copies every month. Do you really think it's so bad, Monsieur?"

"No, as a matter of fact, it's really rather good," said Mûrier gravely, and he saw the bookseller, whom up to this moment he had not really seen. A little man, almost bald, with swollen eyelids, singularly meditative.

"Do you read your merchandise?" Mûrier asked, in an aggressive tone because he was feeling absurdly benevolent. The bookseller owned that he did not have the time, absorbed as he was in studies more important in our epoch, astrology.

"Ah, so am I," cried Mûrier, lying with sincerity. He put his hand on the book of a Parisian astrologer, *1940, Year of Victory*. "That, I must admit, is going a little too far."

"Charlatans, Monsieur, consecrate a science . . . for fools . . . I have much better things."

Mûrier felt the need to name himself, not out of vanity, he thought, but in order to escape, for a few minutes, from the solitude of anonymity. ("Poets, solitary as tyrants. The qualities of solitude . . . let it pass.") "Monsieur, I am the poet whose works you don't carry."

"I had guessed as much, Maître. Once every month, an author comes in asking me for his own works, most often after the full moon; none had come in this month and this is the twenty-ninth. They have a detached way of pronouncing their name, I never mistake it. It grieves me not to know them, or rather, not to appreciate them, they are sometimes excellent authors . . . for the elite."

Mûrier was amused.

"Glory is such a little thing under the stars," the little bald man continued. "And although I have the greatest respect for your person and your profession, you will agree with me perhaps, Maître, that the true poetry of our days is the astral knowledge of destiny. I am not a true initiate, but I can see that you must have a very interesting horoscope . . ."

"Rather flat, as far as the past is concerned. As for the future, muddled constellations."

"I understand. Best not to know, that would be wise. I have given up plotting horoscopes since Munich. Men are not equal to their destiny, the stars are too heavy at this moment. But it is a good time to reread Nostradamus."

"And Saint John of Patmos."

Out of courtesy, Mûrier bought a *Treatise on Scientific Astrology* by a Dutch scholar. From his plebeian ancestors, Isidore Mûrier, carpenter at Besançon, republican under the Empire, and Jean-Paul Mûrier, country doctor, freethinker, Freemason, Dreyfusard, admirer of Combes, of Louise Michel, and of Séverine, he was proud to have inherited the concrete, precise, materialist spirit of a population fed up with being duped, strong enough to have confidence in its own good sense and to consider death as eternal sleep: no flowers or wreaths, a hygienic cremation. Life could be confronted without crutches. To these conceptions Félicien Mûrier added only a reasonable epicurean-ism, intuition, imagination, polypersonality, the divination of hidden realities ... Astrological works are full of poetical insights of the second zone; but everyone knows that the lyrical inspirations of the second zone—unintelligible verbal irrelevancies—are those that cause a book to sell, impress the critics, and bring you the most interesting letters: from the obsessed reader in Guadeloupe, from the young girl studying pharmacy who believes in telepathy and in the numbers of destiny, which she deciphers in prescriptions. When life is on the downgrade and never takes you anywhere except to Dufayel furniture sets, bankruptcies, and mobilizations, a false and mathematically delirious science that permits the intelligence to busy itself with dizzy astronomical heights, with numbers more magic than lottery tickets, with paranoiac lyricism and stellar mystifications, that opens up es-capes ....

Mûrier stopped at General Delivery. He only hoped that there would be nothing from Clémence. And nothing else from Paris. A telegram from Lucien Thivrier called him to Marseille: PERFECT DELIVERY STOP BOY. This meant: "I have found Augustin Charras." This stranger remained the only man whom Félicien Mûrier wanted to see—because of that dawn on the Seine.

25. THE SKEPTIC

FÉLICIEN Mûrier's mood changed: he made plans. This is an incoherent pleasure in which one indulges after periods of depression, as though childish daydreaming naturally followed anxiety. Formerly, Mûrier would have dreamed of a great work that would win recognition, of a "name" borne as they say "on the wings of Fame" (wings of gold-painted cardboard), of a real love, or of women; tempted in turn by a unique soul in a noble body—and by every imaginable face, every conceivable body (one has so little imagination in these things!), especially the most inaccessible, the Cingalese with ovoid breasts, the Mongol, the Dahomeyan, the Biblical Palestinian. The quality of our waking dreams varies with the vigor of our infantilism, the age and ardor of our instincts, but they remain the visions of primitives—on the level of Mohammed's paradise: fountains, houris, sexuality projected into the hereafter. Doesn't the very conception of the hereafter have its roots in sexuality? Now he desired a studio opening out on a garden, somewhere on the Côte d'Azur, tamarind trees, a hairy palm tree, a broad view of the sea, quiet, infrequent visits, books about the polar regions, the Pacific islands, the life of beasts in the jungle...

The inspector passing through the car reminded him that he was living in a police state. "Your safe-conduct has expired, Madame."

The old lady in mourning was frightfully upset. "But, officer, two of my trains were delayed, I am only one day late."

"I'm not responsible for the timetable, Madame, your safe-conduct has expired, that's all I know, you will give your explanations at the gendarmerie, no arguments, eh?"

Mûrier intervened. "It would seem to me, after all, that Madame is invoking what is called in law a case of *force majeure*."

"You mind your own business, I am doing my official duty."

"I am a Frenchman, Monsieur, and what happens in France is my business. I shall accompany Madame to the gendarmerie if Madame permits me."

The lady had given up the struggle, she sat like a threatened insect feigning death. Mûrier's irritation made him hot. He tore open his overcoat.

"Very well, then, we shall see!" His movement revealed the ribbon of the Legion of Honor in his buttonhole. The inspector calmed down, because you can't really know nowadays who is wrong and who is right, whether you should annoy people to the limit or be lenient. And it is very hard to avoid incidents in a mess like this. He adopted an administrative tone: "Madame, the decrees on the movements of foreigners are clear." (Yet he returned the pink paper.) "On arrival you will report to the competent authorities and give your explanations." He neglected to question the other travelers.

I'm an idiot, thought Mûrier. I might have got myself into a fine fix. What if they were looking for me? For a moment he savored his fear. Except in case of criminal indictment, the authorities of the Free Zone did not concern themselves with fugitives from the Occupied Zone. They demobilized escaped prisoners, asking them to keep their mouths shut. But perhaps I am the object of a criminal indictment? A criminal without knowing it? Why not? Or semi-afflicted with persecution mania?

His fear came back toward evening as the train pulled into Marseille. He expected to be picked up on the platform. He should have had the presence of mind to get off at the last stop and take a streetcar or bus. Faces that could only belong to dicks were floating about in the crowd. Several times they seemed to be descending on him, but he kept outwardly calm, though his heart was pounding and his legs had gone soft. Nothing happened. He was reassured. From the top of the monumental stairway outside the Saint Charles Station, he looked down on the spacious boulevard, the low-lying side streets with their shady hotels, and he suddenly felt strong, almost joyful, like an escaped prisoner confident of his luck. Full of defiance, he chose the best hotel, the Splendide, and filled out the registration form. If you are looking for me, here I am.

In the following days he regretted this imprudence. Hearing steps in the corridor at night—pure hallucination perhaps—he woke up shaking, sure that they had come to arrest him. They arrest people at night too—the law forbidding arrests between sunset and the legal hour of daybreak was a product only of high civilization. (The hunted assassin knows that he will sleep out the night undisturbed, even if the inspectors are watching the exits, ready to knock on his door, revolver and handcuffs in hand, at five twenty-five. He has an eternity of several hours ahead of him, a vast respite, and if he is with a woman, he embraces her as if the whole of life were still in his grasp. Daybreak will come later, but nothing can prevent him from having had this night, this woman, this hope.)

At about five o'clock one morning there really was a knocking at the door. Mûrier jumped out of bed, bare-legged, in his pajama jacket, covered with cold sweat. This time they had *really* knocked. He listened. His terror was simple. Again a knocking, this time distinct.

All he could utter was one strangled syllable: "What?"

The soft voice of the chambermaid answered, "It's time for your train, Monsieur."

"What train?" The train for the underworld, for the shooting range at Vincennes. He saw himself executed at dawn, he trembled in his whole frame, ah, it's all over!

Incredibly, the female voice stammered, "I beg your pardon, Monsieur, I got the wrong door."

"Wrong door, wrong door!" he burst out. "It's insane." He thought he was shouting but his voice produced only the murmur of someone being strangled.

He turned on the light, looked at himself in the mirror, his hairy legs, the hair around his dangling sex, his decomposed face—I'm the world's biggest coward, I'm a jerk, an overimaginative maniac. He put on his trousers and rang. The chambermaid appeared. She had yellow, tired skin, and handsome hysterical black eyes.

"Was it you who woke me up?"

She muttered frightened apologies.

"It's no joke," he said, "I can only sleep well in the morning, I won't be able to get back to sleep. Bring me some strong coffee and a sandwich."

"There won't be any coffee until seven o'clock."

He flew into a rage. "Well, bring me whatever you can. You figure it out, it's your fault!"

He was angry because a question was on his lips and he couldn't ask it. "Have people been arrested at night in this hotel, on this floor, in this room?"

"I'll go and see what I can find in the kitchen, please forgive me."

Another chambermaid, almost pretty despite her disheveled hair, brought him a cup of wretched "national coffee" and two dry rolls. Forcing a smile, he thanked her effusively, and took her around the waist.

"I'm a respectable woman, Monsieur," she said without repulsing him.

"Well, I am a very respectable man," said Mûrier, completely relaxed, and kissed her on the ear. She permitted no further advances. He touched neither the coffee nor the rolls, fell asleep, and slept till noon.

In Marseille Lucien Thivrier called himself M. Jasmin and lived in the Rue Thiers. It seemed very fitting that old Thiers should have been born in this narrow sloping street with its barred windows, its monastic bourgeois houses. Félicien rang the bell but the door was not opened at once; he realized that he was being observed from within. A young woman with a high hairdo, a long neck, and singularly bright eyes opened and looked him over.

"M. Jasmin . . ."

"Come in, he isn't home, but he will be here soon. Whom shall I announce?"

Mûrier handed her his card. Her bright eyes became even brighter. "Ah, it's you—Lucien!"

Lucien emerged from the adjoining room. "Welcome, dear poet. My wife is a great admirer of yours, you know."

Florine Thivrier served a tisane in the absurd, freezing living room. "Keep your overcoat on, it's cold."

Involuntarily they spoke softly. "Oh, everything is fine," the Thivriers said both at once. Mûrier vaguely knew that they were doing dangerous work—without fear of arrest at night—or making love warmly despite their fear. "Yes, we've given up teaching. We were suffocating! This idea of religious education without any precise religion! 'Robespierre's supreme being, then?' my husband asked the Inspector of Education. And do you know what he answered? 'Yes, if you like, as long as you don't mention Robespierre.' In the new children's books the French Revolution isn't mentioned: Vercingétorix, Jeanne d'Arc, Henry IV, Louis XIV, the marshal. Louis XVI never had his head cut off!"

They looked at a book illustrated in color: *Yes, Monsieur le Maréchal, or the Oath of Pouique the Glutton and of Lududu the Lazy* by Uncle Sebastian. The marshal, armed with a big peasant broom, was driving out the wicked, represented as spiders. "... He had deigned to take the broom into his noble hands that had wielded the sword ... And at once ... The sky cleared, the sun burst forth ..." Mûrier was amazed. "Why, that's much better than any witch's broom!"

The Thivriers missed their school and the children. You can't imagine what children are like. Thirty children, thirty unknown dramas that will find neither their poet nor their novelist. "In twenty years," said Lucien Thivrier, "the NRF hasn't published a single book about this section of humanity."

"The men of letters are a good deal more than twenty years behind the times," said Mûrier.

Florine reported the remark of Cécile, aged ten: "If I have lice," she said, "it's not my mother's fault, it's her lovers'...What pigs!" And the protest of little Jesus Navarro, when they gave him an airplane to cut out: "Airplanes are filthy machines for killing Republicans. I don't want any... I'd like to smash them all!" And Sneaky Josette: "So what if I do like to tear off insects' wings? They'd tear my fingers off if they could, wouldn't they? You take your pleasure where you find it, right?" Josette, aged eleven, also said, "When I'm big, I'd like to be a kept woman like my aunt. That's the good life." "And Barnabé," cried Lucien Thivrier, "priceless Barnabé. A rascal and a thief, serious as a pope in school, a good student. He already had three girlfriends and what scenes of jealousy he put them through! I lent him a book by Fenimore Cooper and he brought it back next day: No, Monsieur, the Redskins bore me; they're nothing but fake Apaches. Haven't you something by Courteline? Stories about cuckolds for instance?"

"And now, what are you going to do?"

"And you?"

All three of them had the same look of false perplexity, Lucien Thivrier who loved general ideas and "theory"—"Without sound theory, no revolutionary action"—said, "The chips are down, Monsieur Mûrier. Your literature of yesterday is as dead as our teaching. We could try crawling along on our bellies in the shit, we might succeed—with difficulty—and that wouldn't be without its dangers either. A big piece of humanity is being crushed under the steamroller. If the operation succeeds, we're cooked—whether we behave or not. I think it will fail. They are strong but there are great imponderables, Russia, America, Europe itself, us—yes, us."

Félicien Mûrier's fat crooked nose and slightly widened eyes expressed his skepticism. "High politics is like high poetics: both based on little tricks and old delusions. Why not cultivate the mirage? Hurry up and appreciate every nuance of the fairytale soap bubble, because it's going to burst. You are young, Monsieur Thivrier, I admire you sincerely."

"And I'm amazed that you can give me an answer as banal as an alexandrine by Abbé Delille! Even if it's true that my thirty-five years may have something to do with it, there are millions of us on this continent who have not yet reached the age of universal fatigue. Allow me to remind you that what is true for eighteen-year-olds is true for men of sixty. Neither children nor old men will be able to breathe in the immense model prison they are building for us."

"Are you sure? An ultramodern, hygienic prison, tolerable diet avoiding an excess of goose liver; radio, elevating moral movies; permission to sleep with a woman now and then; wouldn't that be an average ideal, highly acceptable to the majority? Propaganda would point to the dangers of the outside world: never leave the country that protects you—if you only knew what perils await you abroad! Besides, the jam ration will be increased in six months. Man would be relieved of the need for initiative, struggle, resistance, or the search for explanations—for everything would be explained. Once he had completed his obligatory tasks, he would cultivate four square yards of garden, free to plant either turnips or hortensias. The radio would repeat every hour: you are happy and free! Movies, posters, novels, and illustrated newspapers would prove it. Your little man would leave his house in the morning whistling the new hit: 'I am happy and free!' Most of our retired people and small rentiers don't dream of any greater happiness! I see on the horizon a black, totalitarian socialism, more of a rationalized barracks than a prison ... Why should it fail? You would teach utilitarian spiritualism, disciplinary materialism, or authoritarian racism—or some mixture of the three—and the state police would make it absolutely irrefutable. Section XX of the General Plan for Literature, drawn up by prosperous, docile academicians, would permit me, during the period of reeducation of intellectuals, to publish six poems a year in small editions subjected to four different censors, two of whom would be indulgent. To make a living, I would correct the proofs of a popular education daily with a circulation of thirty millions; it might call itself: *Order without Shadow*."

The irony in Félicien Mûrier's voice accentuated his desolate look.

"Prove to me that this is impossible and I'll follow you anywhere."

He looked at man and woman in turn, longer at the woman. "I've just discovered that the reign of fear has begun."

Lucien Thivrier leaned toward him and spoke with controlled vehemence: "...the reign of fear—you mean, of cowardice...That may be so, but we will not consent to it, do you understand? We are Europeans and there is no more Europe, unless you mean a charnel house. We are French and there is no more France. We are civilized people and civilization is reduced to scientific murder. We are clean and we wallow in filth. Is that no true?"

"Yes, that is true."

"Well, we will not accept it. Let the great intellectuals acquiesce if they like, and beg little favors that will smother them alive. We shall resist without them."

"Don't be angry, Monsieur Mûrier," said Florine. "My husband esteems you highly."

"Why should I be angry, he is right, he is right. The red corpuscles can't escape from their charge of oxygen."

Mentally Félicien Mûrier added two lines to a poem which was constructing itself in his brain, sometimes as irritating as the rasp of a saw:

> I promise you solemnly
> Ursula a party in the Great Bear

26. THE SUITCASE

FÉLICIEN Mûrier accepted the hospitality of an old friend who owned a villa facing the Mediterranean, surrounded by dwarf palms. This elderly writer preferred to live at a hotel in Nice, keeping to his routine round of bars—which were becoming more and more deserted. "I understand you," Mûrier said to him, delighted at the prospect of being alone in a big house with a lame gardener and an ageless maid. "It's lucky for me. I admit that I have need of solitude... We would hurt each other if we spoke at this moment." Not very polite, but friendly. The two men agreed neither on art nor on the bit of politics that interested them, nor on women, nor on magazines; and their diverse successes, the one famous without fortune, the other rich but little known, made them bitter toward one another.

Nonetheless, before taking leave of him at the garden gate, Mûrier asked his friend what he thought of the future of France.

"Finished for a century!" said the other, tossing his white-checked muffler over his shoulder with a gesture of finality. "And what difference will it make to us in a century?"

"It makes a difference to me," said Mûrier.

"You'd better go inside," said his host. "You'll catch cold. This damned wind— We aren't made for the centuries. Luckily!"

"I'm very grateful to you, you know."

"...Really nothing to be grateful for."

The other man was tall and slender, a trifle stoop-shouldered, sickly, with a face whose hardness was misleading. Weak, he was inclined to be good—for it is tiring not to be. His intelligence was brilliant but superficial—"not the slightest imagination," thought

Mûrier. "The barren fig tree." Lazily egotistical, deserted by his wife, exploited by an unloving ("and certainly frigid . . .") mistress, neglected by his married children, he still wrote, in a style limpid to the point of insipidity, essays on the seventeenth-century *moralistes*. He suffered from liver trouble and was afraid of dying. "I offer a reward of five francs to anyone who will show me the one person (doubtless female) who reads your essays. This disease has no known cure."

With a youthful movement, the essayist turned around. "Do you know where Easter Island is?"

"Yes. Vaguely."

"I would like to take refuge there . . . And I spend my evenings in the Yellow Island bar. We've made a mess of everything, old man. Go inside, I tell you."

Mûrier would have liked to say something friendly, one of those phrases commonplace in appearance that people remember later because they contain a grain of sincerity; but instead, he swallowed down his shame and asked in an anxious tone, "You haven't got a few Gauloises left from the days of President Lebrun, have you?"

The essayist expressed his astonishment with the grimace of an African fetish.

"You've never had a sense of realities, Mûrier. My gardener dries selected leaves, cuts them up, and seasons them with three percent of cigarette butts. It stinks but it's bearable in a pipe."

The essayist opened the door of his car. He looked down bizarrely into a mole hole at his feet, visible only to himself, going down to the center of the earth. He said, "I bore the disasters of the front more easily than the lack of tobacco. It makes me mean. If you knew what a clever rascal my faithful gardener is. Make friends with him. That's my advice. Goodbye!"

The door of the car slammed. The synthetic gas engine sneezed to life. Mûrier thought with a weary grimace, "Old egotist, go on with you. Rationing didn't catch you unprepared. I'll bet you have whole packs of Gauloises and Gitanes and I bet you smoke them all alone in your bedroom, with the doors and windows locked, as if you were masturbating." (Eh, what do I know about it? Where do I get these intuitions of vileness? The desire to smoke, one more abasement...)

Mûrier chose the studio on the second floor, lighted by large bay windows (the sea, the sky), with light-colored wooden furniture, a red carpet, works of art. The other man thought he understood abstract art, dynamic (or dynamist or dynamited) sculpture. On a little ebony stand, a work of this school projected brass tentacles to which black and white semicircles were attached. It was called *Aurora Borealis*. Mûrier laughed—glumly—and, suddenly exasperated, put the piece away in the desolate winter garden. As for the pictures, he left them in place, having noted that he hardly saw them. He donned slippers and a house jacket, reread Dostoyevsky and Stevenson, smoked the gardener's vile mixture of herbs and leaves, though it made him cough, discovered excellent records. "Lord, how comfortable I am. The old Pierrot did well to leave his nest. If I had to see that mug of his every day! I'm not going out anymore, I'm going to live like a monk." And yet he stood by the windows, overlooking the stupid, magnificent sea, murmuring, "Paris, Paris...this war..."

> Oh guillotine incompatible
> with the sea with the sky

It was a misty morning, infinitely light and reassuring. Mûrier was listening to Handel when the ageless maid entered. "A gentleman is asking to see you, Monsieur. He says you are expecting him."

Visibly shocked, the maid drew breath before finishing her announcement. "He has no visiting card. His name is Chavas."

Mûrier sighed heavily: "Ah..." Two impulses clashed within him: a kind of joy and annoyance mingled with fear. I was feeling so good, I was forgetting. I always do something idiotic. Big tomcat by the stove, purring your music—shake yourself!

"...I know. Show him in."

When Augustin Charras reached the end of this strange road with fenced-in gardens on both sides reminding you of a prison walk and burst out onto the seaside drive, he abruptly "cast off his worries": Silber lost, Ortiga in hiding, Justinien hunted, the little suburban house evacuated in haste, Angèle's tense eyes and unsmiling mouth, Dr. Ardatov's anxiety, Hilda's neurotic calm. And the bombings, the rationing, the rackets, the traffic in cigarettes, the growing cretinization of the world! "Calamities come in series and the big ones bring on little ones, to each his own, citizens, and the day to drink it down has come...."

The road seemed white to him, the sea soothed him, he breathed in deeply, everything seemed to brighten... Better not believe in it, but it feels good. The visit to the "great poet" did not particularly move him. Great or small, what poet could find a living word at this hour? It was no longer a time for words. "A time for killing," Justinien would say. This irritated Charras, but the hard phrase encrusted itself in his brain. And what do you accomplish by killing? Where are the guilty ones? You never strike the guilty, they are everywhere, but they are up too high. And their office boys, what can they do about it? The circus horses circling in this infernal circus will never escape. Nothing to do. *Do nothing?*

His fists clenched of their own accord. Christ! Do nothing in this hell, let everything ride?

A few days earlier, he had said to Lucien Thivrier, "All right, I'm with you. There's still a bit of strength in my old bones. They ought to make old men fight the wars, they have less to lose. If it comes to that, I won't make such a bad-looking corpse." And he had thought: it might even be a relief to me. "The little girl has courage. She'll get along. A man can't cling to his children like a coward. You can count on me."

The teacher answered, "Nobody wants you to die, we want you to hold out. Patience and caution. The war with Russia is the beginning of the end for them."

Another country devastated, another youth cut down. Charras liked the Russians and distrusted them. A revolution transformed into a dictatorship, executions on an industrial scale, tons of propaganda rammed down your throat. But they still sang the "Internationale"; the executioners and the executed, even if they were a little crazy—Slavs after all—and they were building a new society together, thousands of factories without capitalists, that was something. The people who work, in Russia like anywhere else, aren't the ones making deals with Hitler, nobody asked their opinion. Now that the borders of the USSR had been broken through, the Russian earth, bleeding red under the red banners, became blindly precious again.

After locating the villa in which the "great poet" lived, Charras idled for a time on the road. "Nowadays, I go visiting in fancy neighborhoods. Suppose I turn around and go home?" But he rang the bell. Though he had never before entered a house of the rich, nothing struck him until the studio. There it was the abundance of light and colors, the red carpet.

"There you are at last!" cried Félicien Mûrier who had a two days' growth of beard. The great poet's woolen jacket was soiled with the ashes of ersatz tobacco.

Charras grumbled, "Delighted to see you again ..."

"Let me stop the phonograph."

"No, leave it on. I like it. I would even like to listen."

"Listen then. Have a seat."

Charras noticed that he had left his hat on (his first felt hat, he had always been faithful to the cap) and took it off.

"I'm not very polite. I'm sorry."

"Who cares about good manners?" said Félicien Mûrier merrily.

"I do."

Charras sat down in a woven-rope chair. Now that's an idea, rope furniture, shouldn't be expensive. Decorators have ideas.

"Didn't you wear a mustache, Monsieur Charras?"

"Yes, but the police are looking for me."

"Why, they're after me too," Félicien Mûrier almost said, but perhaps it wasn't true—he hoped it wasn't true. He only smiled.

"Do you know why?"

"I don't know much. There is no 'why' anymore."

They had nothing more to say to each other.

The record emitted a grave chant, graver than Angèle's music, a profound cry, as though the earth, the sea, and men were singing in chorus on appeased battlefields covered with black wheat...Charras felt that to be polite it was not enough to listen, he ought to say something.

"Do you miss Paris?"

"No, I have it all in my head."

"So do I," said Charras, "but maybe that's what makes me miss it."

"Right."

The great chant was beating its wings: immense wings, somber and transparent. They hid the light of day, then suddenly uncovered it, intolerably bright, a light of sobs. The record stopped.

"Have you something to drink? A glass of water?" Charras asked, "And no more music, that music is too strong for me. It's no time for music."

Félicien Mûrier admired him. The Seine drowns, but when it chooses to illuminate a man it makes no mistake. This is a man, a real one. An old man of the Paris pavement, of the underworld. A complete man.

"I am not of your opinion, Monsieur Charras."

"Neither am I. Sometimes I say the opposite of what I think and I say it sincerely. Batting the breeze, that's all. But silence is a fine thing too, isn't it? Sometimes you'd wish for a monumental silence. Have you a glass of water?"

"I have some *quinquina*," said Mûrier grandly. "This is a privileged house."

"So I see. Does it belong to you?"

"No. I think nothing belongs to me now. And I never had much, you know."

"So much the better for you."

Mûrier went to get the rare bottle and the glasses. They did not clink glasses. Charras looked absently at the modern pictures, which he took for the work of an engineer or an architect. Then he saw the friendly look in Mûrier's eyes and asked, "Are you decorated?"

"Men of letters are always decorated. It's the custom."

"The ribbon," said Charras meditatively, "makes a good impression on railroad trains."

This incoherence appealed to Félicien Mûrier.

"Well, yes…"

"Do you feel like risking your skin?"

Mûrier, funnily enough, felt no surprise. As a matter of form—mechanically—he exclaimed, "Goodness, what serious questions you ask, Monsieur Charras! A little more *quinquina*?"

"It's not me raising serious questions," said Charras with a note of gloom. And added playfully, "It's the music."

They became gay. They felt like exchanging broad smiles but contained themselves. The liquor warmed their hearts.

"Well, Monsieur Charras, explain yourself. I'm moderately attached to my skin, like everyone else."

"I'm not much attached to mine," Charras broke in. "I can't be nowadays. But as for you, it's strictly within your rights."

"I don't know if I care about it any more than you do. But as you say, it's within my rights. The right to be scared, the last right we have."

Now they were smiling. Mûrier sank deep into his chair. Well-being took possession of him. Charras hesitated.

"They tell me you're a great man. In that case your skin is valuable."

"Admitting it for the moment," said Mûrier (flattered). "Would you find it natural for a great man to be a bit of a coward nowadays?"

"No. Anyway, for you the risk is minimal, I think. For anyone without a decoration, who happens to be watched, the risk is greater."

Mûrier mentally composed a newspaper ad:

MINIMAL RISKS
Wanted
men of letters, preferably famous,
decorated … no reward …

"A little suitcase of explosives to be brought as far as Lyon, not very heavy unfortunately. Our man in Lyon is beyond suspicion. It's only the trip."

"What kind of explosives?" Mûrier asked eagerly.

"I have no idea. My line was wood and coal, you know. Four little gray packages, labeled as lye. For making soap. You put them at the bottom of your suitcase, beneath your underwear."

The underworld must burst! Old-fashioned dynamite, gelignite, TNT fermenting under innocent labels. Minds charged with bitterness and hatred, it's the minds that will explode. Mine too. A joyous shudder ran through Mûrier.

"I would prefer to take your little suitcase to Paris."

"Not possible. From Lyon on the liaison is organized, unless something goes wrong. Another time if you like."

"All right. Another time."

Mûrier dreamed of the satisfaction of depositing a briefcase at minimal risk in that hotel with the cream-colored corridors where the office of Major Erich-Friedrich Acker—the 317th Bureau—was located. A package on which he would write PROSE AND VERSE OF THE PRESENT TIME would contain the infernal machine. Major Acker's opaque face would appear, sitting solidly on the collar of his gray-green uniform. Mûrier saw himself saying confidentially, "Monsieur Acker, I don't know why, but I can't be angry with you. You are an old European in spite of everything. Get yourself out of here! Your office building, full of the destroyers of Europe, is going to blow up in seven minutes. It's a little joke of the vanquished, my philological major. An explosive little joke, of cosmic dimensions. Take the elevator, believe me, and beat it without turning around. I'll let you enjoy the charm of Paris for a little while."

> Prose and verse cruel atoms
> atoms pitiless atoms
> burst open seeds of celestial fire
> purifying nebulous

"Atrocious," muttered Mûrier half-audibly.

"I beg your pardon?" said Charras, ready to beat a retreat. "Think it over. I understand that . . ."

"Nothing, my friend. No objections at all. I was answering myself. I talk to myself, an old habit. I have a street organ under my skull. But as for your little suitcase, it will be with pleasure, I assure you."

(Won't I ever find a natural word?)

"...with my decoration, my bourgeois looks, my re-pu-ta-tion, I'd like to see anybody bother me on the train...It's all settled. *Quinquina?*"

"Sure. In case of danger, you can lose the suitcase on the way. It would be a shame, the merchandise is rare. Don't put anything that could identify you in it. No marked clothing or papers. They haven't got your fingerprints?"

The cautious question made both of them laugh. "No, my friend, no, my friend. I used to know the systematic madman named Bertillon, but my hands are innocent. I guess someone else committed my crimes and misdemeanors for me."

"Mine, too," said Augustin Charras. "And, do you know, whatever we do, we shall remain innocent. We didn't want all this. We are against it."

The *we* made Félicien Mûrier feel immensely good.

"Agreed. Let's talk about something else. You've got to relax. Do you like my home? My home for the moment."

Charras rediscovered the bright studio, the carpet, the sea in the windows.

"It's nice."

"It's disgustingly comfortable."

"What do you expect? People who have nothing to do surround themselves with lots of comfort. They take care of themselves."

Charras said, "I can't relax. Would you like me to tell you the story of a Jew?"

"Oh no. I know your story in advance. Unless you know something new about a certain Jesus. He's the one that started the trouble. Should I put on another record?"

Charras nodded, and the full song rose, tragically gay.

"What's that?" asked Charras.

"The song of the little suitcase."

They spoke of insignificant things, the shortest way to the street-car stop, the weather, black-market prices. They noted addresses to be learned by heart.

"Tomorrow, at dawn, I'll bring you the little bag. When you come back I'll bring my daughter, Angèle, to see you, she'll be so happy to hear the records. And by the way, if anything does go wrong, we'll do our best to help you."

"And what about my good luck?" Félicien Mûrier exclaimed. "I can guarantee delivery on our lye."

While Charras was returning to the city, Mûrier continued to listen to Bach and Handel, walking up and down through the studio, between the Mediterranean horizon and the canvases conceived by painters in abstract prisons, who perhaps had forgotten the world and were trying to remember it. "You think it is so simple to hold men by fear? Well, it isn't." With a sense of deliverance, Mûrier looked through a large carton full of reproductions. The nudes and still lifes left him indifferent; but he took out a Van Gogh, *Starry Night, Saint Rémy, June 1889*, and set it on a book rack to look at it at length. This vision, surpassing reason and madness, achieved a lyrical lucidity. The tree in the foreground twisting into a somber earthly flame, a lethargic village singing into the hollow of the hills; enormous stars filling the sky with whirling fires; massive waves of cosmic light rolling in the firmament. The inconceivable explosion of galaxies that carries us through space with human thought its musical emanation. And that thought rediscovered in explosives a primordial power anterior to anything human.

Twenty-four hours later Félicien Mûrier took the train. The molten sky of Saint Rémy was moving in broad daylight above his head. At the station cops in uniform, in the dress of the Legion, in plain clothes, in colored paper, in ebonite, in ectoplasm, gave the poet a wide berth, recognizing at a glance the average Frenchman—thrifty, sly, and respectful of regulations he doesn't give a damn about: "Walking on the flower beds strictly forbidden." Yes, my good man, certainly!

A cosmic power slumbered in the little suitcase. What catastrophic carnival would end the voyage of this bit of distilled courage and righteous anger? What murders? I am entering the realm of murder. There was really no need to tremble.

The lulling rumble of the train shredded the oratorios into fragments. The passengers' flat faces fade into the mist. The smoke of explosions spread in wisps over the countryside, whose foreground sped by and whose horizon barely moved. Café du Saint-Esprit, Cement Factory, À l'Abreuvoir. Timon, Horticulturist—Plato's Soap Factory would come next, caustic soap to cleanse souls and ideas. There was no such factory, but Félicien Mûrier saw moments of the future... Like this:

Stagnant rain, impenetrable night, cyclists in caps gliding furtively between long straight walls. One of them stopped in front of Félicien Mûrier and shook hands with him.

"If anyone appears from the right in the next five minutes, you turn around quickly and whistle softly, very softly, I'll be there."

"No one will come," said Mûrier. "I'll guarantee that. There's going to be quite a shock!"

"Better believe it!"

No one, no one beneath the stagnant rain, in the muddy blackness. Then a long muffled crash splitting the night, a red sun flaring up at the end of the wall, and everything flying sky-high. And then the earth, the night, the rain regained the equilibrium of silence, and Mûrier, frightfully happy, chilled to the bone, went off through the silent streets, closed over fear...

—It seemed to him that he could foresee the rest, right up to the end, but he declined. Dreaming is a drug. He opened a book.

27. ESCAPES

"EVERY time I open the door," said Angèle, "I know that bad news is coming in. When someone goes out you can never tell whether he's coming back. Or if you open the door, you never know to whom or to what or where you'll end up...You never know..." José Ortega answered her, in a cheerful mood, as he always was in her presence.

"Maybe that's the real life ... A great future may come in someday without anyone suspecting it ..."

And that very night he went out towards an infinite nightmare. He had left a tumbledown house plastered with blackened billboards, in the Rue de l'Arbre. He sensed he was being followed and thought of going back to warn the Catalan comrades who lived there, but it was too late to make the least move. He was grabbed by the shoulders, his arms were pinned to his sides, expert hands frisked him. "Where is your revolver?" Disarmed, he said nothing, it was all he could do to restrain the explosions in his muscles. "Spaniard? Anarchist, eh? Let's see your papers." Several oily shapes pushed him behind an archway, into a pissy corner. A famished dog, disturbed by the human intrusion, raised angry jaws. "You're dying, *hijo de puta*, for the same reasons as men." A kick in the teeth sent the dog rolling into the darkness where he set up a bitter yelping. "You have no respect even for dogs?" sneered Ortiga. Now he was calm. A flashlight shed more light on his face than on his papers, which were more or less in order. "What do you want? I'm properly registered. I'm waiting for a Mexican visa, here's a certificate from the Consulate."

"You can wipe your ass with it. No nonsense on the street or I'll make hash out of your face. I know how to talk to anarchists."

"I understand," said Ortiga politely. "I guess I must have shot a baker's dozen of your type."

Nothing would have seemed more natural to him than to be stabbed right there without a sound, and that gave him courage. They fastened some funny little chains around his wrists and walked heavily in a ring around him.

Things were slow at the police station. M. Tremblin, the recently appointed precinct captain, was not happy about it (you realize it would be better to put off promotion until after the wars are over...). He had almost finished carefully reading the newspaper. He was a peaceable man. At home on Sundays he devoted himself to watercolors of flowers and seascapes. He was without opinions—what good are opinions?—flexible in the application of regulations, rigid on the subject of the law. The Law, he said, with two distinct capitals. He wondered unceasingly "how all this would end"—"certainly not as people think." He feared the English, "Albion," detested the Italians, except the naturalized ones, respected with antipathy the "dirty Boches," damn strong, distrusted Spaniards and Africans; he longed with all his soul for his retirement, which was still far off, and turned green at the thought of inflation, which swallowed up two-thirds of your income more quickly than the waterfront whores could empty the pockets of a sailor on shore leave... And you haven't even the compensations of the shore leave, ah là là! The Legionnaire police who brought in Ortiga were disappointed to find M. Tremblin at his desk and unoccupied.

"Here is the accused," said one of them.

"Not so fast," Ortiga protested. "Accused of what?"

Rather stout, despite the rationing, M. Tremblin sighed. "Very well. The what's-his-name case you mean?"

"Exactly."

"Accused of what?" Ortiga repeated in a hard voice. "What what's-his-name case?"

The face of a disinterred corpse, spotted with pink and green, came toward him from one side. It gave forth a corpselike breath and a menacing threadlike voice: "Keep your trap shut!"

The Commissioner picked a typewritten sheet out of a pile. The disinterred face was like a flat fish pickled in rancor; he whispered something in M. Tremblin's ear and M. Tremblin answered neither yes nor no. Ortiga said, "I have an important statement to make immediately."

M. Tremblin gave him a grieved look. He despised Spaniards and feared them at the same time. All sorts of committees interceded in their favor, the Mexican Legation protected them—it would seem—you never knew who was the chauffeur of a former minister who was himself an ex-chauffeur, and they organized mafias capable of knifing you in the back. This fellow, now, was rather a handsome lad, with an honest face, he didn't look like a criminal, but he was doubtless one of those pistoleros of the CNT who . . .

"What have you got to say? Be brief." (The "be brief" was for the principle of authority.)

"First: If you give me the third degree, I won't answer any questions. Second: If you give me the third degree, I'll kill somebody sooner or later, one way or another. That's all."

"We aren't savages," said M. Tremblin calmly. "I merely apply The Laws and decrees of the Go-vern-ment."

"I guess that's not easy," muttered Ortiga, inwardly reassured.

"That's enough. You will speak when you are questioned."

Ortiga had no fear of physical pain; in a fight, blows only spurred him on. They sent seething spirits running through his blood and nerves; they did not blind him, but rather gave him an animal lucidity quite alien to reason. But to be bound, beaten by brutes, tortured without being able to strike back; he feared the desperate humiliation and the lamentable impotence that follows it, when the victim is like a plaintive child that wants only to cry and cry—and he feared the feeling that arises afterward that you must avenge yourself to save your self-respect, risk your life foolishly to take away the shame.

M. Tremblin laid out photographs on the desk as though playing solitaire. The fortune-teller hesitates dramatically before turning over the card of destiny. M. Tremblin collected the photographs of persons sought by the police, he had 4,327 of them, selected in eighteen years of service and classified according to physiognomy. This pursuit gave him a mild cerebral excitement. "I have the soul of a psychologist, you see, I might have been a novelist. You can see a whole life in a photograph, you can surmise words, gestures, the color and cut of the underwear, amazing things." He thought of certain faces when he painted his flowers and seascapes, and for this reason his watercolors, which he seldom showed to anyone, were misty and devoid of innocence, as though painted by someone drunk or high on morphine. He examined the features of a pretty woman named Émilienne wanted for complicity in certain department-store thefts; the face of a matron with a double chin and a vicious look, wanted for traffic in narcotics. It seemed to him that an old man with a twisted nose (offense against morals—previous record) moved his lips almost imperceptibly.

"Do you recognize any of these persons?" he asked José Ortiga absently.

Ortiga bent down over the faces, examined them, and answered sincerely, "No."

With the nail of his index finger, M. Tremblin picked an anthropometric photo from near the middle.

"And what about this person, are you going to tell me that you don't know him?"

"I mustn't get pale or tremble," thought Ortiga, recognizing a wretched Maurice Silber with swollen lips, thick eyelids, chin black with beard, eyes hard and lifeless. Moritz said to him, "This is what they have done with me, poor old fellow." Underneath, a number: 15-25-35 K, and a date.

"Don't know him," said Ortiga.

"Well, you've got balls," said Commissioner Tremblin softly.

"Yes, I have, but I don't know the gentleman. He looks ill."

Having nothing else to do, M. Tremblin might have kept going for reasons of professional pride. But a policeman came in with an affair that had to be settled right away—that is, before the arrival of his colleagues: a lady caught red-handed negotiating the sale of a kilo of coffee beans from the stocks of the Italian Armistice Commission. M. Tremblin, accustomed to affairs of this type, settled them benevolently and profitably. The lady would promise to respect the laws in future and would be sent home with half her coffee—just as she had expected.

Ortiga signed his brief deposition and was sent to prison that very night. To the men of today going to prison is like taking a train or a bus. It's nothing as long as there's a chance of getting out. Ortiga believed in his own chances. His alibi for a certain night—the night when M. Vibert encountered a silhouette—was watertight. The examining magistrate, having approved it, said to Ortiga, "I'm signing your release." And added with amiable indulgence, "You're a sly fox . . ." Ortiga, acquainted with normal procedures, returned to his cell with the step of a free man. He was on good terms with his cellmates, M. Pilâtre, a relatively reputable crooked businessman who deplored being in the clink at a time when there was money to be made, ah, my friends, money by the basketful; with an impassive Kabyle accused of voluntary homicide, who suffered from being unable to perform his Mohammedan ablutions; with a colossus, all jaws and no forehead, apparently a Corsican, who specialized in thefts from abandoned ships in the port of La Joliette; with a young shopkeeper from Oran, accused of concealing his racial origins and expressing anti-national sentiments.

The man from Oran congratulated Ortiga. "I recommended you to your examining magistrate. He's mine, too, and I pay him plenty. Now you will be a modest workman on the Trans-Saharan Railroad . . ."

Ortiga was brought before an official, who delivered an order of deportation issued by the Prefect on the basis of the Law of 1852 relating to foreigners. Transferred to a depot for undesirables, suspects, deportees, internees, Ortiga experienced two dazzling joys in one day. The first was meeting Nihil Cervantes, of the Friends of Durruti group, who had robbed the Bank of the Levant in order to set up farm cooperatives, who had thrown up the last barricade at the Barcelona subway and fought the next-to-last skirmish at the foot of the

Pyrenees: a little man with the waxen face of an ecclesiastic, with long yellow hands, tortoiseshell glasses, and rigid features. He had escaped from the camp at Argèles, under strong suspicion of having organized the execution of an executioner in the secret prisons of the Republic. Recaptured at Martigues, where he had been preparing a getaway by sailboat, Nihil Cervantes (he had completely forgotten his real name) also considered himself destined for the great Saharan construction project.

"*Vive le Sahara!*" he said. "The nights there are magnificent, the most authentic nights in the world. This civilization of scoundrels and idiots has destroyed our nights. By poisoning them with noise and electricity, it has robbed men of half their lives. The desert nights are bitter cold, *verdad*, but the stars form the chorus of Pythagoras. "I'll explain the constellations to you—we will escape and set out for the oases. I have learned Berber and a few words of Touareg. I know how to say 'I am a man and a friend to men' in all the languages of the desert and since it's the truth, it will get us through wherever we go. You'll see."

Nihil Cervantes invited Ortiga to share his straw mattress, which contained razor blades, tools, money, and even excellent maps cut out of the best atlases in the Toulouse library.

Ortiga's second joy was receiving a package of biscuits, frozen turnips, and sardines. The twenty-seven occupants of Barrack 6 gathered around the sardine can and marveled at it as the faithful marvel at a miraculous image. Though faint with hunger, Ortiga dreamed of keeping the can intact because the name "Angèle" was scratched into the metal with the point of a penknife.

"Is that your woman?" Nihil asked him fraternally in a rather hoarse voice.

"No, she will never be my woman," Ortiga replied implacably. He had an intoxicating sensation of staggering at the edge of a precipice and recovering his balance with a single superhuman movement of his knees. Nihil came close to him and looked into his eyes. "Love is the highest living beauty," he murmured. "The abnegation of love is the test of the strongest."

"Don't bug me," exclaimed Ortiga savagely, so full of stormy bitter joy that it disfigured him.

Then he added more quietly, "What you say is true, though."

Nihil suggested that they divide the sardines among the weakest prisoners: each one received half a sardine. Nihil refused his portion but counted out fifteen drops of oil for himself on a slice of bread. "Eat all your biscuits today," he advised Ortiga. "Or you'll have to fight to defend them during the night. These men are half-mad."

That night they lay on the same mattress, devoured indistinguishably by the same bugs. Nihil said to José Ortiga, "You are young. You ought to educate yourself. What is a man without science? A scientific vision of the world is the only source of power. Would you like me to explain the origin of the earth and the goal of mankind?"

"Explain away."

Ortiga scarcely heard the lofty explanations. In his fist he clenched, like an amulet, a small piece of tin with Angèle's name scratched into it. Under the bare December trees she was walking away from him with a fragile, firm gait, like a severe dance step, across moist earth smelling slightly of death. Ortiga suddenly saw her so close that he perceived the redness in the parting of her lips—but what was the true color of her eyes? He ceased to see her, he no longer knew the color of her eyes, the shape of her nostrils, the line of her neck—he had thought that he saw her, now there was nothing but mist in which shapes, colors, reality were vanishing. "I am bleeding in the void . . . Nothing ever begins again." Wearily he summoned to his aid the image of Amparo, who had been his companion for four months, between the beginning of the rout and his internment in France. Amparo, erect, with her hard-muscled thighs, her soft, dry skin, her sharp tongue, relieved for a moment the intolerable absence of Angèle. Amparo had vanished among the crumbling divisions, the motley vehicles of the panic, the last bombings, the first cold winds of the Pyrenees. Vanished in the flood of men, beasts, groaning machines, events. "Don't worry about me," she had said, "I'll always make my way, and if I don't I'm only one woman like so many others who have died . . ." Perhaps she was alive, perhaps she had preferred prison and the risk of summary execution to exile in France; perhaps she had preferred her old lover whom she missed. "I hurt him so much!" she said, bizarrely cracking her thin fingers. Perhaps she was hiding in Aragon with him (a swell comrade he was, too) and often missing her Pepe, Josito, Pepito, whom she probably believed dead... Life passes on, we pass on, the water flows on. The image of Angèle returned, untouched, untouchable, undesired, undesirable, inconceivable, repellent, and alluring, a statue of airy marble, a statue of smoke in the emptiness that also passes on—or remains? Was she still alive at this instant, was it possible that she should really be alive? The cold of unreality and the tomb blew over José Ortiga's stiffened being. He felt his teeth grinding, his head became a death's head, he raised a slab of stone weighing several tons from his forehead, rubbed his eyes, and heard the even voice of Nihil Cervantes.

"Have you been following me, Pepe?" his comrade asked softly, in order not to disturb the restless sleep of the others. "That was the planetesimal hypothesis of Thomas Chrowder Chamberlin."

"I haven't understood a thing," Ortiga confessed. "I'll never be an intellectual."

He said it with pride but underneath with more bitterness than pride. "Do you know what memory is?" he asked.

"An imprint."

"Or an obsession?"

"Imprint and obsession. Consciousness—everything is memory. This instant is already past. We are nothing but memories."

"And our memories are as real as we are?"

"Perhaps. *Quién sabe*? Everything passes on, memory too."

"Then what is real, Nihil?"

Sleepers moaned. A snore arose like a death rattle. Someone scratched himself violently. Someone shouted a vile oath. Nihil said, "They are hungry. Hunger torments their sleep. They drink hot blood in their dreams. I have dreamed that. You kill to eat in your dream. The ancestral beast. The Sahara's the place for us. Sand, truncheons, the molten sun, the stars, death, or flight. All or nothing."

"Yes," murmured Ortiga.

Within him one obsession followed another. At this moment it was the penal colony. The only answer to this obsession was to unleash an irreconcilable will. His voice was ardent: "If they torture me, I'll survive and I'll kill."

"*Sí*," said Nihil.

Sleep is a somber wave that drowns you. It is neither peace nor oblivion, it is sometimes the torment of the far slope of existence.

The months passed, dragged from prison to prison. Classified as "very dangerous," Nihil and José Ortiga were transferred together again and again, destination some forced-labor camp, probably in Africa, dreaded by everyone, the Africa they were longing for. They studied the possibilities of escape, learned the course of the wadis, the position and elevation of heights, the location of palm groves and wells. Captivity made them indistinguishable from the wasting creatures among whom they lived. With them they waited avidly for the anemic swill called soup or a ration of sticky sandy noodles; with them they suffered from stomach cramps, inflated bellies, diarrhea, sore gums. The air was full of news and rumors, alternating between a gleam of utterly incredible hope and irretrievable perdition; they believed them without believing, they were turning into mental cases, patients for Charenton, for a worldwide *manicomio*, walking corpses prepared for the autopsy table of a continental morgue. They were tormented by scabies, further irritated by dirty nails that they could not chew close enough, by dental cavities, by nighttime explosions of sexual heat (another cavity, shit!), of their last nervous energies, of hallucination...

For the rest, feeble furies, jokes, rackets, plots woven around some képi who might be detestable or bearable or humanly corrupt. Few faces resisted famine-induced obliteration; the ugly ones resisted best, just as baseness thrived as characters disintegrated. Danse-macabre figures prowled around the barracks, more famished for tobacco than for food. Le Pourri (the rotten), also known as le Vampire and Bazar de l'Hôtel de Ville (the department store), sold smokes for scraps of bread, banknotes, rags, for the hideous erotic favors of cadaverous boys. To the most degraded of his clients, dying men who somehow kept on their legs for several hours a day, he rationed puffs on butts manufactured from leftover tobacco smoked at least ten times, mixed with the straw from mattresses. "You can smoke while I count to thirty." And according to his humor he counted more or less rapidly, the bastard! The same cigarette served three or four customers, depending on the force of their breath and their good or bad faith, for some consumed almost the whole cigarette while the owner was counting to thirty... Nihil Cervantes and José Ortiga were preparing for their African escape; they did not smoke and they trained themselves to endure thirst. They believed in deliverance by the desert, the sun's fire, thirsty marches, taking their directions from giant constellations of pure steel. This kept them standing, like the spiny thistles that grow on the sand dunes—hard to say whether they're alive or totally desiccated.

A pain in his bowel had Nihil bent double, and he said simply, "Bad joke, old man, I think I've caught dysentery..." For weeks he made his way as best he could, with the step of a sleepwalker, to the abominable latrines and back. He was surrounded by a smell of defecation and organic decomposition. His breath became fetid. He bled out his last strength. And José Ortiga, unwilling to part with him, spent his nights in the stench of death.

"I won't leave you, Nihil," he repeated harshly. "I'll save you. You'll save yourself. You know how to brace your will, you've got to!"

Ortiga could do no more than will, he thought he had discovered the searing power of will. He wanted his friend to live, he wanted will to triumph over excrement, infected blood, microbes, neglect, hunger—for will is all-powerful. Ortiga would have fought like a madman against anyone who denied the power of will, but among the feeble, fever-ridden phantoms with whom he fiercely discussed the matter he met no one who denied its power. He carried black fire in his half-mad eyes, he suffered long hours of insomnia, he hypnotized himself by repeating: I will, I will, I will, until he became totally stiff. He calmly twisted a short bar of iron to prove to himself that will dominates weak muscles.

And then one morning it was all over. Defeated and shivering, Nihil said in an apologetic lifeless voice, "Even my will is all gone, I'm finished. I'm empty. You'll escape alone, old man."

"It's not true," José Ortiga shouted into his ear. "You're lying. You must have the will. I will it. You must live. We'll escape together."

Nihil's big eyes glittered in the face of a child, hollow and covered with red and gray splotches. Ortiga was trembling with exasperation. His throat and brain were fighting back crazy words. "I'm gonna hit you and make you hold firm. I'm gonna smash your face to save you! I'm out of my mind, I'm a brute. Nihil, you can't die like that, you can't, Nihil!" And this was all he had the strength to think as he wiped Nihil's wet forehead.

The dying man recovered the color and the voice of a man nearly alive and said, "I feel better. It won't be long... I know there is all the beauty of the world, I know I should want to live... but I haven't the strength. I'm sleepy."

These were his last intelligible words. At noon he was moaning softly, his eyes open but extinct. Ortiga walked around a barbed-wire enclosure, fifty feet by ten, his head sunk between his shoulders; he exhausted himself with willing, and felt that his will was failing. At frequent intervals he came and bent over Nihil's eyes; strong eyes, cut in quartz, shining with dull radiance. Once he came back running, overcome by an immense joy, and said to the eyes, "You're all right, amigo. The crisis is past. I felt it in my nerves like an electric shock. You're saved!"

The quartz eyes looked beyond all that was visible, the moan died down, Nihil was entering into silence. Ortiga clenched his fists and left him, pushing his way through shadows. He hadn't a single valid idea left.

... Around five o'clock a Pole offered to help Ortiga carry away the body on a stretcher. It was not heavy. They left it in a low shed, where there was already another dead man—a tortured form covered with gray canvas. Ortiga cautiously took Nihil's cold head in his two hands and set it down gently on the earth. He felt lice moving under his palms, he felt the hard fragility of flesh and bone. And he looked away, seeing nothing, a mask of himself. Will, memory, death, the desert, what, what? The Pole made the sign of the cross, joined his hands, and stood for a few seconds in prayer.

From outside a nasal voice cried, "Eh, hurry up in there, it's time for roll call!"

The Pole murmured, "God rest his soul."

"There isn't any soul! There isn't any God!" Ortiga gasped furiously. "There's nothing!"

And he saw the Pole, a tall, bearded boy, dressed in rags that had once been a uniform. Blond, wild, young. Strangely intact. And without transition, still bending over Nihil's remains, he looked the Pole in the eyes, and asked fiercely, "Do you want to escape with me?"

The Pole made a calm sign of assent.

28. FREEDOM DEAR

PASSING by the hotel's office, Simon Ardatov saw figures gathered round the radio. A glacial expectancy fell upon them like an asphyxiating dust.

"Come in, come in, Doctor," said Mme Emma. "Come listen to the news." Several faces without features were lifted toward him for a moment, he felt himself the object of dismal, vaguely sullying curiosity.

"There's war in Russia," said an indistinct figure. "Hitler is attacking."

Ardatov felt cold. Emotivity declines after sixty and it is cold that mounts. He leaned on the counter under the letterboxes and keys. An automaton's voice was announcing the bombing of cities, grotesquely mispronouncing their names: Vinnitsa, Smolensk, Gomel, Vitebsk, Minsk. No relation was conceivable between this voice, these names, and the geysers of smoke, fire, blood, and fear bursting at this very moment over those peaceful cities with their old quarters full of wooden houses surrounded by fenced yards enclosing tall sunflowers. And tall girls walking toward the well with their yokes over their shoulders stopping, terror stricken, and listening to the rolling thunder, the mechanical buzzing of invisible motors in the sky. And...
Then a radio tube gave off a greenish sound, and a charming new voice announced: "Radio-Lyon will now transmit its musical program."

The asthmatic M. Jantolle expressed his pondered satisfaction.

"It was about time for the Bolsheviks to get it in the neck... They'll be wiped out in five weeks. Ah, Hitler really put one over on them.

That's what I call modern politics: I smile at you and I cut your throat! No Reynaud or Daladier would have thought that up."

M. Gauffrin, traveling salesman, answered, "And yet, Monsieur Jantolle, you approved of his policy of peace in the East. You even said, if I remember rightly, that it was brilliant: Never fight on two fronts at once."

"He's not worried about the English and he's right. He was waiting for the proper time, I tell you. Once the Bolsheviks are liquidated, we'll have real peace."

M. Gauffrin seemed to dream as he listened to Verdi. *Ta-ta-ta-ta*, he hummed between his rusty teeth. M. Byrsot looked around the room with a sly look and then spoke into the air, addressing no one, "You can say what you like, the Russians have always been great soldiers, and the steppes, well, the steppes aren't as easy to invade as our departments of the North. And believe me, steppes are one thing the Russians have plenty of! If they can only hold out until winter when the snows come, I wouldn't like to be in a Fritz's shoes, that's all I know."

Demobilized and unemployed, his family still in Calvados, M. Byrsot saw everything in black—that was to be expected. To relieve the tension, Mme Emma asked Ardatov for his opinion: "After all, Doctor, you know the country, what do you think? —Monsieur is a Russian refugee from the revolution," she explained for the benefit of anyone who might not have known it.

And it was at this precise moment that Simon Ardatov became a man doubly hunted. He knew that M. Jantolle would identify him this very day to the scribes at the préfecture who were drawing up new lists of suspects. By evening there would be white posters enjoining foreigners of Russian origin to report within twenty-four hours, etc. He knew that he would not be able to answer any of their questions prudently, that a spark of hatred might be seen in his eyes, and that he might say things full of defiance, which would be absurd—solely to avoid debasing himself... Sometimes it is very important not to debase yourself, even in appearance. Clear out this very afternoon, but where to? Change identities, but would it be possible? M. Jantolle was picking his nose.

"Monsieur Byrsot is right," said Ardatov. "Russia is so vast. No invasion has succeeded since the thirteenth century. I doubt if the best armies could cross the Urals..."

"There are no mountains for airplanes," said M. Jantolle. "Besides, I'll wager Japan will strike, hard, and that won't be any joke, you can believe me."

You can believe M. Jantolle about Japan, obviously. The radio was rhyming "my fair love" with "stars above."

"In any case," M. Gauffrin insisted, "the Boches will be too busy around Moscow to bother much about France. We'll at least gain something out of it."

"They'll steal our last drop of wine for their hospitals on the Eastern front," M. Byrsot announced bitterly. "You'll see."

"That would only be fair," said M. Jantolle. "After all they are fighting for us."

M. Byrsot regarded him without anger. "Fairness without wine or potatoes doesn't appeal to me very much. And besides, you make me piss."

"Come, come, Messieurs, I beg you," said Mme Emma quickly. Ardatov descended the stairs.

That night he slept on a bench at Augustin Charras's place. As he had expected, Russians became prey for internment. They were screened in the police stations and depots, largely by former Tsarist officers more or less affiliated with the Gestapo. These White émigrés, informers for every police force in the world, spoke English, Czech, Serbian, Croatian, Turkish; some were familiar with China, others with Ethiopia. And now they capitalized on their experience of the lower depths of twenty capitals, nightclubs, blackmail rings, terrorist gangs, Cossack choruses, taxi-driving, roulette...They would never forget the calamitous years 1917, 1918, 1920, 1921, the routs of Novorossiysk and Sebastopol, the barracks in Gallipoli, exile in Mukden, the miseries of Shanghai and Ménilmontant, the names of companions-in-arms massacred, their own exaltation in the massacres of times past. And now they had revenge at the tip of their fingers. In six months they would be in Moscow, in St. Petersburg, they would recover their power and their lands, they would cleanse old Russia of the Tsar's assassins. If he fell into their hands Ardatov wouldn't last two weeks.

He had an identity card as a French citizen made. Taking into account the failings and automatisms of memory, he kept the same initials and same date of birth. Doctor Sylvestre Ardateau, why not? Sylvestre dated back for him to a past preceding several deluges. He had gone by that name in Tiflis in 1904 when he was watching the residence of the Viceroy for the Combat Organization. He was living in a little pink house at the foot of the Mount of David, and in his idle hours he had drunk Caucasian wines with the Tartars of Chugureti. Would he recognize himself now in a picture taken in this distant past? He remembered himself as he remembered other people. He was thin and muscular, he did not think of the death he was risking, he was sure that he would not grow old. The idea that a just revolution might open the gates of an unexpected hell (if there had been a mind perverse enough to formulate such an idea) would have seemed to him worse than sacrilege: it would have seemed antiscientific. The thought that, instead of witnessing the coming of a rational society, he would in the course of his long life see two world wars without reaching an intelligible outcome would have discouraged him from living.

Calais was sufficiently destroyed to furnish Dr. Sylvestre Ardateau with an address that could not be verified. Forged documents, though superior to real ones because they are more stylized, can, by themselves, thwart only the most superficial inquiries. It takes professional swindlers, spies with elaborate equipment, ingenious maniacs, to create the false reality capable of withstanding every kind of investigation. Ardatov contented himself with an approximation. The authorities were seriously interested only in men of military age. "I have reached the statesman's age," said Ardatov, "the age when people think you are no more use for anything."

The isolation around him grew. Kurt Seelig was in prison at Casablanca—one sea crossed, one more chance of survival. Our chances from now on are counted by seas, oceans, continents—and they aren't enough. Tullio had been handed over to the Italian authorities. With the help of accommodating, underpaid jailers and worried Fascists (false or real), he had managed to smuggle a letter out of a Piedmontese prison. "My first glimpse of my native land," he wrote, "revealed to me the ingenuousness of its Renewal: a very old prison car, freshly repainted. A hero of the Tripolitanian War first told me with great severity that I would soon bow to the Duce's imperial accomplishments. As soon as we were alone he recommended himself to me in view of the imminent change of regime. 'Do you think, dear Signore, that the monarchy will last?'—'Thank the Lord, I hope not. A rope is the thing, Major, a good mule driver's rope.'—'Speak more softly, Signore, I beg of you. Do you think we are ripe for a parliamentary republic?'—'Ripe as rotten fruit for a plebeian republic, with nothing parliamentary about it, Major.'—I began to improvise oracles, valid perhaps only in the domain of absolute history according to Hegel. As payment I received a ham omelet and some Tuscan wine, not a bad bargain. Probably I shall be sent under house arrest to some hamlet of eternal poverty. When I get there, I will cough up the same oracles for worried old cowards tired of the *Impero* and young scoundrels eager to turn their coats in time. Then one fine day I'll go to the next town and personally arrest the *podestà*. This hierarchy of overdecorated dictators remains decorative, but is completely senile. They make mild jokes about it to calm their colics. The castor oil rises in their throats. They persecute as little as possible nowadays, preferably Jews who have no more money. Our officials are flirting with several different types of cowardice, they know that most of them can survive only by treason. What they don't know is the right time for it. They have restored my confidence in the future and in Europe."

Ardatov envied him his captivity and his optimism: but we do not choose our prisons. After he had given up hoping for it, he was granted a visa to enter the United States—known as a tourist-type or "danger" visa. Actually, we have been tourists in the land of danger for quite some time. His double identity forced him to reduce his contacts with the few political refugees who, by various camouflages, had still managed to keep out of the concentration camps. Bitter young men, recognizing him on the street not far from the American Consulate, would observe among themselves, "Oh, of course, the New York committees run themselves ragged for these old fellows who have nothing left but their biographies (and don't look too close at their biographies) because they're sadder and wiser and no more use, stuffed with rancid pride because Lenin or Kautsky called them an idiot thirty years ago. And we can roll from Gurs to Vernet and from Vernet to Bidon 45! The unknown, the young, who've still got some bite in their teeth, there's no visa for them, just the minimum of interest needed to save the face of the committees and justify the salaries of their officials." (This was not entirely false.) These young men spoke aggressively and loudly enough to be overheard. Ardatov wondered which of these young men had it in them to fight for long for anything but themselves. He avoided them. One out of three, he felt sure, would betray him at the first twist to their testicles. And how could he distinguish that one from the others? This raised the question of courage and torture, the most insoluble problem of our time.

The day before his embarkation, meticulously prepared by savvy accomplices like Chinese artisans chiseling a work of art, Ardatov saw only Charras. Standing on a silent street corner, both of them in a hurry, they said none of the important things they had intended to say to one another—about the war, America, Russia, the possibility of deliverance, the likelihood of death, the masses, the unknown, memories.

"There's not much chance of our seeing each other again," said Charras. "I'm glad for you, Doctor. Try to make them understand over there." Ah, what can they understand over there about the tragedies of the Old World? thought Ardatov. And what can a ship-wrecked man out of the last lifeboat explain to anyone about his experience, his despair, the certainty of his expectations—as certain as the storm in the gathering clouds?

Ardatov asked vaguely, "Is Angèle well? And Laurent?"

"Angèle is a brave girl," said Charras humbly, because he was proud of her. "Laurent sends his regards and thanks."

"Thanks for what?"

"For a disagreeable but useful treatment. Those are his own words. I like Laurent. His eyes aren't so wild anymore, he looks like a man beginning to live again."

"Would you like to leave here, Augustin? I could try to..."

"Never," said Charras softly. "Not for anything in the world."

Augustin bent his head a little to avoid raising it defiantly, he spoke softly in order not to be vehement. He couldn't say what he thought, "I shall die or I shall be resuscitated with what I love. France and I, we won't part. What would become of me anywhere else? An old good-for-nothing, a woodsman without an ax or a forest, a log that no one needs for his fire!" You couldn't say that in front of a man who hadn't the shadow of a country of his own, a foreigner in every land, a citizen of the world, a hunted citizen in a crazy world!—and who had to move on once again, try to live again, try to do something for lost humanity with his old brain that often, no doubt, flickered like a candle under black winds!

"I couldn't," Charras said. "And for what? I'll go and find a corner in the woods, back to the land as they say. And there I'll wait for death like the old animal I am. Unless they come to kill me, and they're capable of that. Or unless I hold out until the day of liquidations and new beginnings. I'll try to. There are men just like me who will hold out by chance until that day, aren't there?"

"There are," said Ardatov. "There's my streetcar. Farewell."

...The coasts of Spain passed the freighter in the distance, solitudes steeped in bloody legends. In the dusk, the ruins of Sagunto lay hidden at the foot of dead mountains. Some of the passengers watched this land recede with the tense calm of men standing by fresh graves. They recognized the escarpments and the fishing ports, scarcely discernible through the haze of forgetfulness; they knew the names and each name marked a massacre, a defeat. A fishing vessel resembling a great plucked bird was bobbing up and down in the low swell. At moments its dark sail grazed the heavy waters, its hull might have been blackened in a fire. Shapes of men appeared to exchange hard, embittered salutations with the emigrants, their fists clenched. Someone shouted: *Muere Franco*. Rather *Muere* than *Viva*! Life to a symbol, an idea. This voyager's farewell to Europe was nothing but cold fury. There was nothing more to cheer for. The republic, a farce—anarchy, you still believe in it, Tonio, either your faith is mighty resistant or your brain is atrophied. Tonio made a megaphone out of his hands and cried out, "*Libertad!*" The fisherman answered with a confused shout, stifled by the wind.

"How sad!" said Hilda. A brightness of insomnia was on her clear-cut features.

"It is only night falling," Ardatov answered, but what did he mean by "night falling"?

At daybreak the coast of Africa was arid, spotted with black brush like a panther skin. Simon Ardatov stood alone and thought of the harmony of the earth, of plants, beasts, and men. The sun stabbed through the morning mists. The enormous rock of Gibraltar opened an ocean, closed a convulsed continent. The Pillars of Hercules. It might have been a fantastic tombstone. Warships lay low on the lifeless sea like alligators in an immobility that was older than catastrophes. A fan of sun opened over the distant fields of Andalusia, prodigious with amber and liquid green.

Displeased with himself, Ardatov went down into the foul air of the after hold, whose bunk beds strewn with ragged clothes were like a prison barracks. A few men were sleeping. Ardatov lay down on his mattress at the end of a narrow stifling corridor close above the keel. He had chosen this place because there was no upper bunk, and a light, burning all night with the yellowish glare of a chronic fever, enabled him to read in his moments of insomnia. The sound of the swirling waters beating against the metal hulk took on the rhythm of a hurricane, so persistent that he felt it even in his sleep. Not for a moment did Ardatov lose contact with this thundering elemental fury of the depths conspiring against human steel. This pleased him.

Perhaps there was some accord between his nerves, his thoughts, and the inconceivable indifference of the waves. How thick was the metal between him and the massive weight of saltwater caught up in apparently chaotic motion, but in fact connected with the equilibrium of the planet? Less than a centimeter probably. Muffled sounds of squalls ending in long streamings and long rustlings of chains. "Prometheus bound under the sea." It was good to feel calmly expendable, attached to being, but by no means revolted by the touch—imminent perhaps—of nonbeing. Liberty, serenity! What dosage did they contain of intelligence greedy for survival yet prepared for death; of tenacious old instincts that would surrender only at the last heartbeat; of fatigued muscles and arteries; and of the weary consciousness imprisoned in this epoch of destruction, obsessed by the suffering and death of others, darkened by the vision of the shadowy years to come—which count so little in history and so heavily in our lives? From all anguish we can yet distill an appeased understanding, from all certainty of personal destruction a confidence surpassing the limits of destruction, a justified confidence—because our universe continues.

Thus cosmic submarine rumblings distracted Ardatov from a more painful obsession. He saw the villages of Ukraine astride the hills, with their broad streets and here and there a garden, under the unmediated vastness of the sky; the church surrounded by birches, the motley crowd at market, the valley of the Dnieper, plains, sleeping forests, the gentle majesty of spaces that seem to breathe a primordial liberty in their sadness. And then suddenly the hard new cities of industrialization, cities of reinforced concrete. Certain crossings in Moscow illuminated by memories of youth, persecution, revolution, the old peasant woman selling apples at the edge of the sidewalk, the Arbat streetcar . . . Plains, planted fields, cities, rivers—colored with death. The well-constructed theoretical analyses that he incessantly elaborated to dispel these images led him inexorably to conclude that disaster was imminent. And then?

At nine in the morning Ardatov went walking on the crowded deck. Greetings were exchanged, pleasantries without wit. The freighter carried four hundred refugees from Europe, selected by pure chance.

The atmosphere was that of a fair, of an internment center with relaxed discipline, of a floating prison—and at the same time it was a pleasure ship on an ideal cruise, impossibly overcrowded, ludicrously filthy. The happy travelers did their best to forget, to pretend to forget: crimes, bankruptcies, griefs, humiliations, mental illnesses—but also bravery, clear-sightedness, authentic heroism, the generosity of great believers. Around the latrines, hastily constructed on deck, excrement mixed with seawater ran into the scuppers. The red carcass of a freshly butchered beast hung on the other side, swinging back and forth against the ocean sky. Ladies in deck chairs knitted and discussed the destruction of family fortunes, government intrigues, summary executions in Berlin, Warsaw, Vienna, Trieste, Madrid, Prague, Paris, and everywhere else. They spoke also of their stomach ailments and of their friends' characters. Spaniards, some in blue overalls, others bare to the waist, burst suddenly into arguments that died down just as suddenly; it could be gathered that they were discussing the independence of Euzkadi. A bold, pink-cheeked little man with gold-rimmed glasses and blue-and-white-striped silk pajamas (like a prisoner in a penal colony for millionaires) greeted the "dear doctor" effusively. He was standing with a desiccated old man in a gray jacket, who turned out to be the Loyalist Canon of the Cordova Cathedral. They were discussing the chances of survival of a Christian Europe: and they are slight, Monsieur; I wrote as much two years ago in a letter to Archduke Otto—and do you think we shall succeed at our age in acclimating ourselves to Brazil? The very destiny of the Church is compromised, we must have vision. "The Vatican has," said the Canon, "but it has committed grave errors, what we need is a social Christianity to stand up to atheistic socialism."

Ardatov agreed politely. The gentlemen offered him black coffee served in a tin can washed in seawater, and told him that the captain's Saigonese steward had agreed to keep them supplied with coffee, rum, and even stew. Ardatov was in a good humor when he left them. He stepped over the rolled cables and greeted Belisario. His name was not Belisario; he was a Czech painter who had become a Spaniard during the civil war in which he had lost his right hand. He had a bewildered, malicious, amusing look: he always seemed to be on his way out of a flophouse after an unfinished alcohol cure (but he never drank liquor).

"Let's go see the businessmen," said Belisario. "They are priceless." Some families of merchants still prosperous were sitting under the captain's bridge, occupying, as if it were only their right, the only places adequately sheltered from the sun and wind.

"Take a look at them," said Belisario. "Look at the tilt of their noses over their omelets. Don't they seem to be saying: we're not political but economic refugees, *please, Wirtschaftsemigranten*. We never fought for democracies or revolutions. We never did anything to upset the powers that be. Don't confuse us, if you please, with this international subversive rabble, or with the Jews without capital—Jews with ideas for which vile persecution holds us responsible.

"Doctor, at least half of these people would be with Hitler if Hitler had wanted them."

"And what are you indignant about?" Ardatov asked.

He looked around for Hilda and she appeared draped in her discolored raincoat.

"Good morning, good morning," she said playfully. "I bet Belisario is running somebody down. Did I guess right, Belisario?"

Belisario was attracted to her. "And why not?" he asked. "I am bitter. I have a right to be bitter. One must be bitter, *my dear*, or throw in the sponge. In New York I'm going to become a *businessman* like the smartest of these fellows, I'm going to be hard-boiled. With one arm it will be difficult; but I have fewer illusions than they have, and that helps. They believe in themselves, in money, I believe in nobody, nothing—that's an advantage for me."

He told them that he was learning how to draw with his left hand and was making progress. "I'm inventing a new deformation, I'm going to be a portrait painter for ladies!"

Hilda took old Ardatov's arm. In passing, they greeted the group of doctors sitting on the iron stairs leading to the forward deck. In the center of the group was a fragile old man in a workman's cap. His little pink hand was trembling, and he was speaking in German about

Pavlov's experiments with conditioned reflexes. The forward deck was the children's favorite spot. At this moment they were standing in a colorful circle watching two laughing young men wrestle. The few young people on board were good to see after the tired faces. The freighter was rolling a little, the heat and the light were becoming more intense from moment to moment, the sea sparkled. To the left the golden line of the Moroccan coast could be seen. Hilda stopped on the last step of the stairs and said in a pensive, aggressive voice, without turning around, "How beautiful young people are. That centenarian anthropologist frightens me. Did you see his hands? He's a corpse."

"Hardly," said Ardatov. "I believe he may live another five or ten years. His intelligence is still lively, especially concerning problems that interest him."

Hilda felt her secret irritation mount. Won't you ever get sick of problems and intelligence? Won't you ever guess that people would like to live like plants exposed to the sun, the rain, the night, with open eyes, asking no questions—that problems are built on muck, that the intelligence struggles in vain against this muck. Have you never felt that the intelligence is made of algebraic signs, that it engenders nothing but symbolic phantoms, that it is uselessly clear like a clouded windowpane behind which—behind which, what?—The two wrestlers stood facing one another, one with his bare legs planted heavily on the deck, his toes black and strong; the other dancing around him, weighing with every muscle the force of an attack. Hilda cast a sidelong glance at Simon Ardatov's square gray face and was aware of her stumbling hostility. She thought, "I wish you were thirty years younger. I wish you were what you are and a brute as well. I wish I understood much less."

"Let's go and look at the ship's wake," said Ardatov affectionately.

They passed through the whole length of the ship, climbed the vertical ladder in the stern, and leaned against the railing, which ended nearby, leaving a broad opening close to the flagpole. The anchor lay on its chains, here one could feel the vibration of the engines, their struggle against the resisting sea, one could see the chasm plowed through the waters by the moving ship. Effervescent waves closed against the hull, creating whirlpools of dense, foaming, strangely mineral substance in which transparence and opacity fused, brewed together with a gentle and formidable indifference. The curved wake fanned out toward the horizon, it was pale green, lighter than the waters around it. Nothing was repeated in this monotonous spectacle, absorbing as a purely instinctive reverie. Nothing in it was connected with anything else. Ardatov said, "At night, under the stars, the wake becomes slightly phosphorescent and strains your eyes. I don't know anymore whether I am seeing things or imagining them. You are no longer able to think. Come tonight, Hilda."

"I'll come," said Hilda, suddenly appeased, understanding her irritation. Why are you in the decline of life? I see it by the wrinkles in your eyelids, by the way you walk, by the thickness of the veins of your hand, I can't help seeing it. And you seem unaware of it, unaware that I see it. Your lucidity drives me to despair, your contact calms me, you give me back a taste for life, and an aftertaste of the end... And it's my fault not yours.

"Willi Bart is on board," she said aloud. "I'd like to know what kind of papers he has. He only comes on deck at night. Don't you think he's dangerous?"

Ardatov shrugged his shoulders.

"Dangerous or not, he's really not worth thinking about."

...The ship was moving almost imperceptibly through a fluid incandescence, between two expanses full of sparkling reverberations. The sea had become uniformly bright, the heavens were afire. The universe was all oscillating immobility, airy glow, torrid. Not far off, the coasts of the Sahara were low, though behind them level heights could be surmised, whitened with solar dust. The desert without mirage presented successive planes of abrupt plateaus, bereft of shadow, without the slightest mist or vapor. The desiccation of the earth outlined an abstract landscape of rudimentary lines and planes delimiting celestial space. It was an elementary splendor of naked combustion, incompatible with everything we know about life. The freighter's roll resulted from the attraction of a central fire.

The passengers were suffocating in the shade of tarpaulins pierced by the merciless radiation of heat. They only spoke lazily. Memory, at times, became an intoxication.

"I wish I could vomit out my memories of the Center," said Hilda suddenly.

She had just left an Internment and Screening Center in the suburbs of Marseille. Located in a small abandoned hotel, it had become a perpetual quarantine for the sick, a Beggars' Row for the persecuted, a brothel for the benefit of a few policemen. Some old women were rotting there, tucked into their shawls: one was a former lady-in-waiting at court, another an intrepid pacifist of yore, yet another the most fashionable go-between on the French and the Italian Rivieras. Bar girls continued their traffic. They obtained the best rooms and passes to go out for calls at imaginary consulates. They were often paid in soap or military rations. "I was waiting to do my laundry until Rita finished receiving her protector." These "receptions" took place on a pile of old carpets and sacks in a room behind the garage, a cool place, decorated with nudes. Drying wash was strewn all about, displaying persistent stains. The children were lice-ridden and deathly pale, but aside from the sick, they lived in an anemic gaiety, shot through with fears. They stole the last crumbs of sugar no matter how well hidden—and the lady-in-waiting wept tears of chagrin. They had noisy attacks of diarrhea.

"Here I am leaving," said Hilda, "and all that still continues. It's intolerable. Can you explain to me, Simon, why so few attempt suicide?"

"I think I could, but my correct explanation would explain nothing."

Drawn back to the crushing landscape, Hilda said, "If death could be represented by an earthly vision, it would be this: the desert, the passive sea, an immense aerial fire without flame . . ."

Ardatov followed the idea: ". . . A blind clarity . . ."

Willi Bart slept most of the day in the stifling hold. A sailor brought him his meals from the officers' mess. He avoided the light, the crowd, pointless conversation, possible encounters. The sultry half-light kept him in a state of tormented well-being, a sleep obsessed by dreams that left behind them only a sensation of anguish and malaise, and monotonous drowsy daydreams: women met in the street, naked, obscene, copulations he suffered from, the humiliation of it, sating his filthy appetite on obedient loins. That was better than ruminating on the disaster like a madman.

Everything that he loved in this world, infinitely more than himself, was in mortal peril, bathed in blood, submerged in defeat. He knew the map thoroughly and was fairly familiar with the country itself. Every day he measured the catastrophe by the ship's bulletins. At nightfall he arose, shaved without a mirror, resisting the temptation to cut his throat, put on a blue canvas jacket which made him look like a seaman, and went out into the air. His espadrilles carried him without a sound, his young anonymous figure dissolved among the shadows. The only bright lights on the freighter were amidships, near the bridge. Some passengers were playing bridge under the lanterns. On the forward deck, Spaniards were singing softly to the sound of a guitar. Refreshed by the coolness and the night, Willi Bart sauntered alone to the stern. Two lovers were kissing in the shelter of a black lifeboat like a great coffin. Afraid of disturbing them, Willi Bart moved on, climbed a vertical ladder, felt the breeze blowing on his back, looked into the starlit darkness. At the end of the little deck he saw a human form standing at the edge of the void, leaning his shoulder against the flagpole. There was no rail in this spot, the shape stood free, calmly balanced over the backwash. Willi Bart recognized Dr. Ardatov by the massive curve of his shoulders, the tufts of hair on his temples. Simon Ardatov was contemplating the ship's moving wake, in which a very faint light reflected crystalline stars.

Willi Bart looked swiftly around: no one. The shadows deepened around the stern lights, the Spanish guitar moaned in the distance. He gathered all his strength and released it in an instantaneous push against the human form standing over the murmuring wash of the sea. The opaque form opened convulsive arms into the air, the torso gave forth an astonished gasp, and it vanished, swallowed up by the night, the void, the wake—as though it had never existed. Willi Bart climbed down the steep ladder. The trembling in his wrists died down, his heartbeat was unhurried, appeased. He gazed intensely at the curl of the wake, invariably the same. He recomposed his face, which a look of desolation might have betrayed.

29. DAWNS BREAK EVERYWHERE

AUBELAC (Dawnlake) does not exist. Dawns break everywhere; the lake has drained through fissures in the ground toward the subterranean waters that have been working their way under this region for thousands of years. Tall stands of trees have grown up from the silt on the bottom. During rainy years, puddles shimmer under the young foliage. Wooded heights, difficult to reach, spread their fleecy foliage toward every horizon, tinged with pale steel, fern green, purply green, tawny green, tarnished silver. In autumn, the spectrum of rusts, ochers, dying reds, breathe a savage sadness. In winter, the snowy scene, honeycombed with dark arrows and populated by crows, is like certain pictures by Pieter Bruegel: you might expect to see an archer appear, dressed in purple, seeking solitude after the Massacre of the Innocents.

There are only twenty-seven houses left in Puysec: and several of them are abandoned. There is nothing to requisition, hence nothing could possibly happen in this somnolence of brambles, brush, chicken coops, ancient walls, crucifixes blackened by time. The squat houses are roofed with slate. Here and there an ancient tree gently demolishes a bit of wall. There is but one witness left on the main street: a very old woman, dressed in black, her stiff lace bonnet primly tied beneath her chin, sits outside the door in her straight-backed chair. Is she interested in the hen pecking on the walk or in the little pig that suddenly begins to roll on the pointed stones? Her fingers move from time to time as though she were counting her beads. Possibly she is asleep with her eyes open. They say that once, when loud voices spoke of the war in her presence, she grew quite agitated, spoke of Monsieur

Thiers and Gambetta, and asked if "it were true that General Bour-baki* had been taken prisoner, Saint Mary protect us." They calmed her down by giving her a half cup of grilled chestnut coffee.

The sour smell of goat cheese spreads through vast rooms in which time—like dust—sifts the light. There must be ironbound wardrobes in these houses that date from the reign of Louis XVI, beds that have seen generations of births and deaths, spinning wheels, pikes (hidden in garrets) from the time of the Great Terror... The main thing is that gendarmes never stray into this hamlet of innocence, where people remember there was a theft of some linen in 1922 committed by a foreigner—that is, a journeyman from Lot-et-Garonne.

Augustin Charras arrived at Puysec with his backpack and metal-tipped walking stick. "The very depths of deepest France," he said to himself, delighted to be there. "If any refuge is possible, this is it..." The sign indicating the Auberge du Coq (Rooster Inn) had been fading for thirty years, but had nonetheless outlived the inn itself: three tables subsisted in a gray room papered with colored calendars of the last ten years, minus those of the last two. The owner of this "establishment," an ex-lumberjack from the Cevennes, gave a cordial welcome to Charras, who introduced himself as a former lumberjack from the Vosges looking for a quiet spot. In our days we knew the proper way to cut an ax handle, each man to own his preference, each to his grip. An ax handle was faithful, each resembled no other, it was really yours, like your wooden sabots. Today they mass-produce your tools in a factory, all identical, they're heavy, they're expensive, they're good for everybody, like whores. And when I say "today," I should really say "yesterday," for at present nothing is manufactured at all, they chop wood any which way, they deforest without thinking of the rains, while in other places they let the wood grow into you might say virgin forests... This damned war, eh? This armistice with-out peace, this world upside down, this universal misery, eh? The

---

*The old woman's war was the Franco-Prussian War of 1870–71. She recalls the conservative Republican leader Thiers, the radical Gambetta, and General Bour-baki, who was the leader of the defeated army of Emperor Napoléon III.

proprietor of the Coq said, "My son was taken prisoner in the Maginot Line without firing a shot... What do you think?"

"Christ!" said Charras. "Oh, I beg your pardon, perhaps you are Catholic."

"In Puysec we're all Catholics from father to son, except for a family of Camisards, and they're no worse than anybody else—but there's plenty to curse about, blast me!"

The cloudy cider they drank was suited to their dull gloom.

"Was a son of yours taken prisoner?"

"Yes," said Charras, to give the other pleasure and without any feeling of lying.

He obtained all the necessary information. "Aubelac is an ideal place to be forgotten in... Even in Puysec you'd die of boredom if you didn't know you were very lucky to be here. Aubelac is on the mountain, the country has gone wild, a pile of crumbling walls, leaky roofs, rooms inhabited by bats... Aubelac is a place that exists and doesn't exist. No food cards unless you go and get them at the district office, a nice trot... There you are, Monsieur."

The house had walls of heavy stones, leaning against outcroppings of rock. The leaky roof held up, the chimney drew—they would make fire only at night and not when the moon was full, or only a little. The gullies of little streams served as steep paths. The house dominated the countryside, and at twenty yards distance there was a real enchanted forest. Angèle put the living room in order. Jacob Kaaden carved stools out of logs. Joris, a Fleming, dug a latrine and built a little stone wall around it. The site became known as Citadel 100. Laurent Justinien prepared hiding places for arms where they would be easily accessible. He also made long trips from which he returned thin and laughing, told stories embroidered on a background of dense silence: "I've got the luck of a lottery winner. Only I never seem to get the first prize. I always get the egg cup that's right next to the gold watch!" ("Besides, I've had the gold watch and I don't wish that on anybody.") —Augustin Charras took trips too; he brought back Julien Dupin.

Aubelac became inhabited. The house became a pleasant place to live in. Crépin, a local boy, and his wife, "La Crépine," took refuge there, bringing with them good bedclothes and a tall looking glass with gilt molding. La Crépine was big with child, but they said, "We'll get married when peace has been made and we've saved up a little something. It's no use going to the mayor before we have our furniture." La Crépine could be seen constantly, with her round face, her squat figure, her hair blown in the wind, going up and down the path leading to the spring, balancing pails on her shoulders, or kneeling by the waterfall which was nothing more than a trickle of pure water spurting over violet rocks. She would gladly have become everybody's servant as long as Crépin was saved from conscription, mobilization, labor service, deportation to Germany, this rotten war without war.

Cornil came mysteriously from the neighboring département. Small and yellow, with sharp observant eyes and an oldish face though he was only twenty, he stepped out of the thicket one morning. He had a good hunting rifle slung over his shoulder and two chickens tied over his chest. He aroused strong suspicions. The severe questioning to which he was submitted by Laurent Justinien and Jacob Kaaden didn't fluster him for a moment. "Nothing is known about you around here and that's why I've come. I've poached the whole countryside, there aren't two like me; but I don't count. I said to myself: Cornil, those are brave fellows, they'll see that you're honest ... here I am and I'm ready for whatever you want." His good faith seemed certain. They kept him, deciding to put him to the test on the first occasion. The Refuge became a home for outlaws, a friendly place, softly lit by candles at night, guarded day and night by a sentry hidden in the thicket.

Some of them found it hard at first to bear the hours of guard in the deep night: the cold earth and sky, the night birds with their sudden cries, the mysterious sounds of the forest in which some shapeless creature seemed to be prowling. The world receded, the house became as distant and unreal as a memory of the past; an animal fear, caused by nothing more than the loneliness of the night, a fear rising from the tangle of roots under the ground, penetrated the sentry's bones. He fancied that he saw monstrous shadows in the darkness, so dense that it revealed nothing but hallucinations. One night it drove Crépin raving mad and he woke up half the house. His teeth were chattering. "There are hundreds of them, they are crawling, crawling, we're in for it!"

"Hundreds of them?" Justinien asked, incredulous. "Jackass, go on!"

Charras armed with an ax, Justinien full of sarcasm but clenching his Browning in his fist, Cornil stammering words that no one understood, checking the two charges in his Winchester, launched into the starless, soundless, charmless, harmless night. La Crépine hid under the covers and wept.

"Where are they?" Justinien scoffed at the trembling Crépin. "Let 'em come and we'll kick their asses."

The clouds broke, a ruddy moon appeared, a pale disembodied face looking down through a gap in the trees, with an ugly deformed smile. "She's laughing at you, Crépin," Justinien cried out. "You had a case of the heebie-jeebies, that's all, there's nothing." And he comforted him: "I've had scares too, old man, worse than you or anyone else. I know all about them."

Crépin went back to his post surrounded by a terrifying Nothing. He repeated to himself over and over again, "I'm a jackass, I'm a jackass, no doubt about it..." He turned into a very good watchman, eagerly looking forward to certain good moments. Toward three o'clock, La Crépine threw a blanket over her nightgown and came out with a warm drink that ran through him like old brandy. He pressed the woman close, ran his fingers over her nakedness. "Ah, you're so nice and warm." He gripped the hairy tufts of her body, caressed the roundness of her belly. "Don't you feel the little one moving about yet?" "I don't know. Listen to the hoot owl." The cry of the hoot owl was like a heavy drop of blue water falling into a pond from high up. "Who knows, when the little one is born, maybe the bad times will be over." "Let's hope so, Crépin."

Augustin Charras would wander during the hours before dawn. The entire earth seemed to him a sleeping creature whose respiration was perceptible. The light, the beings, the events of the day were its dreams... He was participating in its unconscious wisdom and ending up having barely intelligible ideas which he would never entertain during the day...We are earth's dream. I'm beginning to understand things that I can't understand... He filled a pipe with dead leaves and lit it, leaves that had caught the breeze and warmed in the sun, that dew had covered with its pearls and that having reddened the way one grows sad and stiff and old had finally dropped to the ground. When they were about to rot, some aged hand had swept them up, dried them, chopped them, and now that dust glowed with fire that would turn it to ash... the hot ash that he dumped in the hollow of his hand and snuffed out with a finger and blew into space, quietly astonished. Nothing these days was like that anymore— leaf to pipe to ash—because day after day nobody could claim to be anything but an animal scheming to get by, as if we knew what's what. Charras looked forward to these hours on guard duty like a kind of secret feast.

Justinien entered the night the way he might dive into frigid, dark water and swim resolutely in search of... Certain of suddenly discovering in the bed of the torrent luminous crystals, treacherous, alluring quartz stilettoes onto which one might have the impulse to charge, chest extended... Justinien would explore the environs, passing his hand over the rugged back of a moraine, slipping noiselessly between the trees, like wolves when they are on the hunt... His alertness communicated with the movements of the woods and the clouds. And an inner image of Place Pigalle flashed up, consumed by flaming tresses of hair. To put out those flames, Julien would take his binoculars and study the tops of trees—caressed by the sky, black lace on a background of celestial ash...

"Let's get to work," he would say to himself. He had a visual memory as exact as a photographic copy for things inhuman and things to be destroyed, and, like photos, his mental images were almost devoid of color. Projects would take shape in him like engineers' blueprints on which white lines indicated a machine to be constructed, a machine to be destroyed... That convoy of women prisoners spied in a station, their bundles, the withered faces, the young faces one might love, the discreet waves of the hand, the schoolteacher carrying books under her arm, the last group climbing into a cattle car, the discordant voices of those who were starting in to sing—this was engraved inside his skull on a sheet of indestructible steel. On the opposite side of that sheet, the lines of the munitions factory—its environs, the brick surrounding wall, the poorly guarded alleyway where it might be possible to break in—were inscribed in inalterable strokes. Two ladders, a dozen men, and I can bring it off. He shook Kaaden. "It's time, old man, listen, I've made a plan . . ." Kaaden was listening with complete attention. "I'd like to see that again in daylight, with a pencil in my hand. You have the brain of a strategist, Laurent . . ."

"No, I have the brain of an habitué of Place Pigalle, but my record has two sides: suffering on one and rage on the other."

Time passed without Sundays or holidays, better measured by the changing tones of the great waves of motionless foliage on the slopes. Storms surrounded the Refuge with innocent lightning, the lightning struck the earth with jagged broken swords, but the earth remained inexorably tranquil under their white fury, the stricken oaks continued to live. The rains hung veils of obsession over all nature, but then you could light a fire in the house, the veils would conceal the suspicious smoke, and the hearth gave forth its coppery warmth. The London radio repeated so incessantly the same news—bombings, torpedoings, battles in Russia, submarine battles, executions of hostages, cabinet shifts at Vichy—that nothing in the world seemed to change, yet each bit of news had its weight of condemnation and hope. There were French voices so polite that their exhortations to resistance seemed chiseled in a noble and fragile substance.

The Refuge was hungry. They ate rutabaga, frozen potatoes, cattle feed, hawk with herbs, squirrel with fresh roots, weasel with mushrooms *à la sauce maréchale*; there was no help for the menu but laughter. In search of food the men walked for many hours toward the departmental road, where the trucks of the militia passed. When they returned there were real feasts, on top of which they had established contact with the resistance at Thives-la-Rivière, with whom there was a Gaullist officer who promised to send them a submachine gun. This alliance would make them strong, they could attack the railway, intercept the boxcars of potatoes, grain, cattle being shipped out of the hungry country. The Thives people had horses. That night as they meditated on these beautiful plans the usually silent Cornil grew so enthusiastic that he began to sing gay songs in a husky but penetrating voice:

> "*Jeanneton prend sa faucille*
> *Et s'en va couper les joncs.*"*

They all took up the chorus, accompanied by muffled laughter. Perhaps Cornil didn't like them to be too gay, for he paused, looked up into the rafters, thrust out his dried-up neck, and raised a more mournful voice:

> "*Du haut de ma potence*
> *Je re-gar-dais la France.*"†

Evenings were spent drawing a map of the region, based on a set of Automobile Club road maps and each man's own knowledge; the result was superior to the best General Staff maps—which none of the mapmakers had seen—for it marked hideouts prepared by schoolchildren, shepherds' shelters, shortcuts frequented only by poachers, groves known only to lovers, isolated trees, the Spring of the Hare, the Refuge of the Fox, the Brigand's Grotto. The original, traced in pencil and shaded with aniline, was an indecipherable hodgepodge, but Kaaden made a clean copy in ink. It looked like a dense jungle,

---

* Jeanneton took up her sickle
  And went out to cut some rushes.

† From the height of my gallows
  I looked out over France

covered with red arrows and numbers referring to explanatory notes. This masterpiece was put to use immediately for the operation proposed by the Thives-la-Rivière group. Target: a switchman's hut on the railroad.

After the munitions train had quietly jumped the track in the most natural manner, several grenades exploded under the locomotive. (The switchman, tied up with good strong rope, wondered for how many hours he would have to play this uncomfortable comedy—bleeding for real, but only slightly. The engineer had jumped out onto the embankment, in time—even a little too soon.) Cornil was the only one caught. The infallible woodsman who could smell every point on the compass had lost his bearings, doubtless because he had too much joy in his heart. Missing his way, he headed for the viaduct and didn't realize it until the lights of the motorcycles were almost on top of him. He jumped into the ravine, sprained his ankle, and became the prisoner of pain, just like the animals he had trapped. From mouth to mouth, by ways as hidden as the channels of underground springs, the story of his sufferings was faithfully transmitted. "They crushed his fingers with a hammer. The sergeant bellowed at him: I'll make you talk, you scum! Ah, you think you can buckle your lip, I'll make you open it! They opened his mouth with a knife, from ear to ear. They did things to him that you can't say in front of a woman." This was related in the kitchen by the firelight. The smoke of the wet branches, blown inward by the wind, made their eyes smart. Kaaden stretched out a large, clean hand, black on one side, glowing red on the other, and asked, "Did he talk?"

The bringer of the news, a puny lad from the village, murmured, "I don't know. They don't think so. But maybe he did—you can imagine. It wouldn't be his fault. I'm sure he held out as long as he could."

Rare are those who resist beyond the impossible. No more Refuge.

"What's that sergeant's name? Where is his post? Try to remember the bastard's face, the cut of his lousy jib, so there's no mistake..."

With cold fervor, all listened to the description. Augustin Charras's earth-encrusted finger glided over the map. Kaaden slapped the table with the flat of his hand.

"I'll take care of this," he said. "No objections?"

La Crépine uttered a strident little laugh. Angèle repressed a moan. To be finally face to face with torture and the torturer. Kaaden felt cold as stone, yet moved by an implacable certainty. Charras pushed a log with his foot, and said in his most everyday voice, "We'd better get to bed all the same. Double guard tonight. Joris, go and get two bottles of red wine, it's not a night like every other. We'll divide Cornil's things, each of us will have something to remember him by."

The alarm sounded next day. La Crépine returned from Puysec, her fists clenched on her hips, her mouth twisted, fierce as a singer of the "Carmagnole" on a day of rioting. She disclosed that there were twelve militiamen in the village. "I saw them, I saw the Accursed One, I mean that damned sergeant. I'd tear out his eyes with my nails if I could. They're aiming for the Refuge, and they've arrested the owner of the Rooster. They're waiting for reinforcements from the *sous-préfecture*."

From now on they watched the approaches through field glasses. They decided to spend the night and the following morning in the Grottoes, three or four hours away through trackless woods. There were some places that could be climbed only with the help of ropes, a part of the trail led through icy brooks. They would have to reduce their baggage to a minimum.

"Do they have dogs?" asked someone. "Well, if they have, I volunteer to stay behind and get rid of them."

"They haven't any," said La Crépine. "I would have heard about them. Every eye in Puysec is on them. If eyes could kill, they'd all be dead right now."

And leaning toward Crépin.

"Crépin, I'm taking the mirror along. It's the only nice thing we have. You'll tie it to my back under the blankets."

From the Grottoes another all-night march would take them to the Thives-la-Rivière people. The Grottoes appeared on no maps, only that of the Refuge. The evacuation of Aubelac took place under a persistent autumn rain. The heights were shrouded in a white mist that sank lower and lower. The seared leaves were gloomy and hostile.

"A day for the dead," thought Angèle, "but without cemeteries, without flowers, no one but the dead on the whole earth." A resolute young man in a beret helped her carry a basket of cooking utensils, on her back she carried a big iron kettle encrusted with soot. Her companion was bowed down under a sack and kept shifting the sling of his rifle from one shoulder to the other. He joked in a soft voice with Julien Dupin who followed them.

"How will it be after the victory, eh, Julien? I'll go back to school at the Arts-et-Métiers, you'll get yourself transferred to Paris, I'll invite you and your wife dancing the first free Sunday!"

Dupin was tormented by an absurd fear that the other was talking too loudly. He peopled the rain with ears and snipers' rifles. Dupin had changed a good deal; he was convinced that this fantastic, harassing, lost life wouldn't go on for long: he was truly afraid only of what did not exist, but as the nonexistent is the infinite, fear lived tranquilly within him, causing him little emotion. Against his heart he warmed a Belgian Army revolver—it seems that a bullet in the heart doesn't hurt any more than a tooth pulled after an injection in the gum.

He stumbled over a stump and answered stupidly, "I don't like dancing but the day when we can blow ourselves to a movie on the Grands Boulevards, that'll be a day, all right." The memory of his wife made him stumble again, Christ alive!

The student at the Arts-et-Métiers turned around: "Café-crème or vermouth-cassis?"

"A wooden cross or a pit full of lime?" snickered Dupin.

"Don't scratch each other's eyes out," said Angèle.

"Oh no, we're just joking."

Halfway up the mountain, an opening in the bluish cliffs led to the Grottoes for those who knew which crevasse to follow and at what point to cut through the thicket. A narrow, malevolent tunnel. The flashlight revealed nothing but cleft rocks, crannies in which even darkness could not breathe, vague profiles of monsters, beasts, and men, shapes glimpsed that could never be recovered. The coarse sand of a dry brook provided a strangely soft floor. Through crevices opening out on the thicket and the sky, the low chapels of a subterranean cathedral received a diffused light. A star-shaped puddle of black rainwater reflected a crack in the vaulted ceiling: a gray-pink serpent appeared to be moving in it if you looked at it while walking by. The cold limpid air was heavy with the weight of granite. No breath of life entered here, only a silence of crushing security, oblivion, the hereafter, of repose after a death that is no real death but an empty sleep without dream or warmth—or duration ...

Charras spoke first to break this oppressive charm. "It's wonderful," he said. "Prettiest catacomb I ever did see. All that's missing is furniture to go with it. If anyone is dissatisfied, let him speak up!"

His voice came back in echoes, drowning out the other voices and the laughter. In order to be heard, it was necessary to speak more softly than usual. "And if they want to find us here, they'll really have to look for us."

They lighted candles, which created the atmosphere of a church, casting deep shadows and vague sparks on the cliff walls. The kettle was soon singing over a solidified-alcohol heater. Fifteen faces lighted by pale fire returned to their own world. After the meal the next day's risks were studied.

"It will be dangerous to cross the road between the bridge and the farm. It's sure to be guarded. Wonder if they have a motorcycle. We could cross it one by one in the mist, under the protection of a combat team."

"If that's not possible," said Justinien, "I'm for rushing the farm all together. They won't outnumber us. We'll wipe them out."

And an echo repeated distinctly, "... wipe them out."

"Even the stones don't doubt it," said Justinien.

("... don't doubt it ...")

Somewhere the dripping of icy water marked off the seconds.

The combat team was formed of four volunteers, Justinien, Kaaden, the Fleming Joris, and an almost anonymous athlete who insisted on being admitted and offered good strong arguments. "The most important thing, after muscles, is confidence. I have plenty of that. Here"—he tapped his chest—"that's where my confidence is, and I've had experience too. I went through the evacuation of Dunkirk, don't forget it. The boat was leaking, I baled her out with an old leaky boot... I'm immunized."

The immunization decided them. "I believe you," said Kaaden. "But you'd better sew a bag of poison in your undershorts just the same..."

"Anywhere you like, for all I'll need it!" And he added with a wink, "This time at least, because in the long run..."

The sleepers huddled together on the sand and rock. The cold was not sharp but vast. Candles watched over their deathlike forms. La Crépine's fine mirror opened a gilded door on another cave, peopled with the same candles and the same giant shadows.

Dawn found Augustin Charras on guard at the entrance, seated comfortably on a mossy stone, his cap well down over his ears, his rifle dry under his overcoat. The rain had stopped, but the air was still full of a cottony silent mist that penetrated his very brain. He listened and watched, so vigilant that he could not even hear himself live. Thus would it be after the end of the world. Perhaps everything would have to end before everything could begin again differently. It is all over, Augustin, and you keep imagining that you're here. The others are asleep, dreaming that they are asleep, and everything is finished, nothing exists either of us or for us. The world has only to be reborn, will those who have been reborn know what we were? Not much of anything we were. And it's too bad, we might have been able to...

Augustin Charras was furious with himself. What's the matter with me? You're not the man to let go, however late it may be, it's this horrible cottony silence, this mine, this blackness. To pull himself out of his obsession, he tried to get his bearings. Over there is Puysec— I'll never see Puysec again, goodnight, Puysec! —The village road turns right, and there is Aubelac—Aubelac is finished—adieu—and straight ahead lies the cold body of France. First comes the station, the Gatekeeper's bar—the owner is a traitor, bought and paid for, to hell with him. Straight ahead you'd get to the Loire, to Paris. It would be funny to come into Paris by way of the Austerlitz station, to pass by the Jardin des Plantes and the Halle-aux-Vins. Paris appeared to him as a city of the dead, bereaved housefronts pierced by windows that were hideous black rectangles with glacial wind blowing through them. The Seine reflected nothing, as though there were no more sky. A music of fifes and drums blew in gusts over the murdered city. That's a fine case of the blues you've got there, Augustin!

Dawn showed first a moonlight pallor, then instants later a reassuring whiteness. The fog, blown by the breeze, began to disintegrate. On the horizon, Charras perceived a point of red, which he stared at with pleasure. It must be a fire, a beautiful fire—there was nothing so attractive, so healing, as that fire—I bet that nothing has changed on Rue du Roi-de-Naples, that Mme Sage is still selling her herbs, that Nelly Thorah is still reading coffee grounds for fifty francs, the letter you are waiting for is on its way, it was mailed by the blond man who is thinking of you, he has been unfaithful, but he will return! —The fire was distinct now, halfway to Puysec, ah but of course, of course, they've set fire to Aubelac... Farewell, Aubelac. The fire was no less beautiful for that, it warmed from a distance, through the eyes. Everything must end. You still have three or four hours to sleep—it's Crépin's turn on sentinel. "Get up, Crépin, come and see the Refuge burning...The weather outside is good..."

...The penetrating cold awakened Angèle early in the morning. She looked around for her father, he lay rolled in a ball, snoring softly, his head covered by his coat. His dark hand hung relaxed beside his gun. Angèle felt a strangely reassuring anxiety. Laurent was standing a few paces away looking down at her, his tall frame melting into the cliff wall. He said "good morning" with a puzzling smile. "Come." He disappeared behind a massive pile of rock, representing the head of a colossal crouching beast.

"I'm coming, Laurent," Angèle replied in silence. She smoothed her sweater, quickly rebraided her hair, and out of coquetry ran a moistened handkerchief over her eyes. Does he really know my eyes? She pulled on her rubber boots, quite elegant in spite of their holes.

He was so near that she was surprised when he took her hand. "Watch out for the holes, walk along the edge, there—"

This was the first time he had addressed her with "*tu*," he did it with an easy lightness. "I'm taking you to my place," he said softly, victoriously. "Bend down, the entrance is low…"

They stood up again at the end of a short, shadowy tunnel, under a peaceful half-light.

"This is my place, do you like it, Angèle?"

It was a side room of the cavern, illuminated through a hidden fissure way up high. Here was Laurent's bunk; blankets spread out over rock and straw along a bluish wall; on it lay a hunting knife, a small Browning, a big revolver, a striped muffler, and his old raincoat… The decanted light was turning to pale rose.

"What calm, Angèle. Listen to the calm." Inside him a secret voice said, "I am the man of calm, I am drunk with calm…"

"I'm listening, Laurent. Dear God, how nice it is!"

"There's only you and me," he said very softly.

Angèle's clothes were so steeped in the calm and the hovering opacity that he shifted his gaze to her bright hands, which had fallen to her sides, in suspense at the edge of the unreal. Her hands made him feel that she was really there. Angèle raised her chin and looked straight into his eyes (did she see the calm?) and all the increasing light in the cave became concentrated in her white face. But her dark hair melted into the shadows. Much space between them—so little distance and so much space.

"You are at the center of the calm, Angèle," he said in a hard voice.

Laurent's large dry hand seemed to detach itself, it rose to his forehead and hid his eyes, then it fell slowly, revealing eyes which seemed to be looking into the bottom of a well.

"Angèle, if you don't understand," he said desperately, "I'll never be able to tell you."

"But I do understand, Laurent."

The space and the underground calm that separated them brought them together. Angèle felt it in Laurent's warmth and strength, in his arms hard with immobility like powerful roots. He breathed in the odor of her hair. He did not see the radiance of her face. Her eyes still closed, she asked, "You'll be leaving soon, Laurent. Is it dangerous?"

She felt Laurent's breath on her hair.

"Dangerous? A little. I like that. Risk is luck, the only luck there is these days. Now I am sure I'll come back. Sure, do you understand?"

"I am sure, too, Laurent . . . Look, what's that?"

Appearance or reality, play of light and shadow or actual created forms—the stone wall came alive. Curved lines drawn as if in charcoal revealed a massive beast with a narrow muzzle, broad horns, hairy chest, bent legs, frozen in motion. Only half the body could be discerned—dimly yet intensely, flesh tinted with dry blood, immobile and vibrant. More clearly, the feather end of a black arrow was suspended over it, appearance or reality.

"It's a bison," said Laurent. "He is being hunted, but he is strong, he will live."

Wisps of fog whitened the woods. The four of the combat team went out on reconnaissance. From the top of the Grottoes, the ruddy countryside could be seen, surrendered in its entirety to space and light, under a yellow sun that was beginning to distill a feeble warmth. The walkers' feet were sinking into the dead leaves, scaring the birds. Justinien and Kaaden were in the lead. For a moment Justinien contemplated the landscape through the dead branches.

"Jacob, Jacob, will you believe it? Today is a day of joy for me. We'll get through."

Hefting a nameless weight within him, Kaaden measured the distances.

"A day of joy," he answered in a different tone. "Yes."

THE END

(. . . but nothing has ended.)

Mexico, 1943–45

OTHER NEW YORK REVIEW CLASSICS

MEZZ MEZZROW AND BERNARD WOLFE Really the Blues
HENRI MICHAUX Miserable Miracle
JESSICA MITFORD Hons and Rebels
KENJI MIYAZAWA Once and Forever: The Tales of Kenji Miyazawa
PATRICK MODIANO In the Café of Lost Youth
FREYA AND HELMUTH JAMES VON MOLTKE Last Letters: The Prison Correspondence
ALBERTO MORAVIA Agostino
JAN MORRIS Conundrum
GUIDO MORSELLI The Communist
MULTATULI Max Havelaar, or the Coffee Auctions of the Dutch Trading Company
ROBERT MUSIL Agathe; or, The Forgotten Sister
SILVINA OCAMPO Thus Were Their Faces
YURI OLESHA Envy
IRIS ORIGO A Chill in the Air: An Italian War Diary, 1939–1940
MAXIM OSIPOV Rock, Paper, Scissors and Other Stories
LEV OZEROV Portraits Without Frames
ALEXANDROS PAPADIAMANTIS The Murderess
CESARE PAVESE The Moon and the Bonfires
ELEANOR PERÉNYI More Was Lost: A Memoir
LUIGI PIRANDELLO The Late Mattia Pascal
JOSEP PLA The Gray Notebook
DAVID PLANTE Difficult Women: A Memoir of Three
ANDREY PLATONOV The Foundation Pit
J.F. POWERS The Stories of J.F. Powers
GEORGE PSYCHOUNDAKIS The Cretan Runner: His Story of the German Occupation
QIU MIAOJIN Notes of a Crocodile
PAUL RADIN Primitive Man as Philosopher
GRACILIANO RAMOS São Bernardo
FRIEDRICH RECK Diary of a Man in Despair
GREGOR VON REZZORI Abel and Cain
MAXIME RODINSON Muḥammad
MILTON ROKEACH The Three Christs of Ypsilanti
FR. ROLFE Hadrian the Seventh
GILLIAN ROSE Love's Work
RUMI Gold; translated by Haleh Liza Gafori
JOAN SALES Uncertain Glory
TAYEB SALIH Season of Migration to the North
JEAN-PAUL SARTRE We Have Only This Life to Live: Selected Essays. 1939–1975
GERSHOM SCHOLEM Walter Benjamin: The Story of a Friendship
LEONARDO SCIASCIA The Wine-Dark Sea
VICTOR SERGE The Case of Comrade Tulayev
VICTOR SERGE Conquered City
VICTOR SERGE Memoirs of a Revolutionary
VICTOR SERGE Midnight in the Century
VICTOR SERGE Notebooks, 1936–1947
VICTOR SERGE Unforgiving Years
ELIZABETH SEWELL The Orphic Voice
VARLAM SHALAMOV Kolyma Stories
CLAUDE SIMON The Flanders Road
MAY SINCLAIR Mary Olivier: A Life